SHADOWS AND SECRETS

Arcadia Rayne

To those of you who, like Huntyr, need to hear this:

"Do not look back on your past with hatred. Do not look at yourself with anything other than respect for the girl who fought to become such an incredible woman."

CONTENT WARNING

Please note this is an Adult/New Adult fantasy novel written for a mature reader.

This story includes scenes of graphic combat, blood and bodily harm, mentions of parental death and grief, graphic language and sexual content.

Springhallow
Oxhorn
Saltgl
Kilshore
Fae Lands
Amberhull
Bridgemond
Sarria
Vàstile
Kingdom of Covia
LEGEND
Metropolis
City
Town
Road
Sea Trade
THE EVER REALM

Bamora
Montsir
Kingdom of Kedsan
Mortal Kingdoms
Kingdom of Purithia
Kingdom of Velia
Everrock
Lleiria
Roulan
Thornfury
Wastelands
Mistwater
Malaga
0   200   400   600   800   1000 ml

PART ONE

THE CONCLAVE

Huntyr

If I had a gold coin for every man who's begged me for mercy, I could retire to a vineyard and drink myself to death in luxury.

But, alas, life is cruel, and I remain tragically underfunded.

Instead of lounging in a sprawling countryside estate, I'm here, in some nobleman's overly perfumed manor. I pick at the dirt under my nails as Cristoff Angerella Marsten tries, and fails, to escape his own assassination.

One thing I've learned through the years is that if you're going to kill someone, you should at least understand who you're killing.

And I *do* understand Cristoff, or Froggy as I've affectionately nicknamed him.

Shortly after I was given the contract on his life, I noticed the way his smile spreads just a little too far and looks a little too slimy. I've spent weeks following him in and out of dingy brothels and gambling dens. I know which business partners he's screwed over, which nobles he's blackmailed, and which women he's hurt. I even know he likes his wine watered down. Frankly, that might be the most offensive thing about him.

The point is, Froggy and I have been in a one-sided relationship for quite some time now. But tonight, it all comes to a final, bloody end.

He hobbles forward, one hand dragging along the tacky wallpaper of his manor house, leaving a streak of blood over the delicate painted roses.

"Please," he sobs, voice high-pitched and frantic. "You have the wrong man!"

I let out a slow, dramatic sigh, twirling my knife between my fingers. "Froggy, we've been over this. I don't have the *wrong* man. You, however, are a man who made all the *wrong* choices."

His mouth opens, presumably to protest, but his leg finally gives out, and he collapses onto the marble floor with a *thud*. I cluck my tongue, leaning sideways.

"Honestly? I have to admit that I'm impressed. I didn't think you'd make it this far after I broke your ankle."

The first time *I* broke my ankle at just eight summers old, I spent a week crying in bed and demanding Kristona bring me every sweet in the market. It was the worst pain my young mind could imagine.

Granted, I've experienced far worse pain since then: punches, cuts, broken bones, and even a few nasty bashes to the head.

For Froggy, though, this is probably the first time anyone has ever hit him, let alone broken a bone. So, you know, good for him for putting on a decent show in his final moments.

I step forward, planting my boot firmly between his shoulder blades. "Unfortunately," I continue, "this is where we part ways."

"Please," he chokes out, voice hoarse with desperation. "I can pay you."

I roll my eyes, feeling the weight of irritation settle on my shoulders. *They always say that.* "With what, exactly? The money you stole from Kristona Roschoff?"

He stiffens, spine going rigid.

Out of all Froggy's crimes, that was his riskiest. Only a true idiot would steal from Kristona Roschoff, the most infamous assassin in all the Mortal Kingdoms. Just his name alone is enough to send nobles into a cold sweat.

Froggy's gaze flicks to my neck, locking onto the tattoo branded there, visible from where I pulled my hair up. KR. The initials that mark me as one of Kristona's acolytes.

And that's when it happens. That final moment of clarity. The sudden acceptance of what's about to happen.

His lips part, and he stammers, "You're...her, aren't you?"

Ah. *My reputation precedes me.*

"I—I'm sorry," he sighs, resignation ringing in the air.

His shoulders sag, his breathing turns ragged. And he finally stops fighting, he stops pleading.

That's the thing about death: you can't beg your way out of it.

My blade flashes.

And it's over.

◆◇◆

Kristona is waiting for me in his study when I return to deliver Froggy's seal ring as proof of the kill. He barely looks up from the wooden desk as I drop into the velveteen chair across from him, plopping the ring onto the polished mahogany surface between us.

"Huntyr," he greets me dryly. "Nice of you to clean yourself off before stomping in here."

My boots still carry traces of mud from the slum streets, but at least the blood has dried. I glance down at my knuckles, where it crusts and clings to my skin. *Gross.*

Kristona puts on a good show of ignoring me, focusing on the paperwork in front of him, but I don't miss the way his eyes quickly scan over me, assessing for any injuries. Even after all this time, after I've made a name for myself that inspires nearly as much fear as his does, he still worries for me.

It's sweet.

"You'd think the worst part of being an assassin would be the guilt," I muse. "Or the constant brushes with death, or the complete destruction of any semblance of a normal sleep schedule."

Okay, that last one is pretty bad. I, like any other girl, rely on my beauty sleep, but you can't really skulk around hunting your prey in broad daylight.

Kristona peers at me over the contract he's reading. The old man has long since stopped getting his own hands dirty. He tells his clients it's because he's spent his life building enough capital and training enough acolytes that he can now retire in comfort.

But I know the truth. Once the wrinkles started settling in around his eyes and his hair started turning grey, his hands began to tremble. Soon afterward, he'd taken me to dinner and told me he would soon need me to step up and run his empire when his mind was no longer fit to be in charge.

I'd thrown a plate at his head.

I've already lost one father, I won't lose him too.

So he can sit here in this elaborate manor if it makes him feel better, but I refuse to let him give in to old age that easily.

"Please," he says, voice laced with sarcasm, "do enlighten me on what the worst part is."

I grin. No matter how many times I bait him into these conversations, he never fails to indulge me.

For fifteen years this has been our dynamic. I had been the youngest child he'd ever taken in as an acolyte, but I suspect my dark hair and blue eyes reminded him of the daughter he lost all those years ago. The daughter whose murder gave birth to the deadliest assassin in the Mortal Kingdoms.

He'd stepped into the role of my father and I'd stepped into the role of his daughter, both of us filling those gaping voids that had been carved into us against our will.

"It's the blood," I say, glancing at the dried stains under my nails. "It gets everywhere. And no matter how hard you scrub, it never fully comes out of your clothes. Half my earnings go to replacing my wardrobe."

Kristona picks up the ring, turning it between his fingers before tucking it into the top drawer of his desk, where he keeps all his other mementos: other rings, hair ribbons, letter openers. The list goes on.

Then he neatly folds the contract and tucks that away into another drawer.

"I've already sent Flannigan to pick up a new dress for you to wear tonight." He sighs, catching onto what I'm not-so-subtly hinting at.

I smile victoriously as I stand, moving around the desk to press a light kiss to his cheek. "Good, I put one on reserve at Maxine's last week. The blacksmith is also fashioning a new axe for me if you want to have Flannigan stop there as well."

Kristona leans into my touch briefly before pulling away. "You could at least pretend to be surprised."

I gasp, placing a hand dramatically over my heart. "Of course I'm surprised, Kristona. Your generosity *always* astounds me."

He rolls his eyes, gesturing toward the door with a dismissive wave. "Out. I have work to do. I'll see you this evening."

"You could take the day off, you know," I tease, a mischievous grin spreading across my face. "It's a holiday, after all."

He glares as I reach for a caramel toffee from the bowl perched atop a stack of papers.

"Stop that!" He swats at my hand as I grab another, the first already melting on my tongue. "It's not a holiday."

"It should be," I retort playfully. "Everyone in the Ever Realm should celebrate the birth of *the Huntress*."

He chuckles softly, before resting his full attention on me, hazel eyes narrowing ever so slightly. "As much as I love you, Huntyr, I somehow doubt the Fae are celebrating your birthday, my dear."

I bristle at the mention of those immortal monsters across the sea, the ones who slipped into my house so many years ago and murdered my father while I slept in the next room.

No, the Fae aren't celebrating my birthday.

And I certainly don't want them to.

The Fae are the reason I took up this line of work in the first place. That night, when I'd fled onto the streets, I'd sworn to myself that I would make the Fae King pay for what his people had done to me, to all of the Mortal Kingdoms.

Shortly afterwards, Kristona caught me trying to pick his pocket and told me who he was, expecting me to turn and run.

I didn't.

I looked him in the eye and told him I wanted him to teach me how to kill a Fae.

And here we are all these years later.

Kristona watches me carefully, his eyes searching my face. I wonder if his comment about the Fae was a slip of the tongue or if he intended to provoke me and see if my hatred for them still burns as fiercely as before.

"Well." There's a sudden touch of venom lining my words. "They're not invited to my party anyway."

He tilts his head slightly, as if weighing his next words, then nods in acknowledgment. "Very well. Go wash up. I have important people coming tonight, and I can't have my guest of honor looking like she just crawled off a battlefield."

I wink at him as I move toward the door. "Isn't that exactly how you want your guests to see your acolytes?"

"You, my dear, are different from the rest."

Don't I know it.

⚬

I take the long way back to my apartment, dipping in and out of shops along the cobbled streets of Soria. Normally, I prefer walking along the shoreline where the stench of the city isn't as overpowering, but today I have errands, so I'm stuck with the city's rot.

It isn't just the reek of sweat and smoke that puts me on edge though, it's the chaos of the streets. Everywhere I turn, there's someone looking to prey on the weak or the desperate. Madame Cruella's girls linger on every corner, seducing men, women, and even boys barely grown. Peddlers shout, desperate to bully passersby into buying whatever they're selling, while thieves and vagrants lurk in every shadow.

There's a strange sense of camaraderie in it all, I suppose. After all, where else can an assassin feel more at home than in a city full of people just as wretched as I am?

Still, walking through these streets always puts me on high alert. My muscles tense, my eyes scanning constantly as I make my way toward the apothecary. I'm not dumb enough to be caught unawares.

All it takes is the slightest brush of air by my hip to trigger my instincts. My heart lurches and I snap my hand down, catching the wrist of the child trying to lift my coin pouch.

I click my tongue and look down at the little urchin. "I don't think you want to do that."

"Let go of me!" he hisses, struggling weakly.

He's small, the top of his head barely reaching my chest. Thin, too. His thick hair is so oily it looks practically damp from where it sits heavily across his tanned brow.

"If you tried this in the proper part of town, the King would have your hand for it."

"Let go of me, you bitch."

My, what foul language for such a young boy.

Had it been anyone else, I might have taken a more physical approach to teaching him manners, but even I draw the line at hurting a child.

"Okay," I say with a shrug, releasing his wrist and watching him fall backward into the mud. His clothes are already filthy, so a little more splashing on him doesn't make much of a difference. With a grimace, he rubs the back of his hand across his brow to wipe it away.

Rolling my eyes, I pull open the pouch on my waist and flick a gold coin towards him. "You try that on the wrong person and they might not be as nice as I am. And I won't be as nice as I am now if I ever see you call another woman a bitch."

He stares up at me, wrapping his tiny fingers around the coin. Despite his frame, I'd guess he's around fourteen summers. You wouldn't know it from a distance though. He hasn't eaten in too long. Based on how slow he is to stand, the hunger is taking its toll on him. My own stomach clenches.

It's a feeling I'll never forget.

"Thank you," he mutters, staring at the coin in his hand with wide eyes.

I point towards the baker across the street. "Go over there and buy yourself some bread. Tell them Huntyr sent you and ask for a job. The owner owes me a favor."

His face splits into a grin, and with another breathless word of thanks, he sprints away. I watch him go, waiting until the bell on the door chimes closed before I turn on my heels and make my way towards the apothecary. Hopefully that good deed negates the atrocity I committed this morning.

I do love an opportunity to balance out my karma.

"Afternoon, Joneson!" I call politely, announcing my arrival, as I step into the shop and cough against the sudden aroma of herbs and medicines.

Joneson's head pops up from behind the counter, where he's busy sorting through tiny glass jars. "Ah, Huntyr. Come in. I've been expecting you."

We have a routine, Joneson and I. After all these years, he has my usual tonics ready in advance. I'm one of the few customers he trusts enough to allow a tab, and I pay him handsomely for his discretion.

With a grateful smile, I place the three vials into the pouch on my hip: a fertility suppressant for me, a pain tonic for Tyla, and a sleeping draft to chase away the nightmares that plague both of our nights. He watches me carefully, chewing on his bottom lip.

"I've got something new for you this week," he whispers, reaching under the counter, grabbing a fourth tonic, and sliding it towards me.

There's a sudden chill in the air between us.

I eye the amethyst-colored liquid suspiciously. "What is it this time?"

Every so often, Joneson experiments with new herbs, brewing up some new concoction that he hopes will cure Tyla's illness. None have worked and I gave up hope in them a long time ago.

His expression darkens and on quick feet he moves past me to lock the door and draw the blinds, his movements rushed and furtive.

"What the hell is going on?" I demand, as he grabs my arm and begins pulling me towards the back room. I rip my wrist from his grasp so sharply he stumbles back a few steps.

"You cannot tell anyone about this."

He folds the vial into my fingers and closes my fist over it.

"What is this, Joneson?"

"I got it from a smuggler. From the Fae lands."

No.

My grip tightens instinctively, my fingers twitching with the urge to crush the vial right there. There's no way I'm giving Tyla anything touched by those creatures.

"Are you out of your mind?" I hiss.

Joneson grabs my elbows, holding me steady even as my glare promises violence. "We've tried everything else, Huntyr. Say what you want about the Fae, but their magic keeps them alive for centuries. Tyla doesn't have much time left."

I want to shove the vile potion down his throat. Glass and all.

And yet...

"Will this cure her?"

He smiles at me sadly. "I doubt it. The Fae themselves might have something strong enough to cure her illness, but this was all I could get. It should give you a few more months with her."

My heart sinks.

I stare at the vial in my hands.

A few months with her is better than nothing.

So, for Tyla, I let Joneson add all four tonics to my tab and leave the shop without another word.

DERIAN

"You cannot be serious about this!" I snarl, hurling my magic toward my brother. Satisfaction flares in my chest when he stumbles back a few steps.

Luceron raises his hands in mock surrender, swiping away the damp strands of hair clinging to his brow. He's covered in sweat. His years on the throne haven't taken away his love for battle. The Captain of the Royal Guard swears the King comes out to these training yards daily to keep his sword-fighting skills sharp. Pointless, if you ask me, considering the fact that none of his advisors will allow him anywhere near a fight.

But when Luceron asked to talk to me this morning, I suggested we do it here so that I could assess his skills myself. I've come to the conclusion that while my brother is still fairly lean and sharp-witted, his endurance is no match for mine. Not when I've spent every day for decades wielding weapons and magic like this. So, I've been going easy on him.

Without another word, he hands his sword to a squire before reaching for a canteen of water and pushing a hand through his damp blonde hair.

"Deana said you'd react like this," he says between gulps.

Power simmers beneath the surface of my skin, fueled by my growing rage. We've been sparring for nearly an hour, trading blows with both swords and magic, but I feel like I haven't even touched the depths of the energy inside me. I've been stuck inside these castle walls for too long, and it's left my magic feeling restless, yearning for release.

It's been ages since I last endured the rigid structure of Bridgemond Castle, with its endless procession of lords and ladies lurking around every corner. I'm far more accustomed to the wide-open fields of Amberhull, where I can unleash my power and shake the very mountains simply because I feel like stretching the muscle of my magic.

When I received word that Luceron was summoning me back from the battlefields, where I've been training younglings to control their own magic, I suspected he had something unpleasant in store. I never in my wildest imaginings would have guessed it would be for this.

"Your wife has always been perceptive," I mutter, tossing my sword toward the young squire. He misses the hilt, and the blade clatters to the ground. My brows lift in disappointment.

"I'll sharpen it right away!" he squeaks, scrambling to pick it up as he bolts off, clearly terrified by my scowl.

I've never even met the boy, and he's fleeing from me.

"The Queen, you mean," Luceron corrects, his tone hardening.

Pompous ass. He's only two summers older than me, a trivial difference to the Fae. It had never seemed to matter. At least, it hadn't until our parents died.

Then Luceron was crowned King, and everything changed.

The chasm only got wider after he married Deana and started having children. After that, I was deemed nothing more than the immoral prince who was only good for killing enemies and serving as a spare heir in case of a catastrophic emergency.

Luceron tried to maintain our relationship for a while, but eventually his advisors got in his ear, warning him of the precedent that giving me too much leniency set. They warned him what the nobles would think to see that I didn't have to follow the same orders they did.

Now, he's my ruler first and my brother second.

Still, there is one thing that keeps them from fully caging me.

Power.

The kind that I have and they don't.

Neither Luceron nor his advisors can challenge me magically, and that simple fact offers me the independence I need.

All it took was a single complaint that I needed more of an outlet for my powers and the warning that without one the magic could start to get out of control. Luceron then gave me leave to establish the training camp in Amberhull and to oversee the fortress in Oxhurn.

I suppose that independence is officially being revoked now, though.

"We've avoided interacting with the Mortals for two hundred years, brother. Why now?"

The unspoken question lingers heavily between us: Why me?

Luceron has been working toward an alliance with the Kingdom of Velia for some time now. He's been insistent that we explore the Mortal Kingdoms' wastelands to see if they're experiencing the same strange roars and rumbling that we've noted in the patch of dead land in our territory.

I'm not surprised he's secured an alliance through marriage—it's a typical political move. But why *me*? Why not marry off one of our sisters? Both would gladly plan an extravagant wedding just to be the center of attention, even if it meant spending seventy years married to a Mortal.

I, however, have no interest in marriage, to a Mortal or otherwise. I'm bred for battle, not for family.

Since birth, the roles Luceron and I would both have to play have been obvious. Luceron was born with sparkling green eyes and hair that lightens under the sun. He's the one with the winning smile and charming wit. He's as personable as any king should be.

I, however, take after our father, with dark hair and eyes. My temperament is moody at best, and my power unmatched.

He's the brother meant to form alliances and rule a kingdom. His children are the heirs meant to follow him.

My only purpose is to defend them all.

For two hundred and fifteen years, I've honed my power, stamina, and control. There's no place in my life for a delicate wife or the children such a union would inevitably bring. I have neither the need nor the desire for a sweet princess warming my bed.

"Derian." Luceron grasps the back of my neck, pressing his brow to mine. I stiffen under his touch. "There's no one in all the Ever Realm I trust more than you. This alliance grants us access to the Wastelands, but I need someone I trust to explore them. We have to understand what's causing these disturbances or we risk another war."

I exhale sharply, wanting to continue making a case against this. Arguing is pointless, though. This isn't a request from my brother, it's a command from my King.

"When?" I mutter, pushing away from him and snatching the canteen from his hand.

Luceron chuckles and gives my shoulder a playful shove. "Three days. You'll leave for Velia in three days to meet the Royal Family, celebrate the engagement and alliance, and bring your bride back here."

Three days.

I almost choke at the realization. Just three more days of freedom before everything I know changes forever.

I'm not quite sure if I should be irritated by the timeline or consider it a small mercy.

I glance at him as we leave the training yard and walk toward the stone castle Luceron calls home. It stopped feeling like that to me years ago. It certainly doesn't feel like a place of comfort now.

"You're not coming with me?" I ask.

He shakes his head. "Deana says the babe will arrive any day now. The Queen would have my head if I missed the birth."

"Yes, she would," a melodic voice chimes in.

Deana leans over the terrace balcony of their chambers, her pale blonde hair cascading down her shoulders. She wears a loose gown that does little to hide the roundness of her belly. If the royal psychics are right, I'll soon have my third nephew.

I wonder absently if one day Luceron will offer up his own son to be married off in a political bargain like he's doing to me now.

Luceron looks up at his wife with such adoration, it's almost impossible to believe they've been married nearly one hundred and fifty-eight years. That's what happens when you find your mate, though. It's a love that never fades or weakens. Luceron knew Deana was his mate the moment he saw her. For others, it takes longer. Sometimes years pass before the bond fully forms. Luceron was one of the lucky ones.

Mating bonds are reserved for the Fae, though. There would be no bond between my Mortal bride and I.

Not that I'm complaining on that front. I don't need some magical compulsion to protect a female clouding my better judgement. I've seen what that bond does to Fae, and it certainly doesn't make them better warriors.

"You look beautiful, my love," he calls up to her.

Deana raises her brows, exasperation clear in her expression, though a pink blush creeps across her cheeks. "And you look filthy. Come bathe before dinner."

"Yes, ma'am." Luceron bows with an exaggerated flourish before turning back to me, clapping a hand on my shoulder. "This is for the good of the Fae, Derian. I hope you understand that."

The good of the Fae.

How is aligning with the Mortals for the good of the Fae?

They hate us. Their memories are too short, too swayed by stories incorrectly told by their fathers and grandfathers. I have no interest in being the one to correct their biases.

"Just don't expect me to be nice to her."

Luceron rolls his eyes. "You? Nice?"

"Me? Married?" I retort with a raised brow.

He flashes a grin as he backs away, flicking a finger across his brow in mock salute. "Touché, brother."

HUNTYR

"Tyla, I'm home!"

The small apartment I share with Tyla isn't much, but it's just enough for the two of us. A cramped kitchen with the essentials, a washroom that's modest but always spotless, and a bed with well-worn cotton sheets, perfectly sized for us to share. Truthfully, I could afford more, much more, in fact, but Tyla insists on us saving every extra cent I make. She argues that if one day I ever decide to walk away from the business of killing, she doesn't want money to be what keeps me tethered.

Sometimes I suspect she isn't exactly proud of what I do for a living.

Not that I'm *proud* of the blood on my hands, but...

Killing is what put a roof over our heads when we had no one else to rely on. Killing is what pays for the tonics that help Tyla manage her pain. And frankly, I'm good at it. I'm *notoriously* good at it.

So, no, I don't plan on quitting anytime soon.

"I've already prepared a bath for you," Tyla calls from the bed, her frail body barely visible beneath the thick comforter pulled up to her neck.

"You shouldn't have gotten up!" I chide, rushing to her side. Even hidden under the blankets, I can see her arms trembling with shivers. My palm presses against her forehead. She's feverish as usual. Sweat plasters her dark hair to her brow, and her sunken eyes flutter open at my touch.

It's getting worse.

With clinical precision, I pull back the blankets and examine her. The dark tendrils in her veins have crept higher up her arms, extending further than they had just this morning. That inky blackness is spreading over her skin faster than it ever has before.

"What are sisters for?" she murmurs, managing a weak smile as she avoids looking down at her arms.

We aren't sisters by blood, although with our similarly dark hair and high cheekbones, we might as well be. My complexion is darker from more days spent in the sun, and my eyes are a bright blue in comparison to her dark ones, but it's not uncommon for us to be mistaken as relatives.

In truth, I found her two years after I started training with Kristona. I was sent to deal with a husband accused of adultery, and while I was efficient, ruthless even, for my age, I was still just a child. A curious one at that.

So before leaving, I wandered the house. That's when I found Tyla, two years younger than me, huddled in the corner of the kitchen, terrified. The husband hadn't been a cheater after all; his wife simply couldn't stand that he had adopted a little girl without her permission.

We bonded instantly, and I begged Kristona to take her in. He took one look at her small frame and declared that the training yard was no place for a girl like her. At seven summers, though, I had already learned the art of stubbornness and threatened to gut every one of his acolytes if he didn't let her stay. So, he agreed, on the condition that she worked in the kitchens.

The arrangement worked for a while. Until she started complaining about pain in her ankles.

One night, I awoke to her whimpering in the bed across from mine. I rolled up her pant leg, and we discovered the black veins for the first time. It only got worse from there—the pain, the cough, the fever, the fatigue. That's when Kristona told me she couldn't stay any longer. There was no place in the League of Assassins for a girl who couldn't contribute.

So I bought this apartment, took on every job I could, and made it my mission to take care of her.

Because *that's* what sisters are for.

"I brought you something," I whisper, pulling the pain tonic from my pouch. Gently, I lift it to her dry lips, helping her take a sip. Her sigh of relief mirrors my own when the potion begins to work its magic.

"Thank you, Huntyr," she mumbles, resting her head back on the pillow. Her dark eyes flicker closed, the pain easing just enough for her to rest.

This has become our routine: I come home, give her a tonic, and she drifts off to sleep. If I really wanted to, I could just let the scene play out again. I could let her dream and go about my night. She wouldn't even know about the other vial, the one that still sits in my pouch.

I slip the amethyst-colored tonic out, staring at it for a long moment before gently shaking her awake.

"There's something else."

Her eyes open slowly, taking in the vial. "Another miracle tonic from Joneson?"

"Something like that," I force myself to swallow, trying to keep my voice even. "He says it's from the Fae lands."

Her eyes widen, darting from the vial to my face. Tyla knows better than most how much I hate the Fae, how much I distrust them. And she's smart. She understands the significance behind my offering this to her.

She understands this gift implies a sense of urgency.

"You think I need that?" she whispers, her voice thin.

Her eyes flash with sadness as I place the vial in her hands, folding her fingers around it. I won't force her to drink it. If our situations were reversed, I'm not sure I'd want to drink it either.

But I will allow her to make the choice on her own.

"I love you, Tyla," I say softly, brushing her hair back from her forehead, trying to ignore the sudden familiar ache forming in my own temple. "I'll do whatever it takes to make you better. If this is what it takes, so be it."

She stares at the vial for what feels like an eternity, then finally nods. "Bottoms up, then."

With trembling hands, she uncorks the bottle and brings it to her mouth before taking a few tentative sips.

"I think that's enough for now," she murmurs, re-corking the bottle and setting it on the wooden end table beside her.

"Do you feel any different?" I ask.

Tyla shrugs. "I'm not sure."

She extends her hand towards me, turning her wrist towards the ceiling. The dark veins stand out in stark contrast against her otherwise pale skin, and I run my thumb along the path of the largest one before gasping.

It's... fading.

My lips part while I as watch the darkness on her skin recedes slightly. It's working. It's actually working!

"That's impressive," she muses, turning her arm over and watching the magic take hold.

Reaching across her, I tuck the vial into the drawer of the end table. "We'll save it for emergencies?"

She gives me a slight smile and nods encouragingly before patting the bed next to her in invitation. With a happy giggle, I flop down heavily, running through my mental to-do list. Dishes need to be washed. The dining table needs to be tidied. I need to bathe and prepare for the dinner at Kristona's but...

"You look exhausted," Tyla notices, glancing over me as a yawn claws its way out of my throat.

I think of how far I'd had to walk to get from Froggy's house to Kristona's. "Long day."

"Headache too?"

I nod, pinching the bridge of my nose.

Tyla pulls back the covers, unfazed by the dried blood that lingers on me. "Come on, then. There's plenty of time for a nap before your party."

◄◦►

*R*ain.

It batters against the walls, against the windows, howling through the cracks in the shutters. Thunder roars.

The world is too dark, the kind of darkness that seeps into your bones.

I step forward, my tiny feet padding across the cold wooden floor, my nightgown whispering against my ankles. Lightning flashes and for a heartbeat, the room is bathed in white.

Then the darkness swallows it whole.

"Daddy?" My voice is barely more than a whisper against the storm.

Another step forward. The wind screams against the walls.

Another flash of light—

And I see it.

The bed.

The sheets.

The blood.

A sob tears from my throat, but I don't stop. I run.

Slick warmth coats my feet, my hands, my nightgown. My stomach turns, bile rising in my throat. I slip, hitting the floor with a hard thud.

"Daddy!"

He doesn't move.

He will never move again.

Something behind me shifts.

Footsteps. A voice.

"Come, girl, out of here."

Arms circle my waist, squeezing too tightly around me as they tear me from the floor. I don't want to go though, I want to stay with Daddy. I thrash. I kick, I scream, I fight.

Chesain drags me from the room, through the hall, past the shadowy figure of my stepmother.

Her voice drifts toward me, sharp and cold. "What could have done this?"

Chesain sighs, tossing me into my bedroom and shutting the door firmly behind him. The latch clicks shut from the outside.

"I ain't ever seen nothing like this, ma'am."

My stepmother's breath catches. "The Fae. What else could do something like this?"

She isn't crying.

She isn't mourning.

My father is dead, and she doesn't care.

The realization shatters something inside me.

Her heels click against the wooden floors. "What am I going to do, Che-sain?"

For the first time, her voice wavers. But not with sorrow. Not with despair.

With fear.

"We should get the body out of the house, ma'am. Until you can arrange a proper burial."

No.

They can't mean—

Daddy can't be dead.

"Yes, yes. You're right. I trust you can arrange this?"

"Of course." There is a beat of silence before Chesain continues. "There's also the matter of the girl—his daughter."

I don't even dare to breathe.

My stepmother scoffs, and I can feel her glare through the door. "Put her out. She's been nothing but a nuisance to me. I cannot bear to deal with her now."

Chesain hesitates. "She's but a girl, ma'am, not even six summers."

My stepmother laughs.

Cold and unfeeling.

"If it eases your conscience, sell her to Madame Cruella, then. She will buy girls that young to train them, and at least she'll make sure the girl is fed."

The room is too small, too tight, my lungs constricting as I stumble back-ward.

I won't go to Madame Cruella.

I won't let them take me.

I turn. Run.

My legs burn, tremble, slip in the blood still sticky between my toes.

The window. I shove it open. Rain slashes at my skin. The wind howls.

Jump.

I don't hesitate.

The night swallows me whole.

—◆—

"H untyr!" A firm grip on my shoulders, shaking me, rips me from the nightmare. I'm already reaching for the blade on my hip, the instinct to protect myself strong even as I sleep, when Tyla slams her hand down on mine. "It's only me."

I gasp, working to steady my breathing and make sense of my surroundings. It was just a dream.

Just a dream of the most horrific memory of my life.

"You were whimpering," Tyla explains, sadness shimmering in her eyes as she squeezes my hand tight. It's still trembling.

I can still feel the blood on my fingertips, hear the remnants of the storm that night. I exhale sharply, rolling onto my side to face her, attempting to ground myself in her warmth. "It was just a nightmare."

"Was it about—?"

"Yes." My voice is sharp and tense, my mind still whirling from the memories of my past.

"Do you want to talk about it?"

I squeeze my eyes shut, breathing through a wave of nausea. No. No, I do not want to talk about the night the Fae murdered my father. I do not want to talk about the night that changed me from the nobleman's daughter to the assassin's apprentice.

"Not tonight."

She doesn't press. She never does.

Since the day that I told her of my background, she's always understood that the pain of that night isn't something I ever like to acknowledge. She lets me ignore it, allows me that escape, and I love her all the more for it.

She curls closer to me, tucking her head beneath my chin. The feeling of her breath in a steady rhythm against my skin centers me in the present. I let myself breathe her in. Let myself forget that awful dream and that awful night.

"Go wash up," Tyla tells me when my heart rate has finally slowed. "Flannigan dropped off your presents earlier. I suspect Kristona wants you to wear them tonight."

My ears perk up at the word presents, and I launch myself off the bed to the sound of Tyla's giggles. The gifts are stacked on our small dining table, each box ostentatiously wrapped in pastel colors, ribbons and bows piled atop the delicate paper. I pull a card from beneath the largest bow and read it aloud.

"My dearest Huntyr, please do us the honor of pretending to be a lady by wearing these fine fashions this evening."

Tyla's cackling laughter echoes through the apartment, and I shoot her a glare over my shoulder. Kristona and his ever-present sarcasm.

"And if, for any reason, you're considering skipping this evening's festivities, please know these gifts are only a preview to a very special surprise."

I frown, rereading the last line. Kristona has celebrated my birthday every year since he found me alone in my room the night I turned seven, sobbing uncontrollably. He knows how much I love these parties. I would never miss it, so why the sudden emphasis on my attendance?

Carefully, I untie the ribbon and lift the lid of the largest box. Inside is a gown of shimmering silver fabric, folded with precision. I pull it free, momentarily surprised by its weight, captivated by the way it catches the light. The bodice is scattered with crystals, sparkling like stardust.

Tyla gasps, sitting up straighter to get a better look. "It's beautiful!"

I can only stare. This isn't the pale blue dress I reserved at Maxine's.

"It's a surprise," I whisper, unable to tear my eyes away from it.

— ◆ —

My second surprise of the evening comes when I step outside my apartment and find a coach waiting for me, its lacquered frame gleaming in the evening light. The driver greets me with a bow so deep I almost stumble backward. Without a word, he opens the door and gestures for me to enter.

I hesitate for a moment before gathering the heavy folds of silver fabric around me and climbing inside, settling onto a velveteen seat. The fabric is softer than anything I've touched before. With a gentle lurch, the coach quickly pulls away, and I find myself staring at the city lights through the small window, my mind still reeling from the gown, the jewelry, and now the carriage.

This is too much.

Suspiciously too much.

I had suspected Kristona might plan something special for my twentieth summer since this birthday marks my year of maturity. Ballgowns and horse-drawn carriages, though? A custom-made sword, I had thought. Maybe a towering cake.

Kristona doesn't spend money frivolously.

He doesn't do anything frivolously.

And this gown, with its shimmering embroidery, surely costs more than all the birthday gifts he's given me over the years combined. The trinkets in the other boxes, a diamond bracelet, silk gloves, and heeled slippers—were also oddly expensive.

Appreciated, yes, but what use did an assassin have for diamonds? *What is he getting at?*

The coach rolls to a stop, and the driver quickly rounds the front and opens the door, offering his hand to help me down. I eye it for a moment before hiking up my skirts and hopping down with a flourish. Entirely unladylike. He looks momentarily scandalized, so I simply wink and stride up the pathway to Kristona's house, the cool night air biting against my flushed skin.

There's no music, no laughter echoing from the house, none of the vibrant energy that usually fills his home during my birthday party.

Kristona opens the door before I can knock, his eyes sweeping over the gown with a warm smile. He pulls me into a tight embrace. "You look lovely, my dear."

"You look exactly the same as you did several hours ago," I mutter, half-smirking as I scan over his usual attire, an ivory shirt loosely tucked into trousers, hair as uncombed as ever.

He chuckles and drapes an arm over my shoulders, guiding me inside. "I thought we'd do things a bit differently this year."

I gesture at the gown, my voice dry. "Clearly."

Inside, the familiar faces of Kristona's other acolytes greet me, each of them dressed in their usual worn leather and dark fabrics. No one else is remotely as formal as Kristona requested I be.

I stop in my tracks, pulling away from him. "Alright, that's it, what's going on here?"

His eyes flick toward my right hand, where my fingers twitch instinctively. "How many weapons did you manage to hide under that gown, my dear?"

"Six." I list them without hesitation: "A small knife between my breasts, two throwing stars in the bodice, a blade in each boot, and a dagger strapped to my thigh."

A grin spreads across his face slowly before he nods approvingly. "That's my girl."

"Sit down, Huntyr," Flannigan calls from his spot by the wall, pushing off to greet me with a grin and a kiss on each cheek. "No one's killing anyone tonight, especially not the birthday girl."

Flannigan was only a few years older than I when Kristona took me in, still just a boy, but now he's a man in his own right. And a formidable assassin at that. When I refused to be Kristona's successor, no one was surprised that Flannigan stepped in to take on the role.

Truthfully, he's far better suited to the politics of being head of the League of Assassins than I am.

Flannigan guides me to my seat at the head of the table, next to Kristona, and I find myself surrounded by familiar faces. Evora and Althea, the mercenary twins always wearing matching smirks, sit across from me. To my right are Christof and Jacobi, the orphaned brothers Kristona took in after their parents' deaths.

"Tabitha, Chylan, and Brayden send their regards," Kristona says as we settle in. "But tonight is about you."

With a nod, he motions to the staff, who begin bringing out platters of my favorite dishes: smoked meats, roasted potatoes, candied fruits, lemon tarts, and even a bowl of Kristona's prized caramel toffees. My companions immediately start filling their plates, quiet conversations beginning, but I remain still.

Something is wrong.

Why insist that I come tonight, knowing I'd be here regardless?

Why send me this extravagant dress, only to be in a room with others dressed so casually?

Why cancel my favorite party for a dinner with the closest members of our circle?

I rub my temples, trying to ease the tension building behind my eyes.

Just then, a knock echoes through the house.

"Ah, our special guest has arrived," Kristona says, standing.

"Guest?" I look around at the familiar faces, frowning. I thought I was supposed to be the guest of honor. "Who else are we expecting?"

Flannigan exchanges a glance with Kristona, then stands to answer the door.

"Well, as much as I wanted this night to be all about you, my dear, business waits for no one," Kristona quips, a teasing smile tugging at his lips.

I feel a flash of irritation. "You're turning my birthday dinner into a business meeting?"

Before he can respond, Flannigan returns with a tall, lanky man in tow. The stranger's crimson velvet doublet, embroidered with golden thread, catches the light as he enters the room. His polished boots echo against the floorboards. A jeweled dagger hangs from his finely tooled belt, more an ornament than a weapon.

Kristona greets him with a warm handshake. "Mr. Dunklee, I'm glad you could join us."

I raise an eyebrow, a million more questions firing in my mind as I recognize the name.

"A lord?" I whisper, leaning towards Flannigan.

He smirks at me but says nothing.

Mr. Dunklee takes his seat at the far end of the table, unfolding a parchment from his inner pocket as he settles in. "I received the contract this morning. I'm ready to proceed."

A heavy sigh escapes me. "Did this really need to happen tonight?"

I'm not usually one to stand in the way of earnings or good business practices, but why do this now?

Kristona only smiles, gesturing for Flannigan to bring me the parchment. "It did, my dear, because this contract isn't with me. It's with you."

The world suddenly freezes, completely thrown off its typical axis for a brief moment in time.

I blink, taken aback. "With *me*?"

Kristona nods, his eyes gleaming. "It's time, Huntyr."

I open the parchment, frowning at the unfamiliar weight of it in my hands. No one in Kristona's employ ever takes their own contracts. We work under his name... always. Kristona handles all of the business arrangements. He writes every contract. He deals with the clients. We deal with the kills. That's the rule. That's how it's *always* worked.

Even Flannigan has never taken a job on his own.

I stare down at the parchment in my hands, unable to make sense of Kristona's scheming.

Mr. Dunklee's voice breaks the silence, his eyes locking onto mine as he speaks softly but firmly. "I want you to kill the Fae prince."

Huntyr

I cough violently, choking on the bitter wine I sipped just as those impossible words echo through the room.

"Come again?" I ask, my brows shooting up in confusion.

"I want the Fae prince dead," Mr. Dunklee insists, his voice level and calm as if he's simply requesting updates on the weather.

I stare at him, waiting for someone to tell me I'm hearing things or that this is all some sort of joke. This must be some kind of practical joke, a manifestation of Kristona's twisted sense of humor. That is the *only* explanation for this ridiculous turn of events.

And yet, as I look around the room at the familiar faces of my perverse little family, my stomach clenches. Flannigan smirks back at me with a demented little smile. The twins both lean back casually in their seats, watching my reaction with clinical focus. Christof and Jacobi haven't even paused their eating to breathe, let alone marvel at what's happening.

No one else is surprised.

Which means they all already knew this was coming.

"If a Mortal enters the Fae lands, they don't leave them alive," I protest sharply, crossing my arms over my chest.

No one, and I mean *no one,* wants the Fae royals dead more than me, but I am no fool. I do not go on fools' errands.

Kristona tuts. "You won't be going to the Fae lands, my dear."

His tone is entirely too calm and unfazed, and he gestures for Mr. Dunklee to elaborate.

"The King is planning to marry his daughter to the Fae prince," Dunklee explains. His words carry the weight of carefully guarded information, which means only one thing... he's come to us directly from the castle. He's a traitor to the crown. "A delegation of Fae arrived just a few nights ago. A masquerade ball is to take place tomorrow evening to celebrate the engagement. The prince will be in attendance. I'd like you to ensure this wedding never happens."

I narrow my eyes at our guest, scrutinizing every inch of his lanky, noble figure, from the way his lips fold in on themselves in a tight line to the slight tremble in his fingertips. "If the King knew you were here, he'd have your head on a spike," I mutter.

"Some things are worth the risk," Dunklee responds, his gaze never wavering. There's a flicker of something in his eyes, though.

Perhaps desperation?

Ah.

I drain the last of my wine before placing the glass back on the table with deliberate care. I take a moment to dab my lips with the napkin before leaning forward, my voice dripping with sarcasm. "So, how long have you been in love with the princess?"

Dunklee sputters, his face turning a brilliant shade of red. "That's not—I'm not—"

"I've heard enough," I say, cutting him off with a dismissive wave of my hand. I turn to Kristona, trying to keep the growing irritation from my voice. "This is stupid. Reckless. Two things that *I* am not. I'm not going to endanger my life because of some heartsick little lord."

Kristona, always patient, smiles at Lord Dunklee and turns in his seat towards me, leaning in close and whispering for me alone. "You asked me to teach you how to kill a Fae, Huntyr. I've done that. Now, what are you going to do with that knowledge? Because you won't get another opportunity like this."

I bite down on the inside of my cheek sharply, hard enough to draw blood, just as a pulse of something dark and heavy wells up inside me. Based on the glint in Kristona's eye, though, it's the exact reaction he wanted me to have.

Suddenly, I'm not in this room anymore. I'm a little girl again, standing in the doorway of my father's chamber. All these years later, I can still clearly see his lifeless body, twisted and broken. His eyes had been nothing more than horrible black pits sunken into his face. His mouth had been frozen in a scream that never ends. Blood dripped from his ears, staining the floor like a scar on the earth itself.

I press a hand to my temple, willing the memory to fade as the ache in my head steadily intensifies.

"I thought this would be a particularly special way to celebrate your birthday," Kristona says before spearing a sliced bit of meat on his plate and sliding it into his mouth. He watches me intently, a challenge clear in his gaze.

The room is silent as I stare at him, considering.

Kristona has given me everything. He's offered me a place in his home, given me the skills necessary to defend myself against any enemy, showered me in gifts and love, but he's also taught me to be clever. He was the one who warned me to be skeptical of any gift that seems too good to be true.

Even if that gift comes from him.

"Why me? Flannigan is far more experienced, and as your second, it makes more sense for him to begin the business of managing contracts."

A soft cough from Flannigan makes me cut a glare in his direction. He doesn't deny it. No one does.

He's clearly better suited for this kind of mission. Still, Kristona's expression darkens as he quickly glares at the other assassins, silencing any further argument. He pushes out his chair and strides across the room to the large oak hutch that lines the far wall. From its top drawer, he retrieves a folded parchment and slowly lays it down in front of me.

"This came for you."

I hesitate a moment, struggling to command my fingers to move and reach for the letter. It's cold to the touch when I finally grasp it. Silently, I unfold it, scanning the neatly scrawled words across the page. My heart stutters painfully in my chest.

It can't be...

I look up, meeting Kristona's gaze as he explains, "I'm giving you this job because you're the only one who can do it. Your stepmother passed away three days ago, and your father had no other heirs. Therefore, you, Huntyr, are now the Lady Lachlan of Vastile."

The room spins. The letter sits limply in my hands as I force myself to breathe in and out, to stay present despite my every instinct telling me to scream and run from the room.

This isn't real.

How did the crown even locate me? I left that life behind years ago.

I can't be the Lady Lachlan. I don't know the first thing about nobility and, more importantly, I don't *want* to learn.

As if it had burned me, I throw the letter onto the table, needing it away from me. I clench my fists, my knuckles turning white as I try to control the tremors in my hands. Later. I'll give myself a moment to fully digest all of this when I'm alone. As much as I consider these people to be family, I cannot let them see me break, not after so many years of training myself to be invincible.

Kristona's voice softens as he places another item on the table before me. A mask.

"Happy birthday, Lady Lachlan," he murmurs gently.

The mask is silver, intricately crafted with swirling designs that glimmer in the candlelight. A beautiful invitation to step into a world I swore I'd never be a part of again.

I stare at the mask, my stomach churning.

A masquerade ball.

An assassination.

And me, the assassin with noble blood. The irony isn't lost on me.

The only thing standing between me and the vengeance I've been preparing to enact all this time is the identity, the life, that was stolen away from me as a child. My fingers brush the cool surface of the mask.

"I don't care about the title or the land," I confess, my voice weaker than I intend. I don't want it. I don't want to step one foot back into that house. "This changes nothing."

"Doesn't it?" Kristona counters, his tone unreadable.

I glance at the letter again. Lady Lachlan. Just that one extra word before my name opens doors to me that no other assassin would ever be able to walk through. Tomorrow, if I want it, I'll have the opportunity to walk into the ball, dance with the elite, and get close enough to the Fae prince to end him. No one would question the presence of the newly named Lady Lachlan of Vastile.

But Kristona won't force me to go if I refuse my inheritance.

The choice is mine.

The mask glints in the firelight, daring me to take it, to accept the responsibility that comes with it. I hesitate for only a moment longer before finally picking it up, sliding my fingers over the delicate straps.

I am no noblewoman. I am a killer.

But for my father's memory, I will play the part.

DERIAN

Roland bursts through the door with enough force to rattle the antique portraits. His face flashes purple with irritation as he takes in my lounging form on the oversized bed.

"You're late!" Roland snaps.

I glance up over the top of the book I'm skimming. "It's not like they can start the party without me."

I was supposed to join the ball at sunset, but the sun stopped shining over an hour ago, and I still haven't bothered to change out of the loose silk pants I'd slept in. I've been indulging in the capital's nightly distractions since we docked in Velia a few days ago and have spent most of my days in this bed as a result.

Mortals have their faults, but their gambling dens come with enough women and booze to *almost* make up for it.

Almost.

"I knocked two hours ago to remind you of the schedule," Roland continues, hands on his hips.

I shrug, flipping the page of the book.

My brother may be able to force me into this wretched kingdom and demand I marry some vapid Mortal princess, but he can't make me care about impressing her. I keep reading, and Roland releases a frustrated huff as he begins navigating through the mess of my discarded clothes. Piece by piece, he tosses garments in my direction: trousers, a cotton shirt, a black jacket. His muttered curses fill the air between us, and I suppress a smile.

Fifty years ago, my brother named Roland the Delegate to the Mortal Kingdoms, and I haven't seen much of him since. The years apart haven't softened him. He was a friend of my father's, so I've known him since I was a boy, which means he'll always view me as the reckless prince who drags mud through the palace.

"Impressions are everything, Derian! This is no way to endear yourself to your future in-laws."

I stand, slowly and begrudgingly changing into the formal clothes he's thrown at me. The mask I'm supposed to wear lies face-up on the hand-carved desk.

I hate that fucking desk.

The whole room is far too ostentatious for my liking, with towering stone walls and arched windows framing the star-dappled night sky. The high, vaulted ceiling makes the room feel too much like a cavern. Near the empty hearth, the two maroon-upholstered chairs are too stiff, as if they're hardly ever used.

I also hate this mask. Who thought a masquerade ball was an appropriate way to introduce me to my future wife? Surely she'd want to see my face.

Not that it matters.

Whether she finds me pleasing or not is irrelevant.

"Help me with this," I say, holding up the mask to Roland.

He ties it behind my head, making sure to conceal the tips of my ears.

"She'll see them soon enough, you know," I remark dryly. "Their King asked for this alliance with us. I don't see why I should go out of my way to hide the fact I'm Fae."

Roland tuts, straightening my jacket. "You know how Mortals are. Their memories are short. They believe only what they're told."

"They're told the Fae are evil monsters who steal their children in the night," I scratch at my chin contemplatively. "Perhaps I should just act the part they've assigned me?"

Roland's glare could wilt the most vibrant flowers. "Your King wants this alliance, Derian. Do not disappoint him."

Ah, yes. My brother's wishes are all that matter.

I should know that by now.

I'm sure Roland's not the only one waiting for me to fuck this up.

I'm the impetuous, spoiled prince who will never be king. The brother of a great leader who never lives up to his own potential.

Truthfully, I'm not sure why I'm even bothering to go through with all this circumstance. You can't let down a kingdom that already expects you to be nothing more than a brute.

"She's quite attractive," Roland adds after a pause, as if her beauty might console me. He gives me one final once-over before beckoning me to follow. "And well-spoken. You'll be very happy with her."

I doubt that very much.

As we step out of the room, the five Fae warriors tasked with my protection greet us with their usual stony silence. Towering men with thick arms and even thicker expressions, they follow me everywhere like oversized shadows.

As unnecessary as the lavish furnishings of my room.

"Boys," I greet them with a wink.

The warriors, clad in their typical leather armor, stare ahead silently. It's tradition for the royal guard not to speak in the presence of sovereigns, and despite my repeated insistence that I don't care about such formalities, they haven't budged.

They were lovely company on the long boat ride over.

"How come they don't have to wear masks?" I mutter to Roland, jabbing a thumb at the silent guards.

He only sighs and pushes me forward, guiding me through the winding halls toward the ballroom.

They'd better at least serve wine at this party. I desperately need a drink.

———◆◇◆———

"**I**t is my greatest pleasure to make your acquaintance, Prince Silverthorn."

The girl who is to be my bride remains in a low curtsy, waiting for my permission to rise. I glance at Roland beside me, who gives a small, encouraging nod, then clear my throat.

"The pleasure is mine, Alaya."

Roland jabs his elbow into my rib, and I return the gesture with a glare over my shoulder.

"Princess Claristen, I mean," I correct. *Why* exactly are these kinds of formalities necessary if we're to be married in a week's time?

The princess straightens, daring a glance at me, and I take the opportunity to do the same. She looks exactly how I'd expected. Too young, too innocent, too perfect. Golden hair falls in waves over her shoulders. Her hazel eyes, wide and clear under her ivory mask, are empty and unthinking.

They hold none of the sharpness or wit I might have hoped for, the kind of intellect I might have actually respected.

The gown she wears, with its delicate embroidery and shining pearls, is just as immaculate as she is. It clings to her pale skin. Gods. With the light dress, the pale skin, and the golden hair, she looks like a fucking doll. A doll, dressed up and thrown to the visiting prince like a prize.

A few seconds spent in her presence tell me everything I need to know. She's been sheltered in this castle her entire life. She's never seen true darkness, not like the kind I've walked through on more days than I'd like to admit.

There's absolutely no hope for any sort of camaraderie or understanding between us.

Her father, King Eryndor, stands beside her, cheeks flushed from nervous drinking as he grins at me. The King of Velia bears the marks of a man who has grown his borders in battle and maintained them in peace, with deep-set lines and age spots. His thick silver beard frames his jawline as he beams at his daughter and then at me.

"What a pair you two make!" the King exclaims, clapping his hands together.

The princess keeps her eyes fixed on my shoes, but a soft blush creeps up her neck. She's barely said a single word to me or met my gaze at all. I wonder if that will change without her father at her side or if that's simply what I have to look forward to for the next sixty years.

I suppose that is the small silver lining in this arrangement. A Mortal bride will grow old long before I do.

Still, she probably holds the same resentment towards the Fae that all Mortals do. Sixty years can feel like an eternity when you're spending them shackled to someone who loathes you.

"How have you been enjoying your time in our kingdom, Prince Silverthorn?" Eryndor presses a hand to my shoulder, guiding me toward the banquet table set for us. "I was saddened to hear your brother couldn't join us."

"Yes, well, as you know, running a kingdom is busy work." I force a smile.

He chuckles, the sound somewhat hollow. "Of course. Send him my regards and let him know how honored we are to begin this new age of alliance. I am hopeful this will be the first step in easing the tensions between our people."

Even Roland stiffens behind me, and I smirk slightly as I slip away from Eryndor's touch.

No one in this room believes that the King is marrying his youngest daughter to a Fae prince in an attempt to ease the relations between our peoples.

Velia is simply running out of space.

The King has spent much of his reign expanding his territory, but after years of brutal war with Purithia, he's reached his limits. His kingdom is overcrowded, with no room left to grow. After decades of conflict, the other Mortal Kingdoms have refused to take in his people, so he's turned to us.

The Fae kingdom is vast and abundant, perfect for his needs. That's the *only* reason I'm here right now. He obviously isn't happy that we're his only option. It's clear in the way his jaw flexes and the way his nobles glance toward my ears every so often, even while they're hidden under my mask.

"I'm afraid dinner was served some time ago," Eryndor apologizes, though frustration creeps into his voice. "But I can send for the kitchen to bring you something warm if you'd like."

I glance at the remnants of roast duck scattered on the plates around the table, resisting the urge to sigh.

"No need," I reply, shooting him another empty smile. "Let's not alter the night's plans for me. I'm sure the dancing is about to begin."

As if on cue, the strings swell with soft, melodic chords, and laughing couples begin to fill the marbled dance floor. Eryndor looks pointedly at his daughter, who, after a moment, peers up at me through thick dark lashes.

"Prince Silverthorn, would you like to dance with me?" Her bell-like voice makes my skin crawl.

An entire song spent pressed against her, while she stares at me with those empty, doe eyes, sounds somehow less appealing than sitting through a cold dinner with her father.

"Actually, princess," I grab Roland's elbow and shove him forward, perhaps a little harder than necessary. "Our dear delegate is a far better dancer than I. Why don't you allow him to take you for a spin while I find myself something to drink?"

Her wide eyes dart between us. "Oh... I suppose."

"Wonderful!" I praise, practically pushing him on top of her.

Roland leads her toward the dance floor, sending me a glare over his shoulder that promises I'll be hearing about this later.

I'll survive.

I spot the spirits laid out on a wooden table along the wall and waste no time making my way over. The ballroom is a swirling mess of light and sound, the chandeliers overhead casting a golden glow across the room.

Figures in shimmering gowns twirl across the gleaming floor, masks hiding their faces. The music alternates between hurried and slow, as if it can't decide what kind of night this is supposed to be. Above it all, laughter and conversation buzz.

I pour a generous amount of amber liquid into my glass and lean heavily against the wooden table, watching the scene unfold from the sidelines, as far removed as I can get without actually leaving the room.

And that's when I see her.

She steps through the curtains like a ghost from another world, her graceful, deliberate movements entirely out of place among the other Mortals in the room. Her gown catches the light with every movement—an elaborate silver creation that gleams like polished moonlight. The fabric seems alive, clinging to her frame before pooling onto the floor and trailing behind her with each deliberate step. The waiter's voice echoes through the ballroom, the words hitting me like an arrow.

"The Lady Huntyr Lachlan of Vastile."

Every head in the ballroom turns, eyes narrowing with both suspicion and curiosity, as she makes her way forward, scanning her surroundings with what seems to be a practiced awareness. The name means little to me, but there's something about that controlled grace of hers that has my fingers tightening around the glass in my hand.

Her midnight-black hair is twisted elegantly away from her face, a few loose tendrils falling forward and brushing over her shining silver mask. That mask, though it conceals half her face, only sharpens the rest of her features, making her icy blue eyes stand out even more sharply.

I watch those eyes flick over the room like she's marking each and every person, assessing them carefully. She meets my gaze only briefly, before two suitors rush forward, eager to claim her attention, bowing like fools. All at once, her keen evaluation of the room fades away, leaving a coquettish smile behind. She grins at the two men, takes the elbow that's extended to her, and lets them lead her off.

"Well, that's surprising," a voice says beside me. I turn to find a young man pouring himself a drink.

"Lady Lachlan?" I ask.

"The last time I met Lady Lachlan, she had gray hair and a cane."

I frown, glancing back at her curiously. "Her daughter, then?"

He shrugs. "No heirs, last I heard. Her late husband had a child from a previous marriage that they sent away after her father's death. Guess she's back now. Seems like she'll shake up the marriage season, though."

His gaze drifts to the men practically falling over themselves to get her attention. "Who'd have thought the long-lost Lachlan heir would be so… eye-catching?"

He's right. She *is* beautiful. Undoubtedly one of the more stunning women I've seen in this kingdom. And yet, as I watch her catch a glass one-handed that a hopeful suitor stumbles and drops, I can't help but feel intrigued by her for more than her features. She doesn't even flinch, simply smiles and hands the glass back to the poor boy.

The night drags on. The music swells as the couples move across the dance floor.

But I don't care about any of them. I watch Lady Huntyr Lachlan.

HUNTYR

Nothing, in all my years of training with thieves, assassins, and generally the worst people in the kingdom, had prepared me for this. For being so... desirable.

How am I supposed to find and lure the Fae prince away from this party to kill him when it feels like every man in the ballroom is tripping over himself to fawn over me? One goes to fetch me lemonade, only for another to ask for a dance. And when I finally spin out of that one's arms, another appears, attempting to discuss the weather in Vastile.

I don't *know* how the weather is. I haven't been in Vastile since I was a girl. I don't know whether the flowers have bloomed or if that lovely bakery in the city is still open. I certainly don't know how to lead a damn province of the kingdom.

It doesn't matter though, I remind myself. It won't get that far.

Once I kill the Fae prince, I'll shed this ridiculous gown and slip back into the shadows. Back to the life I built for myself before my stepmother's death revealed me as the sole heir to a title I never wanted.

As I half-listen to the man prattling beside me, I glance around the room casually. The princess sits with her father at the head table, her posture perfect and her eyes downcast, but the seat to her right remains empty, as it has been since I arrived. Her betrothed is nowhere to be found.

"Dance with me?" I interrupt, batting my eyelashes at the man beside me with a soft smile.

He sputters softly, caught off guard by my attention. "Oh. Of course, Lady Lachlan. I'd be honored."

I pull him to the center of the floor, easily mirroring the twirling steps of those dancing around us. I've never been trained in court dances, but the movements are easy enough to replicate, and the constant spinning gives me the perfect excuse to scan the crowd.

Men of all shapes and sizes. Some tall and lean, others thick around the middle. A few with gray streaks in their hair, others too young to be at a party this late. But none have the pointed ears I'm looking for. None except the man sitting beside the king, chatting easily.

I recognize him immediately. Roland Jellard, the diplomat charged with maintaining relations between Velia and the Fae Lands. He's not the Fae I'm after, but if I watch closely enough, he'll eventually have to move and speak with the prince. And then I'll have my target.

I've waited sixteen years for this. I can be patient.

⬥

"So, Lady Lachlan," Duke Walter Eyewig purrs my name, leaning uncomfortably close. "Surely a young lady like yourself will need assistance managing such a large expanse of land. Was your mother arranging prospects for you before her passing?"

I stiffen, angling my neck away from the putrid scent of alcohol on his breath. He's been talking at me for nearly five minutes, and the stench is starting to trigger one of my headaches. "She was my stepmother, actually."

The distinction might not mean much to him, but it means a hell of a lot to me.

The young blonde girl hanging on the arm of a gentleman who's been following me like a puppy all night laughs bitterly. "That's right! Isn't it true she sent you away after your father was murdered? What have you been doing all these years?"

She tilts her head, blonde curls spilling over the pink lace peeking out of the bodice of her silver gown. She hasn't bothered to wear a mask, proudly showing her perfectly proportioned face to anyone who cares to look. As she speaks, she presses herself closer to the man at her side, staking her claim.

"I was in school," I lie, offering a half-smile. It's not entirely false. I have been learning after all, just not the kind of lessons anyone here would expect.

"Your father was murdered?" the man attached to the blonde asks, frowning. *What's his name again? Jensen? Jaxon? Maybe Junsin?*

I flinch at the casual curiosity in his voice as pain begins to pulse in my temple. "Yes, he was."

"My," Jenson—no, Janson—sighs. "I'm sorry. Did they ever find who was responsible?"

The blonde laughs, a sharp, venomous sound. "Who else would have done it?"

Walter squints, his words slurring slightly. "What do you mean?"

Her eyes sparkle with malice as she looks at me. "The Fae killed him, of course."

For the briefest of seconds, I imagine how easy it would be to grasp onto the champagne bottle behind me and bring it down onto her head. No one would expect it. No one would move fast enough to stop it.

I feel the men's gazes on me, waiting for confirmation. It takes all the willpower I have to nod as pain explodes behind my eyes. I press my fingers to my temple, trying to push back the throbbing. What started as a dull ache is quickly progressing towards a full-blown migraine.

Not now. This cannot happen now.

"It must be difficult for you, Lady Lachlan," the blonde continues. "Celebrating the creatures who ruined your life."

A hand touches my elbow and I jerk, my fingers instinctively reaching for the weapon hidden in the bodice of my gown, but I slow as the smell of whiskey drifts closer.

"Are you alright, dear?" Walter whispers, his breath rank with alcohol. "You look pale."

"Truly," the blonde agrees with mock concern. "Has something upset you?"

Actually, violence is too good for her. It would be much more satisfactory to dump the champagne atop her perfectly coiled hair and watch her sputter like a fish in shock.

"Just a headache. If you'll excuse me, I need a drink."

"Allow me," Jossan, or whatever his name is, offers, but the blonde's grip on his arm is too tight for him to follow.

"That's okay," I call over my shoulder. "I'll only be a moment."

I hurry away, walking past the drink table and straight out the doors of the ballroom. My head throbs harder with each step as I slip into the hall, searching for an empty room. Any quiet space to find a reprieve in until the pain subsides a bit will suffice.

The first room I push into is a small, darkened office, and I slam the thick wooden door shut behind me, leaning back against the heavy frame and breathing deeply.

Breathe in for four. Hold. Breathe out for four. Hold.

I focus entirely on the familiar technique. Kristona had shown it to me shortly after he'd taken me in and realized I suffered from the recurrent pains. The steady rhythm helps to dull the near-constant pain temporarily, but never seems to make the headaches stay away.

"Am I interrupting something?"

My eyes snap open, my hand instinctively flying to the knife hidden in my gown. I scan the room, cursing myself for being so distracted by the headache that I didn't notice someone was already here. The office I walked into is very much occupied.

The man lounges in a chair behind a large mahogany desk, feet kicked up, arms folded behind his head, his posture deceptively casual. But there's nothing relaxed about the way his dark eyes assess me, sharp and unyielding. His jacket is pristine, his trousers pressed, and a black mask covers half his face. Dark curls frame his features, grazing his neck in a way that should soften him.

It doesn't.

When our gaze collides, a jolt runs down my spine so sharply that I would have stumbled backwards if I wasn't already pressed against the door.

"I just needed a moment away from the party," I say, straightening. I force my voice to remain steady, ignoring the hum in my chest at the way he watches me, eyes unblinking. "I wasn't expecting company."

"You're not the only one," he replies smoothly, his voice low and warm, like velvet stretched taut. I feel it more than I hear it. It dances across my skin like a physical presence.

I step further into the room, keeping my distance as I study him. He looks at me with a quiet intensity I'm not used to. Most men stare too much at my breasts or look away too quickly, unsure how to handle me. Especially those I've interacted with tonight.

He just continues watching me with that appraising expression.

"Shouldn't you be out mingling with the eligible young ladies?" I ask lightly, tilting my head. "Isn't that the point of tonight's festivities?"

"Not for everyone," he states simply, his gaze steady.

Another shiver runs down my spine, and it has nothing to do with the lingering ache in my temples. He's utterly beautiful. All sharp lines and dark features. It's positively distracting.

"Not for you?"

The corner of his mouth tugs up in a barely-there smile. "And you, Lady Lachlan? Shouldn't you be preparing for the marriage season?"

I raise a brow, letting a small, practiced smirk curve my lips. "I've never been one to meet expectations."

He leans forward slightly, resting his arms on the desk. The shift is subtle, but my pulse quickens nonetheless. Even seated, his presence fills the room. He seems... different from the other men from the ball. Those men are either too thin, lacking any real muscle, or too large from being able to afford more than their fair share of meals.

But this man?

Even in the dimly lit room, under fine clothes, I can make out the lines of thick biceps. He's lean and sharp, every inch of him pure coiled strength. His hands, rough with calluses, rest lightly on the desk.

This is a man who has spent time outdoors. This is a man who has wielded a blade and knows how to throw a punch.

A general perhaps? High enough to have earned an invitation to these festivities despite having gotten his hands dirty in war.

"Are you unwell?" he asks, his tone dipping lower, smoothing over the tension like silk.

I jerk my attention back to his face, and his gaze pins me in place. I force myself not to fidget under its weight. It's an odd sensation, being thrown off balance like this. I don't typically get unsettled by other people. More often than not, I unsettle others. Yet here I am, somehow flustered in a way that is both frustrating and maddeningly intriguing.

"Just a headache," I reply, my voice sharper than I intend.

"You should sit." He gestures to the armchair across from him. When I don't move, he slides a glass of water toward me. "Drink."

The faintest edge of command laces his words, and I bristle at it. Still, I give him a sweet smile. "I'm already starting to feel better, actually."

Not entirely a lie.

Apparently, the distraction of an attractive man is enough to soothe the ache.

His lips twitch. It's not quite a smile, but it's enough to tell me I've surprised him. "I used to get headaches all the time as a boy," he says, leaning back again. "They were debilitating. Still get them, depending on where I am."

His gaze flickers, and he studies me with renewed focus. I do the same, knowing that I'll have memorized that face before I leave the room.

The silence stretches, charged and heavy, until he finally says, "You've had them before—the headaches?"

"Since I was a girl," I answer honestly. "They come and go."

"Painful things usually do," he murmurs, almost to himself. "With enough time, at least."

"Usually?" The word slips out before I can stop it.

His eyes darken, and the faint smile vanishes. "When we're lucky," he says softly. "Other times pain can have a tendency to cling to the unlucky."

There's a rawness in his tone, an honest appraisal that feels familiar. The weight of it settles between us while I study him closer, trying to decipher what kind of man carries that much darkness in his voice.

"So, if you're not here to find a husband, what are you here for, Lady Lachlan?"

His clothes are expensive, his posture far too relaxed for someone concerned with offending the wrong people. Whoever he is, he's clearly important, maybe even more important than the men who've been hovering around me all evening.

Which might mean he knows more than the men I've been talking to.

Might as well see how useful this encounter can be.

I reach for my mask, untying it and placing it on the desk in front of me. "Well, it's all rather exciting, don't you think?"

DERIAN

Everything about her is striking.

Her voice isn't at all what I anticipated. It's low and smooth, each word sending a ripple through me. She's a woman of contradictions. All at once, she's serious and strong while also teasing and flirtatious. She bats her eyelashes like any other dimwitted, pretty woman of the court, but her eyes... they burn unnaturally bright.

There's a delectable amount of calculation in those eyes.

Her mind is alive, and, by damn, if that isn't intriguing.

When she reaches those delicate fingers behind her head and begins untying her mask, every part of me tenses, waiting to see what's hidden under the silver lace. Anticipation coils in my chest, and the payoff is even better than I predicted. Blemishless skin, unusually tan considering many of the ladies of court spend their days indoors. Almond-shaped eyes of the brightest blue I've ever seen on a woman. Full lips, more red than pink, and a narrow jawline accentuated by high, refined cheekbones.

Of all the Mortal women I've met since my ship docked in this wretched kingdom, she's the first one who's made my trousers feel too tight just by looking at her.

I've watched her all night. I saw how each time she danced with a man she spent the first two eight counts of every dance watching the feet of those around her before picking up the steps and making it all look effortless. I noticed how she smiled shyly at every man she talked to, only to turn away slightly and roll her eyes or make a face of disgust.

And now, by some magical coincidence, she's here. Alone. With me.

I want to unravel her. I want to tease apart every aspect of her and understand how she thinks. I might even need it. I'm desperate to peel back the layers of her contradictions to grasp why she seems so different from all the other Mortal women who've been grating on me since I arrived.

"It's all rather exciting, don't you think?" she asks, grinning wide enough that the whites of her teeth shine.

I narrow my eyes. "What is?"

"The princess's wedding, of course."

"You're excited by the princess's wedding?"

It doesn't fit the little I know of her. Sure, the other ladies of the court have spent the night gawking at the princess, eyes glittering with jealousy and curiosity. But not her. Lady Lachlan, the woman who herself admits she's not here to find a partner and often doesn't meet others' expectations, hasn't seemed all that interested in the upcoming nuptials. I haven't heard her mention it in any of the conversations I've overheard. She hasn't been sneaking peeks at me the way the other ladies do. She's no wide-eyed dreamer, this one.

And yet here she sits, leaning forward with bright eyes and excited energy.

She's playing a game with me. I just can't figure out why.

"Of course," she scoffs, her voice light and playful. "She looks so beautiful tonight. I don't know how her groom has been able to stay away."

Her groom. Not me.

So she doesn't know.

Most Mortals can sense when they're in the presence of a Fae. That innate otherness makes their skin crawl, their instincts bristle. Lady Lachlan seems oblivious.

Pity.

Maybe she isn't as clever as I've given her credit for after all.

"The prince is somewhat of a solitary creature," I tell her, noticing the way her nostrils flare slightly.

"Oh, you know him?"

"Some days more than others."

Her brows pinch, the tiny crease faint but there. She's waiting for me to clarify my meaning, and I have no interest in doing so.

"What's he like?" she finally asks tentatively.

I turn my gaze to the wall. I shouldn't feel disappointed in her. The simple questions are to be expected of a Mortal girl. She has to be only twenty, maybe twenty-one, summers. Of course she's curious about the Fae. She's likely grown up hearing the stories, the warnings, of how the immortal creatures across the sea have been twice blessed with beauty and power, only to be cursed by their arrogance. We created the Wastelands, they say. Poisoned the world.

And so, like every other immature girl at this ball, she's curious about the Fae prince who's said to be a monster in a beautiful body.

"He's exactly how you might imagine him to be," I say flatly.

Her brows knit further. "And how's that?"

I meet her gaze directly. "You've heard the rumors of Prince Derian, have you not? You know what they say about him."

Her lips part slightly, her sharp blue eyes scanning my face. Searching. She knows I'm hiding something, but she can't yet see what.

"They say he's a monster," she says finally, her tone soft. "That he can kill within seconds and not feel remorse. They say not even his brother, the King, can control him."

There's a careful neutrality to her words, but I don't miss the flicker of something sharper beneath them. Fear? No. Hatred, perhaps. It's subtle, buried beneath the polished exterior she wears so well, but it's there.

"And do you believe everything you hear, Lady Lachlan?" I ask, keeping my voice light, though I lean forward just enough to unsettle her.

Her smile doesn't waver, but her grip on the edge of the table tightens ever so slightly. "Not everything. I've found there's usually some truth hidden in whispers, though."

Clever. Careful. She plays her role well.

"I suppose that depends on the whisper," I reply smoothly, leaning back.

She doesn't look entirely convinced, but she smiles and drops her gaze, feigning demureness.

"If the prince is truly the monster they say," I continue, rising to my feet, "then perhaps it's best to avoid being caught in his path. You never know what he'd do to a woman like you."

Her breath catches so subtly that only someone watching closely would notice. She glances up at me, the playful edge to her expression slipping.

"Perhaps," she says finally, her tone clipped.

She stands abruptly, pushing her chair in. As she reaches for her mask, I'm faster, grasping hold of it and stepping around the desk.

"Allow me," I say, my voice low as I step behind her.

Her shoulders stiffen, and for a moment, she hesitates to give me her back. But after a slight nudge on her shoulder, she turns, letting me tie the mask into place over her dark curls. Her hair is silken, and for a moment, I imagine fisting my hands in it, pushing her forward at the waist and pulling so her spine arches for me.

"You should go back to the party," I say, my voice dropping even lower. "Before the prince notices one of the ball's most intriguing guests is missing."

I run my fingers across her shoulders. Her shiver is so slight it's almost imperceptible, but it gives me satisfaction knowing I'm having that effect on her.

If just a touch on her shoulder can make her quiver, I can only imagine the fun we could have together. I can't help the smirk tugging on the corner of my lips.

"I'm not all that intriguing," she protests.

I step back, letting my gaze linger on her for a moment longer. "You are far more fascinating than you realize, Lady Lachlan."

Her lips part as if to respond, but she simply nods, brushing her fingers against the edge of her mask as if reassuring herself it's secure.

With a glance over her shoulder, equal parts suspicion and curiosity, she turns and slips through the door, the click of the latch echoing softly in the room.

I remain where I stand, a low hum of interest settling in my chest as I turn my glass in my hand.

Intriguing, indeed.

Huntyr

I turn the corner of the hall sharply, pressing my back against the cold stone wall as I struggle to catch my breath, my chest heaving.

What in all of the Ever Realm is wrong with me?

Heat coils in my stomach, and my skin prickles as though I've been caught in a storm. My pulse is erratic, and I'm uncomfortably aware of the dampness between my thighs.

This isn't me.

I'm not some simpering court maiden, entirely undone and left wanting by a handsome man with a sharp jawline and piercing eyes.

Men don't faze me like this. I've never shied away from pleasure, but I also haven't ever romanticized it. I've taken lovers when it suited me and discarded them when it didn't. When you spend your life in the shadows, not knowing which day might be your last, you learn not to waste time on notions like modesty or propriety.

And sure, some of those men have made my breath catch. Some have even made my toes curl. But this...

I've never been so affected by a simple conversation.

One conversation. One man with an enigmatic smile and a voice like velvet, and I'm trembling, my body humming with need.

And I didn't even think to ask his name.

"Get it together," I hiss under my breath, flexing my fingers in an attempt to dispel the tingling that lingers since I left him.

I have a job to do.

I cannot let some beautiful, dark-haired man distract me from my purpose here.

My thoughts shift, grounding me in the present. Based on what he said, the prince isn't at the ball. That means returning to the party is a waste of time. If the prince isn't mingling with the court, where else could he be?

He's a guest here, and a dangerous guest at that. The royal guards wouldn't leave him unsupervised to wander the castle grounds. If he isn't downstairs... he has to be in his chambers.

Closing my eyes, I picture the castle schematics Mr. Dunklee sketched for me in meticulous detail. The guest rooms are on the second floor, tucked away in the eastern wing. I'll need to take the staircase at the far end of this hall, then follow the corridor—two lefts, one right.

I let out a slow breath, my hand instinctively brushing the hilt of the blade hidden in my bodice. My resolve hardens, my vision narrows, and my purpose focuses.

Time to go to work.

Adjusting the folds of my gown, I step lightly down the hall, my ears straining for any sound. The staircase is narrow, made of iron rods with a faint layer of dust. It's likely reserved for servants moving discreetly between floors. It creaks faintly underfoot as I ascend, clutching my skirt.

When I reach the second floor, I freeze, listening carefully. The hall is eerily silent, the faint echoes of music from below barely reaching this space.

Room by room, I search. The first few chambers are pristine, the beds perfectly made, the drawers empty. Guest rooms, yes, but clearly unoccupied.

Where are you, you pompous, immoral bastard?

My frustration climbs as I work my way down the corridor, the silence amplifying the sound of my footsteps, no matter how carefully I step. Finally, at the end of the hallway, my fingers close around a brass door handle. Unlike the others, this one is warm to the touch, faintly polished from use. Anticipation flutters in my stomach, sharp and insistent.

I ease the door open, its hinges groaning softly in protest.

The scent hits me first—a heady, intoxicating mixture of smoked leather and citrus. It invades my senses, wrapping around me like a second skin. It's decadent, bold, and utterly infuriating.

The room is a stark contrast to the empty chambers I passed. Silk pants are draped haphazardly over the bed, as though discarded without a second thought. The desk is littered with parchment, some scrawled in neat but hurried handwriting, others blank and curling at the edges. A book lies open on the rumpled sheets, its spine cracked from use.

The disarray tells me as much about him as the scent lingering in the air. He's powerful, yes, but careless. Accustomed to claiming spaces he enters as his own. Entitled and spoiled.

I take a cautious step inside and close the door behind me, my grip tightening on my blade.

This is it. This is the prince's room.

So where is he?

The floor creaks softly behind me, and I spin, releasing a second dagger from where it's strapped to my wrist as I turn to face the Fae male in the doorway.

He's ridiculously tall, and he wears a brown leather vest and tight breeches, leaving his enormous biceps and thick thighs visible. His chestnut hair falls easily to his shoulders, braided back away from his face. My lip curls as I take in his pointed ears.

"Who are you?" he demands, his voice firm as he reaches for the sword on his hip. "You shouldn't be here."

I grin menacingly. "And you should have gone to your party, your highness."

I waste no time, running forward and brandishing both my blades. He moves impossibly quick, pulling his sword and swinging it down to meet my crossed daggers in the air. Shock reverberates through my arms from the force of the blow, and I lash out, kicking him in the stomach as I twist the blades away and dance to his left.

He hardly even flinches against my strike, his face a picture of rage. He swings his blade again, and I dodge, only for him to seize my left wrist.

I gasp.

After years in this business, I'm no stranger to pain, but *this* is more than simple pain. It takes everything in me not to scream. I'll count myself lucky if my bones don't snap under the pressure.

My blade drops from my hand and clatters to the ground, earning me a taunting smile from the prince.

He releases my wrist, and I back away, subtly flexing my fingers, desperate for the pain to subside so I can finish this.

"You're fast," he compliments, "and obviously well-trained. But you didn't think it would be that easy to kill the Fae here, did you?"

"I don't need to kill all the Fae, just you."

Ignoring the throbbing in my wrist, I lurch to the side, spinning effortlessly so I can wrap my arm over his shoulder and pull his blade-wielding hand hard enough to force his grip to release.

Two can play the disarming game.

I kick his sword to the opposite side of the room and twirl my remaining dagger in my fingers, preparing to pierce it through the gentle flesh under his jaw.

The blow shakes me before I even have time to realize it's coming.

He backhands me so sharply I go flying to the floor, my vision blurring for a moment.

Fuck.

My head spins as I scramble forward. I need to get out of arm's reach. There's no way I'll hold up if that bastard hits me again with his Fae strength.

He stalks forward, wrapping his fingers around my ankle and pulling me back toward him.

I yelp, swinging blindly, my head still spinning, and feel my nails slide down his cheek.

"You bitch," he hisses.

Gripping my arm, he tosses me, flipping me onto my back before crawling over me.

I buck my hips, thrashing as I try to shake him off, but I'm no match for his superior strength. His hands climb to my throat, applying enough pressure to make my chest lock up in panic.

He's going to kill me.

The Fae prince is going to kill me.

My vision blurs, dark flecks swimming in my sight, and in my mind's eye, I see the image that's haunted me since I was a child.

My father's lifeless body in his bed, skin sunken in, eye sockets black and hollowed as though his eyes had melted into his skull. His mouth stuck open in a perpetual scream, his veins black with poison.

That's what the Fae did to him.

That's what they're about to do to me.

All these years of darkness, of murder and deception, and I'm going to die at the hands of the same monsters who took everything I ever loved.

Panic rises in me, louder than anything I've ever experienced before. I gasp, clawing at the Fae prince, smacking his meaty palms as my entire body locks in tension, heat burning suddenly through my spine.

"No!" I groan, pushing my hands against his face.

And light explodes from my fingertips.

⸺◆⸺

My heart pounds like a drumbeat, echoing in my ears, as I hurry through the halls back toward the ballroom, Kristona's instructions looping relentlessly in my mind.

When the deed is done, do not leave the party immediately. It will look suspicious. You cannot be followed. Above all, maintain your calm.

How am I supposed to stay calm after what just happened?

My pulse is a chaotic rhythm, and broken fragments of the memory flash before my eyes. The way he flew off me, his body hitting the wall with a sickening thud. The way his veins turned golden, glowing under his skin like molten metal. The way his eyes turned completely white.

He must have done something, some Fae trick. Maybe he pushed his strength too far, or tried to use his powers against me, only for it to backfire. That's the only explanation.

I slow my pace as I near the ballroom, the music spilling out from under the doors like a seductive whisper. Time for the last phase of the plan.

My steps grow deliberate, my breathing deeper and more controlled. I sweep my hair back over my shoulders, straighten my posture, and carefully school my expression.

Just a little longer, Huntyr. Then you're out of here.

A few more moments. Long enough to show my face, dance a little more, and make an exit without drawing suspicion. Then I can go home to Tyla and leave the cursed Lachlan name behind forever.

My lips twist into a bitter smile. I wonder what my stepmother would think now if she knew I'd just used her name to kill the Fae Prince.

When I step through the ballroom doors, warm light washes over me, and the hum of laughter and conversation fills the air. Happy, expectant grins from eligible men meet my gaze, and I paint a demure smile on my face, allowing myself to be swept into their world once more.

A short man with carrot-colored hair steps forward, extending an eager hand, and I accept his invitation to dance. As we fall into step, moving in time with the music, the rhythm should settle me, should ground me.

But it doesn't.

A prickle dances over my spine, the feeling unmistakable and sharp.

Someone is watching me.

DERIAN

For the second time this evening, I find myself watching Lady Lachlan.

I initially doubted her indifference to the marriage season. In my experience, most women who claim to disdain court politics still play the game just as well as anyone else. And yet, she has surprised me.

She is polite enough to the men who approach her, dancing with those who ask and offering small smiles. She moves through the room with effortless confidence. Yet there's truly no spark of ambition in her eyes. She doesn't scan the room looking for prospective matches like every other woman here. She is truly indifferent to it all.

Perhaps, having been sent away to school at such a young age, this is her first time at a social engagement like this. Maybe her lack of enthusiasm isn't an indication of disinterest, but rather a reflection of being overwhelmed.

But I don't think so.

I want to know for sure.

I want her alone again. Our time earlier wasn't nearly enough for me to move past this sudden infatuation. I want to strip her mind bare, pick apart every thread of her thoughts, and weave them back together until I understand everything about her. I want to know what makes her so different from every other Mortal woman I've met in this kingdom.

If I'm honest with myself, though, I want her alone for far more reasons than that.

I'm not shy about my appetites—most Fae aren't. Since landing in this kingdom, I've made no secret of the women who've shared my bed during long, wine-fueled nights. Still, even I have to admit that bedding another woman on the night of my engagement celebration would be highly inappropriate.

And yet, as I watch her sip her wine, her full lips stained crimson, her tongue darting out to catch a stray drop, I think maybe, just maybe, she'd be worth breaking the rules for.

My self-restraint dwindles the longer I watch her eyelashes flutter over those impossibly cerulean eyes. I'm on the verge of moving when a sharp touch on my elbow distracts me.

I turn, already scowling, to find Roland standing beside me, his face drawn tight.

"What?" I snap.

"We have a problem."

I lift a brow, waiting for an explanation.

"Kai is dead," he says, leaning close. "His body was found in your chambers."

The words hit like a blow to the chest.

How?

Power rushes to my fingertips, eager for release.

We've brought our people here under the guise of a truce, an alliance, and now one of my people has been murdered in the castle? My eyes seek out the King, drinking himself silly and laughing. He'll be dead before he even realizes what's happening.

Roland grasps my arm as I move to instep forward. "We need to handle this situation carefully."

I level my glare at him, my voice cold and sharp. "Do not presume to counsel me, Roland."

Roland may be someone I consider a friend, someone who's known me since I was a boy, but he is still under *my* chain of command. I will handle this however I damn well please, even if it means interrogating every person in this room and burning the guilty party alive in front of everyone.

This alliance was a fool's errand. A reckless decision made by my brother, a King who's forgotten the ignorance of Mortals. He may be willing to get on his knees for the creatures who have spent centuries villainizing us, but I won't. I won't stand for their cruelty against my people. I won't allow the Fae kingdoms to become a joke here.

Roland's mouth opens to protest, but I'm already moving. Over his shoulder, I catch the eye of the guard standing against the wall. The guard stiffens as I speak.

"Seal the doors. No one leaves this room until I return," I order, my voice like steel. "If anyone tries, they'll answer to me."

Roland stiffens beside me. "The treaty—"

"Fuck the treaty," I growl, grabbing Roland by the arm and pulling him toward the door.

The music fades behind us as we slip into the room where I sat with Lady Lachlan earlier. Rage claws at the edges of my control, and the thrum of power beneath my skin grows more desperate with each passing moment.

"Tell me everything," I demand, my voice tight with barely restrained fury. "Now."

His explanation is short. He went to my chambers to see if that's where I'd disappeared to, only to find the room destroyed and Kai's body lying there. No sign of the perpetrator. No evidence to suggest who they might be.

"Where's the body?" I demand.

Roland hesitates. "I had it disposed of."

"You *what?*"

His dark eyes flash with indignation. "You may not care about this alliance, Derian, but your brother, the King, does. We can't allow anything to jeopardize this. Kai's death is... unfortunate, but nothing more than a symptom of the tensions between our peoples. Tensions that can only be eased by you marrying the Mortal princess."

Lightning cracks outside, a storm rolling in. Roland's gaze shifts nervously to the window. "Control yourself," he warns.

I inhale deeply, forcing the lid back on my power. "His death is more than unfortunate. I refuse to bow to Mortals who kill us while we're here offering to help them."

"So what would you do?" Roland huffs, folding his arms.

I clench my jaw, fury coursing through me. "Were there witnesses?"

"A maid found a sliver of silver fabric in the room. It had bits of lace and pearls. Could it have come from one of the women you've entertained?"

No, the women I brought into that room certainly weren't wearing ballgowns.

A woman?

A Fae male brought down by a Mortal woman.

"She must be found," I announce. "And held accountable."

Roland's chest lifts and falls in an exaggerated sigh. "The alliance must stand, Derian."

I turn the information over in my mind, weighing every possibility, every path, until only one remains. A path that allows both problems to be solved. It's potentially controversial and definitely reckless.

But it just might be effective.

"You have a plan," Roland notes, watching me closely.

"It's not one you're going to like," I reply.

⚬

"You cannot do this!" Roland insists, hurrying to keep pace with me as I stride back toward the palace ballroom.

"I can, actually." My voice is clipped, my patience thinning. "I may be a prince, but I am a Silverthorn warrior first and foremost. This is precisely within my Gods-given rights."

I actually don't know why I didn't think of this sooner.

It's been decades since anyone in my bloodline has called a Conclave. It's only happened once since King Almayi died without an heir, and his most trusted guard, Omari Silverthorn, was named his successor. Since then, our family has been royals first, warriors second.

But I have always looked better in armor than wearing a crown.

Roland presses on, undeterred. "Your brother will never allow this." His breath comes quicker now, his shorter strides working twice as hard to keep up with mine.

I cast him a withering look. "My brother isn't here right now, is he?"

His mouth presses into a firm line. He knows as well as I do that King Luceron's absence is to my advantage.

"I don't see how this solves our problem," he argues. "Even if you force every woman here into the Conclave, one of them will still win. And if she's strong enough to kill a Fae guard, she's strong enough to win."

"No one can predict who wins the Conclave," I counter. "And besides, I only need to bide my time until I uncover who's responsible for Kai's death. Then we ensure she doesn't win." I glance at him. "I get my revenge. The king gets his marriage. No one is the wiser."

Roland exhales sharply, his face reddening. "I simply don't like it."

I arch a brow. "I don't recall asking for your approval."

Nor do I need it.

With that, I push open the ballroom doors.

The room stills. Every head turns toward me. The only ones who remain unmoved are the Fae guards stationed at every exit, preventing anyone from leaving.

"Prince Derian!" King Eyrendor rises from his seat, his face flushed with barely contained anger. "What is the meaning of this? Your guards have no right to bar the doors!"

A prickle of awareness runs down my spine. I turn my head just slightly and lock eyes with Lady Lachlan.

Her expression is carefully blank, but those brilliantly calculating blue eyes narrow slightly as my name registers and she connects the stranger she met in the office with the prince from the Fae Kingdom. Even in the face of a brewing storm, though, she remains composed and unshaken.

Fascinating.

Despite the severity of the moment, I can't help myself. I wink.

She doesn't react, but I don't miss the way her fingers tighten around the stem of her wineglass.

"King Eyrendor." I sweep my arms wide as I approach the dais, my voice smooth and practiced. "You'll forgive me, but I didn't want anyone to leave before my announcement."

A crease forms between the king's brows. "Announcement?"

Roland murmurs under his breath, "I would be remiss if I didn't caution you one last time."

I ignore him.

I ascend the steps deliberately, standing before the king as the weight of the room presses in around us.

"There's been a slight change to our alliance."

Eyrendor sputters. "What?"

"No need to worry," I say with an easy smile. "We are still willing to open our borders to your people, just as we expect you will still allow our people to explore the Wastelands off your border."

The ballroom erupts. A collective gasp ripples through the gathered nobles.

Ah. So the good king hasn't told his people about that part of the deal.

I smirk. I'm not surprised.

"You cannot do this!" someone shouts from the crowd. "The Fae will expand the Wastelands! They seek to kill us all!"

"Silence!" the king roars, his expression darkening. "King Luceron assures me this will not happen! The war between our peoples ended centuries ago. It is time to move forward."

"Which is exactly what we'll do," I agree.

Eyrendor eyes me warily. "Then what about the alliance is changing?"

"There is an ancient tradition among my family," I explain. "My brother overlooked it when drafting the treaty, which is understandable, as it is a custom more common among the warriors of our bloodline. Luceron has always been more of a politician." I allow a slow, wolfish smile. "And I have always been... well, the more violent of the two of us."

I practically feel Roland rolling his eyes behind me.

"Anyway," I continue, turning slightly to address both the king and the crowd. "I'm officially calling for a Conclave."

The princess speaks unprovoked for the first time, her voice careful but clear. "What is this Conclave?"

Roland, ever the diplomat, answers before I can. "It is a competition, Your Highness," he explains, keeping his tone gentle, as if softening the words will dull their impact. "To determine who will wed Prince Derian."

The king's face purples with rage. "You have already agreed to marry my daughter! It is signed!"

He should count himself lucky I'm not forcing his daughter into this competition.

I purse my lips. "Don't you consider all the citizens of your country to be your children? In a manner of speaking, at least."

Eyrendor opens his mouth to protest, but then closes it.

I know I've won.

He is too desperate for our land, our resources, to fight me on this.

"So," he says, his voice tight. "How do we proceed?"

My guards are already moving through the crowd, pulling forward every woman adorned in the slightest bit of silver. One by one, they gather before me, six in total, each looking unsteady on their feet.

It is hard to believe any of them could have killed a Fae.

But Mortal hatred has taken many of my people before. I will not allow the guilty party to slip away this time.

"The prince has chosen these young women to compete in the Conclave," Roland announces. "They will leave with us for the Fae kingdom."

"How will we come home?" a blonde woman in a navy-and-silver gown cries, her voice thick with fear.

Roland stiffens beside me.

m"You won't return," he says simply. "The Conclave is to prove your strength. It is a fight to the death. Only the strongest can marry a Silver-thorn warrior."

Chaos erupts.

Shouts of protest and confusion echo through the ballroom. The king rages as the nobles demand answers. My guards hold firm, barring the exits as some try to flee.

But I barely hear them.

Something is wrong.

My instincts tingle as I scan the gathered women, searching for the source of my unease.

And then...I realize.

We're missing one.

I straighten, my gaze sweeping the room until it lands exactly where I expect it to.

Lady Lachlan.

She remains seated, her glass of wine still poised delicately in her grip.

Her expression is unreadable, but those eyes...

I smirk. "Lady Lachlan will also be coming with us."

Her gaze flickers.

Not with fear, or even shock.

No, that cold calculation is back.

10

HUNTYR

I killed the wrong damn man.

I wasted my time flirting with the actual Fae prince, only to drive my blade into a guard instead.

How had I ever found him attractive? Really, I should have known just from his cocky arrogance alone.

Even now, Derian watches me with that infuriating smirk plastered on his face, gesturing lazily for a guard to come and collect me.

I rip my arm from the male's grasp before he can touch me and stride to the front of the room on my own, ignoring the way the Fae track my movements.

"What if we don't want to marry you?" I challenge, my voice cutting through the tense silence.

His gaze follows me, unyielding, as I step beside the other women gathered at the front. He descends the steps, coming to stand before me, suffocating me with the scent of leather and citrus.

"Doesn't every girl want to marry a prince?"

I lift my chin, meeting his eyes without flinching. "I've never been one to meet expectations."

Our gazes lock in silent confrontation.

"So you say," he finally murmurs quietly.

Derian turns toward the crowd, angling himself between them and the King. "There are many benefits to winning the Conclave beyond marriage. Winners are among the most respected warriors in the Fae kingdom. My wife will have my protection. She'll live in my castle, never wanting for jewels or riches."

He glances at me again, as if measuring whether his words sway me. I arch a brow impetuously. I grew up slinking through the slums. I never cared for wealth, and now that my stepmother is dead, I have more than enough to last a lifetime.

This prince is sadly mistaken if he thinks diamonds will get me to fall on my knees for him.

Derian inclines his head, almost as if acknowledging my lack of interest.

"The winner of the Conclave also gets a gift of her choice from her betrothed."

"Anything?" the girl to my left whispers, wide-eyed.

I glance at her. She's short, the top of her red hair barely reaching my shoulder. I noticed her earlier because the white and silver gown she wears is eerily similar to mine.

"Anything," Derian confirms with a charming grin. "You could ask for the biggest estate in the world, and I'd set sail the next day to find it for you."

His eyes find mine again, as if waiting to see if *that* entices me. I'm distracted though, too focused on noticing the women standing near me.

The redhead's dress is almost identical to mine. And the brunette next to her? Her gown mirrors the redhead's.

I scan the line of women, my stomach twisting as I do. We're all different. All varying in height, complexion, and hair color, but there is one thing we share. The silver threaded through our gowns.

Well, fuck.

Someone saw me.

Every muscle locks into attention as I mentally scan my body, confirming that all my weapons are still in place. My pulse hammers.

And yet...

The Fae aren't arresting me.

Derian still watches me like I'm a puzzle he's trying to solve, not a murderer he's suspicious of.

I exhale slowly, forcing my shoulders to relax. Someone might have noticed my dress, but they didn't see enough to know exactly who I was.

Which means I have a choice to make.

I can fight my way out, expose myself as the Huntress, and likely die in the process. Or I can stay Lady Lachlan for a little while longer and go along with this stupid contest.

Play along, find the right moment, and kill my real target.

I weigh the options in seconds.

"What if I don't want jewels or land?" I ask, my mind spinning with possibilities.

Derian steps toward me again, closing the space between us until he's so close a simple shift forward would press my breasts against his chest. The proximity sends a rush of anticipation over me, but if he's as affected, he doesn't let it show on his face as he stares down at me. His attention is absolute, like no one else in this room exists.

"Win the Conclave," he says, his voice low and sure. "And I'll give you *anything* you want."

And with that, my decision is made.

Not only does this Conclave give me a second opportunity for revenge, that prize sure sounds tempting.

I don't want a damn thing from him, but I might *need* something. Or rather, Tyla needs something.

That Fae potion only bought her a little more time. Joneson seemed sure the Fae had something stronger, though, something that might even be able to cure her. Without even realizing it, Derian just gave me the perfect opportunity to kill two birds with one stone.

A plan takes shape, sharp and clear.

I'll compete in this Conclave. Win. Take the healing tonic for Tyla.

Then, once she's cured, I'll kill my brand-new husband on our wedding night.

Maybe I'll even get lucky and take out his bastard brother, too.

A slow smile spreads across my lips as I stare up at the prince.

"Let the games begin."

His lips pull into a slight grin. "The game has already begun, Lady Lachlan."

⸺◆⸺

We're forced to spend the night in the castle, locked away in separate rooms like prisoners. I suppose they're worried we'll try to sneak out, or maybe even try to kill each other before the Conclave even begins.

I wake to sunlight glittering through the window, sore from sleeping on a mattress that was too soft while still trapped in the suffocating gown from last night. My ribs ache from the corset's relentless grip, and a sharp, familiar pounding in my temples nearly blinds me. Without my tonics, the headache is unbearable, each throb shooting stars across my vision.

Pinching the bridge of my nose, I try to focus on anything but the pain. My thoughts quickly wander to Tyla, and guilt twists in my gut. She'll be worried when she realizes I didn't come home last night. Maybe Kristona will check on her, though I doubt even he can save me now. By the time anyone realizes what's happened, I'll already be on my way to the Fae lands. Too late for rescue.

Not that I want it.

As ridiculous as this competition is, it's also my chance to get everything I've ever wanted: a cure for Tyla and revenge for my father.

All I have to do is kill six noblewomen and claim my prize. Easy.

I sit up, wincing as I reach behind me to fumble with the laces of my corset. I'm halfway through tearing the gown off when a knock sounds at the door. It swings open before I can respond, and a servant enters, bowing slightly.

"Good morning, Lady Lachlan."

"Call me Huntyr," I snap. Lady Lachlan will always be my stepmother, and I want nothing to do with her cursed name.

The servant hesitates, blinking as if she's unsure how to handle my tone. "Very well, Huntyr. I've been asked to deliver something appropriate for your journey."

She steps forward, a gown draped over her arms. It's green velvet, simple and sturdy, with thick fabric to keep me warm on the voyage. Practical, yes, but the skirt is too narrow, too restrictive.

"Is there another option?" I ask, raising a brow.

Her lips press into a thin line. "Is the color not to your liking?"

"It's not just the color," I say, waving vaguely at the gown. "I need pants."

"Pants?" Her tone is incredulous, like I've just asked her to fetch me a dragon.

"Yes, pants. Trousers. Something I can actually move in."

She stares at me, clearly trying to decide if I'm joking. "The other ladies will—"

"I don't care what the other ladies are wearing."

The servant sighs, bowing again before leaving the room, locking the door behind her. Rolling my eyes, I strip off the silver gown, letting it crumple into a heap on the floor. I rip the pins from my hair, groaning in relief as the dark waves tumble down my shoulders.

When the servant returns, she opens the door cautiously, her arms laden with garments. "I've brought—oh!" She squeaks and nearly drops the bundle, her cheeks flushing as she slams the door shut behind her.

I grin at her embarrassment. "It's just a body. We all have them."

She mutters an apology, avoiding my gaze as I scoop up the leather trousers and gray blouse from her arms. The loose top slides over my head easily, a welcome reprieve from the suffocating corset. The pants are snug but comfortable, the soft leather molding to my legs. The belt fastens securely around my waist, its pouches perfect for stashing weapons.

"That's better," I sigh, running a hand down the fabric.

The servant hands me my boots without a word, watching as I tug them on and lace them tightly. Once finished, she curtsies awkwardly and scurries out. By the time the guards arrive to escort me to the docks, I've slipped a dagger into the waistband of my pants and tucked another into my boot.

The castle halls are quiet as I follow the guards, my boots clicking softly against the stone. Salty air coats the back of my throat. Silently, I pull my cloak over my shoulders, tying it at the neck as we step onto the dock and I scan over my surroundings.

"Stay here," one of the guards barks, depositing me among the other contestants.

I cross my arms, glancing at the women gathered. Three look terrified, one looks half-asleep, and two are practically buzzing with excitement. They glance at me, their expressions turning sour as they take in my outfit.

"Do you see what she's wearing?" one of them whispers loudly.

Of course, it's the blonde who brought up my father last night. She looks me up and down with a sneer. "They probably didn't teach her how to dress properly at that school of hers."

No, but Kristona taught me how to kill, which will be far more useful.

I blow her a kiss, flipping her off for good measure before turning my attention to the ship.

Derian stands near the ramp of a sleek, obsidian ship, carefully decorated with Fae symbols. He's dressed for travel, in a loose-fitting tunic and versatile trousers that hug his muscular thighs. I keep my appraisal of him short before glancing away to hide the fact that I'm listening in on his hushed conversation with his advisor.

"They're not going to like this," Roland warns.

"They don't have a choice," Derian replies, his gaze sweeping over the dock. "The Conclave has been declared. It cannot be undone."

With a flick of his wrist, he signals for us to board. Guards push us forward onto the ramp, and as soon as my boots hit the ship's deck, I feel it... a strange hum of power beneath my feet.

There are no oars, no sails. Just magic, pulsing through the vessel like a heartbeat.

They waste no time in undoing the ropes that tie us to the dock, and the other women and I are herded towards the center of the main deck. I refuse to shudder, forcing my expression to remain neutral as the ship eases free and starts moving along the waves. The port district fades behind us, until Velia is nothing more than just a shadow on the horizon.

Then, with a sudden lurch, the ship begins to rise.

Gasps ripple through the women as the deck tilts slightly and the vessel lifts itself into the air. They clutch the railings and each other, their fear evident in their wide eyes and trembling hands.

I stand firm, though, simply adjusting my footing and keeping my eyes on the horizon.

Let them gape at the Fae magic. Let them all marvel at the wonders of the world they barely understand.

I refuse to be impressed by any of it.

I need to stay focused. I need to nurture the fiery rage boiling in my stomach, because the time is coming when I'll finally be able to release it all. And when I do, Prince Derian is going to regret ever laying eyes on me.

Derian

Dinner is served below deck.

The women chatter amongst themselves while they eat, tossing flirtatious glances my way. The bolder ones lean in closer, their voices honeyed, their smiles practiced. Like I said, every girl wants to marry a prince.

I simply ignore them.

In truth, I want a wife less now than I did before this damned contest began. No amount of fluttering eyelashes or feigned shyness is going to change my mind.

I eat in silence, half-listening to Roland prattle on about my brother's plans to explore the Wastelands. The conversation should interest me, and yet it doesn't. At first I'm not even sure why I'm so uneasy and struggling to pay attention to him. Then it hits me.

I can't seem to relax because she's not here.

Lady Lachlan.

I scan the room again, slower this time. But there's no dark curls, no sharp blue eyes narrowed in suspicion. I've been busy since we started the voyage, discussing the Conclave with Roland and meeting with the ship's captain to get updates on when we should arrive. The other ladies seemed to always be nearby, watching me from a distance, but she went straight to her cabin and stayed there.

It didn't bother me at first, primarily because I figured she would eventually emerge and join the other women at some point. She has to eat, after all. Doesn't she?

I'm on my feet in an instant.

"Excuse me," I say abruptly, grabbing a plate of untouched food and climbing the steps to the top deck.

Power rushes through me when I finally spot her, and wind blows suddenly, brushing back the hair from her face and rippling the soft fabric of her blouse. It's an odd choice of wardrobe for a noblewoman.

The black leather of her pants catches the faint glow of the setting sun, the snug fit a stark contrast to the flowing skirts of the other noblewomen, and Gods, does she fill them out.

I'd had to physically stop myself from staring at the curve of her ass when she'd climbed aboard the ship.

She's seated on the deck, leaning back against the rail, as she stares up at the starry sky. When the wood creaks under my feet, though, she jumps to alertness.

"You expecting trouble?" I tease as I lower myself next to her, setting the plate between us.

"Trouble seems to have a way of finding me." She eyes the food suspiciously. "I find it best to remain prepared."

"And what kind of trouble are you expecting, exactly?"

She finally glances at me, holding my stare. Those sharp blue eyes flick over my face, then down to where my arm rests on my knee, assessing and shrewd.

She's always watching. Always thinking.

I wonder if that mind is ever at ease.

"There's plenty of dangers on this boat," she murmurs.

I smirk. "The Conclave won't officially begin until we're in the Fae kingdom. I think you're safe enough for now."

Lady Lachlan rolls her eyes, and I suspect she wants to refute my claim, but she holds her tongue as I nudge the plate toward her. She glances towards it but remains still, not taking it.

"So." I stretch out my legs, crossing them at the ankles, making myself comfortable despite the way she glares at me. "Are you really so desperate to avoid your competition that you're willing to miss meals?"

She exhales slowly, the wind lifting the edges of her hair. Her scent curls through the night air, winding around me, settling low in my stomach. Dark, floral, and faintly sweet.

The woman doesn't have to do anything but sit here, and I want her.

As subtly as possible, I trace over her figure with my eyes, memorizing the line of her breasts and curve of her hips. That dress at the ball had managed to hide a delectable body, but now, even while sitting, it's impossible to deny the perfect proportions of her. And Gods, that mouth. Full lips, tinted nearly red despite the fact that her face is free of cosmetics. I barely know the woman, but I can just imagine the things she knows to do with that mouth.

Fraternization with the contestants of the Conclave is encouraged. It's expected that I would want to bond with whomever my future wife will be. Intimate relationships, however, are forbidden.

Again, though, she might be worth breaking the rules for.

"Who says it's the women whose company I want to avoid?"

I bark a laugh. "No need to lie."

Those blue eyes narrow at me slightly before she turns away, all too effectively dismissing me as if I'm not a damn prince, a powerful Fae prince at that. She returns her gaze to the sky, content to sit in silence and wait for me to leave.

"I didn't peg you to be so boring."

She bristles, twisting towards me with a look of frustration. "That's a bit rude."

"And staring at an empty sky for hours is a bit uninspiring."

Her mouth twitches. Those full lips pucker ever so slightly while her jaw works, and I'm practically holding my breath waiting for her retort.

But then she turns away again.

Magic rises in me, bringing another sharp breeze that rustles back her hair. She's a stubborn little creature. Self-assured, seemingly unafraid, entirely unlike the dim-witted girls below the deck. Entirely unlike most people I interact with actually. There aren't many souls in this realm that would risk annoying me.

My eyes trail over her. I'm lost in her presence, filled with equal parts of lust and interest. It's an intoxicating mixture, and so help me, she doesn't seem to be feeling anything close to what I am.

"I'm weighing my odds," she finally says, snapping me from my thoughts just as I was about to give up on trying to draw her into a conversation.

"And?"

She looks at me, the silvered moonlight catching her hair, turning it nearly purple.

"Better than most." She shrugs, the left half of her lips quirking up slightly.

I chuckle, staring at her as she turns back to the sky and leans her head against the wood of the railing. "Confidence looks good on you."

She rolls her eyes again, an action that sends a bolt of need through me, and the wind catches her hair again, blowing it back over her collarbone to expose some more of that perfectly tanned skin to me.

Lady Lachlan looks to me from the corner of her eyes. "You should save your flirting for someone who's impressed by it."

"You liked my flirting at the ball."

"I did not," she scoffs, her brow pinching in irritation.

"It's okay if you aren't willing to admit that you think I'm cute."

"I think you're arrogant."

"Two things can be true."

She shakes her head before turning to me with a wicked grin. "You know, if your idea of flirting is not admitting who you are, and telling women that you find yourself cute, you might need to practice a bit more."

"Oh I've had plenty of practice flirting with women. Among other things," I purr, enjoying the way her eyes darken ever so slightly as I lean towards her. "Want me to prove it?"

"I want you to go away."

"And I want you to eat something."

She glances towards the plate quickly before watching me with such intense scrutiny, it's as if she's the royal and I'm the one vying for her affection. I've never seen anything quite like her eyes, neither in their color nor their thoughtfulness.

Finally, with a frustrated huff, she reaches forward and grabs a cube of cheese from the plate and pops it into her mouth. A small, unexpected satisfaction blooms in my chest.

"Happy now?"

"Ecstatic."

"Great, then you can leave."

Not yet. I'm having far too much fun to leave. Her eyes narrow, and for a moment, we're in a silent standoff.

"What did your advisor mean earlier?" she asks suddenly. "When he said they won't like it?"

I lean back on my palms, watching her carefully before I look pointedly at the plate again. "Try the sugared pecans."

It takes a moment, but eventually she gathers that I'm not going to tell her anything unless she continues eating, and she scoops a handful into her palm with an irritated growl. I huff a quiet laugh. "So not just a loner, but an eavesdropper too?"

"I have excellent hearing."

"You're nosy," I counter.

She doesn't even pretend to be apologetic as she gives me an exaggerated shrug. "I prefer observant."

That's one word for it.

I consider before answering. "Let's just say the Conclave hasn't always been open to Mortals. Some of my people won't like it."

She doesn't react right away, but eventually I see it—the faint tightening of her jaw, the flicker of awareness in her eyes, the way her fingers tighten into a fist around the nuts before releasing softly. She understands exactly what that means.

Good.

She'll stay on guard.

I don't know why I felt the need to warn her, to prepare her for the harshness of the fortress I'm bringing them to, but something uneasy in me settles as she nods softly.

"Well, I guess they'll just have to get used to us Mortals walking around."

"How's your head?" I ask suddenly, smirking when she frowns in confusion. I lift a hand, tapping my temple. "You get headaches."

She blinks, as if only just remembering. "Oh. I've had an awful one all day, but it's finally getting better."

I nod. "That's good. If you get one when we dock, you can send for pain tonics."

She doesn't answer, just stares at me with that same expression of suspicion and thought, as if she's searching for hidden meanings in my words.

I push off the railing and stand, stretching, before glancing back down at her. "You should get some rest, Lady Lachlan."

She scowls, her jaw tightening and her fingers twitching slightly. "Huntyr."

I pause.

"My name is Huntyr," she corrects again, her voice sharp.

The spark in her voice strikes odd feelings within me. Confusion, of course, but curiosity too. It's not that she wants an air of familiarity between us. No, she's drawing a line between her and her title. It's a feeling I'm familiar with, but have rarely seen in others.

A slow grin spreads across my face. "Very well," I say. "Finish your food and get some sleep, Huntyr."

"I don't respond well to orders," she says, a wry look in her eyes that makes me want to laugh.

"Hasn't anyone told you I'm a prince? You have to do what I say."

"As you said, two things can be true. You can be a prince *and* a Fae bastard."

I lean forward, grab the plate, and push it closer towards her. "Ah, but I'm a Fae bastard you might just marry."

Then I turn and leave her there, still watching the sea.

The ship glides into the harbor at Oxhurn under a thick veil of mist, the hull slicing cleanly through the water. The fortress rises from the cliffs ahead, its jagged towers clawing at the gray sky.

Already, the dock is teeming with activity. Soldiers, merchants, and dockhands scurry about, their movements precise and deliberate. Unlike the Mortal harbors in Velia or Covia, which bustle with trade and luxury, Oxhurn operates like a well-oiled machine. People move with purpose, all of them aware of the dangers that exist just beyond the borders of this fortress.

I lean on the railing at the bow, arms crossed, watching the organized chaos below. The sharp bite of salt in the air mingles with the faint metallic tang of weaponry being sharpened somewhere in the distance. My gaze sweeps across the dock and lands on a familiar figure. Caldren. My oldest friend stands with his hands on his hips, his broad shoulders stiff with tension. Sunlight glints off his auburn hair. Even from here, I can see the frown etched onto his face.

He looks pissed. But then again, when is he not?

As the ship bumps gently against the dock, I make my way down the ramp, boots thudding against the wood. Caldren's frown deepens as I approach, but there's a flicker of relief in his dark eyes.

"You're late," he grumbles, his voice rough. The sound of it grounds me in a way I hadn't realized I needed.

I clap him on the shoulder as I pass, leading the way toward the fortress without slowing. "Aw Cal, did you miss me?" I tease.

"I'm considering throwing you back into the ocean." His tone is flat, but I catch the faintest twitch at the corner of his mouth. "Please tell me the rumors aren't true."

"Unfortunately, they are." I glance back at him with a grin. "I *am* as devilishly handsome as I am menacingly powerful."

Caldren groans, exasperation rolling off him in waves. "You called a Conclave. Here."

He doesn't phrase it as a question, and the weight of his words lingers between us as we pass through the gates of the fortress. The stone walls rise around us, cold and unyielding, but the familiar clang of steel from the training yard offers a strange sense of comfort. The air here is warmer than the sea breeze, heavy with the scent of sweat and damp earth.

I breathe in deeply, luxuriating in the smell of home.

Fortresses like this, and that of the one in Amberhull, will always be more of a home to me than my brother's castle.

"Where else would I have it?" I ask, keeping my tone light.

"You shouldn't be having it at all," Caldren snaps. His voice drops lower, his frustration barely restrained. "People are already on edge. The Wastelands are growing. We're fighting back more Velkai every day, and you think dragging Mortals into our kingdom, involving them in our sacred traditions, is a good idea?"

We step into the training yard, where rows of soldiers spar in pairs, their movements precise and controlled. A blacksmith hammers away at an anvil in the corner, the rhythmic clanging punctuating Caldren's words.

"I think I was placed in a difficult situation," I say evenly, my voice hardening. "And I made the best decision I could."

Caldren falls silent, his lips pressing into a thin line. He knows better than to push me too far, but I can feel his disapproval radiating off him like heat.

"The Fae won't like it," he mutters after a moment. "They'll object. Your brother—"

"The Conclave is law," I interrupt sharply. "Let them fight. Let them object. I'll deal with it."

He follows me through the stone corridors of the fortress, his boots echoing against the floor. The tension between us is palpable as we make our way to my quarters and I shove open the heavy wooden door.

The room is exactly as I left it. Weapons are scattered across the floor, their edges dulled with disuse. I'll have to send them for maintenance. The bed is unmade, the blankets tangled. Papers clutter the desk in the corner, their contents long forgotten.

"It's not just me you'll need to convince," Caldren says softly, leaning against the doorframe.

I turn to him slowly, narrowing my eyes. "What does that mean?"

He hesitates, his gaze flickering away from mine. "Seraphina's here."

For fuck's sake.

I drag a hand through my hair, irritation bubbling just beneath the surface. Of course, she's here. Because dealing with the Conclave wasn't already enough of a headache.

"I hope you know what you're doing," Caldren says after a long pause.

"I always do," I mutter, though the words sound less convincing than I'd like.

He raises an eyebrow, but he doesn't push. Instead, he nods toward the corridor. "She's in the war room. I believe she's expecting you."

Of course, she is. Where else would Seraphina be?

I exhale sharply, already bracing myself for the conversation ahead. "Thanks for the warning."

Caldren smirks, the tension in his posture easing ever so slightly. "Good luck. You'll need it."

I shoot him a withering look before stepping out into the hallway, the weight of the Conclave, and everything it represents, settling heavily on my shoulders.

<hr>

I can already hear the voices as I near the war room, irritation bubbling beneath my skin. That room is meant for strategy, not idle chatter. Seraphina has never cared much for rules, though, least of all the ones that don't serve her.

My boots echo faintly against the stone as I step inside, taking in the scene.

A map of the Wastelands sprawls across the war table, littered with tiny wooden markers denoting strategic locations. It's supposed to be one of our most valuable resources.

And Seraphina's *ass* is on it.

Perched on the edge of the table, she flicks a dagger between her fingers, laughing at something one of her warriors has said. Her fire-bright hair catches the torchlight, making her seem even more untouchable, even more dangerous. The three Fae warriors before her look up immediately as I lean against the doorframe, and the air noticeably warms when Seraphina glances over her shoulder and meets my gaze.

Her smile vanishes.

"*Out. Now!*" she snaps.

The trio hesitates for half a second too long.

"Did I stutter?" she growls, and the torches lining the walls flare with her temper. "*Out!*"

They scramble to their feet, hurrying past me as I shut the door behind them.

I turn back to her, crossing my arms over my chest as she stands slowly, deliberately. The air crackles with the scent of smoke. She's dressed in her usual training leathers, though she's notably carrying fewer weapons than usual. Not because she needs less, but because she doesn't need *more*.

"I can see you think we have some things to discuss."

She shrieks, hurling the dagger at my head.

I dodge, frowning when the blade *thunks* into the wood above my shoulder.

"Was that necessary?"

A wooden marker follows. I step aside, watching it sail past.

"You called a Conclave," she hisses, grabbing another marker and chucking it at me.

This one I catch midair, setting it back onto the table where it *should* have stayed in the first place.

"You seem upset," I observe drily, stepping around the table just as she grabs a metal letter opener and lunges for my chest.

I catch her wrist before the blade can pierce the skin, my grip tightening just enough to still her movements.

"You didn't even tell me you were going to the Mortal Kingdoms," she accuses. "I was gone for *two days* and came back to find you'd vanished. And then I find out, secondhand, might I add, that you've called a Conclave and invited *Mortals* to compete?"

I let my voice drop into a suggestive hum. "Yes, well, I *do* regret that we didn't get a proper goodbye before I left."

Her nostrils flare, and for a moment, I think she might actually set something on fire. Cal is going to kill me if she ruins another set of curtains.

"How could you do this?" she snaps, yanking her arm free. "The Conclave is *sacred*, Derian! It's for warriors! Not a bunch of simpering court girls who wouldn't know the difference between a pommel and a blade!"

"I'm *aware* of what the Conclave is," I reply smoothly. "It's my family's tradition, after all. Not yours."

She steps closer, invading my space like she always does. She's toe-to-toe with me now, her chin tilted up in that defiant way that would make most men flinch.

"I'm not going to just accept this, Derian."

A slow, dangerous smile tugs at my lips. She likes to play this game with me. She likes to see just how far she can push me, and she even likes when I have to remind her she's no match for me when she goes too far. "I wasn't aware I needed your acceptance."

Her jaw tightens. "If this were a real Conclave, I'd already be the winner. You know it. I know it. Everyone knows it."

There it is.

I arch a brow, waiting.

She doesn't disappoint.

"I'm entering."

I purse my lips, glancing away as if considering. "I'm not sure if—"

"*Any interested party is permitted to join the Conclave,*" she cuts in, voice sharp as a blade. "Unless, of course, you're planning on changing *more* of the rules while you're already breaking our traditions."

I chuckle, leaning against the table. "You want to join the Conclave, Seraphina? Compete for my hand?"

She scoffs, crossing her arms. "Don't flatter yourself. I couldn't care less about your hand."

I press my lips into a line to hide the building grin.

Seraphina turns pensive, twirling a blade between her fingers. "I've sacrificed everything to become the warrior I am. I've killed more Velkai than I can count in service of you and my king. I deserve the respect that comes from winning the Conclave. That honor is *mine.*"

"No one said your service to your kingdom hasn't been appreciated."

"You appreciate me." She gives me a bitter smile. "But you expect me to simply stand aside for this?"

A throat clears from the doorway.

I glance over my shoulder to see Caldren standing there, his arms folded, frowning at the blade sticking out of the wood next to his head and the wooden markers on the floor.

"This is why I hate it when you two are in the same room together," he mutters.

It's not uncommon for Seraphina and me to leave a space in ruins. Usually, though, we do so in *much* more entertaining ways.

She doesn't bother looking at Cal, her attention still fixed on me. "I'll kill them all, you know."

She slams her second blade onto the table, slicing through the map beneath it.

Cal exhales sharply. "*That* was important."

"You can leave if it bothers you," I say over my shoulder.

Part of me hopes he does. Bedding a contestant in the Conclave might be forbidden, but Seraphina hasn't officially joined. I could take her right now, work off the heat that Huntyr caused in my blood.

"I'd rather not return to find the fortress in flames." Cal sighs, unmoving from his position. The glare he levels at me tells me he knows exactly what I was thinking and disapproves.

"You're right," I acknowledge with a sigh, turning back to her and watching the satisfaction flicker across Seraphina's face. "If you want to join the Conclave, I can't stop you. But the Mortals *stay*."

Her grin is slow and vicious. "That's fine."

She yanks her blade from the table, spinning it idly between her fingers. "If you insist on putting them in the same arena as me, I'll simply have to remind them where they belong."

I tilt my head. "And where is that?"

Seraphina flashes a wicked smile.

"Lying on the ground, dead, of course. At my feet."

With that, she turns on her heel and stalks toward the door.

"Careful, Sera," I call lazily after her. "Would be *terribly* embarrassing if you lost after all those grand declarations."

She flips me off over her shoulder without missing a step, and I swear the torches flare hotter as she leaves, but I'm too distracted watching her hips to say for certain.

Cal watches her go, then bends down to start gathering the fallen wooden markers from the floor. "You've really got a death wish, don't you?"

I shrug. "She'll calm down."

"I don't see why you put up with her."

Wordlessly, I arch a brow. I would have thought it's fairly obvious why I put up with her.

He sighs with all the exasperation of a Fae three times his age. "There are millions of other women you could bed, Derian. Surely you can find someone who doesn't set things on fire when she's angry."

"She sets things on fire *other* times too." I grin cheekily.

"That is *exactly* my point. You should find someone else to work out your proclivities with."

My thoughts drift to another stubborn woman, a Mortal in leather pants who I'm fairly certain had a blade hidden in her blouse.

I smirk. "You might be right about that."

Cal's hand wraps around my bicep as I move to walk past him, an expression of warning on his face. "She's right. She will kill them all."

I know that. I'm counting on it, actually.

If Seraphina enters, the Mortals will all die. Including the assassin.

I'd been planning on it since the second I called for the Conclave.

"What happens to this alliance then?" Cal continues.

"The Mortals want our lands. I don't see why we need wedding rings to ensure that happens."

"Still, you should be careful with her. It's not just your reputation at stake, now. It's the treaty."

I've kept Seraphina under control for years. This Conclave will be no different.

HUNTYR

We're shuffled off the ship and into the fortress like livestock, a guard escorting each of us through the winding stone corridors before depositing us into separate rooms.

"You should dress for the welcome ceremony," the guard instructs brusquely before leaving. "Gowns are provided in the wardrobe. The bathing chamber is through that door." He'd gestured toward a flimsy wooden panel hanging unevenly in the corner.

He's gone before I can bite back with a smart-ass comment.

"Well, alright then," I mutter, casting a critical glance around the room.

The door clicks shut behind him, and the lock turns with a finality that feels suffocating. The room is cramped, more a cell than a guest chamber, with a narrow mattress covered by a coarse wool blanket, a warped wooden wardrobe leaning against the wall, and a single standing mirror that has seen better days.

I open the creaking wardrobe to find an array of pastel gowns in shades of soft pink, lavender, and pale blue. Absently, I wonder where they came from. They hardly seem like the fashions I'd seen the female Fae wearing as we'd walked into the fortress. My upper lip curls in disgust with every fluttering chiffon sleeve I push aside.

Finally, my fingers land on something black. I pull it free and study it in the dim torchlight. The fabric is sleek and heavy, the kind that clings to the body without weighing it down. The slit runs high up the side of the skirt, catching my attention, and I feel the faintest flicker of approval.

The other gowns, pretty as they are, are gowns for women who expect to be kissed on balconies by dashing princes. This dress, though…

This dress is suited for someone who's spent more time killing in alleyways than she has being courted.

"I guess you'll do," I murmur.

After stripping off my travel clothes, I make my way to the bathing chamber. The stone basin inside is shallow and unadorned, the water within cold to the touch. I brace myself before pouring it over my skin, hissing softly as the chill seeps in. It's enough to scrub away the salt and sweat from the journey, but not enough to leave me feeling truly clean. Still, I've made do with far less before.

Once dry, I pull on the gown and glance at my reflection in the mirror. The bodice molds to my torso like armor, structured and sharp, emphasizing the narrowness of my frame. The heavy black fabric gleams faintly, catching the flickering torchlight like liquid shadow.

The skirt cascades in smooth, deliberate folds, but it's the high slit on my left leg that makes me smirk. It gives me freedom to move, even to fight, if necessary. Sliding the matching lace gloves up my arms, I watch the intricate patterns slide over my skin.

Tilting my head, I examine myself in the mirror.

"Yes," I murmur, running my fingers down the bodice. "You'll do."

A guard comes to collect me shortly after I finish dressing, offering no explanation beyond barking that it's time for dinner before he turns on his heels and marches away. I follow him through the fortress halls, staying alert as I do, and count the number of paces it takes to get from my room to wherever he's leading me.

I can't afford to get lost here.

We stop outside a set of heavy wooden doors, the faint sounds of clinking dishes and muffled laughter filtering through the cracks.

"How should I announce you?" the guard demands, turning to me with a sharp expression.

"Huntyr," I reply, my tone deliberately flat.

He tilts his head, unimpressed. "Your title, Mortal. What is your title?"

I meet his gaze, my expression hardening. "My name is Huntyr. That's how I wish to be referred to."

Whatever he sees in my glare must convince him to drop the matter, or perhaps he simply doesn't care enough to press further. I'd wager it's the latter.

Velia might be one of the more tolerant of the Mortal Kingdoms, but our hatred for the Fae still runs deep. Even though centuries have passed since the war between our peoples and the creations of the Wastelands—the dead areas of land that refuse to grow any crop. Based on the guard's attitude, and the glares I've felt since setting foot here, it seems the Fae aren't particularly fond of us either.

Any delusion of a happy coexistence between our kingdoms is laughable. Whatever fragile peace this alliance claims to offer won't last long.

The guard shoves the doors open and steps aside, his voice booming. "Mistress Huntyr."

I step into the dining hall, every sense sharpening as I take in the scene before me. A long stone table stretches down the center of the room, piled high with food—roasted meats, fruits gleaming like polished gems, platters of cheese and bread. The flicker of torches casts a golden glow over the space, their light catching on the silver goblets and ornate serving dishes.

The women are scattered along the table. Some chat animatedly, their laughter too loud and forced to be genuine. Others sit in stiff silence, their gazes flitting around the room like mine, assessing every detail, every threat.

At the far end of the table, Roland is already tearing into a loaf of bread. Beside him, a copper-haired man built like a lion leans close, whispering something in his ear.

But I hardly notice either of them, because the second I step through the doorway, there's a shift in the air. My spine stiffens before my mind even catches up, and my instincts pull me to look at him.

Derian has cleaned up since the voyage. As much as I hate to admit it, a bath has done him well. The shadow lining his jaw is gone, and his dark hair still glistens faintly, damp from water. Like the other Fae males in the room, he wears leather armor, its dark surface polished to a fine sheen. But somehow, his fits differently... *better*. The way the leather molds to his broad shoulders and muscled frame is almost distracting.

I shove that thought aside before it lingers.

Of course he's attractive. All the Fae are attractive. That just makes them all the more deadly.

But then his eyes find mine, and it's as if I can smell that smoky citrus scent as easily as if he were standing right next to me.

Derian's gaze locks onto mine, dark and unrelenting, as if he senses my presence as easily as I do his. A faint smile tugs at his lips, one that's more knowing than welcoming, and I resist the urge to bristle under its weight.

He's a Fae, I remind myself.

A beautiful, incredibly tall Fae with excellent bone structure and a scent that seemingly drives me mad.

But a Fae.

Which makes him the enemy.

"Now," he says, his voice cutting through the noise like a blade. "We can begin."

I guess that means I'm the last to arrive.

I take a seat in the last remaining spot at the large stone table, between the annoying blonde from the ball—I really should learn her name—and a short Fae woman with tawny skin and a shaved head. I recognize most of the women from the journey from the Mortal lands, but I'm unpleasantly surprised to see an equal number of Fae women joining us at the table.

The meal proceeds almost immediately after I sit down. A feast of roasted lamb, herb salad, and crusty bread. It's not a particularly elaborate meal, but anything seems like a luxury after days of cheese and nuts aboard the ship. Shadows flicker across the room from the candlelit torches. Derian, thankfully, directs his attention to the two men beside him, the three of them chatting quietly with intense expressions. No one's attention is on me, at least not in any meaningful way. Several of the Mortal women already know each other, not surprising since they likely grew up within the same social circles.

The same circles I would've grown up in, had my father not been killed by the Fae.

That thought is enough for me to catch my gaze wandering towards Derian. I quickly direct it back to the plate of food in front of me.

The Fae women all seem familiar with each other too, laughing and discussing weapons. I can hear their conversation from where I sit on the far side of the table. The Mortal women to my left are being led by the blonde, while the Fae women to my right are talking amongst themselves.

One of them, with fiery orange hair, keeps narrowing her amber eyes in my direction every so often.

Roland clears his throat. "Yes, well, now that we all have food in our bellies, perhaps we should begin."

"Begin what?" asks the hook-nose Mortal woman three chairs down.

The Fae next to me rolls her eyes. "This is why you shouldn't let Mortals into the Conclave."

Roland glances at her with admonishment in his eyes. "I'll be serving as the overseer of the Conclave. Tonight, I will remind you all of the rules."

"No need," the orange-haired girl says with a menacingly sweet smile. "*We* already know the rules. And the Mortals will be dead long before they even get a chance to break one."

"Seraphina," Derian growls, his eyes darkening in warning. "Do let the games start before you put a target on your back."

She grins at him, fingers twitching slightly. "The games already began when you left our bed to bring back Mortal pets."

I keep my face carefully neutral, even as a million thoughts run through my head, even as my grip on the knife tightens, even as Derian's eyes flicker to me for the briefest of moments.

"You didn't tell us Fae would be competing in the Conclave!" the blonde next to me huffs. "That hardly seems fair."

Seraphina shrugs, unfazed. "It's not, Mortal."

"My name is Alexandria," the blonde snaps, and I make a mental note of it.

Seraphina leans forward, her fingers curling around her dinner knife before she begins cutting into her meat. Too slowly. "Your name is meaningless. The dead don't need names."

Alexandria pushes back her chair, the wood scraping against the stone floor. There's fire in her eyes, bravery even, but before she can stand in indignation, Seraphina has already grabbed the carving knife and tossed it across the room. It lands deep in Alexandria's shoulder, and the small girl lets out a hiss of pain.

Though, surprisingly, not a scream.

Good for her.

The Mortals around me immediately stand, some crying, others enraged. The Fae women just laugh and make snide remarks to each other.

Derian leans back and watches it unfold, his eyes narrowed and his expression guarded.

I don't bother intervening either, though. That wound is going to be nasty, but it's in my best interest to simply let them destroy one another. It only makes my job easier.

"Ladies!" Roland exclaims, his voice sharp.

"Someone get her a healer!" orders the auburn-haired man beside him as Alexandria continues to scream at Seraphina, clutching the blade in her shoulder. Her pink gown stains crimson as she reaches for it.

I frown. "I wouldn't—"

Too late.

She yanks the knife out, blood splattering onto the table. Rookie mistake. The auburn-haired man sighs and places his face in his hand, while Derian chuckles and gestures for a Fae guard to carry the sobbing Alexandria away.

"Are you just going to let them kill us?" another Mortal screams at Derian, waving her hands at the Fae women.

He doesn't lift a finger. He doesn't chastise Seraphina, nor does he comfort the bleeding girl. Derian's expression shows no mercy, no sympathy.

"Yes," he answers her, that deep voice positively menacing. "I intend to watch you all kill each other while all the other Fae in the room bet on which of you will die first. You're not in Velia anymore. You'd better get used to that fact."

Silence settles over the room.

And Derian watches.

He watches how we react to him.

"As I was saying," Roland continues. "Welcome to the Conclave. It's time to go over the rules."

DERIAN

The rules of the Conclave are simple.

One: Go where you're told and do what you're told leading up to the trials.

Two: You will eat as a group. You will train as a group.

Three: Violence between competitors outside of trials is strictly prohibited.

Inside the trials—well, the objective is to live. The easiest way to ensure that is to ensure that everyone else dies first.

That said, the rules of the Conclave have always been a bit... flexible.

A competition meant to weed out the weak often consists of spitfires like Seraphina, individuals who have been bred and raised to be strong, brave, and resilient. Those skills usually come with a fair bit of arrogance and unreasonable tempers.

So, as Seraphina just demonstrated, it's not entirely unusual for the "no violence" rule to be broken.

And there's no real punishment for breaking the rules. Why would we need to kill you in punishment when the Conclave will more than likely result in your death anyway?

I watch the women as Roland delivers the rules. The Mortals' faces turn several shades of red and gray as the weight of the competition finally starts to settle in. Even some of Seraphina's lackeys, those who've also decided to join the Conclave, look less sure of themselves now. They've all come for their own reasons. Whether it's my favor they're after, or something else, it won't matter. Only one will survive.

Eleven dead women.

"Training begins tomorrow," Roland tells them. "For the Mortals who are joining us, you will all be given appropriate clothing and weaponry."

Seraphina, predictably, is unbothered by it all, flicking a flame between her fingers with a nonchalant ease while twirling her hair with the other. It's a rather obvious display of indifference meant to intimidate everyone else in the room.

For the first time in years, her arrogance is starting to annoy me.

And then there's Lady Huntyr Lachlan. Her presence is like ice to Seraphina's fire. She barely even blinks as the rules are laid out, as if she had been expecting them all along. Those sharp blue eyes of hers shift, dimming, then brightening, catching the light for just a moment.

She eats quickly, but with purpose. Small, controlled bites, and all the while, her attention never leaves the people settled around the table. The knife in her hand, resting on the table as she finishes, stays in her grip like it's a part of her.

I still don't know what to make of her yet, and the mystery is starting to get under my skin.

Eventually, the conversation dies down, and the warriors from the day guard begin filtering in, taking the remaining food with rough hands as they reach over the girls' shoulders.

In the corner, Lyra, one of the fortress cooks, picks up her guitar and begins strumming a slow, lilting melody. A few of the wine-drunk men and women rise to their feet, encouraged by the music, and pair off to dance. Two Mortals glance at me, unsure of how to act now that the mood has shifted.

"Dance if you want," I tell them, waving a hand dismissively.

Without hesitation, they rise and take the hands of two Fae males, twirling toward the makeshift dance floor.

"You do know your role in all of this?" Cal leans over Roland, smirking. "You're supposed to charm these women."

If this were a normal Conclave, yes. My responsibility would be to court them, ensure that I have the strongest bond with my future bride, whoever she may be. That's the way things are done.

But this isn't a normal Conclave.

The king didn't sanction this. My brother will be quite disapproving, in fact, when he finally finds out.

Still, I suppose there is one woman I'm interested in entertaining. I push back from my chair, slide it away from the table, and cross the distance to where Huntyr sits.

I place my hands on the back of her chair, leaning down just enough to speak into her hair.

"Dance with me."

She doesn't even glance up. "I'm sure there are plenty of other women eager for your favor."

Sure enough, I can feel their eyes on me.

"Oh, I will dance with all of them by the end of the night," I reply. "I have to be fair."

"Of course."

I can hear the sarcasm dripping from her words, and it makes the corners of my lips twitch upward.

"But first," I wrap my fingers around the iron rail at the top of her chair and tug it back, "I'm going to dance with *you*."

She remains still, not even breathing. I'm not entirely accustomed to women having no reaction to me.

"You'll have to put down the cutlery if you're going to dance, Huntyr."

Her gaze flickers to the knife, and for a brief moment, I see a flash of surprise, like she forgot it was even in her hand. She slams it down onto the table, and I can almost hear her mutter under her breath as she stands and grudgingly accepts my hand.

I lead her to the dance floor just as the tempo slows, and I can't help but bite back a grin as I pull her into the dance. She's smaller than I expected up close, more delicate. The top of her head barely brushes my shoulders, and her waist fits perfectly in my grasp as we begin to move in time to the music.

"You're good at this," I compliment.

She shrugs, boredom etched on her features. "I'm a noblewoman."

The tone in her voice, however, suggests she doesn't believe her own words.

"And yet, you don't look like you're enjoying the dance."

Her lips curl into a smirk, her eyes lighting up with mischief. "Is it that obvious that I'm not desperate for your attention?"

I can't help but chuckle. "It'll be terribly awkward at our wedding then."

Her smirk falters for just a second, and I see the tension in her body, a small line forming between her brows. I fight the urge to smooth it away with my thumb.

"I know," I admit, "getting ahead of myself again."

My hand tightens around her waist without meaning to, and I can feel my magic humming just beneath my skin. It's harder to swallow it down when I'm so distracted by her.

"Have I told you how ravishing you look tonight?"

She glares at me from under dark lashes. "Is this another one of your attempts at flirting?"

"That depends on if it's giving you butterflies."

"*Nothing* you could do would give me butterflies."

I don't bother to fight the grin that spreads across my face as I pull her ever closer and lean down, letting my lips brush against the shell of her ear. "I doubt that very much."

She breathes heavily. Just once, a deep inhale and exhale, before she mutters 'Fae bastard' under her breath and looks away.

There's a beat of silence as I lift my arm to twirl her before pulling her back into me. She follows my lead effortlessly, steadier on her feet than some of the other women I've had to dance with throughout my life.

"So, if you win the Conclave, what are you planning?"

For some reason I can't quite understand, I need her to keep talking to me. I need whatever insight I can glean into how this woman thinks.

She stiffens under my touch. "What do you mean?"

"Chocolate cake or vanilla for the party? I'm partial to vanilla."

A breath escapes her in a heated rush as she meets my gaze. "I don't particularly care."

"Come on now, doesn't every woman dream of her wedding day?"

She doesn't answer right away. Instead, she shifts in my grasp, her voice sharp as she cuts through the banter.

"I've never been one to meet—"

"Expectations," I finish for her, tightening my grip around her waist just enough for her to feel it. "I'm aware."

And then, to my complete and utter shock, the little thing lifts her foot and slams it down on top of mine.

"I can finish my own thoughts, thank you very much."

"Did you just—" I blink in surprise. "Step on me?"

"You deserved it."

I can't suppress my laugh. "I think I liked it."

Her shoulders stiffen, but I'm ready for it now. I move my foot out of the way with a quiet chuckle.

"Fool me once."

She's fuming now, but I notice the way her lips twitch upward in spite of herself. There's fire in those ice blue eyes, and damn if that isn't enticing.

"Has anyone ever told you that you're insufferable?" she questions with a tilt of her head.

"Several people."

"And have you ever considered... *not* being that way?"

Once again, I spin her in my arms in time with the music, but this time when I pull her back, I let the momentum bring her flush against me. Her chest rises and falls against mine, and I'm suddenly aware of eyes on me. Cal's and Roland's—but also the other women's, too. "What would you suggest?"

"Well, your arrogance could be toned down for starters," she suggests, shoving backwards to put space between us.

"Is there a difference between arrogance and confidence?"

"One is deserved."

I raise my brows at her. "You hardly know me, how do you know it's not deserved?"

The wicked thing takes a slow look down my frame, trailing from my eyes all the way down to my boots and then back up, lingering at the space where my cock twitches for her for just a moment before she pulls her lower lip between her teeth and bats those eyelashes at me. "I suppose you could call it a hunch."

My body is instantly on fire, every instinct telling me to pull her from this room and show her exactly how wrong her hunch is, to fuck her until she's assured that my arrogance is *well*-deserved. Until she's begging me to bed her over and over again.

And she knows it. She knows exactly what she's doing by leveling *that* look at me.

The music slows, the song, and our dance, coming to an end. I don't want this little game between us to end, though. I want to keep playing with her, to keep wrestling our wits to see who will come out on top.

Perhaps we could take turns.

She simply steps back and glances to where the other women have all turned their sights onto me.

"Your adoring fans await you."

I smirk down at her, letting my eyes trail over her with the same intensity that she examined me. "Until next time then."

I follow her movements as she walks back to the table, waiting until she's seated and focusing on the plate in front of her before I let the next woman pull me into a dance.

I've been settled into my room for no more than thirty minutes when there's a sudden banging on my door, urgent and demanding. I groan. That's never good.

I rip it open and find Cal waiting for me, his eyes wild, lips pressed into the tight, thin line he wears when something is truly wrong. Wind cracks against the window behind me.

"What?"

"Garrick's been hurt."

I don't stop to grab my shirt before pushing past him, moving toward the fortress doors. Magic flares out of me, stilling the water in the air, shoving the storm clouds away.

A man shouldn't have to die in the rain.

"How?" I demand.

Cal follows on my heels. "Two attacked near the western walls. Garrick and two others were on patrol."

"They came this close to the fortress?"

It's been nearly thirty years since the Velkai last left the Wastelands, let alone approached our strongholds. We knew the Wastelands were spreading, inching over our lands in a slow, merciless corruption, but an attack this close?

"I'm as shocked as you are," Cal mutters.

"The others?" I ask as we cross the threshold into the courtyard.

"Dead."

Of course. Two more names to add to the scrolls.

My boots splash through puddles, but I don't slow. By the time we reach Garrick, he's already writhing on the ground, a gaping wound in his lower gut.

Jaylin, one of his closest friends, crouches beside him, looking pale and grim. Garrick's wife, Amora, cradles his head in her lap, her tear-streaked face twisted with desperation.

"Your Highness," Tarin, the fortress healer, greets me somberly. "Thank you for stopping the rain."

I incline my head, more interested in his assessment. "Can anything be done?"

Tarin exhales slowly. "You know the answer to that."

Fae magic was a beautiful thing, but we had our limits. Not even our most talented healers would be able to help him now.

"I can do it," Cal offers, already reaching for one of the twin swords strapped across his back.

"No!" Amora's shriek cuts through the night, raw with fury and grief. Her hands tremble as she presses her hands against her husband's stomach, determined to keep his innards from spilling out. "You will not touch him. You will *fix* him."

I crouch beside her, letting Jaylin meet my eyes. He knows what comes next. We *all* know what comes next. She just hasn't accepted it yet.

"Amora," I say, low and steady.

Her breath hitches. "Your Highness, please."

I can't remember how many children they have. I should know that.

She chokes on a sob, shaking her head.

"He's already gone, Amora."

Jaylin gently pulls Garrick's head from her lap, while Cal steps in to lift her to her feet. She fights at first, but when her legs give out beneath her, she lets him hold her upright. Her heart is breaking in front of us, and there's not a damned thing I can do about it.

"Let's get you back to your children," Cal murmurs, guiding her away. "You don't want to see this."

She doesn't respond, just lets him lead her back inside.

"I'm so fucking sick of killing my friends," I growl, picking up Cal's sword from where he left it on the ground for me.

Garrick sputters on the ground, his eyes saying everything his mouth can't.

"You fought well, brother," I say to him. "Amora and the children will be cared for. You have my word."

I don't allow myself the grace of hesitation.

I swing, forcing all the rage in my heart into that blow, and I don't flinch as blood splatters across my bare chest. I don't blink as his head rolls along the ground.

There's a choking sound, but I'm not sure if it's coming from Jaylin or Tarin.

I exhale sharply, tossing the blade to the ground.

"Clean it up," I order before turning on my heel and walking away.

The storm rolls back in, angrier than it was before.

HUNTYR

The next morning, I wake to pounding on the door.

And I know it's him before I even open my eyes.

Barefoot and barely awake, I push off the thin quilt and pad over to yank it open, already irritated.

Derian stands in my doorway, looking infuriatingly smug and smelling so strongly of citrus, metal, and something earthen that I tense, forcing myself not to react.

"Well, don't you look lovely in the morning," he drawls, eyes scanning down my body and lingering on the exposed skin of my legs.

I groan, rubbing the sleep from my eyes and shifting uncomfortably. "Do you have any idea what time it is?" I point to the window, where darkness still blankets the world outside.

Still, his eyes linger on me, darkening slightly with their appraisal. And though I'm not embarrassed of my body, or consumed with the need for modesty, I can't help but shift under the weight of his attention. My skin prickles, and I shiver.

He shrugs. "Not my problem."

Why does he look so *chipper*?

No one can be this awake this early. There's not even a hint of grogginess on his chiseled, far-too-smug face. He leans against the doorframe casually, relaxed like he has all the time in the world, muscular arms crossed over his broad chest and one ankle kicked over the other.

Despite having *no* reason to care how this man sees me, I'm suddenly very aware that I probably look like a sleep-deprived banshee.

I run a hand through my hair. Not that it helps.

"Is there a *reason* for this morning visit?" I grumble.

He tilts his head toward something behind him. I follow his gaze to a large wooden trunk, locked with a golden clasp. My brow lifts in question.

"I brought you a present," he says, winking as he bends to unlatch the trunk. The lid creaks open, revealing neatly stacked daggers, leather armor, and even a bow and quiver of arrows. "Weapons, as promised. They're being delivered to all the candidates as we speak."

"How *lucky* am I to have the royal delivery service."

I narrow my eyes. Why *him*? If everyone is getting these weapons, why is the Fae prince at *my* door, personally delivering them?

Derian smirks. "You look skeptical."

"I am."

He chuckles, then lifts the trunk as if it weighs nothing and carries it inside, not bothering to seek out an invitation. "Good. Trusting too easily is terribly immature."

I fold my arms. "As you pointed out last night, I don't know you very well, Derian, but I imagine *you're* not the pillar of maturity."

This space is too small for the both of us. It's suddenly cramped and too warm with him inside.

He sets the trunk down beside the looking glass and turns, stepping just a little too close. "I suppose you'll just have to get to know me better, then."

"Or die first," I counter, reminding him exactly *why* I'm here.

He snorts. "I do hope you make it through the first trial. It would be a terrible letdown if you didn't. Who else would fill my life with such interesting sarcasm?"

I track his movements with my eyes. "Why me? Why not bother someone else this morning?"

"So far, you're the one who gets the most riled up around me," he muses, tilting his head. "That makes you the most fun to poke at."

I scoff. "Not Seraphina?" The words slip out before I can stop them.

Derian's smirk falters, just for a second. His gaze flickers, and I briefly wonder if I'm imagining the flash of irritation I see before that careful grin slides back into place.

"Jealous?"

"Just *annoyed* that I got dragged into a twisted competition so you had an excuse to marry your girlfriend."

His jaw ticks, and the teasing light in his eyes vanishes.

"I'd recommend focusing on surviving the trials before you worry about who *used* to share my bed," he says, rolling his neck like he's shaking off the conversation. Then, as if he hadn't just bristled at my words, he throws a lazy smirk over his shoulder. "Get dressed. You're expected in the training yard in thirty minutes."

And then he's gone, leaving me standing there with my bare feet, messy hair, surprisingly quick heart rate, and the undeniable realization that I *definitely* hit a nerve.

T ilting my head back, I let the morning sun warm my face, its light chasing away the lingering shadows of sleepless nights. My eyes flutter closed as I savor the simple, forgotten pleasure of being grounded in my own skin.

The armor left for me in the trunk fits like it was crafted just for me. It hugs my frame like a second skin, stitched with reinforced plating across my chest, shoulders, and thighs. Every vital area feels shielded, yet I can move without restriction.

Straps crisscross my torso and hips, securing the array of weapons that accompanied it. Twin daggers rest snugly in their sheaths against my thighs, the smooth hilts brushing against my fingers with every step. A quiver of black-feathered arrows sits firmly against my back, paired with a curved bow slung diagonally across my shoulders. My utility belt, buckled tight at my waist, holds an assortment of pouches and holsters, one containing the short sword that juts out from my hip, gleaming faintly in the sunlight.

I laced my knee-high boots tightly this morning, appreciating the thick soles that will grip any terrain, no matter how unforgiving. My dark hair is pulled back into a tight braid, falling down the center of my back, neat and practical.

As comfortable as it all makes me feel, though, it takes only about two seconds after opening my eyes to realize I've made a mistake.

While all the Fae women look similarly armed and ready for war, the Mortal nobles are laughably out of place. Their hair is worn loose and messy, their armor ill-fitting, if they're wearing any at all. The few who bothered to bring weapons carry them haphazardly, straps dangling or buckles undone.

One of them stares at me with wide-eyed shock. "How did you figure out how to put it all on?"

Alexandria snorts, unfortunately healed from yesterday's injury. "Because she's a freak."

I breathe deeply, silently vowing that she's going to be the first person I kill when the trials begin.

The training yard is alive with action. Weapons are being sharpened and organized into a rack in the far corner under the high stone towers. Along the far wall, two Fae males are currently sparring, the sound of their steel swords clashing together echoing throughout the courtyard. Fae magic clouds the air.

I felt it sink into my skin the second I'd stepped into the yard.

The ground under my boots is a mix of uneven cobblestones and packed dirt, worn smooth in places from constant footfall. Even some of the weapons seem dull and blunt from overuse.

I can't help but wonder what the Fae are training for.

The war between the Fae and Mortals ended a century ago. The Fae kingdom has just formally aligned itself with Velia.

So what threat are they preparing for?

A sudden sharp clap echoes across the training yard, pulling my attention. Three Fae warriors stand at the edge of the courtyard.

In the center is the tallest and broadest of the group, with a dark beard and skin that gleams in the sunlight. His leather armor is cut into a sleeveless vest, leaving thick, muscled arms on display.

To his right is a man with short blonde hair tied neatly back, his pointed ears visible against the pale strands. On the left, the youngest of the three, about my age, stands with shoulder-length chestnut hair and spiraling tattoos down his neck and arms.

"My name is Taric," the bearded warrior announces. His voice is sharp and authoritative. He gestures to his companions. "This is Rhen." He nods toward the blonde. "And Parker."

I make a mental note of their names, storing them with the growing stockpile of data I've been collecting about everyone and everything related to these trials.

"I'll be preparing you for the trials," Taric continues. His face is a mask of stern indifference. By contrast, Rhen grins openly, like he's eagerly waiting for someone to cause trouble. He reminds me of Flannigan in that way.

The sudden memory of Flannigan tugs at my black heart. I miss my home, my friends in the League of Assassins, Kristona, and Tyla. I miss Tyla so much it feels like a bone has been ripped from my body.

"What are your qualifications?" Alexandria asks, her snark unmistakable. The training yard seems to fall silent around us, the clang of blades pausing as everyone turns to look at her just as the girl next to her elbows her subtly. Even the banners hanging from the parapets above us seem to stop fluttering in the faint breeze.

"What?" Alexandria shrugs. "If he's going to train us, I want to be sure he's the best."

Taric doesn't react, though his patience must be wearing thin.

"He won a Conclave, idiot." One of the Fae women laughs, her voice sharp and mocking. "And besides, you don't *have* to train. Dying comes naturally to your kind."

I shift my weight onto the balls of my feet, anxious energy rolling through me. I'm getting really fucking tired of these Fae bitches acting like killing us Mortals will be as easy as snapping their fingers.

The girl next to me goes to step backwards and stumbles.

She quite literally trips over her own feet.

I sigh. On second thought, maybe killing us off *will* be as easy as the Fae snapping their fingers.

"Why don't you all introduce yourselves?" Parker suggests, his tone mild as he gestures toward Seraphina.

She steps forward, flicking her orange hair over her shoulder. It's styled in elaborate braids that cascade down her back. Her leather armor is finer than anyone else's, though the scratches and scuffs of battle are still evident.

"Seraphina," she says, her voice haughty. She meets my gaze with a smirk that's more of a challenge than an introduction. "Fire-wielder."

Is that supposed to impress me?

The other Fae women follow her lead, all of them wearing the same cocky grin.

"Lirael. Air-wielder."

"Mara. Metal-wielder."

"Thalara. Stone-wielder."

"Sylvana. Air-wielder."

"Elise. Memory-wielder."

Every eye in the courtyard turns to us Mortals. A small part of my soul shrivels at the sight of my companions' wide-eyed fear.

No wonder the Fae women are so arrogant. These girls aren't even going to *try* to fight back.

Even Alexandria looks shaken, her frown betraying the realization that, to marry the prince, she'll have to survive Fae opponents armed with magic.

I sigh heavily, embarrassment for all of Mortal-kind creeping over me.

"Huntyr," I say, breaking the silence as I let my gaze travel over the Fae before landing dead on Seraphina. "Smart-ass."

Rhen snickers, and even Taric's stony face softens with the faintest hint of a smile.

The rest of the women introduce themselves, though their voices are small and hesitant. Taric explains that today's session will focus on honing our skills and selecting our weapons for the first trial. Sparring is encouraged, but killing is not.

I, however, will not be sparring.

The other Mortals around me clearly have no idea what they're doing, which means if I don't want to expose myself as the assassin who killed a Fae guard during the masquerade ball, I need to pretend I'm just as clueless.

Taric barks out a command to begin, and the group scatters. Mortals cling to one another, while the Fae women head toward their preferred training areas.

"Keep running your mouth, Mortal," Seraphina mutters as she passes me, her shoulder jutting into mine. "We'll see how long that attitude lasts."

It takes everything in me not to drive a dagger into the back of her knee.

Kristona would never believe I showed that much restraint.

Still, just because I'm trying to avoid violence doesn't mean I can't poke her just a bit.

"Hopefully it lasts long enough to see how upset you get watching a man who doesn't want you flirt with everyone else."

Seraphina whirls around, her righthand lighting up in flame. My pulse rushes at the sight of it, but I keep my expression calm and my stance casual, my arms crossed over my chest.

"What did you just say to me?" she hisses.

She steps forward, and I prepare myself to fight, readying myself to grab the dagger strapped to my belt, but I feel the presence behind my back before she glares at the male behind me.

"Go train, Seraphina," Rhen orders her. "It's day one. Let's try to make it a little longer into the Conclave before you lose your shit."

With one last glare at me, she stomps away to join two other Fae women who'd been watching our encounter. I don't dare take my eyes off her even as Rhen steps forward.

"I wouldn't piss that one off," Rhen warns. "She has a tendency to go off the rails."

"She'll try to kill me either way," I point out, finally looking up at him, noticing how the wind blows his hair about. He really should tie that back or cut it. "I might as well have some fun taunting her first."

He looks down at me for a moment before tilting his head in acknowledgement. "Fair enough."

DERIAN

"So, what all have you gotten into in my absence?" I ask Cal while skimming over the fortress reports from the past few weeks.

Three expeditions into the Wastelands while I was away in the Mortal Kingdoms. All three led to fights with Velkai.

Either their numbers are growing, or they are moving towards our land.

Both options are concerning.

"The renovations on the downstairs barracks are mostly complete," Cal mutters, his focus entirely on his hands as he meticulously sharpens his blade.

I roll my eyes, glancing out the window to see that the women have started their training. Wordlessly, I stand to file away the papers before heading to the door, clapping Cal heavily on the shoulder as he stands after me. "I wanted fun updates. You know, women? Bars? Fights?"

He frowns, following me into the hallway and out of the space I've taken over as my office. "I won three sparring matches."

I stifle my laughter behind a small smile. He's far too serious for his own good. Gods bless the woman who finally brings him out of that steely shell one day.

Torchlight flickers, casting long shadows on the stone walls as we make our way through the winding corridors towards the courtyard. I breathe in deeply as we step outside, enjoying the fresh spring air. It won't be this nice for much longer.

"Which ones do you like so far?" Cal asks softly, crossing his arms next to me as he examines the women. He stares at them, watching as if he's choosing the next warhorse to invest in.

Several are sparring amongst themselves—mostly the Fae. Taric, Rhen, and Parker are all with the Mortals, teaching them how to hold the weapons and where to strike the body to cause the most damage.

Almost accidentally, my eyes lock onto Huntyr from where she stands with Rhen. She's attempting to shoot an arrow, missing the mark terribly, and Rhen steps in behind her to adjust her hold on the bow.

"Mara's a strong metal-wielder," Cal notes, watching as she throws a sword, using her magic to aid it in finding dead center in the chest of a dummy. "Lirael is quite deadly with daggers, though. Sylvana has always been superior in simple hand-to-hand."

"You're not mentioning the Mortals," I notice aloud.

He stares at me, brows furrowing as if he's trying to decide if I'm joking or not.

"Why would I?" he asks simply. "You know, it's a shame Elise volunteered. Her powers are useless inoffensive maneuvers. It'll be a tragedy to see such a rare power killed off."

We watch as Seraphina drags a Fae male to the sparring arena, demanding she needs a challenge. And yet, when she launches at him, running full speed before jumping an impossible height and wrapping her thighs around his shoulders, twisting her momentum to bring him to the ground, it hardly looks like he's a fair match for her.

Huntyr pulls the bow taut again. She doesn't struggle with the weight of it the way most do when they're learning, but her aim is still shit.

Sniffing, I slide off my leather jacket and toss it onto the bench beside us.

"What do you think you're doing?" Cal asks sternly, as if he already knows the answer.

I'm not subtle enough to *deny* the fact that I'm relishing the opportunity to show off, but this isn't strictly for the benefit of the women. "I've spent weeks away from here, in Bridgemond and then in the Mortal kingdoms. I feel like I'm going to explode."

Keeping my magic in check has always been a challenge for me. It's why my parents sent me away to Amberhull as a child. A young boy with that much unruly magic couldn't be trusted in a castle with important people, as they liked to remind me.

Maturity had brought a certain amount of control to my powers, but still, going too long without ridding myself of some of the buildup often left me on edge.

I lift my hands, fingers flexing as I reach for the sky, for the silver threads of magic that shimmer just beyond Mortal sight. They hum in my veins, an ache, a craving, a call to be wielded. Holding back from that is like trying to cage a hurricane.

Which, technically, I am.

The wind howls as dark clouds gather overhead, rolling in thick and heavy. Strands of hair tear free from their bindings as the women in the yard still, their training momentarily forgotten.

And then, I let go.

Rain comes first. It's a sudden, violent downpour, and fat droplets hammer the earth in heavy sheets. It soaks through my clothing and drenches the training yard in seconds.

A breath later, lightning splits the sky.

The strike hits just feet from me, the brightness so searing I know it leaves ghostly imprints in the eyes of those who dare to watch. Thunder follows, a booming crack that rumbles through the ground, shaking stone and bone alike.

The Mortals reel. Some scramble backwards while others clutch at their ears, wide-eyed in terror. In complete contrast, the Fae stand steady, smirking as though they'd expected nothing less from me.

"What is he?" someone whispers.

Thalara grins. "Storm-wielder."

The words settle over the courtyard like an unspoken warning.

With a deep belly-breath, I release my hold on the storm, letting the sky clear and allowing the warmth of spring to bleed back in. The rain slows, then stops. In minutes, the sun is hanging high in a blemishless sky, as though it had never happened at all.

I don't need to stay and hear what they say. I already know. They'll marvel over how rare my gift is, how powerful I must be.

Then they'll remember who I am.

And they'll realize that my reputation as the deadliest Fae alive isn't just hyperbole.

It is a title that has been rightfully earned.

I turn on my heel, mud sloshing under my boots. The weight of their stares follows me as I shrug my leather jacket back over tingling skin. The storm's lingering energy will thrum in my chest for hours.

"Show-off," Cal mutters.

I give him a lopsided grin. "Let's go eat."

But as we walk back toward the fortress, the familiar needling pressure at the back of my neck alerts me to a gaze that hasn't wavered.

I turn, my eyes finding Huntyr's.

She stands rooted to her spot, watching me with an unreadable expression. Unlike the others, there's no fear in her eyes. No wonder. No awe.

Just something cold and sharp.

Something that might even be hatred.

And Gods help me, I want to know *why* she's looking at me like that.

I glance at Cal over my shoulder, keeping my voice low. "Huntyr Lachlan."

He frowns and follows my gaze. She's already turned away, resuming her attempts with the bow, her jaw clenched in what might have been determination.

"What about her?"

I keep my tone casual, but there's an edge to it. "She's different from the other Mortals. I want to know why."

Cal studies her for a moment longer, his fingers tightening briefly on the hilt of his blade. "I'll look into it."

I nod once, turning away.

Whatever she's hiding... I'm going to figure it out.

16

HUNTYR

A full week passes in the fortress, each day slipping into a mind-numbing rhythm. Breakfast in the morning, weapons training afterward. Lunch in the early afternoon before hand-to-hand combat. Dinner in the evening, then baths and bed.

It's all terribly dull.

The Fae women continue to endlessly complain about the Mortals and preach their superiority. To be fair, while the Mortals are learning, they're not doing so at a speed that will prepare them for these trials. Still, the Fae are grating on my last nerve, especially considering their own glaring weaknesses.

Seraphina is all fire. She's too hot-tempered and too reckless. She strikes first, thinks later. It makes her far too easy to bait.

Lirael has shit aim with throwing knives and is somehow even worse with a bow.

Mara... well, Mara makes me wonder if she's ever had a formal education. She's a strong fighter, sure, but half the things that come out of her mouth make me question if she has a single thought behind those bright, vacant eyes.

We're kept largely separate from the Fae, likely to prevent them from slaughtering us in training. Among the other Mortals, I hide my skill, spending my nights practicing in the cramped space next to my bed. The door to my bathing chamber has become my target, it's surface peppered with tiny divots from my throwing knives.

I've grown tired of the same spaces and faces. The stone has all started to blend together, one notch seeming to mirror all the others. If the feeling of the walls closing in wasn't bad enough, we're watched constantly. I've completely given up hope of moments to spy or learn more about what the Fae are doing here. Everywhere I turn, someone is always watching.

And throughout it all, Derian has been noticeably absent.

Roland mentioned something about "business" outside the fortress, but assured us he'd return in time for the first trial.

Business.

What, exactly, does a Fae prince do when he disappears for days on end?

I'd bet my favorite sword that it has to do with whatever they're training so carefully for.

They're careful not to speak freely around us. The fortress warriors rarely interact with us at all, in fact, leaving Taric, Parker, Rhen, Roland, and Caldren as our only real sources of information. And they're maddeningly tight-lipped. I listen constantly, desperate for any scrap of knowledge, but they guard their secrets well.

No matter. My plan remains the same. Win the Conclave. Get the tonic for Tyla. Kill the Fae prince.

My heart twists whenever I think of Tyla, of what she must be going through. I can only hope Kristona is looking after her, that Joneson is still providing her tonics on my tab, that she isn't making herself sicker with worry.

On the evening of my fifth night, I trudge to the dining hall, dreading another round of posturing and one-upping from the other women.

I rarely speak during meals, choosing instead to observe and listen. It doesn't stop Seraphina from glaring at me each night. Somehow, I've become her favorite target. I've barely settled into my seat before she fixes me with her usual cold stare.

The soup in front of me begins to bubble violently.

Across the table, Caldren sighs. "Seraphina."

She smiles, slow and satisfied, and the soup stills. "I just thought the Mortal would enjoy a warm meal, considering it might be one of her last."

Deliberately, I take a spoonful and swallow without flinching, ignoring the burn that scorches the back of my throat. It hurts like hell, but it's worth it for that flash of confusion in her eyes.

"I find your power interesting, Seraphina," I murmur, still not looking at her.

She tenses. "And why's that?"

I finally lift my gaze to hers, painting on a sweet smile. "Well, it's a bit ironic, don't you think? That you'd wield fire when you're such a frigid bitch."

Parker chokes on his soup. There's a sound of a sharp slap as Rhen claps him on the back, barely suppressing a grin.

Seraphina looks ready to lunge across the table and throttle me, and Gods, I almost wish she would. Despite how much I keep reminding myself that I need to lay low, I have days of pent-up frustration to work off, and I can't seem to stop imagining sliding her own dinner knife between her ribs.

I arch a brow, daring her to make a move.

She nods to the sword strapped across Caldren's back. "I can just as easily gut you with that as I can burn you alive. You'd do well to remember that."

With a flip of red hair over her shoulder, she turns away from me, and I can't help but to snicker under my breath.

"*What?*" she hisses.

For a moment I debate letting it lie. I remind myself, *again,* that flying under the radar and not drawing any further attention or making any additional enemies is the smarter, and far wiser, course of action.

But she's looking at me with that sneer on her face, and I *swear* I can see the lashes on her left eye flickering ever so slightly. I just have to know if it will start twitching if I push her any further.

"It's just," I pause, stifling a laugh as Caldren drops his head into his hands. "You might want to consider improving your threats. You can never underestimate the importance of timing. Drawing out the tension before immediately going to death could go a long way."

"Can we ever just have one peaceful meal?" Caldren mutters.

I don't even think Seraphina is breathing. She's frozen in place, as are the Fae women that all seem to flank her. From my peripheral, I see Rhen move his hand to the pommel of the blade at his hip.

"But hey," I give her a sickeningly sweet smile, "I'm more than happy to workshop it with you if you need help."

"I see nothing has changed during my absence."

His voice slides over me like molten lava, making the room feel suddenly smaller.

I force myself not to turn, but I don't need to see him to feel the shift in the air. Derian strides in, exuding that infuriatingly easy dominance, his dark hair tousled and his fighting leathers slightly rumpled. He claps a hand on Caldren's shoulder as he passes, his sharp gaze sweeping the room before landing, inevitably, on me.

"Making friends?" he asks.

I ignore the way my stomach tightens under his scrutiny.

"Where have you been?" Seraphina asks, voicing the question I've been turning over in my mind for days.

He winks at her as he unfolds a napkin, setting it neatly on his lap. Without answering, he reaches across the table, helping himself to the mashed potatoes.

"Wouldn't you like to know," he says casually.

The torches lining the walls flare. Seraphina clenches her jaw. Derian smirks behind a bite of his chicken.

He's riling her up on purpose.

I can't tell if it's flirtation or if he, too, gets some sort of satisfaction from pushing her.

"So, ladies," he says, voice light but laced with challenge. "How go the preparations?"

His gaze flicks to me, daring me to respond, to match the sharp retort I'd given Seraphina moments ago.

But I don't rise to the bait.

I retreat back into silence, simply listening as the others begin various conversations. Seraphina glares at me like she isn't quite finished with our argument, but the time for antagonizing her has officially passed.

Derian being back means the first trial is soon.

Living through that trial is step one.

Then I kill him, and wipe that insufferable smile off his face, once and for all.

When our eyes meet, everyone else seems to blink out of existence. There is only the Fae prince and I, and the future that lays before us. This little game will end in death, either his or mine. When everything is said and done, only one of us will be walking out of this fortress.

He stares at me, a question in his eyes, and for a moment I hold his gaze. I stare into those dark eyes and wonder what exactly he's thinking.

But then I turn back to the bowl in front of me, focusing instead on finishing my soup so that I can return to my bedroom and get on with my nighttime routine.

17

HUNTYR

Anxiety curls in my stomach the morning of the first trial.

It reminds me of the first time Kristona sent me out alone with a target and a mission. That day changed the course of my life and undoubtedly led me right here to this moment.

But just like I've done every day since, I dress in silence, letting each layer of leather settle over me like armor meant to protect me. Not just against blades and claws, but against the fear, regret, and trepidation that threaten to crawl up my throat.

I'm the Huntress. I can do this.

I lace my boots tightly, strap an assortment of daggers onto my body, and pull my hair into a tight braid, throwing it over my shoulder.

I will not let them know who I am today.

But I will not let them take my life, either.

We meet Taric, Rhen, and Parker in the training yard, their faces impassive as they lead us silently beyond the fortress walls.

The cold morning air feels heavy with magic.

I've almost adjusted to the constant feeling of it against my skin, but this morning it feels suffocating again, like it did that first day I stepped foot into this cursed kingdom.

Grey clouds hang in the sky, blotting out the morning light and sending an ominous fog rolling around our ankles. A storm is rolling in, and either Derian's creating it, or he's doing nothing to stop it.

We walk in silence, the absence of any sound just adding to the overall dread curling around us. The Mortals, thankfully, have all dressed in protective leathers. Their weapons, strapped haphazardly in some cases, glint under what light peeks through the clouds.

I glance at Alexandria. She walks with her head held high, but there's tension in her jaw... fear.

Good. She should be afraid.

Fear will keep her sharp.

I see that same fear mirrored in some of the Fae women, too.

Everyone understands the seriousness of what is about to happen.

The moment we step into the arena, the ground beneath our feet seems to change. This dirt is packed and worn, as if it has seen countless battles, countless deaths. How many other men and women have died on this ground in the name of this ridiculous competition?

The stands surrounding us are already filled. Fae warriors have gathered to witness the trial, their faces impassive. In the raised box above them, the fortress's elite have taken their seats.

Even from a distance, I spot Derian. He lounges back, one arm draped over the side of his chair, as if this is nothing more than a spectacle for his amusement. His friend Caldren sits beside him, along with the Fae I've begun to recognize as those who lead the fortress.

I make the mistake of meeting Derian's gaze.

The bastard winks.

I don't bother hiding the way I roll my eyes before I turn away. Even after I've directed my attention elsewhere, though, I still feel his eyes on me.

"Roland will explain the rules," Taric announces, nodding toward the older Fae who steps forward, his golden tattoos gleaming under the torchlight. "Follow them or die. The choice is yours."

That's all that's said before our trainers retreat to the stands. No words of encouragement or last-minute advice. Rhen is the only one to linger slightly, giving me a small nod when he catches my gaze before we're left alone with Roland.

He studies us in silence, his steely gaze sweeping over our faces as if already predicting who will survive and who will not.

I wonder where I fall on that list.

When he finally speaks, his voice is sharp and emotionless.

"Today, you will face your first trial. Today's trial is known as the Labyrinth."

The ground trembles beneath us. Some of the women stumble, looking down in confusion with anxious gasps, but I keep my balance. I refuse to respond to the feeling of something ancient awakening around us.

"This is not a game," Roland continues. "Nor is it a test of beauty, grace, or charm. This is a Conclave, where strength alone is rewarded. The labyrinth you will navigate is built for one purpose: judgment."

His eyes flick across the group, measuring us.

"Once the trial begins, you will see only the labyrinth. The walls will rise around you. The path will close behind you. The shadows will move when you are not looking."

The magic in the air makes itself known again, tightening around my skin. It squeezes me uncomfortably.

I keep my breathing even, though. I hold my hands steady at my sides.

I will not show weakness.

"We will be here. Watching. Waiting. We will not help. If you hesitate, you will die. If you choose wrong, you will die."

Seraphina lets out a quiet snort, a smirk curving her lips.

"That's it?" she asks, a challenge laced beneath the words.

Does this girl have a death wish? No one can be that confident. No one can feel this tension in the air and not have a healthy sense of appreciation for the gravity of the situation.

Roland turns his gaze to her, eyes like sharpened steel.

Then, his voice drops, quieter and heavier than before.

"At the end of your journey in the labyrinth, you will stand before the Eshari."

Another ripple of magic pulses through the arena, and my stomach roils.

A hush falls over the competitors, the Fae going deadly still. Finally, Seraphina has the good sense to press her lips together and flex her fingers in the slightest indication of hesitation.

Their reactions only make the Mortals more nervous.

"For those unfamiliar with the Eshari," Roland continues. "They were the companions of the Vaereth, our Fae Gods. Their watchers. Their hunters. Their executioners. And today, they will be your judges."

A chill skates down my spine at his words, and I clamp it down under a controlled breath. Magic fills the air once more, and this time I can't stop the way my fingers twitch once, then still against my thigh.

The women all look around at each other warily.

Roland lets the silence stretch, lets the tension choke us.

Then—

"Some of you, they will find worthy. Some of you, they will not. And the Eshari do not offer second chances."

Another pulse rolls over the ground in warning.

Then, it strikes.

With a sudden force that knocks the breath out of my lungs, magic curls around me, locking my arms and legs, twisting slowly from my feet, up my thighs, and around my torso.

Roland steps back, his amber eyes burning. "The trial begins now."

That coiling magic finally climbs up to my eyes, and the arena dissolves, melting into nothing more than shadows. Before my eyes, the stands fade away as the walls rise sharply around us, stone and shadow twisting together until they're shifting, warping. The air changes, becoming heavier and darker. The scent of damp earth and ancient magic forces itself down my throat until I gag on it.

We are alone inside the labyrinth.

And there is no way back.

DERIAN

I had been barely older than a boy during the last Conclave, when Taric won my Aunt Ulna's hand in marriage.

That Conclave had been relatively quick, thanks to Taric's rare abilities as a blood-wielder. If memory serves, he killed all his opponents in the very first trial. He'd been remarkably brutal in his efficiency. It had only taken twenty minutes for the bodies to drop, blood leaking out of their eyes, ears, and mouths.

This time feels different, though. The presence of Mortals changes everything.

I suspect that's why so many have gathered to watch. Some have even traveled quite far just to be here and see who will live through this trial and who won't. All around me, they're exchanging bets on the lives of the women, none choosing to favor any of the Mortals.

"How was your trip?" Cal asks under his breath, careful to keep his question neutral with so many listening ears nearby.

"You were right."

Cal suspected there was a growing power in the Wastelands, so I'd gone to check it out myself. The second I crossed the threshold into that dead land, I could feel the oppressive magic against my skin.

Velkai magic.

Stronger than I've ever felt before.

Then I'd felt the ground shake under my feet as if it knew I was in their territory and wanted me gone. I'd ventured only a few more feet before the sound of a feminine scream suddenly echoed through my mind, nearly bringing me to my knees.

Days later, I still couldn't quite place that voice.

Eventually, her cries stopped. The magic around me settled, the echoes ceased. I walked another few paces into the Wastelands, just to test if that dark force would attempt its attack again, but the world around me remained quiet and dead.

Still, I'd seen everything I needed to.

"Would you like to send for additions to the barracks?" Cal asks, hiding his true question.

Reinforcements.

If we called for reinforcements to Oxhurn, we might as well announce to the entire Fae kingdom that the Velkai were returning. It would cause a frenzy of fear.

I sigh. "Not yet."

Cal looks at me for a long while, contemplative, as if he doesn't quite agree with my decision, but finally nods. "Have you talked to Luceron?"

My brother's name leaves me on edge. "No, but I'm sure someone's already alerted him to what's going on here."

Not just about the Wastelands, but about the Conclave too.

It's only a matter of time until he makes his opinion on all this known.

"You think he'll summon you back to Bridgemond before this is over?"

"He can't." Even a King can't stop a Conclave once it's started. "When it's over, I'll go to Bridgemond with his new sister-in-law in tow, and he can scold me then."

Cal snorts and turns his attention back to the arena where Roland is finishing the last of his instructions to the women.

"It's starting," he says.

So it is.

I'd been watching absently as Roland explained the trial to them, my attention split between the women, the Velkai, and Huntyr. The last of which seems to be, annoyingly, avoiding my gaze.

The second Roland announces the beginning of the trial, though, I focus in on the arena, watching as the women's bodies all go rigid. Magic cascades through the air as their muscles lock and their eyes go unfocused. They stand right before us, and yet their minds are somewhere else entirely.

It's begun.

I glance at her again.

If I was a smarter male, I might turn my attention to the Fae who had a stronger likelihood of winning these trials. I might watch Seraphina, who will most likely be my wife at the end of this.

But I can't deny that Huntyr's the only one I care to watch.

I notice the moment she steps forward into the illusion. Her body remains locked in place, but her jaw clenches, her fingers flexing subtly. Still, her muscles are relaxed and loose compared to everyone else. She's ready for whatever she's about to face.

Good.

Leaning forward, I rest my elbows atop my knees, not daring to even blink.

"How long do you think it will take?" Cal asks from beside me, running a hand absentmindedly across his jawline.

The other women stiffen suddenly, each of them beginning to face the challenges of the labyrinth. The Mortal next to Huntyr stumbles, her breathing turning shallow, fingers twitching as if reaching for something that isn't there.

She's already losing, and she doesn't even realize it.

I'm sure she's only minutes away from death. She'll be the first.

Groans echo across the arena from those who lost bets of who would fall first.

"Not long," I answer, watching Huntyr's every move. I note the twitch of her brow and the purse of her lips. Her chest rises and falls evenly, her breathing steady. "I don't think this will take very long at all."

HUNTYR

We're in a long corridor, shadows dancing along the walls around us.

And it's quiet.

Oppressively quiet.

The floor beneath us is solid stone, but there are no torches. No visible source of light. And yet, we can see. It's unnatural.

We stand shoulder to shoulder, all twelve of us, barely breathing as we wait for something to happen and alert us to what comes next. The air is thick, unmoving, as if the very walls are holding their breath with us.

I swallow, my throat dry.

The Fae women stand poised, assessing the space with sharp, calculating expressions, some already gripping the weapons at their sides. The Mortal women, by contrast, shift uncomfortably. Hands twitching, breathing shallow. One girl rubs at her wrist, another clenches and unclenches her fists.

The air is too still.

Then—a sound.

A deep *growl*.

Low and guttural, vibrating through the very stone beneath our feet. The sound curls around us, menacing and bloodthirsty.

And from the depths of the shadows in front of us, a beast emerges.

It moves slowly, stepping into the dim light with haunches raised. Its hulking form is massive, resembling a wolf—mostly—but still four times larger than any I've seen before. Its hide is dark and leathery, stretched over pulsing muscle and its jaw hangs open, dripping fangs bared in a hungry, vicious snarl.

But it's not the size of the creature that unsettles me most.

It's the fact that it has no eyes.

The monster steps forward, claws dragging against the corridor floor as it tilts its head, ears flicking forward, nostrils flaring. I watch its slow and deliberate movements carefully, noting the way its head rotates from side to side. And the realization dawns suddenly.

It's listening.

The beast can't see us, but it can most definitely hear us, and the slightest whisper of a sound will tell it exactly where to charge.

The Mortal girl next to me, Taylina, stumbles backward as it gets closer to her, and her boot scuffs against the stone.

The sound echoes.

My muscles lock.

And the beast's head jerks toward her.

She doesn't even have a second to inhale before it lurches forward. Tension holds me steady as I stand frozen while it locks that impossibly large jaw onto her throat. Blood splatters along the side of my face, but I simply squeeze my eyes shut and hold tight to my resolve.

I do not move.

I do not breathe.

And I most certainly do not make a sound.

When her body falls to the ground, I risk a glance to my left. Most of my competitors stare wide-eyed, shaking hands pressed tightly against their mouths to prevent themselves from screaming. Some of the Fae have started taking advantage of the beast's distraction, though, and move forward with light and measured steps.

Fine.

I can do this.

I breathe through my nose, shallow and slow, shifting my weight forward onto the balls of my feet with each step. I have moved like this dozens of times before, through darkened alleys or candlelit halls, through crime-ridden streets when I couldn't alert my target to my presence.

The beast lingers to my right, turning its head back and forth, waiting for another sound.

I give it nothing.

Instinct and muscle memory take over, keeping my steps light. It feels like it takes me an eternity to make my way down the dark hall. Like I've aged years by the time my hand wraps around the knob of the door at the end of the corridor and pushes it forward, but I do, and no one else dies.

For now.

Energy rushes over me the second I step through the doorway. The darkness dissolves instantly, swallowed by near-blinding light. My stomach lurches as my surroundings shift, and it takes a moment for the burning in my eyes to recede and my vision to adjust. When it does, I find myself somewhere new.

The corridor is gone. The beast is gone.

And the eleven remaining women are scattered around me, their expressions as disoriented as my own.

Fucking Fae magic.

Ahead of us now is a single pathway of blood-red stones, surrounded on each side by thick fog.

"Do we just move forward?" Caris whispers next to me. She's another Mortal. The only one who's been semi-nice to me.

"Good question," Seraphina breathes. "Why don't you try it out?"

Caris' eyes widen suddenly, as if she regrets giving voice to her questions, but she pushes her shoulders back, steels herself, and begins to step forward onto the path.

Seraphina snickers as she does, likely understanding as I do that it's *not* going to be that simple.

My blood hums in anticipation, waiting for the catch.

The fog presses against the edges of the path, thick and curling, but it does not cross onto the pathway. It moves like a living thing. Writhing. Breathing. Waiting.

"Do you hear that?" Caris asks suddenly, her head turning sharply to the left, eyes looking off into the distance.

I look to the other women, each of us frowning in confusion, and something heavy settles in my gut.

"We don't hear anything, Caris," Alexandria tells her, voice thick with suspicion.

Caris stills, body locking tightly as she keeps staring into the fog. The mist is rising, climbing, filling every inch from the floor to the ceiling even as it leaves the red path untouched.

"It's my brother," Caris whispers, a tear slowly falling down her face. "I see him right there!"

I step closer, my pulse hammering. There's nothing there.

"Caris, *don't*!" I scream, but it's too late.

She steps off the path.

The moment her foot touches the mist, the barrier shatters. The fog surges forward, consuming her.

A second later, her shrieks split the air, blood-curdling screams that I'm certain will haunt my nightmares. Alexandria's hands fly to her temples, squeezing tightly over her ears to block out the horror.

It seems to last forever.

Her screaming goes on and on.

Until all that's left is a whimper.

The fog dissipates, clearing off the path again, but Caris doesn't return. There's nothing left of her. No body. No blood. Gone, as if she was never even there at all.

There's only a moment of silence before Lirael clears her throat next to me, suddenly grinning. "Well, this looks like a job for me!"

She lifts her arms, and wind pours out of her, pushing the fog aside easily until it's nearly gone.

Right. She's an Air-Wielder.

"Simple enough," she shrugs, stepping forward. She struts down the path, smug, barely paying attention.

She only makes it halfway before the fog rushes forward, swallowing her whole.

The Fae, her friends, cry out her name. One even launches forward, and Seraphina moves in a flash, wrapping her arms around the woman's waist and holding her back as tears pour down her face.

When the mist recedes, Lirael is gone, just like Caris.

But this time, there's a pool of blood and what might even be shreds of skin left in a pile where she had been standing.

Alexandria doubles over and vomits.

Gods, I don't even blame her. My own stomach is twisting uncomfortably. I obviously knew the stakes when I stepped into the arena, but even I'm uneasy seeing the gruesomeness of this carnage. This fucking Conclave doesn't just want us dead, it's determined to kill us all in the most brutal way possible.

"We can't use magic against it," Seraphina murmurs to the Fae. "It seems to be against the rules."

"Oh Gods," Alexandria wails.

"Pull yourself together," I bark at her, grasping her arm and ripping her away from Seraphina, who is rubbing her fingers together in the way she does before starting a fire.

"I can't do this," Alexandria whispers to me. Her breathing is rapid. Her eyes, wild and unfocused, won't stop darting to the blood-soaked stones ahead.

It's the first time I've seen real fear in her.

"You're going to do this," I tell her, my grip tightening around her arm. "You're going to walk down that path, and you're not going to stop. No matter what you see, no matter what you hear...you *keep moving*. That is how you live."

"Why don't you try it then," Seraphina chimes in from over my shoulder. "If you're so confident."

I glance at Alexandria. Part of me thinks Seraphina might just wait until the second I step on that path to slit the girl's throat. The thought gives me a momentary pause until I remember how much it doesn't even matter.

Whether it's today, or after the second trial, or the third... only one of us is going to live through this.

"Fine," I spit through a locked jaw, and I place my foot on the first red stone and start moving.

At first, it's easy. One step, then another. Nothing happens.

I pick up the pace, hoping if I can just run through, I won't give the fog time to attack.

Then the pull starts. It's subtle, just a whisper of resistance around my ankles. Then, like hands clawing up from beneath the stones, magic wraps tight, dragging me downward.

I slow.

Then I hear that small voice I know better than my own.

"I need you," Tyla calls to me.

Every instinct in me tells me to look, to go to her. To assess her illness and how bad it's gotten in my absence. She needs me. I just know it. She's always needed me, and I've *always* been there for her. I've always chosen her above everything else.

"You left me!" she cries, as if sensing my thoughts. "I'm going to die without you."

It's like razor blades across my heart. Torture even as I remind myself that it isn't real.

Tyla is safe. She's in Velia. Kristona is taking care of her.

One step at a time.

One step forward, then another.

"You know she needs you."

That voice is enough to make me still.

That voice sends chills down my spine and roots my feet to the ground.

That voice draws my attention over my shoulder, to where my father stands, looking at me with that same patient smile I used to know so well.

"Daddy?"

"Hey, bug."

It's been so many years, and still I remember him so clearly. He's just as tall and broad-shouldered. His hair is that light chestnut brown color that seems odd considering how dark mine is.

"I've missed you," he says, tucking his hands into his pockets.

I sway slightly. His voice is so warm. It's familiar. His presence is *so real* it makes my chest ache. My vision blurs, the heaviness in my gut spreading to my ribs, pressing into my bones.

I've missed him so much.

Daddy.

My father is *here.*

I feel my eyes misting. "There's so much I have to tell you."

"Huntyr!"

Alexandria's scream pulls me from the trance, and I look down in just enough time to see my own foot lifting off the path. I slam it down again and steady myself, breathing deeply until the pull of the magic fades.

"Thanks," I mutter over my shoulder.

She nods.

I need to get off of this path. Now.

I rush forward, keeping my gaze locked ahead, my gait strong. And I'm just nearly at the door on the other side when a prickle of awareness rushes down my spine.

His voice is suddenly all I can focus on.

"Huntress," he purrs, and this time when I turn, it's Derian's dark eyes that I stare into.

I freeze.

And for the briefest of seconds I'm...confused.

The mist had shown me the two people I cared most about in this world. The only two people who had earned the smallest parts of life from my cold, dead heart.

Derian has not done that.

And yet, here he stands, hands tucked into his pockets, dressed in all black. The leather clings to him, his dark hair falling just slightly over his eyes.

"Why you?" I whisper.

He tilts his head to the side. "Don't you know?"

"What am I supposed to know?"

He smirks, stepping forward as his tongue darts out over his lower lip. "Maybe you don't know yet."

"Know what?"

Derian runs a hand over his jaw, contemplative. "Maybe you're not ready to know. Maybe neither of us are. I do wonder though."

His gaze locks onto mine like a tangible weight.

"I wonder what it'll feel like."

The words wrap around me like silk and shadows.

"What do you mean?" I demand, but my voice is quieter now.

"I wonder what it'll feel like when we're finally together. I think part of me has always wondered about it, even if I've never felt like I deserve it. Don't *you* wonder?"

An icy shiver rolls down my spine, leaving my body tingling and my mouth impossibly dry. Heat coils under my skin like an ember about to catch fire, and a tapping on my thigh is the only indication that my fingers are trembling.

I clench my fists, letting my nails dig into the skin hard enough to draw blood. Hard enough to remind me what's happening right now.

What's real and what most definitely is not.

"No, I don't," I tell him, and then I grasp onto the door and pull it open.

That same rushing sensation takes over me, spinning my body, my mind, my very soul until I'm standing in the center of a circle of doors.

In a few moments, the other women begin to appear next to me, each of us standing before single doors. I glance around rapidly, noticing that all the other women successfully made it down the path. There's still nine of us here.

"They have our names on them," Alexandria notices with a whisper.

I step forward to my door, between Seraphina's and another Mortal.

Burned onto the wood in front of each of our doors... are riddles.

Next to me, the Mortal reads her riddle aloud. "What can fill a room but takes up no space?"

I frown, brain overturning the possibilities.

"What does it mean?" she asks me desperately.

Seraphina scoffs from the other side. "Why would we help you? Your death only improves our chances."

I glance at Seraphina's riddle. *The more you take, the more you leave behind. What am I?*

"Footsteps," she answers without a second of hesitation, and the door opens before her.

She gives me her haughtiest smile before flicking her hair over her shoulder and stepping through. The door disappears.

The girl next to me watches the spot where Seraphina stood for a few moments before turning back to her own door. "Um...a shadow?"

I cringe. She's wrong.

The moment the words leave her lips, the ground groans beneath her.

A rush of searing heat explodes. Sudden, blinding, and unstoppable, singeing the side of my arm so sharply that I stumble backwards.

She barely screams before the flames devour her.

"What was the answer?" Sylvana wonders aloud when the girl is finally gone.

"Light," I tell her, before turning to look at my own riddle.

I was here before the Gods, but even they fear me.

I am patient, but I never sleep.

I take kings and beggars alike, I do not discriminate.

Who am I?

A grin pulls at the corner of my lips.

Finally, an aspect of this trial that doesn't seem impossible.

The answer comes as easily as recognizing myself in the mirror.

"Death."

The door creaks open.

HUNTYR

The moment I step through the door, I fall, landing heavily on my hands and knees as if I've been dropped from midair. I struggle to suck in a sudden gasp of air as I look around.

I'm in the fortress courtyard.

And yet, it's wrong somehow.

I stand slowly, glancing around me as I do, searching out any of the other competitors. The entirety of the courtyard is empty though. Not only are the other women missing, but there's no sign of any life at all. No sharpening blades, no sparring, no sounds of throwing knives and arrows slamming into targets.

The night sky above is starless, but the air around me is thick, charged with Fae magic. I turn, the ground crunching unnaturally under my feet as I do. I stumble backwards as I take in the scorched black land, cracked and dead under my feet.

A single pathway remains untouched by the blackness.

A pathway that doesn't belong in this courtyard.

My brows draw together in a frown as I stare at the alley across from my apartment in Velia.

It's exactly as I remember. There's the turn in the stone path, the shadowed doorway that leads to a staircase, the stacked crates just left of where I had once killed a man.

I inhale sharply.

The silence presses in, nearly unbearable.

And then, the shadows shift.

And from them... emerges a panther.

It's massive, sleek as oil with a shining black coat. Its eyes burn golden with an alertness that's unnatural for an animal.

Because it's not an animal, I realize.

It's an Eshari.

I freeze, not allowing myself to feel fear. It would be pointless to be afraid of the beast. I may not be as familiar with the Eshari as the Fae are, but I understand that there's no escaping what's going to come next. No way to outmaneuver or out-think it. None of the training and skills that have carried me so far in this trial matter now.

The Eshari will judge me for *who* I am and what I've already done leading up to this moment.

The panther watches. Unblinking. Assessing. There's only a few feet between us, but it doesn't pounce or growl. It simply watches me with that strange intensity.

Slowly, it moves closer to me, circling where I stand, close enough that I can feel its warmth and hear the gentle puffs of air as it breathes in the scent of me and then huffs it out.

It circles again, and this time I feel its tail flicking against my leg.

I don't flinch, don't move. I don't even breathe too deeply.

"Strange."

My body locks as I hear the feminine voice, coming not from the panther's mouth, but from inside my own mind.

"You are unlike the others."

I clench my jaw.

Realization hits me with brutal clarity. My time in this Fae competition is coming to an end.

Because if anyone will fail to meet the judgment of the Eshari, it's me.

The Eshari were the guards of the Vaereth, the Gods who protected the Fae, and I'm an assassin who tried to assassinate the Fae prince.

It's definitely going to kill me.

"So?" I force the word out.

The panther steps forward, tilting its head in appraisal. *"You do not flinch before the death you feel is imminent."*

"Death is imminent for us all." I shrug.

A huff that sounds suspiciously like a laugh. *"You do not beg for my mercy."*

I've seen dozens of men and women alike beg me for mercy that I didn't have to give them. Their pleas didn't make a difference then, and mine won't now.

"You wouldn't show me any."

The words hover between us, and the panther continues studying me. *"You are strong. Brave. Pure of heart—though your soul is touched by darkness."*

I frown. I don't think I've ever been described as pure of heart before.

"Strangely, you remind me of my masters."

She circles me again as I stiffen. What does that mean?

"And yet, you are not entirely like them."

"Why don't you get it over with?"

She pauses, looking up at me. *"You wish to be judged so desperately?"*

"I need no judge to tell me who I am."

A laugh echoes in my mind. *"Brave words for a woman who is no more than a wounded child. A woman who hides behind weapons and violence because of how deeply she fears being hurt again. A woman who loves few, so that she may not suffer too many more losses."*

She's crawling through my mind, seeing all the dark and twisted parts of me. "You don't know me."

"I know you, Huntress."

My blood runs cold, and like I've seen in so many of my victims, the rush of acceptance falls over me. I know what comes next. Just as I know that I cannot stop it.

"I am Kaia. I was once a hunter, a seeker of souls, a companion to the Vaereth."

She meets my gaze, golden eyes burning into mine.

"I will choose you to be my new companion."

Her words strike through me. I stumble backwards, struggling to maintain my balance as the world starts to move around us and the ground shakes violently beneath my feet. My stomach twists painfully, and a pulse of something ancient and unbreakable starts moving under my skin.

"What does that mean?" I demand, my voice rough and unsteady, doubling over as my entire body locks in cramps.

Kaia comes to my side as I fall forward, landing heavily on my hands and knees.

"I shall stay."

My heartbeat slams against my ribs. My blood boils. When Kaia presses her forehead against mine, heat rushes over me. Power courses *through* me.

It's neither painful nor comforting.

It's a connection formed by something far more powerful than any Fae magic I've ever felt before.

The world slams back into place in a dizzying rush, and the coiling magic that held me in the labyrinth releases me. I curl my fingers into the dirt of the arena, letting the sounds of the crowd wash over me and bring me back to the here and now.

Only Kaia is also here. Now. With me.

She presses against my side, offering another grounding sensation as I feel like I'm about to shatter apart.

I force myself to breathe through the nausea and fully take in my surroundings.

Two more bodies, two of the Fae, are lifeless on the ground next to me.

The Eshari must have killed them.

That leaves seven of us. Three Mortals, four Fae.

Five of the twelve of us dead within the first trial.

I struggle to look up, to breathe through my body's reaction to whatever magic kept me in the labyrinth. When I do finally gain the strength to pull my head up, Roland is watching me, a concerned expression evident on his features.

"This..." his voice trails off as he turns to look at the panther pressed against me. "This has never happened."

It takes me a second to make sense of it, to look around and realize that the other women are standing alone, the shock on their faces mirroring that of Roland's. There are no other Eshari in the arena.

Kaia isn't supposed to be here.

"No one will tell me where I am supposed to be. I will go where I please."

I whip my head at her so sharply a cramp forms at the base of my neck.

Great. The ancient magical creature can read my thoughts. That's not creepy at all.

She flicks her tail, smacking it against my back.

"They are unhappy," Kaia tells me. *"You will stand."*

Bossy.

I drag myself to my feet.

Murmurs echo around me, the warriors in the stands all talking at each other in a rush. The other contestants stare at me, wide-eyed and open-mouthed, their expressions equal parts confusion and rage. Silently I look up, searching for Derian, only to see he and Caldren already on their feet. They pause for the briefest of moments before rushing down.

"How has this happened?" Taric demands, stepping into the arena with Rhen and Parker close on his heels.

Roland sputters, glancing between Kaia and Taric. "An Eshari has never remained."

So much for my plan to hide my skills and simply fly under the radar. Kaia's presence just put a massive target on my back. I glance at her in my peripheral.

"Felt like being dramatic today, did you?" I push the thought in her direction.

She rolls her golden eyes.

"This is ridiculous!" Mara cries from across the arena, clutching an area of her thigh that's visibly bleeding from a bite mark. She might have been judged to be worthy, but obviously she'd had to earn that judgement. "An Eshari is an unfair advantage!"

"This cannot be allowed!" Thalara agrees next to her.

"It shouldn't be allowed," Seraphina tells them, stepping forward with malice firing in her eyes. Her hands light up in flames. "Let's just kill the Mortal and be done with her."

Kaia puts herself between us, growling, a low and deadly sound that seems to echo around us. *"You will not be harmed by this viper."*

"I can handle her."

"You can," Kaia agrees, even as her eyes remain locked on Seraphina, her lips curled back over sharp teeth. *"But the Fae must all know that I will protect you. That I have chosen you the way I once chose my masters."*

Derian steps onto the hardened ground of the arena, his presence effortless yet absolute. He doesn't rush. Doesn't even look concerned.

"Why did *you choose me?"* I wonder, looking away from him while I can still force myself to do so.

Her tail flicks against my ankle. *"It has been a long time since I have seen a creature who is capable of the bond, whose soul is strong enough to meld with that of my kind."*

I frown. *"I'm just a Mortal, though. How was I capable of it when the Fae weren't?"*

"I do not know. I only know that when a bond is possible, it must be honored. That was the will of the Vaereth, and so it is the will of the Eshari."

"Something must be done, your highness," Parker says cautiously, snapping my attention back to the chaos unfurling around us.

Every Fae in the stands is on their feet, watching their prince casually stroll towards us. Half of them are seething in anger, the other half is simply staring at me like I'm a prize they want to claim for themselves. My fingers twitch towards the blades on my hips.

Derian's lips quirk as he takes in the scene before him. Kaia stands with her hind legs between my feet and her menacing glare directed at Seraphina, who stares at me with both of her hands on fire. Meanwhile, my muscles are poised and ready to launch these blades at the slightest indication that I need to.

Derian drags his gaze to Seraphina. "If you'd like to continue challenging an Eshari, you're welcome to do so."

His eyes flick to Kaia, who snarls as if she welcomes the possibility of a fight.

"Though, I do believe it looks ready to eat you."

Kaia flicks her tail again, her voice curling in my mind. *I would never allow such filth to fester in my intestines.*

I snort, unable to stop myself, and earn a look of pure hatred from Seraphina. If I haven't made enough of an enemy in her already, I can almost guarantee she's going to cause problems for me after this.

Derian turns back to the crowd. "The trial is complete. The Eshari are servants of the Vaereth and above our rule. If it wishes to stay with the Mortal, it may."

"She," I interrupt pointedly, suddenly feeling overwhelmingly protective of her. "Her name is Kaia, and *my* name is Huntyr. Not Mortal."

I feel Kaia's approval float over me.

Derian stares at me, not even bothering to acknowledge the ancient predator standing between us, the panther who glares at him as if she is now considering letting *him* fester in her intestines.

Nothing else in the world seems to matter as we stare at each other in this silent standoff.

I practically dare him to fight against me.

"Very well," he acknowledges with a tilt of his head. "*Kaia* may stay with Huntyr."

"I will stay because I have chosen to, regardless of what the Fae prince thinks on the matter."

I grin down at her. *"I think I'm going to like you."*

She begins moving out of the arena, waiting for me to follow after her. *"Your approval is also unnecessary. I will stay because I have chosen you, and that is the way of the bond."*

I stare after her a moment before I follow her swishing tail, suddenly not sure how I feel about being bonded with a grumpy cat for the rest of my foreseeable future.

21

Derian

My office is frigid. The window hangs open and wind tears through it haphazardly, wild enough that it just might rip the shutters off their hinges.

My powers haven't been this difficult to control since I was a boy.

And it's pissing me off.

This Conclave was a bad idea. I should have married the damn Mortal princess, left her in one of my lavish homes in Bridgemond, and gone back to the training yards in Amberhull.

Had I just done that, my life would be back to normal by now.

Nothing has been normal since the second I called for this fucking contest.

No, that's not quite right.

I sigh heavily and rip a hand through my hair. The strands are already slightly tangled from me repeating the action over and over since I'd sat myself behind my desk.

It's not the Conclave that's fucked everything up. It's the fact that nothing has been quite right since Huntyr Lachlan walked into the dark room I was hiding out in.

Kaia's arrival is an anomaly. No Eshari has ever chosen to stay with a Conclave competitor. Fuck, I've never even *seen* an Eshari before.

But suddenly there she was, standing next to Huntyr Lachlan of all people. Defending her. Claiming her. Placing herself between Huntyr and anyone who might wish her harm, myself included.

Of course, it was *Huntyr* who had been chosen.

The woman is an anomaly herself, a girl who acts wiser than her years. A noblewoman who can't shoot an arrow straight but somehow seems more intelligent and quick-witted than any of the other Mortals. Why wouldn't the Eshari choose her?

I push out from behind my desk and stand, walking five paces to the window and back. Then to the window. Then back.

Maybe it was simply curiosity.

Maybe the Eshari also saw what a conundrum she is, and now the beast is just as desperate to figure her out as I am.

A knock at the door halts my movements, an eerie sense of precognition settling over me that my day is about to get worse. I move to open the door, a growling creak filling the space as I do.

Parker is standing with tight shoulders and a wary expression, a letter clutched in his palm. Without a word, he simply extends it to me.

Fuck me.

I have a very strong suspicion of who that letter is from.

"What?" I bark.

Parker clears his throat, clearly uncomfortable having to be the messenger of this news. "It's from Bridgemond."

Of course it is. Once again, I run a tired hand through my hair, waving at him to get it over with. "And?"

"The King is on his way here."

Lightning cracks outside, and Parker glances at it nervously.

Control, I remind myself, before breathing deeply and pushing down that power once more. The storm seems to settle a little outside. As much as I can settle it, at least.

"Tell him to stay exactly where he is."

It's not safe here. Not for a King. Oxhurn is far too close to the Wastelands. And with the Velkai coming closer and closer to our territory, with their numbers seemingly growing, I cannot allow my brother here. If Luceron wants to lecture me for calling the Conclave, then I can simply go to him.

"He's already en route."

So much for control over my magic. The storm outside intensifies, thunder booming so loudly that even Parker flinches. I don't bother quieting it.

Of all the stupid, reckless fucking things my brother has done, this might take the cake. How he managed it is beyond me. I can practically hear Deanna nagging him from here, insisting her mate stay with her and the children.

Guess that mate bond doesn't stop a man from making idiotic decisions.

"Move," I command Parker, pushing past him and making my way towards the dining hall, where the celebratory dinner is being held for the victors of the first trial.

If I have to suffer through this Conclave and my brother's wrath, I can at least do so with a drink in my hand.

The dining hall is already buzzing with energy and the rush of survival, so no one thinks twice about the strangely intense storm raging outside the fortress walls. Candles flicker against the stone walls, and plates are piled high with roasted meats and golden fruits. Both the fortress warriors and the Conclave contestants are drinking heavily, celebrating, and enjoying themselves.

I can't wait for the evening to be finished.

Without a second glance at anyone in particular, I stalk towards my seat at the head of the table. A full glass of wine has already been poured and sits waiting for me. I pull it to my mouth and drink deeply, running the back of my hand against my mouth once finished.

Appearing from the throng of people, Cal drops heavily into the chair beside me and folds his hands behind his head. I feel his eyes on me even as I avoid his stare.

"You look fairly unhappy for a man who has seven beautiful women fighting over him."

"Shut up," I practically growl, downing the rest of my goblet.

Cal simply refills my glass, more than accustomed to my moods. "What's got you so testy?"

Only one word is needed.

"Luceron."

His eyes flash in understanding. He knows my brother well enough to have also known this was just a matter of time. "I suppose we should prepare the finest room in the fortress for him."

I glare at him. "The finest room in the fortress is my own."

He nods, brows raised pointedly. "That's because this fortress is no place for a King."

"You don't have to explain that to me!" I reply sharply. "I'm not the one who invited him."

"I don't think a King needs to be invited to travel within his own king-dom."

I'm silent for a long time, simmering in my irritation, until I finally mutter in response. "Yes, well, while I would have cautioned him against those travels, my *brother* hasn't considered my wishes in some time now."

I think there's a flash of sympathy in Cal's eyes. Either that or pity. I need neither.

Cal and I watch the revelry for some time before he finally turns back to me, head cocked sideways. "Well, not to risk making your bad mood worse, but I did some investigating on your favorite Mortal."

My heart rate spikes as I arch a brow.

"She isn't who she says she is, Derian." His voice is low and laced with caution.

"Meaning?"

He begins piling food onto his plate, talking subtly out of the side of his mouth. "Her father was, in fact, a nobleman. He managed a rather large province in Velia. Mother died in childbirth, and he remarried shortly afterward."

"That doesn't sound all that suspicious."

If anything, it's rather... common.

Cal narrows his eyes at me before continuing. "The suspiciousness start-ed after his death. From what I can discern, it's as if she disappeared. The stepmother was never seen with a daughter. There was no governess employed at the manor. She never attended any society gatherings."

I take it in, considering his words. "Until the masquerade."

He nods. "The stepmother died and she suddenly re-emerged, claiming her title and spinning a story that she'd been sent away for schooling after her father's death."

I frown. That is a slightly less common turn of events, but it's also not entirely unbelievable. The idea that a widowed stepmother sent away her husband's daughter to avoid having to raise a young girl is certainly not impossible.

"You don't believe it?" I ask him.

He pauses for a moment at the sudden cacophony of laughter and swelling music from the revelry. "I couldn't find a record of her education or what school she attended. I used all the resources I have, but I haven't the slightest idea where she has been since her father died."

I tap my fingers against my goblet, considering his words. After decades of friendship, I've come to trust Cal's instincts. I've grown to rely on them as carefully as my own. If he doubts the story, it's because there's a good reason to.

Still, there's a strange feeling coiling inside me, a mixture of suspicious apprehension and undeniable... interest.

"She's dangerous, Derian," Cal says, watching me closely, as if he can sense where my thoughts have turned. "I can't put my finger on it exactly, but there's something unnatural about her. And I think you know that."

I scoff, drinking deeply again.

He only shakes his head in frustration. "You really think she was locked away in a finishing school for all those years? Because I don't."

Where else could she have been? And what difference does it make, anyway? She is a Mortal woman for Gods' sake. Oxhurn sits on the edge of the Wastelands. It's home to the fiercest, deadliest warriors in the entirety of the Fae kingdom. Even *if* Huntyr is the one who managed to kill Kai at the masquerade, a Mortal woman stands no chance against me or the warriors here.

Cal sighs, his exasperation evident as he runs a hand through his auburn hair. "Look, I get it."

I turn to face my best friend, annoyed by the way his voice sounds cajoling, as if he's trying to calm a child throwing a tantrum. "You get what?"

He pauses. "You want to bed her, Derian. Practically everyone in this room does."

A snarl rips out of me before I even realize what I'm doing, along with a sudden rush of... possessiveness. I clutch the goblet too tightly as the storm outside intensifies for a brief moment before calming.

He only grins at me knowingly. "And if I'm going based on how she responds to you, you might be the only one who actually stands a chance with her."

"She's a contender in the Conclave." I'm not sure if I'm reminding him or myself of the rules. "And she's unlikely to live through the next trial, anyway."

"Even still, she—"

I don't mean to stop listening to him. I don't mean to turn away.

But I do.

My attention snaps to the door just as she steps across the threshold.

She moves through the room easily, confident and assured. Dressed in deep red, her leathers have been replaced with something smoother. Sleeker. The gown clings to her figure, the slit along her leg revealing just enough to stir something deep inside me.

Her dark hair is pinned up, a few loose curls framing her sharp features and brushing against her tanned collarbone. The flicker of firelight catches on her skin, painting her in warm, golden light.

The Eshari stalks silently at her side, golden eyes sharp and watchful. The panther's presence is as commanding as hers. Together, they're a formidable pair, and they draw practically every eye in the room.

Cal is right. It isn't just fear or mistrust in the eyes that land on her. There's a fair bit of desire in this room as well.

"You were saying?"

"What?" I rip my attention back to Cal. Taking my eyes off her is surprisingly painful.

He nods to Huntyr. "You were staring."

I scowl, irritation bubbling again. "I was assessing someone you just implied is a potential threat."

He snorts, stabbing a cut of meat with his fork. "Assessing her curves, maybe."

I don't even bother responding. There's no point in denying it when I'm already seeking her out again. When I'm already assessing the way the dress lies on her figure, imagining what she would look like out of that dress.

Huntyr catches my gaze and holds it, those blue eyes so impossibly bright. Unnaturally bright. We hold that stare for just a beat too long, and I swear I can see the heat burning through me mirrored in her eyes.

But then she smirks.

Mocking me. Entirely unbothered.

And suddenly I want to kiss her just to wipe that look off her face.

Or rip her skirt up, find the dagger I know is strapped to her thigh, and slam it through the table between us. Either would work.

But I don't move.

I watch as she takes a place next to the blonde Mortal that's always been rude to her. I watch as she grins at the girl. Somehow the girl, who has done nothing but make her life difficult, has managed to earn a smile from Huntyr that is both light and genuine. She's earned the kind of smile that Huntyr has yet to direct at me.

And that bothers me for the entirety of the time that I pretend to eat my meal, even as I remind myself that it shouldn't matter. Her smiles shouldn't matter. She shouldn't matter.

⸺◆◇◆⸺

I don't know what it is about this woman that prevents me from being able to pull my attention away from her.

My evening proceeds in a dull haze, pretending to pay attention to the words being spoken to me while I watch her from across the room.

I watch with satisfaction as she finishes the meal.

I watch as she drinks deeply from her goblet, noting that it's the first time I've actually seen her drink any of the wine we offer.

I watch as she stands easily and chats with Rhen and some of the other warriors.

She's relaxed.

I don't know if I've ever seen her relaxed.

Scratching the side of my neck, I wonder absently if it's the presence of the Eshari trailing her that has her feeling more at ease. Despite the fact that the beast arrived only a matter of hours ago, the two already seem intimately attached to each other. The Eshari's tail flicks easily around Huntyr's ankle, and she reaches down to scratch the soft area between the panther's ears without missing a beat of her conversation. It's as if she doesn't even realize she's doing it.

And all too suddenly, I'm moving, pushing back from the table.

I'm not even sure why.

I just know that I need to be closer to her. And I can't stand another second of watching Rhen stare at her with lust burning in his eyes.

He might as well be shouting his intentions to the sky for as obvious as he's making it.

While intimacy with contestants is forbidden for me, it's certainly not for the women. Hell, they're *encouraged* to enjoy their last nights.

But I'll be damned if I watch him pull her out of this room.

"Your highness," the warrior greets me, bowing his head respectfully.

I nod, barely keeping my frustration intact while thunder cracks outside. "Please consult with Roland regarding the next trial for the Conclave. I want to be sure everything is prepared."

The bastard has the audacity to glance at her out of the corner of his eye, as if he's unhappy at being sent away, before he follows my order.

Gods help me, if he had said anything to her before leaving, I might have killed him.

Huntyr turns, glancing up at me through dark lashes with a wry smile. Her gaze flickers quickly to my mouth before bouncing up to my eyes, and I can't help my smirk.

"You look like you're considering murdering someone," she says.

Perceptive little thing.

"I just might," I acknowledge, reaching for the decanter on the table beside us to refill her glass. "The night is young."

She rolls her eyes, the motion sending a burst of need through me, before she glances pointedly at the window. She's the only one that seems to notice I'm the cause of the booming outside. "It's a party, Derian. It would be a shame if you lost your temper."

I'm distracted. I want to listen to her, to play this game with her, but it's really hard to fucking concentrate when she's dressed like that. Where did she even get that dress? None of the other women are dressed in anything near as tight or revealing. None of them would have the confidence for it.

Seraphina would, but only because she *wanted* every eye on her.

I don't think Huntyr has the slightest idea of the effect she's having.

"You like testing me, don't you?" I ask, leaning over her.

"You make it easy." She grins up at me, and fuck, I can't think straight when she's peering at me from under those lashes. "What was it you said the other day? You're the one who gets most riled up around me, which makes you the most fun to poke at."

She's just a Mortal. And yet she meets my gaze without a shred of fear. She calls me by my name instead of my title. She doesn't want to win for the benefit of my hand.

She's a complete anomaly.

"Believe me, you're getting plenty of people riled up tonight."

She chortles softly, turning away to scan over the room, before glancing up at me with an arched brow. "Jealous?"

"Yes." What would be the point in denying that?

She leans back against the wall, rolling out her neck, and *fuck,* this angle lets me look right down the neckline of that dress.

Red is officially my favorite color.

The woman should have an entire wardrobe of nothing but this color.

"Good," she says softly, taunting me. "It's probably the first time in your spoiled princely life that you've been faced with wanting something you can't have."

She stares at me, those eyes burning through me, and I swear I can feel a spark of magic in the air. I don't dare step back away from her, and she doesn't either.

For someone who claims not to be interested in me, there does appear to be a faint blush coloring her cheeks.

"And would this be *your* attempt at flirting?" I ask, resting a hand on the wall above her head, leaning over her, noticing the way her fingers tighten on her glass.

She laughs, the sound shooting arrows of heat through me. "I don't flirt with Fae bastards."

I narrow my eyes. "Liar."

"You *really* do think that everyone is obsessed with you, don't you?"

The cat at her feet lays down, resting its head on its paws. Apparently, she's decided that Huntyr is safe enough for now.

My gaze lingers on her mouth, on the curve of her full lips. "And you really like pretending that you're not attracted to me, even though we both know you are."

Huntyr downs the rest of her drink and rests it on the table next to her before twisting—still leaning against the wall, but now fully turning back to face me.

"What could possibly make you think that?"

"Could be the way you just arched your back." I lift my hand to rest upon the curve of her hip. She tenses slightly, her eyes darting over my shoulder to the room around us, where I'm sure plenty of eyes watch our every move. But then her attention is on me again, and I savor the feeling of those eyes on mine. "Or it could be the way you bite your lower lip every time you talk to me."

"That's all it takes for you to convince yourself that a woman wants you?"

"Those are typically signals that send a certain message, yes."

She grins, those lips pulling back over perfectly white teeth, and she leans forward, tapping one finger against my chest and leaving it there. "Trust me, when I want a man, there's no question about it. There's no need to ask whether or not I'm flirting or debate the signals. When I want a man, I make sure he knows. And when I do finally take a man to bed, he leaves so satisfied that the separation is almost painful for the poor soul."

Dear *Gods*.

Does she have any idea what she's doing to me? She must. Surely she's trying to murder me with need.

Because I am more desperate than I've been since adolescence.

I'm practically ready to get on my knees before this creature.

I glance towards her empty glass. "Are you drunk?"

She smirks. "No, you idiot. I have an Eshari at my feet who swore to bite through the spinal cord of anyone who tries to hurt me. That knowledge brings me a fair amount of comfort."

The panther looks up at me, the promise of that threat obvious in her golden eyes, before she rests her head back on her front two paws.

"The Eshari won't be with you during the trials," I remind her, voice low, ignoring the soft growl at our feet.

The sound of a clearing throat pulls my focus, and Parker approaches us, another message clutched in his palm. My stomach drops heavily.

Our game has ended for the evening.

"How soon?" I ask, already dreading the answer.

"His majesty will arrive in a fortnight. Likely after the Conclave has finished."

Well that's a relief at least.

Not even he has the power to end a Conclave once it's been called, but still, I'd prefer not to have to deal with his criticism while this is all still happening. By the time he arrives, the Mortals will be dead and Seraphina will have won.

There will be nothing to be done at that point but write to the King of Velia, praise the strength of the Mortal competitors who showed bravery until their last breaths, and offer to maintain the alliance in honor of the women's sacrifice.

I take the note from Parker and fold it in my pocket to read later. I'll save it for after I finally manage to calm the storm outside. "Tell Caldren for me?"

Parker nods and heads to the table where Cal is somehow *still* eating.

I turn back to Huntyr, stiffening slightly when I notice that alertness in her eyes again. She watches Parker retreat, her expression... calculating.

Her features turn teasing once more when she returns her attention to me. The change is instantaneous, effortless, as if I'd imagined the whole thing.

But I hadn't.

I narrow my eyes. "You wouldn't be hiding something from me, would you?"

The Eshari rises, pressing against Huntyr's leg and angling between us. She reaches down to pet the beast. "Wouldn't you like to know?"

I would actually.

I would like to pin her against the wall and use whatever means necessary to make her confess everything to me.

But with a wicked grin, she pushes off the wall, murmurs something to her pet beast, and walks away without a single word of explanation. She returns to her spot at the table, next to the blonde, and the Eshari sits behind her, its golden eyes staring directly at me.

Cal appears at my side, smirking. "That might be the first time I watched a woman reject you."

I glare at him from my peripheral. "You know as well as I that I cannot show favoritism."

"Well you're doing a terrible job following that rule," he points out. "It's quite obvious that you want her, *and* quite obvious that she wants nothing to do with you. It's admittedly fun to watch."

Gods help me.

"Find out where she was during those years," I order him, running my tongue over my teeth as I continue watching her. "You just might be right about her."

"About the fact that you want to fuck her?" he asks with a raised brow.

"No." *Yes.* "She is different from the others. She's not what she's pretending to be, and that might just make her dangerous after all."

He pauses, looking between her and me, consideration heavy on his face as he crosses his arms above his broad chest. "What happened to *she's just a Mortal?*"

Quite a bit, actually.

She faced that first trial without a single misstep or show of fear.

She bonded an Eshari.

And the version of her I saw when my brother was mentioned was not one that I've seen before.

The dread that curls through my stomach is like a physical force coming over me, because as intoxicating as Huntyr Lachlan might be, I must defend my brother and King against any threat.

Even if that threat is her.

HUNTYR

K aia is curled on the edge of my bed, licking her paw lazily and ignoring me. She's been ignoring me for what's felt like hours.

Which is fine.

I'm preoccupied anyway.

I have been all day.

We didn't have training today because today has been reserved for something called the *Bonding Procession*, which requires Derian to spend one-on-one time with each contestant. Apparently, it's to allow him to better get to know his future bride. Whoever she may be.

So Kaia and I have been sitting in this tiny room all day, waiting for the Fae bastard to decide to sweep me off my feet for a romantic escapade.

I gag at the thought.

Still, the time alone has been helpful. It's given me plenty of time for scheming.

King Luceron's impending arrival is a strike of luck. The inclusion of Fae in the Conclave has made my victory less certain, but if I can manage to still win then I'll have both the Fae King and Prince within reach. What better revenge could there be than wiping out two key members of the monarchy?

"You're not going to kill the King," Kaia chastises in my mind, her voice filled with impatience.

I glare at her from where I'm crouched by the dresser, sharpening each blade in the chest of weapons. *"Do you doubt my abilities?"*

She looks at me, her ears flicking. *"I doubt your resolve."*

"You don't understand." If she knew how much suffering my kingdom had experienced at the hands of the Fae, if she knew about the nightmares that have haunted me for my entire life, then she would know that absolutely nothing is going to stop me from plunging my blade through the King's heart.

For myself and for every single Mortal who has ever suffered at the hands of a Fae.

"I understand more than you think." Her voice is exasperated.

My grip on the blade in my hand tightens, irritation curling in my gut at her dismissal.

"This need for vengeance is beneath you. You've been distracted all day."

"I have not been distracted," I protest. I've spent the day exercising, sharpening weapons, and creating plans. Those are all incredibly useful ways to pass the time. *"I wisely used my day to devise a rather brilliant plan for once Luceron arrives."*

She raises that feline brow at me. *"If you insist."*

"You don't believe me."

"You may claim whatever you want, but your mind is no secret to me. You've spent far more time today thinking about the king's brother."

I've grown rather attached to her since the trial, but I don't think I'll ever be happy with her constantly listening to my thoughts. *"I was thinking about killing his brother."*

A chuckle echoes through my head. *"Yes. You thought about killing him. Then, you thought about what he was doing with the other women. Then, you thought about bedding him. Then, you thought about killing him again. Your mind is an endless circle that leaves me dizzy."*

I'm just about to tell her off when a sudden awareness falls over me, a warmth deep in my bones, just before a knock sounds at the door. Kaia doesn't even bother to get up.

"What if that was an attacker?" I point out as she begins lazily licking her paws.

"Then I would trust that you could use your very plentiful skills to handle them."

Rolling my eyes, I stand, just as he knocks at the door again. Of course Derian is incapable of showing patience.

"What exactly is the point of this bond?" I ask her.

"I am your companion. I will fight by your side, until one of us leaves this realm, but I am not a common guard dog. I will not take care of problems you can easily manage on your own."

Fair enough.

I open the door, ready to greet him with an attitude, only to suddenly lose any ability to speak clearly.

Fuck, he looks *good*.

He's obviously always been attractive. And I'll admit, the fighting leathers do add a certain appeal. But somehow this is even worse. My gaze trails over him, tracking the loose, dark shirt, with the sleeves rolled up over his forearms. He leans against the doorframe with a careless smirk. His dark eyes are heated, promising all sorts of wicked—

I need to snap myself out of this attraction before it becomes a serious problem. It's already become too much of a distraction.

"Nice of you to finally show up," I spit out. "Have a fun day with all your other girlfriends?"

"Good job snapping out of it." Kaia's voice rings in my head.

"Shut up," I hiss back at her.

It's late. The sun went down hours ago. I was just starting to think I was going to luck out and not have to go through with this ridiculous ceremonial outing.

"No, you weren't."

I glare at her over my shoulder. *"Would you quit it?"*

Derian's eyes sparkle as his lips quirk up. "Aw, were you missing me?"

"Hardly."

He tilts his head, the small motion pulling him closer towards me. His leather scent falls over me in an intoxicating rush that leaves my head dizzy.

And my lower stomach clenching in anticipation.

When did my body become so traitorous?

This is simply an artifact of general longing. It's just been too long since I last laid with a man. Derian is reasonably attractive and close enough that he's the target of pent up energy. It has nothing to do with *him.*

"Really? You sound like you were waiting around all day thinking about me."

"You sound like a Fae bastard who can't get over this obsession you have with yourself."

He laughs, the sound surprisingly genuine, and damn if I don't kind of like the sound of it. Before I know it, his hand snakes out and grabs mine, pulling me forward. "Come on, I have something special planned for you."

"What does that mean?" I stumble over the threshold, hating the tingle of energy that surges through my palm.

"You don't strike me as a 'flowers and picnics' kind of girl."

Well that's... perceptive. I suppose.

I glance back at Kaia, who still lays lazily on the bed, her head resting on her front paws and her eyes growing heavy.

"You're not coming?"

She glances between Derian and I. *"I have no need to spend my evening watching you two salivate over each other."*

I tense. I had assumed Kaia would come. If she doesn't, I'm going to be left alone with the Fae prince and this incredibly inconvenient desire for him.

"And what if there's danger?" I practically whine.

"We just went over this."

Still, I stare at her with wide eyes.

With a heavy sigh, she rises from the bed and prowls forward, tail flicking as she positions herself between us. She bares her teeth, releasing a low, warning snarl as she levels her eyes at him.

Derian holds up a hand in mock surrender. "Bring her home safely. Got it."

She doesn't move.

Doesn't even blink.

"Can you talk to him the way you talk to me?" I wonder.

She turns back to the bed, tail flicking from side to side as she does. *"No. But sometimes words are not necessary to send a message. The prince is aware I will feast on his entrails if harm comes to you. Now go so I can finally sleep without your girlish thoughts keeping me up."*

I frown at her.

"Unless there's another reason you long for my presence?"

I fight the urge to throw something at her, even as I hear her laughter echoing in my mind.

Feeling utterly defeated, I turn back to Derian, only to find him staring at me with an expression that looks like it borders the line between confusion and awe.

"Lead the way," I tell him, beckoning us forward.

◆◇◆

We ride out of the fortress into a small nearby town. When we finally arrive, he throws himself off his horse, grabs my waist, and helps pull me from mine, a gesture that is neither needed nor wanted. When I make that point very clear, though, he simply ignores me and takes my hand in his. He leads me through the winding streets until we're stepping into a tavern that's nearly filled to the brim with people.

Not people.

Fae.

My hand twitches to the blade strapped to my hip, and I rest it atop the hilt as I scan the room quickly, clocking the Fae that have weapons strapped to them, assessing the nearest exits and calculating the overall number of people in the small room.

"Relax," Derian whispers in my ear, putting a hand on the small of my back and guiding me towards a booth in the far corner of the room. "You're perfectly safe with me."

I don't bother hiding when I roll my eyes. "You're a Fae."

I wouldn't trust him if we were the last two souls alive.

"I knew you were starting to like me," he teases, reaching up to squeeze my shoulders playfully as I begin walking through the room. The touch sends small shivers down my spine. "You just called me a Fae and *not* a Fae bastard."

"It's not too late to correct that." But it most definitely is.

We sit on opposite ends of the booth, and even though he promised we were safe, I watch as he, too, assesses the room with the same careful precision as I did.

The tavern is rowdy, filled with sounds of laughter, clinking glasses, and fiddle music. The smell of ale and sweat lingers in the air, the temperature warm from too many bodies pressed together. It's not entirely unlike some of the taverns I frequented back in Velia.

Those establishments were typically hubs for criminal activity. They were places where brothels and gambling dens thrived, which meant they were invaluable resources for assassins. Those were the places where I would be sent to trail a target. And when the job was done, those were the places where Flannigan and I would go after particularly brutal assignments to drink away the memories.

I smile as I remember one of those nights when I'd climbed on a table to sing off-key and demanded that he join me. He hadn't, but several other men had. And when one had gotten a bit too handsy, I'd knocked him out with one well-aimed punch. Flannigan and I had instantly looked at each other, very aware of the brawl that was about to break out. We moved quickly, dodging blows and landing those of our own, until he pulled me off the table by my waist and we ran from the pub laughing at the chaos we'd caused.

This place looks... calmer than that. There's no hint of violence hanging in the air. No one else seems to be watching for threats. No one is exchanging money or forbidden substances under the table. Everyone simply seems to be enjoying themselves.

How boring.

Derian waves over a waiter and orders two pints of ale, handing over a gold coin in payment before turning to me with expectant eyes.

"What?" I sigh. How long are we expected to make this little outing last?

He purses his lips, his attention focused entirely on me. "You're dressed in leathers."

I glance down at myself. "Am I supposed to be impressed by your observational skills?"

"The others wore gowns. You are wearing fighting leathers and are strapped with at least three weapons." His eyes heat slightly as his gaze slides down my torso. "I suspect there might be more that I can't see, though."

There are.

The waiter brings out our drinks and I pull mine to my mouth, suddenly feeling the overwhelming need for something to calm my stomach. "Would you have preferred if I dressed up for you?"

He laughs softly, the sound sending a rush over my skin. "I care very little about what you wear, Lady Lachlan."

"Huntyr," I remind him, barely able to keep the irritation from my voice.

His eyes narrow and he watches me for a long time as I continue nursing my drink.

"Huntyr," he finally agrees with an incline of his head.

"And who's the liar now?"

"What makes you think that's a lie?" he asks with a furrowed brow, the question genuine and not teasing.

I smirk. "You clearly enjoyed the gown I wore last night."

He doesn't try to hide when his gaze drops to my breasts, now perfectly covered. "That was a sight indeed, but I wasn't lying. Whether you wear leathers, a gown, or a burlap sack makes no difference, I'd still prefer to see you naked."

My breath halts, even my heartbeat seems to skip a bit.

Has this game between us come that far?

Not to be outdone, I lean forward, determined to throw him just as off-balance. "I do look my finest without anything hiding my best assets, but I'm afraid you'll just have to use your imagination."

"Oh I do." He smiles softly, the expression positively wicked, and I ignore the rush of wetness between my thighs as his eyes spread warmth to every place they trace over me. "I use my imagination every single night."

The thought of that—of him pleasuring himself to imaginations of *me*—should disgust me. It really should.

But it only fills me with a sick satisfaction and an unhealthy amount of curiosity. Suddenly, I'm picturing him, on the brink of release, his plentiful muscles tensed, his eyes closed, my name on his lips.

My voice is a bit breathier than I intend when I respond. "What a shame you have only your imagination to keep you company."

"Why bring another woman into my bed when the one in my mind is so much more intriguing?"

I snort. "Well I do hope the woman in your mind is fulfilling, considering the real one won't be joining you anytime soon."

He tilts his head in a soft acknowledgement that suggests the version of me in his head is *not* fulfilling at all before he drinks deeply. "And you, Huntyr? Is the Eshari the only thing keeping your bed warm?"

Wouldn't he like to know.

"That's a rather forward question to ask a Lady, don't you think?"

"Yes it is. It's a question a Lady would never expect to be asked, but you have never been one to meet expectations, if memory serves me right."

Fine, two can play that game. If I was going to be left flushed and unable to remove that image of him from my mind, then it was only fair for him to have to suffer, too.

"Well," I bite my lip slowly, knowing he notices every time I do. "You have us training every day in that courtyard."

"I do."

"And there are so many other Fae training there."

His jaw works. His knuckles twitch slightly before tightening on his glass.

"I can't help but to notice them," I continue, a smile playing at the edges of my lips. "They're all so beautiful and so strong. So many of them fight shirtless, and when they're finished, they're covered in sweat. It's quite the sight."

"What exactly is your point, Huntyr?" He growls. The window next to us rattles with a sudden gust of wind. I fight my laughter. He really does make it too easy to rile him up.

"Well, after such *stimulating* days, I'm often very tense when I return to my room in the evenings. So, to relax, I usually strip the leathers off of my body, crawl into my tub, and let the hot water rush all over my skin."

I don't even think he's breathing. His knuckles on that glass are white. "And then what do you do?"

Slowly, I lean forward and run my forefinger across the line of his jaw. He leans into my touch, eyes trailing to my mouth, his gaze dark and filled with desire.

"Use your imagination," I say, before flicking his nose and leaning back in my seat.

He stares at me for a long moment, at first with lust, then with frustration, then with something that looks a lot like wry amusement as he shakes his head. "What a tease you are."

I fight back laughter and shrug, satisfied with having won this little round of our game.

"So," I draw out the word as I glance around the room, needing to change the topic. "Is this how you impress most women?"

I earn a mischievous grin from him.

"No," he says. "You're special."

"Lucky me," I reply sarcastically, watching three Fae males at the bar race to finish their drinks. One yells victoriously as he finishes, slamming his glass on the counter while a second sputters and begins coughing violently.

"Tell me what Velia is like," he commands suddenly, pulling my attention back to him.

The question is innocent enough, but there's something hidden under the words that makes me bristle. Perhaps it's the seriousness of his eyes, or the way he leans forward ever so slightly, like he's too eager for my answer.

"You visited," I reply, keeping myself guarded.

"I didn't grow up there," he grins. "What was your childhood like?"

Violent. Bloody. Tragic. Traumatic.

"Like any other Mortal girl. What was childhood like in the Fae kingdom?"

Derian leans back in the booth, crossing his hands behind his head, before giving me a nonchalant shrug. "Fae live longer than Mortals. I'm nearly two hundred and sixteen years old. I hardly remember my childhood."

I feel out his words, letting them fall over me as I assess him and tilt my head with narrowed eyes. "You're lying."

He grins. "So are you."

So, we're going to be playing another game, then.

I roll out my shoulders, matching his relaxed posture, painfully aware that this game is remarkably less fun and more dangerous than our simple flirtation.

"Did you have many friends when you were at school?" he asks.

I thought of Kristona, Flannigan, and the other members of the League of Assassins.

"A few," I answer, mixing truth into the ruse. "They were all a bit older than me, but as close as family."

"But you didn't have family," he reminds me, his expression unreadable. "Right?"

This outing is starting to feel more like an interrogation than an opportunity for *bonding*.

I don't like it, and I certainly don't want this conversation to turn towards my family.

The family I lost at the hands of his kind.

"Why all the questions?"

"We're bonding," he says nonchalantly with a shrug.

"Are we?"

A pause of quiet settles between us, both of us on edge and trying to suss out the other. Derian takes a sip of his drink, his eyes never leaving mine.

"How are those headaches of yours? You haven't asked for any pain tonics."

A wave of surprise hits me, both that he remembers my headaches and that I'd managed to forget them. I've been getting them a few times a week for years, but haven't had a single one since we arrived in the Fae kingdom.

"They haven't been bothering me," I answer him truthfully. "I'm sure they'll come back once life settles down a little."

If I live through the Conclave, that is.

Derian watches me again, that strange expression on his face, as if he's thinking through a million different things at once. As if he's trying to figure out a mystery he can't quite solve.

"Have you eaten tonight?" he asks with furrowed brows. Once again, I'm stunned by the sudden change in topic.

I frown. "Why?"

"You haven't, have you?" He stands, out of the booth before I've even had a chance to answer. "Stay here."

And then he's gone, making his way through the crowd effortlessly to approach the barkeep. I watch him for a moment, noticing absently that he's nearly a foot taller than everyone else in the room.

It's not just his height that sets him apart, though. It's the magic that seems to drip off of him, so much stronger than anyone else's. It's the sheer confidence with which he moves through the space. It's the way the torchlight catches on the skin of his jawline.

I shouldn't be so desperate to watch him, and yet, I can't turn away.

I'm not the only one either. Several of the Fae females eye him. I can't tell if it's because they know they're in the same room with their prince or because he's impossible to *not* look at.

Probably both.

The thought leaves me with a sticky, uncomfortable feeling that I wash down with another chug of the ale.

"This table free?"

I glance at the Fae male who points at the table next to our booth. His copper hair is dry and scraggly, overgrown near his ears, and his shirt is too tight around his waistline. He looks to be middle-aged by Mortal standards, but I'm not sure what that equates to in Fae years. His companion, another male, looks to be about the same.

"Go ahead," I motion toward the table.

The two sit, placing their drinks on the table and settling in. I'm content to turn back to Derian when the sound of their conversation suddenly catches my full attention.

"They found another body on the outskirts of town."

The copper-haired man stiffens. "Like the others?"

"Exactly like the others," his companion says. His voice lowers as he leans towards him. "It's the first time I've seen one of the victims myself. After five hundred years and a war, I thought I'd seen it all, but this was something out of a nightmare."

I frown. Why are bodies being found here?

Is someone else here hunting the Fae?

Or is this what all those warriors at the fortress are training for?

Bowing my head, I try to look inconspicuous as I shift further to the left. Close enough to hear them clearly.

"Black veins and sunken eyes," the man continues in a hushed tone. "Really, all that was left of his eyes were darkened pits. And his jaw was hanging wide open, broken I think. And Gods the *smell*."

Something cold washes over me.

I can't hear them anymore. I can't hear anything but the rushing of my own blood in my ears. And I certainly can't stop the flashback of a memory that locks me in place, even as I clench my hands onto the table in front of me.

Bloodied sheets.

Blackened veins.

My throat raw from screaming.

"Fucking Velkai," the copper-haired male says with a snarl.

My knuckles are turning white. My heart is pounding. I'm desperately trying to suck in air, and yet nothing is coming. Nausea pours through me, nearly sending me doubling over, and for a moment I think there's a very real possibility that I might be sick.

It's been ages since I've been this affected by the memory of my father's death, but what they're saying...

Fae magic was what left bodies like that, drained of life and energy.

I know that because Fae magic like that is what *killed my father*.

The sound of a plate dropping heavily onto the table before me snaps me out of the memory, and my hand flies to my blade instantly, before fingers land down atop mine, squeezing gently.

"It's only me," Derian says.

"Is that supposed to make me feel better?" I snarl.

It sounds breathless though.

I've never seen another body like my father's.

Did all Fae kill like that or was this magic specific?

Was my father's exact murderer just walking around? Were they in this very tavern right now?

"I don't think I've ever seen you caught off guard," Derian tells me, sliding into the booth across from me with an evident air of concern. "What's wrong?"

My stomach is in knots as I stare at the plate of broiled vegetables and overcooked chicken. A single plate. Just food for me, not him.

"I've already eaten," he tells me, as if sensing my thoughts. "You're pale. Tell me what's wrong, Huntyr."

Not a question. A command.

His voice is apprehensive, and when I look up at him, there's suddenly no teasing in his gaze. His shoulders are tense, his fingers sprawled on the table, tapping against the wood.

"What are Velkai?" I blurt out, ignoring every bit of careful training that Kristona drilled into my mind.

Don't let your enemy know what you're thinking.

Wait until you have all the information before you reveal your intentions.

Never let your opponent know if something is important to you.

Derian sighs heavily, glancing quickly over his shoulder to the two men still engaged in their discussion.

"I knew you were an eavesdropper," he quips, an odd mixture of both relief and trepidation on his face as he points to the plate in front of me, a silent order to eat.

"Food first." He pushes the plate to me before reaching down to unwrap my fork and knife from the napkin and passing them to me as well.

A second command.

He's used to people doing exactly what he tells them to, used to everyone around him following his orders. I stare at the cutlery that he presses into my hands. I don't want to eat.

I want answers.

"Velkai?" I insist.

His expression is stern, unwavering, and he glances pointedly at the plate once more. The bastard isn't going to say a damn thing until I have food in my stomach. I bite into a piece of broccoli, not bothering to hide my irritation.

"What do you know about the Wastelands?" he asks me, carefully watching my expression.

"They were created during the war between the Fae and the Mortals."

He rolls his eyes. "They were created during a war, yes, but the Fae weren't fighting the Mortals. You were fighting us."

I curl my lip back over my teeth. "Semantics."

"It's not, actually." The seriousness in his voice gives me pause. "Your people blamed us for creating the Wastelands when we had nothing to do with it. The Velkai created them."

He keeps his voice low, and I watch as his eyes dart from me to the room and back, as if he's overly mindful of who may or may not be listening to our conversation.

"What are Velkai?" I repeat, the word feeling unnatural on my tongue.

"They're an ancient breed of creature, older than both Fae and Mortal alike, and most certainly not from this realm. No one is quite sure where they came from, actually. For centuries, they were largely a solitary species, until they suddenly organized under the rule of a queen. Shortly afterwards, the Wastelands were created, and the Fae began fighting back against them."

I listen to him quietly.

"I've never heard of these creatures."

How could there be an entirely separate species from the Fae and Mortals that we Mortals knew nothing about? No secret could be that well-kept.

He nods, unsurprised. "And yet, in order for stretches of Wasteland to exist in the Mortal Kingdom, your Kings had to be well aware the creatures were there."

His implication, that the Mortal Kings kept this a secret on purpose, is clear. But if it were true, they would have had to have fabricated the entire propaganda against the Fae people. Lied to us all and made us view the Fae as enemies even though they aren't.

And, according to Derian, we fell for it.

"And why would they have wanted us to fight the Fae?"

Derian watches me, brow lifted in a challenge. "You're smart enough to know the answer to that, Huntyr. To the victor go the spoils."

The land.

The Mortal Kings wanted to take advantage of the fact that the Fae were already fighting another war in order to take their land.

That's a big accusation to make.

"And where is this Velkai queen now?" I ask, unable to relinquish my doubt.

"The Vaereth killed her." He shrugs, as if this were common knowledge.

"Why should I believe you?"

"Because I have no reason to lie. Now, eat."

Derian leans back, throwing an arm over the back of his chair and scanning over the crowd of people. He takes a slow sip of his ale before turning back to me, looking first at the plate and then at me.

"Why are you always so concerned with whether or not I've eaten?" I grumble, spearing a carrot and pulling it into my mouth, still tossing over the idea of Velkai in my head.

Someone is lying.

Either the Mortal Kings lied to their people in an attempt to steal Fae lands, or the Fae were lying about monsters in the Wastelands to try and avoid blame for their own mistakes.

I know which one I believe to be more likely.

Mortals didn't kill my father.

Derian watches unabashedly as my lips wrap around the fork and pull. Noticing his attention, I run my tongue over my lower lip and bite down gently.

The chastising look he gives me sends a wave of warmth through my body.

"Food is a privilege not everyone has access to. I won't allow you to go hungry."

I snort, washing down the food with another sip of ale. "What would you know about being hungry, prince?"

"More than you do, lady." His eyes glaze over slightly, as if he's not quite present at this table. Absently, I notice the sound of thunder rolling in the distance, and I wonder if it's him causing it. "I didn't grow up in the castle."

I lift a brow. "So you *do* remember your childhood."

He smiles, the expression oddly genuine. It doesn't quite reach his eyes, but I can't help the rush of energy that flows through me when I earn that quick quirk of his lip.

"As well as you remember yours. If you want to hear about it, you'll finish what's on that plate."

I bite the retort that bubbles up my throat and continue eating.

"I'm the most powerful Fae in centuries."

Unable to stop myself, I snort, the sound far too loud to be considered ladylike. "Humble, too."

He lifts a single shoulder in a shrug. "It's simply a fact. Storm-wielding is a rare power, and my magic is stronger than most. When I was six, I got into a fight with Luceron, and a tornado tore through a wing of the castle."

I narrow my eyes at him. Since I've arrived here, Derian has made no secret about how far the lengths of his power go. Even in the Mortal lands, he's more legend than man. The cruel and powerful Fae prince is a story told to misbehaving children.

I suppose, though, that I hadn't ever stopped to think about the fact that he was once just a child with far too much capability for destruction.

Derian pauses, refusing to say more until I resume eating. I do so with an irritated huff and a wave of my hand.

"My parents sent me to Amberhull. At the time, it was a mostly abandoned forest region. For a hundred years I lived with a distant uncle, another storm-wielder. He taught me to control my magic through any means necessary."

"Meaning?"

"Starvation," he confirmed, heaviness in his voice as his gaze drops to his folded hands atop the table. "Beatings. Humiliation. You name it."

The thunder rolls again outside, and this time I *know* he's controlling it. I'm just not sure if he's even aware that it's happening.

I try to picture him as a child. Try to picture that sharp jawline with the roundness of youth. That head of silken dark hair, shorter and curlier.

"It's not something you forget," he continues, still staring at his nail beds. "It doesn't matter how many years pass or how many hot meals you have, that feeling of hollowness, of your entire body caving, it doesn't go away. You can't understand it unless you've experienced it. In the worst of it, you don't even feel hungry anymore. You just can't think clearly, and all you want is to sleep, but you know if you do that you won't wake up again."

What he doesn't know though, is that I *have* experienced that. If I hadn't picked the pocket of Kristona Roschoff, I would have gone to sleep, and we wouldn't be having this conversation.

No. That feeling isn't something you ever forget.

"I'm sorry." Before I know it, I'm reaching out, resting my hand atop his.

His attention jerks to mine, a frown of confusion painting over his features even as his fingers wrap around mine.

I jerk my hand back.

"Plenty of people have worse upbringings." He stares into my eyes, and for a split second it's as if he sees right through me, as if he knows my childhood was just as unspeakable.

And it was.

My childhood was filled with more horrors and pain than I can ever begin to articulate. It was filled with moments that stained my soul so black that I'll never be able to wash it clean. And *his people* were the reason why.

Not some mythical creatures that no one has ever heard of.

It doesn't matter if the prince had a tortured childhood not unlike my own. It doesn't matter if his presence is intoxicating. It doesn't matter if the touch of his hand in mine sends shivers down my spine.

Derian's story about the Velkai only served as a reminder of what the Fae are. Liars and murderers.

The Velkai are just another lie.

He is the enemy.

He is my enemy.

Derian

She's distant.

She responds to my questions easily enough, still just as evasive as ever, but her eyes are withdrawn, her mind elsewhere.

If I wasn't so curious about what preoccupied her, I might be a little offended.

Still, I make her stay seated at the table until every bit of food is cleaned from her plate. Then, I order her an iced cinnamon bun and watch as she eats that too, stealing bites every now and then for myself, much to her chagrin.

I thought my interest in her was purely sexual, but I have to admit that just sitting with her, eating and drinking, swapping teasing barbs at one another, is oddly... nice.

It really is a shame she won't survive the Conclave.

I keep reminding myself of that.

I know she's hiding things from me, and at this point I'm pretty sure I know *what* she's hiding. Still, even if she somehow managed to kill my guard in Velia, there's no way a Mortal girl is surviving a Conclave. It's simply not possible.

When she finishes eating, I grab her hand and pull her to her feet.

"Let's go," I instruct, keeping her fingers locked in mine even when she tries to pull away. If I only get one night with her to pretend that her death isn't inevitable, I want to soak in every second of her skin touching mine.

I lead her through the tavern, through the throngs of patrons, out the back door to our horses, and guide us back to the fortress wordlessly, feeling the impending end of the evening like a pressing weight.

The grounds of the fortress are quiet when we arrive. Night patrols have started, but the majority of the warriors are already in bed for the evening, leaving the space empty and illuminated only by the faint torchlight of the sconces along the wall.

"Well, I'll show myself back to my room," she says, tossing a leg over the back of her horse and dismounting easily. I don't offer to help her. I want to. I want to grasp hold of her and pull her body towards mine, but it doesn't seem wise after she nearly bit my head off when I reached for her waist earlier.

She pats the horse gently when she's steady on her feet again, smiling at the steed. She rode the beast straddled the whole way, rather than the sidesaddle way the court ladies typically prefer.

And she rode it comfortably.

She'd done it like she'd ridden a horse straddled a thousand times before.

Huntyr glances at me over her shoulder before taking a step back towards the path that leads to her room, and I don't even think before I'm reaching for her.

"I'm not done with you," I tell her, taking her hand once more.

She looks down at our intertwined fingers with suspicion in her eyes, but she doesn't remove her hand from mine. "I can follow directions, you know? If you tell me to walk, I will, you don't need to drag me."

I fight the urge to smile as I pull her along behind me. "Maybe I just like touching you."

"Liar," she grumbles.

That actually hadn't been a lie.

I lead her to the throwing targets, unsure of *why* I've brought her here. The logical part of me says I did it just to assess her skills, to see if she's hiding some talent behind a pretense. That other part of me, the part that I'm choosing not to acknowledge, just doesn't want to send her back to her room quite yet.

I need a little longer in her presence. A little longer with her scent filling my nostrils. A little more of this verbal sparring that keeps me constantly on my toes.

I'm certainly not ready to go back to my bed with the memory of her fresh in my mind and only my *imagination* to satisfy me.

It's been hours since that little comment, and I haven't been able to get the image of her touching herself in the tub out of my head. It's the exact reaction she'd wanted me to have, and damn if she hadn't been successful.

There's no sum in the kingdom I wouldn't pay to be able to watch her do that, her skin illuminated by candles, blue eyes locked onto mine as she falls into oblivion.

I shake my head, pulling myself forcefully back to reality.

She looks at the targets with a frown, that line forming between her brows. The wind blows slightly, blowing back the tendrils of dark hair that have escaped her braid and fallen near her ears. Even in the darkness of the night, her eyes are brilliantly bright, as if lit up by some unnatural force.

"Are we practicing?" She nods towards the targets.

"We're playing," I tell her, reaching down to pull out my blades—two from my waistband and one from my boot. Gently, I sit them on the wooden banister that separates us from the throwing range.

Then I eye her, and before I can stop myself, I wrap an arm around her waist and rip her to me, pulling her right thigh high against my hip.

With speed that's remarkably impressive for a Mortal, she wraps her delicate fingers around one of the daggers I've discarded and presses it to the skin of my throat, the pressure gentle but threatening, nonetheless.

She doesn't flinch, doesn't blink, doesn't show the nervousness others might when faced with the possibility of having to harm another. Her fingers are completely steady.

I grin.

Slowly, deliberately, I slide my fingers up her thigh.

Huntyr stiffens but doesn't move. She doesn't pull away, nor does she move her blade deeper into my skin.

Without breaking eye contact, I trace the leather that sits tight around her leg. I run my hand down that muscled thigh pulled against my hip, so tightly I can feel the warmth of her. And I savor that slight hitch in her breath.

Then I wrap my fingers around the hilt of the dagger strapped to her leg and pull it free, sitting it next to the others.

She glances towards it quickly, but then those icy eyes are back on mine. I hold her to me for just another moment, memorizing the feeling of her body in my grip, before I release her. She takes a stumbling step backwards, her cheeks flushed.

"Two throws each," I explain, nodding to the blades.

"I could have gotten it myself." There's an attitude in her voice, but a hint of breathlessness too, and that impressive speed seems to have vanished as she slowly takes another step away from me.

"My way was more fun," I tease, lifting a dagger and tossing it with nothing more than a quick glance at the target.

I hear it sink into the wood and don't bother looking away from her to confirm that it landed in the center. That much is obvious from the purse of her lips and the way she lifts one brow in irritation.

"Do you always feel the need to show off?"

Wiggling my brows, I gesture to the blades. "Your turn."

She rolls her eyes, picks up the blade, and tosses it carelessly. It doesn't even make it to the target before losing air and falling to the ground.

I click my tongue admonishingly. "How embarrassing for you."

She whips her head towards me, her braid flying over her shoulder as she does. "Don't be rude!"

Her cheeks have flushed with her irritation, a slight rush of pink on her tanned skin. It seems unhealthy for me to be even *more* attracted to her when she's angry with me, but here we are.

Reaching past her, I invade her space once more to pick up the next blade. This time, she doesn't step back. She's adjusted to this game, and she's unwilling to surrender a single inch. I look at the board before I throw again, the dagger hitting true once more. Exactly where I wanted it.

Glancing at her sideways, I pick up the last blade and press it into her palm. Before she realizes what I'm doing, I slide behind her, trailing my fingers up her arm as I do.

She tries to hide her shiver, but I feel it against me nonetheless, and that gives me no small amount of satisfaction.

"It's polite to let the Lady win," she says in a hushed, breathy tone.

That sound. That is the way I'll imagine her voice sounding once I'm alone in my room tonight.

"You don't strike me as the kind of creature who likes to have things handed to her easily."

She huffs, and I take a step closer so that my chest is flush against her backside. She fits against me perfectly as I grasp onto her hips and pull her against my body.

"I could teach you, though," I say softly, leaning down to speak into her ear. Her breathing seems to halt entirely, and I don't bother fighting against my self-satisfied grin. She leans back against me slightly, so subtly that I'm not even sure she realizes she's doing it. But I certainly do. I'm aware of every single move this woman makes. Slowly, agonizingly slowly, I drag my hands up her waist, making my way to the wrist of the hand that grasps the dagger with white knuckles. "It's quite simple—"

The blade is flying through the air, splitting the wood of the target with a heavy thud before I can even finish my sentence.

Dead. Fucking. Center.

"Guess I'm a quick learner." She shrugs, stepping away from me with a smirk that lights my blood on fire.

Magic roars in my veins, and I don't quite know if it's from anger and my suspicion about her or if it's just a reaction to *her*.

Because, Gods, if watching her throw that dagger with her ass pressed against me wasn't the hottest thing I'd seen in a decade.

"Good throw," I compliment her dryly. I wonder if she knows what she's doing to me. If she's playing with me the way I am with her. "But I still won."

"Too bad we weren't playing for anything."

My lips quirk into a grin, and I walk forward, forcing her back against the railing, and place my arms on either side of her. Boxing her in. "I always play for prizes."

The air is thick between us. Her tongue darts out over her lower lip, and suddenly I know in my bones that she feels it too. She's just as affected as I am.

She doesn't want to be, but she's just as caught up in this crackling energy that exists between us.

"Well then, what do you want, Derian?" Huntyr asks softly, her eyes dipping to my lips for just the briefest moment.

Without meaning to, I'm leaning down, angling my head towards her. Feeling her breath against my lips.

What do I want?

I'm not quite sure I know.

Her, of course.

But do I want her secrets, or do I simply want her laid bare beneath me, screaming my name?

Both?

"What would you be willing to give me, Huntyr?"

She's breathing deeply, but she doesn't shove me away, not even when I push past that final inch between us so that our hips are completely aligned. Her body is small next to mine, delicate even while she's strapped in leather and muscle.

I could kiss her right now. Close that gap between us and tangle my tongue with hers. Finally find out what she tastes like. Lose my hands in her hair and hold her exactly where I want her. And if how she's looking at me right now is any indication, I actually think she'd let me. I think she might push herself onto that railing, hook her legs around my waist, and kiss me so thoroughly I wouldn't be able to stop myself from taking things further.

She wouldn't be a gentle lover.

She's built of the toughest form of steel, covered in ice, and hardened into something positively unbreakable. Huntyr wouldn't want a lover to coddle her and gently kiss her.

She would want to fuck as hard as she fights.

It would be so easy to finally release this tension that is eating me alive.

We're walking the line, threatening to dance right over it.

I'm just about to do it. She's tilting her head backwards, the invitation silent but undeniable. And Gods, I *want* to.

But if we go there, I'm not sure we'd ever recover.

Not sure I'd ever recover.

"I'll save my prize for another time, Lady Lachlan." Stepping away from her is undeniably painful. "You should get to bed for now. Big day tomorrow."

She bristles when I use her title, but after a moment's hesitation she nods and walks back through the courtyard to the stone pathway that leads to her room without a single word of goodbye.

I watch every step she takes, staring unabashedly at the sway of her hips. I'm still looking at that pathway long after she's left, idly tossing one of the blades between my hands.

I shouldn't want her as badly as I do, not when the truth of her involvement in the assassination of my guard seems to be so obvious.

She's been careful. She's kept her cards close to her chest.

No one else would suspect a thing.

But *I* do.

I see the assessment in her eyes whenever she steps into a new space.

I see the careful calmness that takes over her when she's faced with danger.

I see the calluses on her hands and the ease with which she picks up weapons.

I see her clear hatred for my kind.

Huntyr Lachlan most likely murdered my guard.

And despite that suspicion, it takes every bit of resolve in me not to follow her, push her against a wall, and memorize every inch of her body.

I want *her*. Desperately. Impossibly.

Magic rushes in me again with a mind of its own, nearly pushing me after her. Wind rushes through the courtyard, and the air thickens with humidity. Lady Lachlan may have just found herself in the eye of my storm.

Gods help us both.

HUNTYR

Once again, we're standing in the arena. The air today is misty with a heavy fog and overwhelming humidity, leaving my skin damp and uncomfortable. I'm wearing my typical training clothes, leather pants tucked into heavy-soled boots and a tight cotton tunic covered by a firm corseted leather vest. Blades are strapped to nearly every inch of me, two on my waistband, two on my thighs, and a sword across my back.

Thus far, the setup for the second trial is much the same as the first. Derian and Caldren are watching, along with all the warriors from the fortress. Although, there might be more common folk present for this trial than before. Taric, Rhen, and Parker are ahead of us. Roland stands at their side, looking nervously between the sky and Derian.

Wait, is he responsible for the shitty weather?

I glance at the stands and catch his eye. His face is a mask of unhappiness, his brow furrowed and lips pinched as he stands, leaning over the banister.

A gust of wind suddenly blows against me, brushing my braid back over my shoulder before fading. Though it lingers against the back of my neck just a bit too long to be natural. As he meets my eyes, he bows his head in acknowledgement.

"Let's begin," Roland announces, handing a heavy satchel to Parker. "Today you will face the shadow maze. The task is rather simple. All you have to do is make it out alive."

Alexandria shifts awkwardly next to me. "I doubt it will be that easy."

That's pretty much a guarantee.

Parker begins pulling crystal balls from the satchel, handing one to each of us. As he places it into my waiting palm, a glowing light emerges from the center.

"These orbs will be your only source of light within the maze," Roland explains. "They are controlled by your thoughts. If you want it brighter, simply think about it. If you want it dimmer, try the same."

Doing as instructed, I think the simple phrase *no light* and the glow from the orb extinguishes in my hand.

"That's so creepy," Alexandria mutters.

I nod my agreement.

"Why would we want to dim them?" Mara, the metal-wielder, asks.

Taric's grin can only be described as mischievous. "Because the brighter the light you use, the faster the magic in the orb runs out."

He leaves the rest unsaid, but the message is pretty clear. Good luck finding your way out of the maze without any light.

Great. Dark maze, filled with enemies, and a light that has a timer on it. I roll out my neck, loosening my muscles.

"Are you ready to begin?" Roland asks us.

Alexandria sighs heavily. "Do we have a choice?"

No, no we do not.

"Any advice?" I ask Kaia. She sits at the edges of the arena, behind Roland. She isn't allowed to help me through the trial, but there was no way she was allowing anyone to force her to stay back at the fortress.

She tilts her head towards me. *"Do not fall. Do not injure yourself. Kill anyone who attempts to harm you."*

Sage words.

I can't help myself. I look up one last time towards Derian before the ground shifts under my feet, before I feel like I'm falling weightlessly as walls of earth climb around me. Magic slides around me just as it had for the first trial, and I brace myself against it. Clenching my fists at my side, I breathe in deeply, and surrender to the darkness that begins clouding the corners of my vision.

— ⬥ —

I'm alone. I sense that fact far before I send a dim light into the orb in my hand and glance around. Whatever magic brought us into this maze also managed to scatter us throughout it.

Around me, the shrubs rise nearly twelve feet high, surrounding the space to the left, right, and behind me, making the only path possible that which comes before me.

And I have a good suspicion why.

They want to lead us in a direction where we might stumble upon each other.

After all, if the only way through the maze is to use our lights to make our way out of the darkness, then turning the light all the way up would help us move through as fast as possible.

But if I were to turn my light all the way up, it would eventually run out.

And what was a girl to do if her light ran out?

Take another from someone else.

We aren't just fighting the maze, we're fighting each other.

Before I can even come to terms with that, I feel something wrap around my ankle, pointed and biting. My sword is in my hand in an instant, slicing through the vine that had launched itself out of the shrub wall—just as another comes soaring through the air towards my throat.

Shit.

I duck, feeling the sudden urge to send light to my orb so I can see where the attacks are coming from, but I stop myself from doing so. Instead, I run, focusing instead on the sounds and changes in the air to alert me to danger.

I neither want to lose my light or alert anyone to my location.

I sprint, feet falling lightly on the ground as I weave, duck, and leap over the vines that continue snapping out at me, each one faster than the last. I can practically sense their hunger for me. When the path finally splinters, I hesitate for only a second before rushing into the shadowy darkness to my left.

The air stills.

The vines stop attacking.

I nearly choke on my sigh of relief, searching left and right for the next danger... when I hear a voice.

"Come on now, Mortal, just give me your orb and I'll make it quick."

The light in my hand goes out completely as I sink backwards into the shadows, becoming a part of the darkness as easily as I always have.

It takes a quick moment for my eyes to adjust, to seek out the spark of light down the path, about two hundred yards away. My steps are light and silent as I creep carefully towards it, to whoever holds it.

Mara is standing still, her back towards me, with three blades suspended in the air around her. Jeseina, another Mortal, cowers close by, trying helplessly to climb the shrub wall that blocks her from escape. I can't see for sure, but based on the small hisses of pain I hear, I imagine those shrubs are cutting into her hands.

"Please," Jeseina whines.

"Please what?" Mara laughs darkly. "You knew it would come to this."

She's going to kill her. Jeseina has no hope of fighting back, and Mara is going to send those blades slicing through her. I only have a few moments to move. I palm the dagger on my hip, pulling it slowly, breathing energy into my muscles before I—

"*Stop!*" Kaia hisses in my mind.

I startle slightly at the sound of her, pausing my movements. *"She doesn't deserve this."*

There's a pause. A pause that feels like an eternity.

"None of you do, but she will die. Do not risk your own life by attempting to stop the inevitable."

Her declaration pounds down on me, cutting off my airway until I swallow down the sudden lump in my throat. Kaia's right. Even if I do rush out to help Jeseina, to save her, Mara will just turn those weapons on me. As a metal wielder, she'll turn my own weapons against me.

And if I manage to kill Mara? It won't actually save the girl.

This Conclave is a fight to the death, and there is only one winner. Nothing I can do will save Jeseina now.

I feel Mara's haunting laughter in my bones as she steps forward.

No. I may not be able to save her life, but I can at least save her from this torment.

My fingers tighten around my dagger again. I move—

The blades hiss as they fly through the air, punching into Jeseina's back in a split second before I can take even a single step towards them. She falls, sputtering, to the ground, and I feel the crash of her knees against the ground deep in my stomach.

Mara stalks forward, tutting her tongue at the girl who lies bleeding out on the ground at her feet. She doesn't even bother to ease her suffering before she picks up Jeseina's orb and prowls off into the darkness.

I'm frozen to my spot, not daring to move until I'm sure Mara's gone, until I can no longer hear her boots smacking boldly against the ground.

I wait until the only sounds that remain are my own pounding heartbeat and Jeseina's labored breaths.

Then I rush to Jeseina.

"Huntyr?" She pants. Her head turns toward me just as I send a dim spark into my orb, just enough to illuminate our faces. Just enough that the poor girl doesn't have to die in the dark. "She took my light."

"I know," I smooth down her auburn hair, keeping my voice light and calming. "That's okay, you don't need it."

She's fallen forward onto her stomach, and now her wounds leak blood onto the ground, coating my fingertips in a familiar red sheen. Based on how labored her breathing is becoming, this won't take much longer.

"It hurts," she whispers. "Can you help me?"

Of course it does.

Disgust rolls through me as I glance at the positioning of the blades still pressing into her back. Mara isn't stupid, she has to have known what she was doing by striking these areas. These were fatal blows to be sure, but none that would cause immediate death.

Mara wanted the poor girl to suffer.

A cold stillness washes over me, the kind of icy focus that narrows in right before a fight, before a kill. Because now I don't just need to win this Conclave in order to save Tyla and earn revenge for my father.

No, now there's another tally on the list of reasons why the Fae need to pay for their injustices.

This Mortal noblewoman, who now bleeds out under my touch, had just wanted to find a handsome suitor.

She is only here because she happened to be wearing a dress that looked like mine on the one night I'd accidentally let myself be seen.

This was on me.

And if I can't save her, then I can at least avenge her.

"I can help you," I promise her. "Close your eyes."

She obeys.

"Thank you for—"

I jam my dagger into the thick vein of her neck, without hesitation, relieving her from what would have been a drawn-out, agonizing death, even as I feel the mark of her murder ingrain itself as another splotch of darkness inside of me.

"I will help you get your revenge," I whisper to her as she releases the heavy exhale of death. "I vow that to you."

When I rise, blood dripping from my hands, it's not Lady Lachlan who lifts the orb and sends brightness rushing into it without fear.

No, it's the Huntress who now marches on.

DERIAN

"She's doing well," Cal says from beside me, his voice rougher than normal, a clear indication of his frustration.

Unlike the previous trial, which took place solely within their minds, we can actually look down into the maze this time. I'm not sure if that's better or worse, though.

I've barely moved since it started, barely even breathed. And I haven't bothered being discreet about where my attention lies.

"Who's left?" I ask, entirely unable to look away for long enough to assess the standing of the others myself.

"Seraphina, Alexandria, Elise, and Mara."

And Huntyr, but he doesn't need to tell me that.

She's been smart so far. She handled the vines effortlessly, has stuck to the shadows so expertly that she's avoided the attention of any of the Fae, and has only been using her orb in small bursts to light the path ahead of her. Even just now, when the maze started closing in around her, she hardly flinched, just ran forward and rolled at the last minute when it looked as if she might be locked into those walls forever.

Something's changed about her, though.

Ever since she put the Mortal girl out of her misery, it's as if a shadow has fallen over her features. Her eyes have hardened into something firmer. Colder. Like twin forms of unbreakable ice.

"She is indeed impressive."

"Too impressive," he reminds me pointedly, leaning forward over the rail and matching my stance. I can feel his tension like waves falling over me.

She's just about to reach the center of the maze.

I look ahead to the fountain that lies in the direct center of the web and nearly choke.

Seraphina is circling the blonde Mortal.

I recognize the viciousness of her smile.

The blonde, Alexandria I think, stares at Seraphina, her posture firm and alert. She must be terrified. Even I would be off balance if Seraphina looked at me that way. But the Mortal just grasps the blade in her hand with deadly force, her knuckles white.

Seraphina's eyes flicker towards the blade before she sends an orb of fire soaring forward with nothing more than a flick of her wrist. The fire singes Alexandria's fingers, and she drops the weapon with a hiss. Fear flashes across her features.

"She's going to play with her," Cal says disapprovingly, with an irritated shake of his head. "She's always been wicked that way."

Yes, she has.

The battle isn't quick. If you can even go so far as to call it a battle. Seraphina lets it drag out like a cat toying with a mouse. We all know she could kill the Mortal with a simple wave of her palm, but she takes her time, beating the girl bloody, until she's nearly unrecognizable.

Seraphina looks up to the audience, a glint in her eyes. She's enjoying every second of this. She's putting on a show and reveling in being everyone's favorite entertainer.

The crowd roars for her as she shoves the girl face first into the fountain and her magic sparks. The water boils rapidly, and the Mortal's body thrashes, splashing water all around them. Even underwater, I can hear her screams.

Eventually, she stops kicking.

It's gruesome. Disgusting.

My fingers curl around the edges of the banister, gripping tightly to steady myself.

"*That* is why your brother didn't want you to marry her," Cal says, irritation thick in his voice. "You're going to make her the next princess of this land. Gods, she'll be in the line of succession."

The thought turns my stomach sour, but I can't respond, can't move, can't *think,* because Huntyr is getting too fucking close to that fountain and Seraphina is still there.

And Gods help me, I don't think I can stand by and watch her do that to Huntyr.

Storm clouds thicken above us, humidity rising in the air so suddenly that it's nearly suffocating.

Cal tracks my gaze, putting a warning hand on my shoulder.

"You can't intervene," he reminds me under his breath, careful of who might overhear.

"I know that," I hiss, even as magic pounds through me, angry and wild.

Demanding.

Primal.

Huntyr's beast sits outside the maze, staring at the high shrubs as if she can see right through the magic. Slowly, she turns her feline eyes to me, as if she's challenging me to do just that.

To intervene.

To blow a gust of wind towards Huntyr, or to send a crack of lightning ahead of her in a magical warning.

I shouldn't. It goes against every ancient rule of the Conclave.

But I don't know if I can stop myself.

The rising tide of magic in my veins is almost painful.

I've never felt my power respond to another person this strongly.

My stomach clenches.

My fingers twitch.

And then—

Seraphina grabs Alexandria's orb of light and leaves before Huntyr finds herself in the clearing.

Before I'm faced with the choice of what I'm *supposed* to do and what I feel like I *must* do.

I relax as much as I can while she's still trapped in that death maze.

# Huntyr

I feel like I've been walking for an eternity, winding through this maze of never-ending twists and turns. My feet are aching, my ankle tender from where I twisted it rolling out of the closing walls of the maze. I hardly feel it though, thanks to the anger that's still coursing through my veins.

The pure, unadulterated rage.

Every step since I left Jeseina feels heavier, more burdensome.

And now, I find myself looking at another body.

When the maze opened into a clearing with a large white stone fountain, I practically *felt* the presence of death. I had sent a pulse of light through the air to get a sense of my surroundings as I stepped towards the center of the maze.

And then I halted.

Because hanging from the side of the fountain, unmoving, is a body topped with characteristically long blonde hair.

I approach her slowly now, careful of any Fae that might be lingering in the shadows.

Steam still rises from the pool of water. The heat of it pushes against my skin, and even though I brace myself, my stomach still sours when I lift her head and see what remains of Alexandria's face. It's nothing more than raised red blisters and melted flesh.

Seraphina burned her alive.

Like a tide rushing in at a breakneck pace, white-hot fury pours through me, lighting my body aflame. The orb in my hand sputters before suddenly lighting up with an intensity that seems unnatural. It's a beacon, shooting towards the sky and alerting everyone to my presence.

For a brief moment, I stare at it in my hand until the brightness causes an ache in my eyes. When I finally look away, I find myself eye to eye with the crowd, watching in the stands above me. I meet the furrowed brows and confused expressions of every single Fae watching me.

They think I'm stupid for sending that much light into the orb. They're already turning away, writing me off as the dumb Mortal that's going to draw the attention of someone who will happily come kill me.

I don't care what they think of me, though.

Let them come.

Let the Fae come and meet the Huntress of Velia.

⊰◈⊱

Ultimately, it isn't Seraphina or Mara who eventually emerges from one of the dark pathways. It's Elise. The memory-wielder.

Her dark hair is tied back tightly, leaving her pointed ears clearly on display. She's bleeding from shallow cuts around her arms, likely from thorns or some other manner of chaos that the maze holds hidden in its depths.

When she approaches, I don't even bother rising from where I sit, leaning against the fountain. She subtly glances at the dagger I twirl effortlessly between my fingertips.

"You're not who I was hoping for," I tell her, barely recognizing my own hardened voice.

She looks at me as if I'm out of my mind, and maybe I am. Maybe I always have been. Maybe madness is the price for all the souls I've taken.

Elise is broader than Seraphina and Mara both, muscle packed on her biceps and thighs, but she's not much taller than me, and she's not carrying nearly as many weapons. Just a bow and arrow and a dagger on her hip.

She must be pretty deadly with that bow and arrow if that's all she brought in here.

"If you know what's good for you, Mortal, you'll leave that orb where it is and run."

A laugh escapes me, the sound dark and menacing. "Why would I do that?"

She looks me up and down. "Because you're not the kind of person who can kill. You're better off taking your chances at running. The maze will certainly be kinder to you than some of my people will be."

That darkness in my soul grows, expanding with a sense of inevitability. It's been kept on a leash for too long, and it's ready for release. Ready to finally claim another victim. "You have no idea how capable I am of violence."

Elise stares at me, pulling an arrow from the sheath on her back and hooking it to her bow, aiming it at my heart. "Last warning. Run or I *will* end you."

A beat of silence, tension hanging thickly in the air.

The charge of an impending fight dances across my skin.

I finally feel like I'm home.

"You're going to try," I whisper.

She releases the arrow, and I'm already moving, rolling through the air and throwing the dagger in my hand. It buries itself in her thigh, and she sucks in a sharp gasp of air. The orb in her hand falls, shattering, but mine is still as bright as the sun, illuminating the air around us as I sprint towards her.

Elise is attempting to hook another arrow, but I'm already upon her, shoving my fist into her nose and savoring the crack under my knuckles as I wrap my fingers around her bow and pull.

The fact that she's caught off guard is the only reason I'm able to wrestle the bow away from her and snap it over my knee, but after the momentary hesitation, she jumps to alertness, punching into my stomach with enough Fae strength to make my lungs spasm.

Grunting, I stumble back, needing a second to regain my breathing, and she takes the pause to wipe away the tears from her eyes after my punch. Her thigh is injured from my blade. She tries not to let it show, but I can see her favoring it. I can tell she's putting slightly more weight on the other side.

It gives me a sick satisfaction knowing I've caused that pain.

"Fighting me is pointless, you worthless Mortal." She spits blood onto the ground at her feet as she unsheathes a blade on her hip.

Huh, hadn't seen that there.

Elise runs forward, all speed and anger and absolutely no skill, the sight of her own blood making her unruly. Perhaps she didn't expect a *worthless Mortal* to accomplish that.

I block her blow with my forearm, the force making me grind my teeth as I spin and drive my second blade deep into her back.

Elise roars.

Before I know it, she's backed up a few steps and is kicking me with that unnatural strength.

My hair falls out of my braid as I go flying through the air before crashing violently into the fountain. The stone cracks against my back and crumbles, landing around me in the pool of still-warm water.

Fuck. That *hurt.*

My ribs might be broken.

It won't be the first time if they are, though. Kristona broke my ribs himself at thirteen summers with a few well-aimed punches. He told me it was to prepare me for a moment like this. A moment when fighting through pain would be what it took to stay alive.

I snarl, pushing off the crumbling remains of the fountain to stand.

Only, the world is tilting and—

My ear is pressed against the wooden door, hands still trembling as I listen to every word of the conversation.

"There's also the matter of the girl—his daughter," Chesain says.

I hear my stepmother scoff, hear her heeled shoes pacing across the tiled floor of our home. "Put her out. She's been nothing but a nuisance to me. I cannot bear to deal with her now."

"She's but a girl, ma'am. She's only seen six summers."

The air is frigid, but I'm not cold. I can't feel anything. I can barely feel my own legs.

"If it eases your conscience, sell her to Madame Cruella, then. She will buy girls that young to train them, and at least she'll make sure the girl is fed."

The room is too small, too tight, my lungs constricting as I stumble backward.

I turn. Run.

Ringing in my ears is the only thing I'm aware of as the magic suddenly pulls away from me, leaving me stumbling backwards into the fountain once more as I blink back into awareness.

Elise's laughter replaces the ringing. "Were you a whore in your Mortal lands?"

She's clutching her side where my blade still hangs out of her, her eyes glazed over as she struggles to continue stepping towards me. I bare my teeth in disgust at the smell of her magic still filling the air.

Fucking memory-wielder.

I gasp, or try to—air is hard to pull in. It's like breathing through cracked glass.

This time, I feel her magic in the seconds before the memory hits, but I'm helpless to fight back against the pull to the past.

"You want me to kill Christopher?" I whisper the words, hardly believing what I've been asked to do.

Kristona looks at me without mercy. His eyes are hardened and filled with anger. They have been since he barged into my room and found Christopher in my bed last week.

"It seems your lover owes quite a few people a lot of money. So, yes. I want you to take care of it."

My chest feels hollow. I've always done everything Kristona has asked of me. I've always trusted him, listened to him, believed he would keep me safe even if no one else would.

But he's never asked me to do something like this.

He's never asked me to assassinate someone I know personally.

Someone I care for.

"I can't do that," I sputter.

He grabs my arm, pulling me from my seat so roughly my muscles protest against him. "You can, and you will. This is what I taught you to be, Huntyr

Lachlan. If you wanted to be a whore, I could have sent you to Madame Cruella's brothel. But you wanted to be a killer, and I made you one."

My stomach heaves, pouring out its contents onto the ground.

"Stay the fuck out of my head!" I fling the words aimlessly, still struggling to come back to reality. My breathing is shallow, straining against the pain in my ribs.

"Dear Gods. Do they know what you are?" Elise is panting.

I know the Fae can see us. I know they're watching, and Elise is one sentence away from exposing me.

"You have no idea what I am."

I pull myself to my feet, hissing against the pain that flows from my side into every inch of my body. Blood is running down my forehead and chest from the cuts earned when the fountain stone crashed down upon me. Nausea threatens to overtake me once more, but I don't give in.

I don't stop.

I can't.

"How do you think Prince Derian will react when I tell him—"

I tackle her, throwing my weight forward, until we're both falling to the ground. We're on our knees in a second and I'm palming a dagger, launching it towards her face. She grabs my wrist, and I roll to the side. I toss the dagger in the air. Catch it. Shove it forward.

And pierce through her chest into her heart.

"You want to know what I am?" I whisper, wrapping my hand around the back of her head and pulling it towards me. "I'm something more than a worthless Mortal. I am something much, much darker."

Her eyes search mine, and I can sense the tiniest sparks of her magic attempting to crawl over me as I twist the blade in deeper.

Her eyes go wide.

She gasps.

And then her eyes glaze over, and a final breath releases from her mouth.

I let go of her head, and she falls limp. Dead.

The second Fae I've managed to kill.

I roll my neck, pain sparking through me as the adrenaline from the fight fades. It's so much worse than I initially thought. It takes all my strength to pick up my orb and stand.

But I do.

Even when my vision blacks out for a minute. Even when I realize there's a jagged piece of stone sticking out of my stomach. Even when the feeling of trying to take another breath feels impossible.

I put one foot in front of the other.

And I walk out of the maze.

DERIAN

She emerges from the maze beaten and bloody.

Dark hair falls loosely in a curtain around her as she clutches the wound in her stomach, where a shard of stone is still deeply embedded. She's limping slightly on her left leg, and blood seeps from wounds on her chest and shoulders. I'm particularly worried about the gash on her forehead, though. She had to have hit her head hard based on the swelling knot that's already forming.

The Eshari rushes to her side, allowing Huntyr to lean against her, but Huntyr only gives herself a brief moment before straightening and pushing away from the panther, unwilling to show any sign of weakness.

A kernel of something that feels suspiciously like pride flares in my chest. Smart girl.

She looks first to the other remaining competitors, Seraphina and Mara, who both escaped the maze relatively unscathed. Then she looks to Roland, as if trying to confirm that the trial is truly complete.

Then she looks at me.

I swear something sparks in the air between us.

A frown pulls at her lips, and there's a flicker of confusion in her eyes, like she didn't quite realize what she was looking for until she saw me.

Our gazes lock. Her blue eyes flash with some unnamed emotion, and fuck me, I simply can't look away. After a moment, she turns back to the people in front of her, and it's like the air around me deflates.

"Do you believe me now?" Cal asks under his breath, just as focused on her as I am. "She just killed a highly trained Fae!"

"I saw."

More than that, I *recognized.*

It had, admittedly, taken me awhile to identify what it was that had changed in her. Even with all of Cal's warnings, I hadn't been ready to admit the truth of what that shadow that had fallen over her features was.

But then she killed Elise, and I *recognized* that hardness in her eyes.

There was no innocence in that expression.

No shock. No regret.

She'd killed Elise as if it were routine.

As if it were easy to watch the life fade from another's eyes.

I know from experience that it takes quite a few dances with death before you stop feeling the weight of it.

Cal shifts next to me, frustration rolling off of him as he grabs my arm and forces me to face him. "It's like you didn't even listen to me this morning!"

Oh, I listened.

When he showed up at my door at dawn, sat me down, and told me what else he had learned about her past, what truth he'd started to piece together, I listened to every word.

Memorized them all.

I took in every piece of evidence he dropped at my doorstep and felt the truth of it all in my bones. When she finally delivered that killing blow to Elise, I swallowed down the fact that Huntyr Lachlan is an assassin.

A rather infamous one, if Cal's sources are correct.

And still, even after knowing that without a shadow of a doubt, for whatever gods forsaken reason, it isn't stopping me from facing the arena again, glancing at her every five fucking minutes while Roland speaks to her and the others.

It doesn't stop me from watching her.

It doesn't stop me from checking that she's still standing steadily.

It doesn't stop me from tracking her shallow breaths.

Cal rips at my arm, forcing me *again* to turn towards him, to turn away from her.

"She's here to kill you," Cal spits the words, as if he can force them into my ears. As if he can force me to take this situation more seriously. "Don't you understand that?"

I watch as she subtly clutches her ribs with a trembling hand. The Eshari seems to notice too and nuzzles its head against her thigh, angling itself so that it stands between her and the others. Like a shield.

"An Eshari wouldn't bond with her like that if she was a true threat to me."

I'm not sure if I'm reasoning with him or myself.

As if the beast hears me say it, it turns and pins me with a glare that makes my magic crackle protectively.

Cal sighs, rubbing a hand over his face. He drags it down slowly, pulling at his tanned skin. "I'm not going to convince you to stay away from her, am I?"

Huntyr turns, following silently as Taric leads the three women back towards the fortress.

Even injured and favoring her left side, her hips sway with feminine grace.

I can't move, can't think, can't even *breathe,* until she's out of my sight.

And the second she's gone, the humidity in the air lifts as my magic relaxes.

And yet, even as the power in my blood settles, my mind still spins, concerned with whether or not she'll make it back to her room, whether she needs medical attention, whether she'll rest tonight as she should before the final trial.

I shouldn't care.

I do.

Fuck, it's unbearable.

"It's only responsible for me to confirm your suspicions," I tell Cal, leading the way out of the arena stands. "That's my duty as a prince of the Fae kingdom."

He grumbles under his breath. "I take it that's a no, then."

That was most definitely a no.

Already, I'm feeling that pull towards her. Again.

I've faced starvation, fought in wars, been deemed a monster by some of my own people, and none of it seems as painful as the idea of avoiding her tonight.

Especially since it's the last opportunity I'll have.

"You're worrying over nothing, Caldren. Just because she managed to kill Elise doesn't mean she stands a chance with Mara and Seraphina. By this time tomorrow, Huntyr Lachlan will be dead."

The words taste like ash on my tongue and land heavily in my gut.

I'm going to have to watch Seraphina kill her tomorrow.

I'm going to have to sit in those stands and watch Seraphina brutalize Huntyr the same way she tormented Alexandria.

And then I'm going to have to marry the fire-wielding bitch and spend the rest of my impossibly long life replaying the memory of her killing the woman I—

The woman I... what?

Lust after?

Cal is silent beside me as we descend the steps and make our way towards the dirt path that leads back to the fortress. The scent of roasted meat hangs in the air as the fortress comes into view. Warriors are swarming back to their posts, bowing their heads respectfully as we pass.

"Fine," he agrees. "At least allow me to go with you?"

I let the request hang between us.

Because I'm not quite sure that's a request that I can honor.

I was burning alive when I said goodnight to her last night. Even in the middle of the night, when I took matters into my own hands, the release had been hollow and unfulfilling. Then she'd found me in my dreams and lit that fire once more. When she strode into the arena wearing those skin-tight leathers, it took all my focus to concentrate on the trial and not spend the entire time picturing her naked.

So help me, something must be seriously wrong with me, because when she'd walked out of that maze covered in blood and looking like a fucking warrior goddess, I'd been so hard it was painful.

Cal wouldn't be coming to interrogate her with me, because if by some stroke of luck Huntyr Lachlan offered to spread her legs for me tonight, I wouldn't be a strong enough man to say no to her.

Cal glances at me suspiciously, as if he knows exactly where my thoughts are. "She's not just another woman you can bed and discard. She's our enemy. I'm serious, Derian."

"I know you are."

He lingers for a moment, watching me, before announcing that he's needed to patrol the borders. He sends another warning glance over his shoulder as he leaves, and I'm careful to stand still.

Even as everything in me screams to turn around.

To find the path that leads to the barracks.

To her room.

To her.

HUNTYR

Everything hurts. From the lacerations that linger on my arms, to the muscles that were pushed past their limits, to the bones that had taken hits harder than they should.

Even combing through my hair feels like torture.

After I'd been returned to my room by Rhen, he'd seen to it that healers came to tend to my most immediate injuries. They'd been silent as they assessed the wounds and stitched up the gaping hole in my stomach. Then they'd left, thankfully leaving behind a tonic that had taken away the most severe bites of pain.

It hadn't, however, dulled the edges of my anger.

I'm tired of playing these games. I'm tired of being spoken down to by the Fae, and I'm tired of watching Mortal women die in the most gruesome ways.

Because of me.

Every single one of those Mortal women are dead because of me.

I worry my lip, combing out the last knots in my hair as I play the fight with Elise over and over again in my head.

"That victory had been hard-earned."

I sense Kaia's hesitation at my words. *"You will not give up."*

After she was confident my wounds weren't life-threatening, she left to hunt down some dinner, and I hate how much I need her presence now.

As angry as I am, I'm also dangerously close to accepting the inevitable defeat of this Conclave.

Elise's powers, as invasive as they were, weren't offensive in nature. Yet it still took every inch of my strength, training, and strategy to beat her. How could I hold my own against a Fae who could control my weapons, and another who could burn me alive with a single thought?

Even if I managed to get them to fight each other first, I would still have to face the victor.

And neither of them would go easy on me.

Seraphina, especially.

Maybe taunting her so much hadn't been my best idea.

A sharp knock sounds at the door, and somehow I'm aware of who's decided to bother me before I even twist the doorknob.

"What do you want?" I snap, cracking the door just enough to see his face.

Derian leans lazily against the frame, smirking as his eyes dart to my hand, my grip tight on the wood.

"You know I could just push it open, right?"

"You could try."

"Let me in, Huntyr."

His voice is quiet, carrying a heaviness I'd only heard that night in the tavern, when he'd spoken of his years training his powers.

"I don't think I will," I tell him. "I'm not interested in playing games with you tonight."

I can't.

This is my last night before the final trial.

My last chance to plan and strategize.

My last night to stare at the stars outside my window and imagine I'm back home with Tyla.

It's just... my last night.

He sighs heavily, his patience wearing thin. "The other ladies will get terribly jealous if they see me at your door in the middle of the night. They might think I'm showing you favoritism."

"There's a simple solution for that: you can leave."

"Oh, but I can't." He steps closer, his body nearly brushing mine. The mint and leather scent of him floods my senses, his heat pouring off him in waves I struggle to ignore. "I have something I'd like to discuss with you. So, let me in, before I'm forced to be a little less than gentle with you."

A vivid image burns in my mind suddenly. His hands on my hips. The door slamming shut behind us. His mouth against mine.

Nothing gentle about it.

"Ask nicely," I whisper, tilting my chin defiantly.

His lips quirk into a crooked, dangerous smile, and I know he's relieved that I've given into the teasing that's become so characteristic of our interactions. "So, you like a man who begs?" He leans closer, his voice a low purr, his mouth only a breath away from mine. "I'll have to remember that."

Rolling my eyes, I step aside, holding the door ajar and allowing him entry. He chuckles softly as he walks past me, invading my space as easily as if it's his own.

"What do you want?" I repeat.

He wanders to the window, staring out at the night sky as raindrops streak across the glass. Moonlight spills over him, making his shoulders seem broader, his skin brighter, his dark hair impossibly more enticing.

This would all be so much easier if he weren't so damned attractive.

"Your performance today was surprising," he says finally.

I shiver, wrapping my arms around myself.

"Yes, well, it was a terrible experience, and I'd like to sleep now," I say coolly. "So, if you wouldn't mind—"

"You're the last Mortal in the Conclave."

Unease travels down my spine. "So?"

"So," he draws out the word as he turns to face me, arms crossed, "I find it odd that a noblewoman fights well enough to survive a competition meant for only the strongest Fae warriors."

I mirror his stance. "I told you, I'm a quick learner."

His gaze rakes over me, lingering on the curve of my hips. The intensity of his stare leaves me feeling bare and exposed.

"I don't think so."

There's a heaviness to his words, and a chill sneaks down my spine.

He knows.

Derian takes a step closer, forcing me to look up to meet his gaze as he towers over me. "Do you know why I called the Conclave instead of marrying the King's daughter?"

I run my tongue over my teeth, crossing my arms across my chest. "I assume you enjoy the idea of women fighting over you."

"Oh, I do, but that's not why, and I think you know that." His voice darkens as thunder rolls in the distance. "On the night of the ball, one of my guards was murdered."

I keep my face neutral, my posture relaxed.

"You wouldn't happen to know anything about that, would you?"

This is how it was supposed to have happened all along.

Just him and I.

The Fae prince and the assassin sent to kill him.

My eyes are steady on his. "Why would I?"

He studies me for a moment, then smiles coldly. "You have quite an interesting story, Lady Lachlan."

"That's *not* my name," I snarl.

He smirks, backing up a few paces. "See, that right there was the first thing that tipped me off. What sort of noblewoman insists on being called by her first name instead of her title?"

"Someone with a complicated history."

He nods, pointing a finger at me in acknowledgment. "Now that, I believe. Your father died when you were six, right?"

"Five." My fingers twitch toward the blade on my hip.

"Five, that's right. Then you were sent away to school. Except no one seems to know where you went to school or what school it was."

My stomach churns as he rubs his jaw thoughtfully. I really should have seen this coming. All this time, his attention had been so obvious. I dismissed it as whatever sexual tension existed between us, when all along, he'd been digging into my past.

And it appears he may have circled too close to the truth.

"I did some research on Velia recently," he continues, leaning back against the wall with his hands tucked into his front pockets. "Your kingdom has quite the crime district. Overpopulation and a lack of resources breeds desperation, after all."

"I imagine that's why we decided an alliance with the Fae kingdom was worthwhile," I say, my tone icy.

"I also learned quite a bit about the slums in your kingdom, all run by some pretty nasty gangs. The kind of people who will do anything to accomplish their goals."

"Fascinating."

His lips quirk into a quick smile as his dark eyes burn into me. "I'm glad you agree. It seems there's a very promising league of assassins willing to do their dirty work."

I stiffen.

How does he possibly know *that*?

Even if he's managed to figure out what I do, why I was at that ball, he shouldn't know about the others. There are only two ways to know about the league: you're connected enough to hire us, or you're unfortunate enough to be killed by us.

Exactly how deep did the prince investigate?

"One assassin, in particular, caught my attention," he says softly.

Here it comes.

I spread my feet, letting my hands drop to my sides, closer to my blades.

"Her first known kill was about five years after you went to school. Odd timing, don't you think?"

My jaw tightens.

My stomach sinks.

This is the moment where it all ends, where I either kill the Fae prince or he kills me.

"And," he adds, pushing off the wall to step closer to me. "Her last known kill was just before the ball."

He reaches out, catching a strand of my hair and running it through his fingers, tugging slightly as he reaches the end. His touch sends a shiver down my spine.

"That's quite interesting," I say dryly. "Can I go to sleep now?"

"Not just yet." He takes a deep, slow breath before finally releasing it. "You see, every good history lesson ends with a test. So, here's my question for you." He pauses. I tense. "What's the assassin's name?"

Time freezes.

In truth, I've never actually publicly claimed the name.

It had started as a pet name from Kristona.

Then it became a legend among the streets of Velia.

Huntyr. Lady Lachlan. The Huntress.

Three different roles that I've never managed to reconcile into one identity.

"Well?" he prompts.

Time stops. Sound quiets. There is only the male in front of me and the secret that has existed between us since the day we met.

"She's known as the Huntress," I finally whisper.

Derian's grin widens, wicked and triumphant, even as his fingers remain tangled in the ends of my hair. "Oddly similar to your name, don't you think?"

—◦—

A deep grounding breath in. A slow steady exhale out.

I let the oxygen move through me, filling my mind and muscles with everything they need for what's about to happen.

A quick glance out the window shows a clear night sky, peppered by sparkling stars painted across the sky. No rain. No wind. His magic is controlled. Or perhaps he's saving it just for me and whatever punishment he plans to enact.

Derian is silent as he watches me, that knowing smile still on his lips. I feel the spark of every place his eyes trail over me. My brows. My eyes. My nose. My lips. My throat.

Will he do it by magic or by the blade? How exactly will the Fae prince end my life?

"Coincidence," I mutter, sounding more than a little breathy.

Blood is about to be spilled.

"Who's lying now," he growls, the teasing lilt gone, his tone low and rough. His fingers release my hair, trailing slowly down my ribcage, pausing just above my hips... where my blades are.

I shove him, palms pressed hard against his chest. "What do you want, Derian?"

"The truth, preferably, Huntress."

The word is a blade, and he wields it like he knows exactly what it will do to me.

"Oh, I'm sorry," he mocks. "Is that another thing I'm not allowed to call you?"

My blades fly before I even realize I've drawn them. They cut through the air, aimed with lethal precision. One for his heart. The other for his right eye.

And the bastard *catches* them.

One hand clenches the blade that should have pierced his chest; the other grips the dagger that should have blinded him.

He doesn't even blink.

"Tsk tsk," he tuts, shaking his head. "No need for violence."

He sets my blades down in the chest of weapons he had delivered to me, turning his back to me as if to remind me he doesn't believe I can actually hurt him, which only infuriates me more.

I reach for the dagger on my thigh, lunging forward, but he spins with unnerving speed, catching my wrist mid-swing.

"Huntress," he chastises, his voice heavy with boredom.

I growl, slamming my boot into the back of his knee. It barely buckles, his body only slightly shifting under the blow. Unwilling to give up, I drop the dagger from my right hand, catching it with my left and driving it toward the tender spot above his kidney.

But he's so fucking fast.

Far faster than either Elise or his guard.

I've never actually seen him fight, I realize. I've heard the rumors and watched him wield storms like a child playing in a sandbox, but I've never seen, with my own eyes, the skills that have made him infamous.

The blade clatters to the floor as he twists my wrist, his other hand gripping my hip to pivot us. Before I can react, my back slams against the wall, his forearm pinning me at the collarbone.

I gasp when he steps forward, and I feel him *everywhere.*

"Do I even need you to confirm it at this point?" His tone is sharp, cutting.

"You want me to say that I killed him?" I spit, glaring up at him, leaning into the rage and pain that burns through me. "I *did*. Happy?"

His eyes burn into mine, heated and unrelenting. "Not quite."

"What do you *want*, Derian? Details? Fine." My voice rises, even as I keep struggling against him. "You were wrong about my first kill. It wasn't when I was ten. I was seven. Sent into the home of some rich couple as an orphan before I stabbed them both in their sleep."

His expression doesn't falter, even as I keep going, my darkness spilling out of me into pools of tragedy all around us.

"Perhaps you want to hear about the more gruesome kills? I've had two decapitations—messy things, by the way. Once, I cut off a man's hand and had tea in his parlor while I watched him bleed out. The worst was the owner of a fight ring. Big guy. Threw me around until I lost my weapons and had a nasty head wound. So, I had to improvise." My lips curl in a humorless smile. "Cake platters are surprisingly effective."

Derian raises a brow. "A cake platter?"

"I'm remarkably adaptive." I surge against him, trying to push him away, but he only leans in closer, his body pressing mine harder against the wall.

"Is that what you wanted to hear?"

"You never cease to intrigue me, Huntress."

His grip shifts, fingers wrapping around my throat firmly. The heat of him radiates through my skin, igniting something deep inside me that I desperately try to suppress.

And then I feel it.

Him.

The hard length of him presses against my lower stomach.

How is he turned on by this?

How am *I* turned on by this?

I level my hands on his chest and push. I can't *think* when I can feel the hardness of him pushing against me, desperate for me.

He doesn't even budge, even as lightning cracks outside.

"You'll have to try harder than that," he tells me, that infuriating smirk dancing on his face.

I roar in anger, forcing my focus away from the shape of his mouth, the lines of his jaw, the curve of his hair around his ears.

"How many?" he asks suddenly, his head tilting inquisitively to the side.

"What?" The question jars me from my thoughts.

"How many have you killed?"

My thoughts scatter, trapped somewhere between defending myself from what's clearly about to be a fight to the death, and the pressure against my stomach sending waves of unbearable need down my spine. I shift, clenching my thighs together, and the bastard's lips twitch like he notices.

I glance toward the sword propped against my bed, calculating, but his body blocks every clear path.

"Don't make me ask again," he says, his grip on my throat tightening just enough to pull my eyes back to his.

My lips part, and the truth spills out before I can stop it. "Forty-one. Well, forty-three if you count the two from today."

I never forget the running tally.

His eyes heat and his gaze flicks to my lips sharply before he chuckles softly. "Not as many as I thought."

He's a monster. A bastard. He's the epitome of everything that's wrong with the Fae.

"So why don't you get it over with, then?" I shove him again, cursing when he doesn't move. "If you want me dead as punishment, then kill me."

"Why would I do that?" He purrs. "The Conclave will take care of that for me tomorrow."

My gut twists, bile rising in my throat.

"Then leave," I snap. "Either fight me or get out."

He tilts his head. "You tried to fight me. You lost."

"Then go!"

"I don't want to."

The sound that rips out of my throat hardly sounds human. I level my glare on him, needing him out of this room before I do something that could only be described as a mistake. "*I* want you to."

"I think it's time we both stop lying," he murmurs, his voice low and intoxicating.

Once more, I hopelessly try to shove against him, but he's simply un-movable. His hips are a solid force pinning mine to the wall. "I'm not lying!"

"Oh, but you are." He leans closer, his breath brushing my cheek. "You're a good liar; I'll give you that. I suppose you have to be in your line of work. But your body *can't* lie. The way your hips press against me, the way your breath caught when I wrapped my hand around this pretty throat of yours, the way your pulse is beating under my fingers." His lips quirk into a smirk. "Not even you can hide that, Huntress."

My traitorous breath quickens, every desperate inhale bringing my chest closer to his. Wind slams against the window, the now-growing storm outside mirroring the tension between us.

"I hate you," I whisper, painfully aware of how hollow the words sound.

I *should* hate him.

But hate is most definitely not what I'm feeling right now.

Every part of me hums in anticipation. My blood is boiling. My need is all I can think about, and there's only one being in all the world who can get rid of the ache inside of me that's been growing since I stepped into that darkened office and found the masked stranger sitting behind a desk.

"That doesn't make what I said any less true," he points out, his other hand squeezing my hip.

He's a Fae.

A fucking Fae prince.

"Still want to lie and say you want me to leave?" he asks.

I clench and release my jaw. "Why exactly do you insist on staying?"

He doesn't move. Neither of us breathe.

I can't look away from those dark eyes.

"Because if this is your last night alive, I'd like to help you spend it screaming in pleasure."

His people are the reason my father died.

And no bedtime story is going to convince me that his people aren't the cause of the Wastelands.

"And I think you might want that too." His voice is nothing more than a whisper.

I hate him.

With every part of me, I hate Derian Silverthorn.

And I'm going to regret this the second it's over, but regret isn't enough to stop me.

Because, even though I despise him, he's right.

I do want that.

I desperately want him.

He leans towards me, and my resolve *snaps*.

If I am to die tomorrow, then I'll let him ruin me tonight. My fingers curl into his shirt, and his mouth quirks into a crooked, genuine smile when he realizes he's won. I pull, yanking him down to me, my lips crashing into his with all the fury I can't put into a blade.

HUNTYR

I am on fire. Derian kisses me like a starving man, and I meet each thrust of his tongue with the desperate push of my own. Any thoughts, any reservations, melt away the moment his mouth claims mine. All I have left are monosyllabic desires.

Yes.

Him.

More.

His grip on my throat tightens, his thumb tilting my jaw to hold me exactly where he wants, and I go willingly. He ravages my mouth with a relentless push and pull that leaves me breathless, my chest heaving against his. My hands tangle in his dark hair, fingers spearing through the soft strands that feel even better than I ever imagined.

He breaks from my swollen lips, guiding my head to the side to expose the tender space beneath my ear. His mouth descends mercilessly, and then he's kissing, sucking, and biting, until every nerve in my body screams for release. Until I can't stop the breathy whimper that escapes.

"Fuck," he groans, his voice rough against my skin. "You whine so prettily for me."

His hands slide lower, gripping my ass as he lifts me effortlessly, pinning me harder against the stone wall. And oh, yes, he is right there. Every hard inch of him is pressed against me, separated by only a few maddening layers of fabric.

I lock my ankles behind his back, rolling my hips as I pull his mouth back to mine.

Our kisses are feral, driven by a desperate need for each other that neither of us wants to acknowledge. There is no softness, no tenderness. There is only the consuming fire of mutual hatred and desire colliding in a way that leaves us both on the edge of combustion.

His hand moves to my breast, palming it over the thick leather of my protective vest. I arch into him, but the material is too firm, too restrictive. I need more.

So much more.

"Put me down," I demand, my voice hoarse.

"I like you where I have you." His hands knead my ass as his mouth trails hot kisses along my collarbone.

"Put me down so I can take my clothes off."

He doesn't even look up. "What if I want the pleasure of that?"

Does everything always have to be an argument with him?

"Put me down so I can take *your* clothes off."

Finally, he pulls away, his lips curling into that infuriating smile. "If you insist."

I waste no time ripping his shirt from where it's tucked into his leather trousers, and yank it over his head, baring the expanse of his toned chest. The sight stops me, my breath hitching as I take him in.

This man's body deserves to be painted, sculpted even, and set in a gallery for all to admire.

I trail my hand down his stomach, feeling the hard ridges of muscle, wanting to take my time for the first moment since I've felt his mouth on mine, but he isn't content to let me linger. He's just as desperate for me as I am for him. His fingers tangle in my hair, pulling sharply, forcing my head to the side so he can continue his assault on my throat.

And, damn, that feels like bliss.

My hands find the buttons of his trousers, working them loose. When I slide my hand inside, grasping him and stroking from root to tip, he shudders under my touch, a quiet curse escaping his lips.

His response sends a thrill racing through me. I want to pry out every sound and tremble I can get from him.

Derian's hand slides to my right thigh, hitching it high against his hip just as he did on the courtyard. Gods, I had wanted him so badly in that moment. I hadn't allowed myself to embrace that need then, but I couldn't stop myself now. Not when death is so close to claiming me.

He crouches to undo the laces of my boot, sliding it off with ease, then repeats the process with the other.

"Spin for me," he commands, his hands firm on my hips as he turns me to face the wall. His fingers move to the laces of my corseted vest, working to untie it with careful precision, his movements deliberate and tender around the spot where my ribs are bruised.

"You don't need to be gentle with me," I remind him, no longer feeling any pain as he brushes aside my hair and places a soft kiss on the back of my neck.

"You're covered in bruises," he counters, his voice low and steady.

"It's not the first time."

His breath tickles my skin as he chuckles, and I lean into it, into him.

"Not gentle then," he murmurs, lips brushing the shell of my ear. "I'll remember that, too."

With skilled fingers, he makes quick work of my corset, sliding it over my head. The cotton shirt beneath follows, though he pauses briefly to take my breasts in his hands, his thumbs teasing the hardened peaks before pinching sharply.

"Oh," I gasp, arching back into him as a jolt of pain-laced pleasure lances through me.

He moves lower, undoing the buttons of my pants and sliding them down my legs. His hands linger as he rises, tracing featherlight paths up my thighs, his fingers brushing dangerously close to that burning core of my desire, and a gentle sigh escapes me.

"I can't wait to see how many sounds you'll make for me."

To prove his words, his fingers dart between my thighs, circling my clit with sudden precision. I cry out, my nails sinking into his arm.

Pleasure sparks through me, radiating until every nerve in my body is alight. This. *This* is what I need. This is what I've needed for so long.

And yet, it still isn't enough.

Yes.

Him.

More.

"I need—" I pant, the words faltering as he alternates his pace, shifting between slow, agonizing circles and sudden overwhelming flicks.

He is frustratingly good at that.

I really shouldn't have expected anything less.

"Yes?" His voice is a low rumble, amusement laced with desire. "Tell me what you need, Huntress."

He says the name not as a slur but in reverence.

Suddenly, I need everything. Him, everywhere. But my body is already trembling, teetering on the edge, every stroke winding me tighter.

"Do you need this?" he whispers, sliding his fingers through my wetness and pushing two inside.

"Yes," I gasp, the word spilling out as the feeling of him overwhelms me.

The sensation is unexplainable—his thumb working that bundle of nerves even as his fingers move inside me, slow and deliberate before quickening their pace. I am a wire pulled too taut, a storm ready to crash against the shore, a fire burning too brightly to contain.

"That's it," he coaxes, his fingers relentless as they drive me higher.

And then, finally, the pleasure explodes.

I gasp his name, the release hitting me with unspeakable fury. Stars burst behind my eyelids as I ride the waves of pleasure, my body trembling and weightless. Only his arm, still wrapped firmly around my waist, keeps me from collapsing.

He holds me there for a moment, his arms steady around my waist, until my legs stop trembling enough to bear my weight again. I hear the slap of his pants hitting the floor before I feel him, hard and hot, pressing against my entrance.

"Grab the wall," he orders, his voice low and commanding.

I brace my palms against the cold stone as his hands grasp onto my hips.

"Should I be impressed that you actually did as you were told?"

I arch my spine further, pushing back against him. "You should stop talking and fuck me."

A growl rumbles in his chest as his hand snakes into my hair, gripping it and pulling sharply. I moan against the sting of pain, and he rewards me by slowly pushing in, giving me just enough time to adjust to the stretch.

"Not gentle?" he confirms.

"Please, no," I pant.

"No need to beg," he murmurs. "I aim to satisfy."

And then he slams into me.

The force shoves me away even as his hand on my hip pulls me back into him. He uses his hold of my hair to guide the rhythm as he moves, and I savor every sensation, the delicious friction of each thrust driving me closer to oblivion.

"*This* is what I want, Huntyr," he says roughly. "I want you like this. I want you on the bed. I want you in the tub. I want you on your knees."

He punctuates each claim with sharper thrusts, his pace walking the line between pleasure and pain.

I am breathless, mindless, unable to do anything other than take what he gives me. My nails scrape against the stone as I desperately try to brace myself, pushing back to meet him with a roll of my hips, loving when he groans in pleasure.

And it's so good. The pace, the pressure, the stretch. It's all perfect. Too perfect. I am already climbing again, the release building far too quickly.

He yanks my hair again, pulling me upright so his mouth can claim mine, his teeth catching my lower lip. I cry into him, my hand reaching back to twist behind his head and pull him impossibly closer.

"You're so fucking sweet," he mutters against my lips. "So sweet, so wet, so desperate for me."

Lightning cracks outside, the flash illuminating the room as his hand slides between my thighs once more.

It's all too much. I'm not sure I can take any more. The depth of him, the rhythm of his hips, the relentless stroke of his fingers against my clit. Every nerve in my body screams for release.

"Come for me," he breathes, lips grazing the hollow of my throat. "Let me hear you."

I feel his teeth scrape against my shoulder just as he rolls his hips, slamming into me deeper than ever before, and I do as I'm told.

I shatter.

Screams pour from my throat, a mixture of helpless moans, slurs of his name, and pleas for more spilling over and over as bliss ravages my body.

When it finally subsides after what feels like an eternity, I am limp in his hands, sated but still greedy for more.

I can't be done.

I need him to fall apart the way I just did.

Derian pulls out of me, spinning me around and lifting me by the thighs. He pushes me against the wall, not wasting a single second before he sheaths himself inside me with a growl, his face buried in the crook of my neck.

He moves harder, faster, every thrust driving him closer to the edge. His breathing grows ragged, his grip on me tightens, until finally, he stills, groaning a curse as he finds his release, too.

And it's glorious to witness.

For a moment, we stay frozen, chests heaving as the world comes back into focus.

He pulls out carefully, his gaze meeting mine, oddly serious. "Are you alright?"

My mind spins, my body buzzing.

I want to say yes. I want to say no.

Truthfully, that felt like the most natural thing I've ever done. We'd fit together as perfectly as if we'd been made for each other. The pleasure still lingers in my limbs, even as my body begins to hunger for more, like it would never have enough of him to feel satisfied.

As the world begins to fade back into view, though, so does the betrayal of what I'd just done.

I just fucked the Fae prince.

The man I am supposed to kill.

The man who is supposed to be my vengeance against all the Fae I've hated for my entire life.

But... I don't hate *him.*

And that confuses me more than I'm willing to admit.

So I simply smirk and force my voice to steady as I answer. "I'm perfect."

This time when he grins, it doesn't infuriate me as much.

Without explanation, he carries me to the bed, pulling back the covers before settling me against the pillows. My nightgown sits discarded on the floor from the night before, and he picks it up and slides it over my head, careful of my ribs as he pulls it down.

I settle against the blankets. My body is more than ready to sleep, but I watch him as he dresses, his movements slow and deliberate.

He comes to sit beside me, his hand resting on my hip. "I suppose I should clarify if you're planning to try to kill me again?"

A soft laugh escapes me. "I'm too tired for murder. Ask me again tomorrow."

The mention of tomorrow sends a shiver down my spine.

Death is hiding in the dark corners of this fortress, just waiting for the final trial of the Conclave.

A shadow crosses Derian's face as he realizes the same. "I should let you sleep. You'll need your strength."

I shrug. "It doesn't matter."

"Don't say that, Huntress," he murmurs, standing and pressing a surprisingly gentle kiss to my temple. He smooths the blanket over me and brushes my hair back over my shoulder, his touch soft. "That arrogance of yours is one of the things I like."

I toss a pillow at his retreating back. "You're one to talk."

He laughs softly, throwing a wink over his shoulder.

"Sleep."

An order, not a request.

He slips out of my room and closes the door behind him.

As I curl up against the pillow, a strange ache settles deep in my chest.

Because suddenly, I can't tell which was the bigger mistake—letting him touch me, or letting him leave.

DERIAN

Fucking her was a mistake.

I knew it the moment it was over, because one time isn't enough. Not nearly enough.

I could fuck her a hundred times, a thousand, and still need more. I could memorize every inch of her body and still need to see it spread before me. I could hear every moan and sigh pour from her mouth and still need the music of her pleasure.

I could have her beneath me, above me, wrapped around me, and still need *her*.

Since the moment I saw her in that silver gown, I thought I just needed to get it out of my system. I thought that once I had her, I would be able to move past this inconvenient obsession I have with the assassin.

I'm starting to realize that I have been so terribly wrong.

I started all of this, called the Conclave, with a simple goal. I just wanted to ensure the Mortal responsible for killing Kai would die without implicating my people in breaking this ridiculous truce.

Tomorrow I'm going to accomplish that.

So why the fuck am I sitting here now, hours after I've left her arms, still staring at the faint half-moon bruises on my arm, unable to stop thinking about her? Aching for her? I'm practically desperate to throw aside my blanket and return to her.

In just a few hours, the sun will rise and my plan will work. The guilty party will be punished. Justice will be served.

And yet—

I can still feel her fingers in my hair. Still taste her on my tongue. Still see the way she looked when she came undone.

I stare at the ceiling, exhaling sharply.

I called this Conclave to kill her.

But now, I'm not sure I want to see her dead.

Huntyr

I wake suddenly to the sound of my door hinges creaking open.

Before I even open my eyes, my first thought is of Derian, wondering if he's come back.

But as I blink awake, I realize Derian wouldn't do that.

He's not some lovestruck boy desperate to sleep beside me just because we shared a moment of passion.

This is someone else.

Still half asleep, instinct takes over. My fingers wrap around the dagger under my pillow, and I sit up straight as a board, calculating the distance between me and the shadowed figure entering my room before I fling the dagger.

The blade stops mid-air, hovering, before clattering uselessly to the floor.

Metal-wielder.

That has to be…

The intruder steps further into the room. The starlight from outside the window catches against her skin, her hair, the leather of her armor.

Mara.

Three more Fae warriors file in after her, each scanning over the room quickly.

"Where's her Eshari?" one hisses, scanning over my room.

"Not here, grab her before it comes back."

My muscles tense. Not fucking happening.

I launch, diving for the weapons chest, just at the same time that Mara assesses what I'm doing.

"Kaia!" I scream in my head.

"Do not let them harm you!"

Mara's elbow slams into my face and snaps my head back. Stars explode behind my eyes as I stagger, the metallic taste of blood filling my mouth. My head was already spinning from the earlier head wound, and now it's practically impossible to focus through the pain.

"Yeah, doing my best. I could use some help."

"What do you think I'm doing?" she snarls, her voice thick with tension. *"Just hold them off for now."*

I lash out, aiming a jab at Mara's throat, but she's faster, more alert, and the other warriors are already making their way towards me. I'm ridiculously outnumbered.

These are not good odds.

"Hurry!"

"Grab her!" Mara hisses over her shoulder, raising her arms defensively.

Like hell am I letting them take me anywhere.

Mara dodges my strike, but I'm already moving again, slamming my bare foot into her knee. One of the warriors lunges behind me, but I feint back, driving my elbow towards him.

I manage a crack to his cheek before the third warrior slams a fist into my side, hitting my already-injured ribs.

Agony streaks through me, blinding and all-consuming.

I gasp, doubling over, clutching onto my side.

My attackers take advantage of that momentary lapse and an arm wraps around my throat and squeezes.

My stomach rolls in dread, and distantly I wonder how far away Kaia is. I almost don't want her to come. There's too many of them here, I don't want to risk her getting hurt either.

"You will not stop fighting! Surrender is beneath you."

Her voice snaps me back into the fight. Grunting, I push off the ground, twisting to flip my attacker, a move I've done a thousand times before, but Mara's hand snakes out, catching hold of my ankle.

"See," she says pointedly to the men. "I told you she knows what she's doing."

She shoves my legs toward the other male who hooks an arm around them, pinning me completely. I thrash wildly, desperate to shake myself out of his grasp, but he lifts my legs, and I'm suddenly suspended in the air between them.

"I'm going to kill you all," I growl right before that arm on my throat tightens even more, cutting off any hope of air.

I claw at his flesh, nails scraping uselessly against leather armor.

Kristona's most important rule in assassin school?

Never get yourself in a situation where you're outnumbered and over-powered.

He would be so disappointed.

Fae bastards, all of them.

Mara walks towards the hall and glances through the door. "Let's go before the cat comes back."

"They'll suffer a fate worse than the most brutal of deaths," Kaia growls in my head.

A hand presses over my mouth, silencing any screaming, as the two Fae men carry me out of my room and through the dark hallways of the fortress.

Desperately, I glance to my left and right, searching for someone to intervene, but can't spot a single soul. I'm in an entire fortress full of Fae warriors and there's not a single one patrolling the halls at night? No one who heard the struggle and is coming to investigate?

"Where do we take her?" the one at my feet asks as we step outside.

The night air bites against my barely covered skin. The only illumination comes from the moon and the splattering of stars across the expanse of the sky.

Mara gestures towards the archway that leads to the stables, the dog yard, and the bird-houses with a vicious laugh.

"We'll leave her body among the shit of the other animals," she sneers.

White fury claws through me, infecting every part of me with a sudden burst of strength and defiance. I open my mouth and clench down hard on the hand silencing me.

The salty taste of blood floods my mouth.

The warrior howls, ripping his hand away.

"The bitch bit me!"

Gods, I hate that word.

I twist, thrashing free, before my shoulder slams into the ground. Pain slices down my spine but I roll into it, shifting my weight and pulling one foot free. Then the other.

His blood drips down my chest, sticky and staining the white of my nightgown as I drive a vicious kick into the warrior's gut, sending him stumbling.

Then I rise.

Mara. The two that were holding me. Two more reinforcements.

I should be flattered that she thinks she needs this many to kill me.

They draw their weapons, and I brace myself for what will inevitably be a fight to the death.

My death.

Even at my best, I wouldn't be able to take on this many Fae, but I'm not at my best. I'm exhausted, injured, mentally drained. I don't stand a chance, but that doesn't mean I won't put up a fight.

"These odds aren't in my favor," I tell Kaia in my mind. *"But if it's any consolation, I'm going to at least make this hurt for them."*

Just as I'm prepared to face down the Fae, a vicious snarl tears through the air, raising the hair on the back of my neck and destroying any semblance of silence in the courtyard

I've never heard anything like that roar. It coasts through the air and rattles my very bones. Based on the widened eyes of the Fae in front of me, they felt that too.

I whip around. She stands by that archway, ears flattened, haunches raised, lips curled over gleaming fangs.

And behind her—

Derian.

His hands are tucked into his pockets, stance casual and unbothered.

His eyes, though. His eyes promise death as he stares down my attackers.

Kaia pounces, rushing forward at impossible speed and launcher herself at the Fae nearest to me. Her jaw clamps down onto his hand with animalistic strength and more blood stains my dress as he screams.

The air shifts, suddenly freezing, before a brush of warmth floods over my arms like a gentle touch. Humidity falls over us, and the hair on the back of my neck lifts slightly with static electricity.

"There are so many better ways to spend your nights," Derian tuts, walking towards us. My attackers all wide-eyed, not daring to look away from their prince.

With a final snarl, Kaia releases her grip on the Fae male, and returns to my side, licking her maw as her victim clutches what remains of his hand.

"I, for example, was sleeping after a *very* enjoyable evening," Derian continues.

My stomach flips.

"What a shame this is how you all chose to spend your last night alive."

I sense the attack before it happens.

I feel the shift in pressure.

The static crackling in the air.

The sudden stillness that comes before—

The sky splits open, blinding light suddenly falling around me.

Four bolts of lightning strike down simultaneously, exploding against the Fae standing alongside Mara.

I lift my hand, blocking out the brightness of the shining lightning, and when I lower it, the smell of charred flesh and burnt hair hits me instantly. It's so distracting that I barely notice Kaia brushing against my legs with her head.

Their bodies lie in heaps on the ground, covered in burns, small flames climbing up from what remains of their clothing. The smell of it is pungent, practically suffocating. One moment, they were standing there, and an instant later, they've been brutalized. It's... horrific. Unspeakable. Unimaginable.

I've seen all manner of death before, committed many atrocities myself, but I've never seen anything quite like this.

My mouth is suddenly dry, tasting overwhelmingly of copper.

"Your majesty," Mara simpers, falling to her knees and averting her gaze.

She has the audacity to tremble.

Derian moves toward her slowly, never taking his gaze off her, even as I feel that brush of warmth against me again.

He taps her chin, a silent instruction to look up at him, which she obeys.

"Doing it quickly like that would be a kindness you do not deserve."

He is death incarnate. The wildest of storms shoved inside a single body. It's no wonder his family sent him away. Magic rolls off of him, leaving the air charged, and I just *know* that he is barely holding back the hurricane of his power. Darkness settles over the space, ever more oppressive, as clouds black out the moonlight.

Derian Silverthorn is not like the other Fae. He could destroy this entire fortress in a single breath.

But he's not going to do that. No—he's set his sights on one Fae in particular. He's going to kill her. I know it in my bones, just as clearly as I know I can't let him.

If he killed her, he would be intervening in the Conclave.

Who knows what will happen to him if he breaks that rule?

"Don't."

I don't even realize I've spoken until he looks at me.

His gaze drags over me, eyes scanning slowly from top to bottom.

There's nothing but darkness in those eyes. Darkness, rage, and *power*. Pure, unmatched power.

This is not the man who had been in my bed hours ago.

Finally, I was seeing the prince whose brutality made him infamous.

This was the monster capable of killing hundreds—*thousands* with his storms.

This was the Fae bastard capable of destroying kingdoms.

"She was going to leave your body discarded in the stables, Huntress," he intones, as if I needed the reminder, his eyes lingering on my still-bleeding nose. "You would stop me from punishing her?"

A shiver crawls up my spine.

I can't help but wonder if he would have still responded with such anger if this had been done to anyone else... or if this type of reaction was reserved for me specifically.

"Why kill her when the Conclave will take care of that for you tomorrow?" I repeat his earlier words back to him, voice steady despite the disapproval that curls on his face. "If she's cowardly enough to think that she needs the help of others to murder me straight out of my bed, how much of a challenge could she really be?"

Mara's nostrils flare at the insult, but she doesn't dare speak.

He considers me for a long, unbearable moment. He looks at me with such intensity that Kaia shifts between us, subtle but protective.

Then he moves.

He fists his hand in Mara's hair, yanking her to her feet as she gasps in pain.

"Very well," he agrees. "But you better hope you don't win tomorrow, Mara, because if you do, and you end up my wife, then I will make sure every day is a fresh torture for you."

He shoves her away, sending her sprawling. She scrambles, jogging back towards the barracks without another word, leaving me alone with a version of Derian that I don't quite recognize.

The air shifts again, the icy chill suddenly leaving.

He glances towards me, but remains rooted to his spot, not moving a single muscle. "Are you hurt?"

The question feels strange. It's a simple question that's progressively getting harder to answer each day I spend in the Fae kingdom.

I lick the blood from my lip.

"I can take it."

He simply stares. No smart remark. No laughter. Just that dark appraisal.

Until finally he comes to me, reaches forward, brushes aside the blood from under my nose with his thumb, and tucks my hair behind my ear. "You shouldn't have to."

I shiver. "You realize the odds of my living through tomorrow are minuscule?"

What will he do with all this anger then? He can't very well bring down the entire arena with lightning.

His jaw works as he avoids my gaze. "I will send a pain tonic in the morning for you. Then you will go to the arena, and you will use every bit of training you have. You will use their weaknesses against them. I know you've studied them closely enough to figure them out."

Even as he looks anywhere but at me, I can't tear my gaze away from him. There's worry in his features. It's abundantly obvious in the pinch of his brows and purse of his full lips.

Lips that had burned themselves onto me only hours ago.

"I know their weaknesses," I whisper, trying to reassure him.

Seraphina is impulsive, too easily manipulated by her emotions. She relies on her powers too much, so she isn't as good at fighting in close contact.

Mara doesn't think things through. She acts without understanding the consequences of her actions. Tonight is a perfect example of that. Her control over weapons is formidable, but she has remarkably terrible aim when targets are moving.

"You are just as much a warrior as they are." Derian reaches out to cup my cheek. "You are just as deadly as they are."

"Why do you care?" I ask as I stare up at him.

Finally, he meets my gaze. He looks at me for an impossibly long time, an eternity measured in heartbeats, before he answers. "I don't know."

And I know that he's not lying.

He steps back. "Get back to bed."

With that, he turns on his heels, walking not towards the barracks, but instead towards the training courtyard. Another bolt of lightning streaks through the sky, and thunder cracks violently.

I'm still standing there, staring after him, when the rain starts to fall, soaking me almost instantly.

"Why did you bring him?" I ask Kaia.

"I was hunting, the prince was nearby. You needed help."

I glare down at her before I start stomping back towards my room, shame flowing over me in waves. *"He's not our ally."*

Kaia is quiet, following after me almost silently, and I hold my door open for her once we're back inside.

"Do not judge the prince for turning to violence in the name of protecting you. Not when that same potential for violence exists in you to defend those you care for."

"Derian doesn't care for me."

She allows me to settle into my blankets before she settles herself in front of the door. *"He cares as much as you do."*

DERIAN

I'm on edge all morning. I lay in bed well past the time when I should get up. Truthfully, I'm paralyzed, tossing over every possibility in my mind of how the next few hours are going to go.

I don't think I'm going to be able to do this.

When the Eshari came to my room last night, clawing at the door and releasing a roar that shook the furniture, I knew something was wrong. I *ran*. Followed that damn cat without even thinking. When I finally saw her, barefoot and bloodied in the nightgown I had left her in, ready to take on five of them by herself, I wanted to tear them apart limb by limb.

Then, when Mara was on her knees in front of me, I wanted to carve her punishment out of her flesh forever raising a hand against *her*.

How am I possibly going to survive watching her battle two highly skilled Fae warriors by herself?

She's just a Mortal.

That's what makes my obsession with her all the stranger. The Gods know I've had plenty of women before. All willing, eager, beautiful Fae who knew exactly how to please me.

Huntyr is different, though.

Despite the fact that she's just a Mortal, weak and easily broken, she meets me as an equal. Not once since I met her at the masquerade has she ever feared or chased me.

Even Seraphina, for all her fire and independence, had initiated our relationship with the eager desire for the status that I would bring her. It was that desire that kept her coming back. I wasn't delusional enough to think it was because of any affection for me. Still, over the years, there have still been times I've recognized hesitancy in her eyes when my temper escaped me.

Huntyr didn't look at me with fear last night.

Anger, maybe, possibly even disgust, but she hadn't been afraid.

She could be greeting death himself, and she wouldn't cower.

There's a knock at my door, and I finally pull myself out of bed to answer it, tugging on a shirt as I do. The knock sounds again, and I rip it open, only to stumble back at the sight before me. "I didn't know you were coming," I tell the woman with a grin.

My Aunt, Ulna, seems shorter than I remember her. Or I've gotten taller. Either way, I have to stoop awkwardly to hug her before stepping aside to let her into the room.

By Mortal standards, she appears to be in her mid-thirties. She puts on a show of being any other married woman, wearing flowing skirts with her hair tied back, but she's as formidable as they come. She'd called her own Conclave, refusing to tie herself down to anyone other than the very strongest.

She examines the dishevel of my room with a disapproving tut. "It wouldn't kill you to tidy up once in awhile."

I run a hand through my hair and gesture to the seats by the hearth. "I've been a bit busy lately."

"So I've heard." She smooths her skirts before sitting. "Aren't you going to offer your dear old Aunt a drink?"

I chuckle under my breath with a shake of my head. "Whiskey?"

"Gin, if you've got it."

I've got everything, and she damn well knows it.

"You're sent to bring back a Mortal princess and you show up with a host of them? Just to force them into a Conclave with the Fae? It hardly seems fair to those girls."

That thought had been sitting heavily on me lately.

I'd sentenced those five women to death. They'd never stood a chance. Huntyr survived this long because she'd been trained for this, honed into a weapon since she was five summers old.

The other women were just fodder, whom I destroyed in my misguided attempt at vengeance.

I hand her a glass, the gin filling nearly half of it, and she scoffs as if it's not quite enough for her.

"I had my reasons at the time."

"And now?" Ulna lifts her brows, as if she already knows the answer.

I sink heavily into the chair opposite her, running my hands over my face. "Now, I think I regret it."

She's quiet, letting me sit with that admission, that realization. She lets me fester in it until I down my own glass and drop it heavily onto the table beside me.

It's my second of the morning, and it is doing absolutely nothing to calm my nerves.

"Taric tells me you seem fond of the Mortal girl." Her voice is soft, inviting, offering me the space to talk through whatever I need to. She's offering me the opportunity to come to terms with what I'm about to witness.

My mouth is locked shut, though, my jaw tight. Even if I want to open up to her, I'm not sure I can. I'm not sure I can let myself articulate the raging storm that is building inside me.

"It will be difficult," she warns me, setting her own glass aside and folding her hands in her lap. "In my five hundred years, I have watched two Conclaves besides my own. The final trial is always the worst. The competitors become ruthless. It's a bloody fight to the death, and the crowd will feed off of it. They will expect *you* to enjoy the show."

"What if I can't?"

She meets my eyes, her gaze a mixture of understanding and sympathy. "You will know when it's about to happen. You will close your eyes for that brief moment. Let your magic reach out to her so that you're there with her in her final breath, and then you say or do whatever you need to until you are back in the privacy of this room."

I stand suddenly, my strength pushing back the chair behind me. Ulna flinches slightly but keeps those hands calmly folded, her position neutral even as I begin pacing, even as my magic stirs inside me.

She speaks as if it's that simple, as if she has any real insight. She was in love with Taric the moment she saw him, and there was never any doubt that he would win. She has no idea what *this* is like.

She has no idea what it feels like to have your every instinct draw you to protect a woman, despite the fact that you know she's about to be slaughtered, and there's nothing you can do about it.

"Roland asked me to speak to you about what happens afterwards. He says you've refused to have that conversation with him."

I scoff. So that's the real reason she's here. Not just a visit from my favorite aunt, but an official matter. "I'll deal with that when it's over."

"People will look to *you*, Derian. You called this Conclave. You made that choice. Now, it's your responsibility to uphold its traditions as every warrior in our family has done since the creation of the Fae."

Her voice is sharp, snapping out like a whip and not leaving any room for negotiation. And even though I know she's right, even though I know that I have to be prepared for the next steps, I can't bring myself to focus on it, not when half of my mind is still somewhere else—with *someone* else.

"There will be a memorial for the fallen competitors," she explains. "Both you and your betrothed will be expected to make offerings."

"Fine," I mutter, pulling my chair back to its normal position and returning to my seat.

"Typically, the wedding is held in Bridgemond, but ultimately that is your choice."

No, not there. After all this, that cold castle—which holds nothing for me but sour memories—is the last place I want to go.

"My house in Springhallow. That will do."

Distaste colors her features, but she nods ever so slightly.

"Then there is the matter of the favor."

Gods, I'd nearly forgotten about that. Forgotten that whoever won would have the ability to demand whatever they wanted of me.

"Do not allow her to ask for the favor until you are prepared to give it to her."

My brow furrows. "Why? What do you mean?"

She sighs. "The favor is a powerful magic. Almost primal. Those who came before me described it as being nearly as powerful as a mating bond. When she demands it of you, you will think of nothing else, *want* nothing else, until it's done. Everything else will stop being important to you."

I let the words settle over me. Let their meaning echo through my head. "You're telling me that the favor will draw me away from here and I will be powerless to stop it?"

She nods, brown eyes tracing over me. "It could, if that's what your bride demands of you."

Which means that if Luceron is still here, I'll be leaving him undefended far too close to the Wastelands.

I can't do that.

So whatever favor my bride wants is going to have to wait until Luceron returns to Bridgemond.

I hear the distinct sound of Cal's heavy footsteps traveling down the hallway, and every muscle in me tenses. The dead heart inside my chest clenches.

"Good to see you, Caldren," Ulna greets him, looking over my shoulder.

I don't bother to look back at him.

"It's time," he says, his voice measured and quiet. It's filled with the same sympathy as Ulna's voice.

Pity. They pity me.

I stand and Ulna follows me, taking my face in her hands and forcing me to look down at her. "Remember what I told you."

Her advice is good, well-thought out, and appropriate.

I can't do it, though.

"I won't close my eyes," I tell her. "She wouldn't want me to. She would want me to watch every minute just as I would for any other warrior's death."

Huntyr

R hen doesn't say a word to me as he walks me to the arena. It's good that he's the one walking me in. Over these past few weeks, training for the trials, he's become somewhat of a... friend.

As much as I can befriend a Fae, at least.

I've become somewhat comfortable in his presence. In the training yard, he's the one who's spent hours taking the time to teach me the proper way to handle weapons and take down enemies. I hadn't necessarily needed the lessons, but I appreciated his patience nonetheless. And outside of the yard, at dinners or in the halls of the fortress, his smiles have always come easily, almost constantly joined with a teasing greeting.

Which makes his silence now all the more uncomfortable.

"What?" I goad, sending him a grin I don't feel. "No heartfelt good-byes?"

I can't let myself think about what's about to happen.

In these final moments before I step into the arena and face what awaits me inside, I need the distraction. I need someone to engage in a sparring match of wits with me.

The kind of push and pull I have with Derian.

I don't have the Fae prince with me now, though. I have Rhen.

And Rhen doesn't seem to want to play along.

He just looks at me with a small smile that looks uncomfortably like a grimace. "It's been a pleasure getting to know you, Huntyr. You have fought well."

Such finality.

My gut clenches unhappily.

He doesn't believe I'm going to live.

No one thinks I'm going to live.

Not even Derian.

He'd looked me right in the eyes last night, gave me every bit of advice he had to give, and still walked away with what seemed to be dread in his eyes. He'd walked away with his shoulders slumped, and the thunder had echoed on for hours afterwards.

I know my odds. I'm smart enough to realize when the outcome of a situation doesn't look promising. Still though, it would be nice for at least *one* person to have a little faith in me.

"Do you think I'm going to die?" I ask Kaia. She's already gone ahead to the arena after announcing she wanted to be sure she was close enough to strike Mara or Seraphina if they attacked before the start of the trial.

"I think it would be a terrible shame to have waited hundreds of years to bond again just for you to die so quickly."

"That's not a vote of confidence."

"My confidence in you is meaningless. It is you who must believe in your own capabilities."

Right.

I could do that.

Kristona taught me dozens of ways to kill. He'd taught me every pain point in the body. He'd trained me to withstand any injury.

I've made it this far. The least I can promise myself, after all these years of pain and darkness, is to not surrender without a fight. I will not allow myself to bleed without taking a piece of flesh myself.

The roar of the crowd reaches us even before we reach the arena. As we pass under the stone archway that leads onto the competition floor, I almost see it shaking above us.

My blood echoes that tremor, sparking to life in anticipation as I prepare to step through to the killing field.

Rhen grabs hold of my wrist, pulling me back.

"Prepare yourself," he warns me, looking over my shoulder into the arena. "Once you step inside, the trial begins. You will not be able to leave until only one of you remains."

"It was a pleasure knowing you, too," I say to him with the smallest of smiles that I manage to muster. "Do me a favor and don't bet against me."

There are obviously wagers happening on this trial.

And yet I pause, tilting my head as I think. "Or if you do, just do me a favor and don't bet on me being the first to die. I suppose you deserve to get a *little* money out of it."

He gives me one of those easy grins. "Get in there, smart ass."

He takes a few steps back, and I know he's been instructed not to leave until he sees me step forward. I wonder if anyone else has stood at this threshold, regretting their choices before trying to make a break for it.

"You do not run," Kaia purrs in my mind. *"You are the Huntress of Velia, the noble-born assassin that strikes fear in the hearts of Mortals across the*

kingdoms. You do not run. You do not cower. You will look your fear in the eyes and not tremble before it, just as you did the day I chose you."

I'd done that the day I jumped from the window of my childhood bedroom into the dark of night.

Done it when I stared up at Kristona and asked him to make me a killer.

Done it when I'd faced the Fae prince and agreed to come here without a fight.

And yes, I'd done it when I had met Kaia.

I can do it again now.

I breathe deeply, pull the twin daggers from my belt, roll my neck, and take two steps forward, walking through that stone archway into the arena for one final time.

The sun is blinding when I step inside, and I raise my hand instinctively to shield my eyes as they adjust. It's swelteringly hot, the air pressing against the leather on my skin oppressively. This world, through whatever Fae magic inhabits the space, is an entirely different climate than the one I'd been in just a few steps before.

I look around me, taking in my surroundings, doing everything I can to ignore the chants and jeers from the crowd. I don't even bother looking up at them. I can't afford to be distracted.

The arena is filled with uneven stones, tiny mountain peaks of dark stone covering the entire space. Between the rocks, red liquid flows, steam rising slowly from it. Along the ground under the mountainous boulders, large obsidian spikes stick up at jagged angles.

It would only take one bad fall from those rocks and the spikes would kill me without Seraphina and Mara even having to lift a finger.

Wait—

Lava rolling down the rock.

And metal rising from the ground.

In an arena where a fire-wielder and a metal-wielder are to fight to the death.

The arena is devised after the powers of the remaining Fae.

And here I am.

Just a Mortal girl with my daggers.

Not even deemed important enough for any of this arena to reflect me.

Well that's... rude.

I strip off my leather jacket, not wanting it to impede my movements if it sticks to my slick, sweat-covered body. Then I adjust the sword on my back, and leave the jacket at my feet. The feeling of the weapons strapped to my body, their weight, is a precious familiarity.

I'm Huntyr Lachlan, the noble-born assassin, I remind myself over and over.

I have lived through far worse monstrosities than the two spoiled Fae, who have relied on their magic more than their brains.

I invite that frozen iciness into me. Let it spread through my body, hardening everything it touches. I let the cold spirit of death fill me just as I have a million times before, and I welcome its embrace like that of an old friend.

I become a shadow, a ghost, a killer.

I become the Huntress.

And then I go hunting.

The plan had come to me in the middle of the night. After spending hours tossing and turning, puzzling over the advice Derian had left me with, it came to me in a sudden flash of awareness.

Kaia had purred her approval, proclaiming that it was one of the few moments since we'd bonded that she felt impressed with me.

Which was... a backhanded compliment, but I took it anyway.

I spent the entirety of the morning planning every single minute detail, thinking through every contingency and possibility. Calculating. Scheming. Planning.

That was what I was good at.

I start walking, inspecting the rocks for small purchases that I can tuck my hands and feet into. And I climb. Higher and higher, ignoring the moments I slip and have to claw into the stone to steady myself, and the moments when the impossibly hot stones burn or tear my skin.

Kristona's lessons echo in my mind. Pain is nothing. Pain is manageable. Pain's only purpose is to spur you on.

I climb up and up, impossibly high. Until I'm high enough that I have to blink rapidly in the bright sunlight. Until I'm panting and my biceps are straining. Until I can look out and see *everything*.

And finally, I allow myself to take it all in.

The stands are filled to the brim with Fae, packed so tightly that they're nearly falling over the railings into the arena themselves. The roar of their shouting is almost deafening, nearly impossible to parse out their words amidst the ring of it all.

I hear enough, though.

I hear the laughter. The mocking.

Die, Mortal.

Run, little Mortal.

Burn, bitch.

When my eyes finally lock onto their target, I know without question that the sudden brush of cool air against me is no accident. His eyes are wide, his lips pinched tightly. He leans forward, clutching onto the railing like his life depends on it. Like my life depends on it.

Die, Mortal.

Run, little Mortal.

Burn, bitch.

I let every single insult fuel the beast inside of me.

And without breaking eye contact with Derian, I rest the palm of my left hand on the pommel of my dagger and lift my right hand high into the air, giving the entirety of the arena my middle finger.

Even at this distance, I can see him crack the smallest of smiles, and the heaviness in my chest lightens marginally.

The crowd fades out then, my attention shifting to the ground of the arena, tracking over the space quickly.

Seraphina is several leagues away from me, trying to pick her way through what appears to be a net made of chain mail. Mara, on the other hand, is only a few boulders down to my left, searching carefully.

If I overshoot her path, I can land right in front of her.

Time to test out this reckless little plan of mine.

I take off at a sprint, leaping across the gaps in the rock, keeping one eye on the path in front of me and one on my target. When I reach the right angle, I lower myself into a crouch, rubbing my hand across my sweat-slicked brow. I unsheathe the sword from my back carefully, quietly, and leave it tucked between the two boulders I shelter behind. I take a single steadying breath, bracing my arms on the stone under me, and throw my legs over, heavily landing in a crouch.

When I lift my eyes, I meet the gaze of Mara, and I know she doesn't fully recognize me, not really.

She pauses, stepping back, thrown off by the hardness of my gaze, the wickedness there.

The monster that lives within my Mortal shell.

She regains her footing. "You must really have a death wish, don't you?"

I let that wickedness pepper the grin I give her as I push off the ground and stand to my full height. "I think the words you're looking for are 'thank you'."

Mara sneers, shifting her feet apart into a more balanced position. "What in all of the Ever Realm should I be thanking you for?"

I purposefully kick one ankle up over the other and lean back against the rock behind me, a picture of relaxation. An easy target.

"Do you need me to spell it out for you?" I mock. "Boy, they really don't teach much at Fae schools, do they?"

Her brows lower. Her lips twitch. There's the slightest scent of Fae magic in the air.

"Repeat after me," I continue. "'Thank you, Huntyr, for stopping the big scary prince from slicing my head off last night when I very immaturely stole you from your bed because I was too afraid to actually face the Conclave like a true warrior'."

Mara hisses just as a gust of wind brushes sharply against me, blowing back my hair.

No time to think about that, though.

I've set my trap.

The blades strapped on my hips, my thighs, in my boots, tear free of their sheaths, flying to join Mara's own daggers, already assembled in the air around her.

"You talk too much," she growls.

And the first blade flies.

Then the second.

Then the third.

Quick, precise strikes. One at a time, because she has to focus on her aim. Still, she's fast enough between throws that it takes every ounce of my skill and experience to duck and swerve out of the way. I hiss sharply when a blade catches the front of my thigh and slices through leather and skin. Still, I go on. Even when the blades that fall return to her. I continue dodging.

"Are you even *trying* to hit me?" I tease, keeping my position carefully close to the boulder at my back.

The wind blows against me again, as if to question what I'm doing.

"You can't dodge forever!" she shouts, her voice thick with anger.

"Not forever, just until you tire yourself out."

The daggers are dragging themselves across the ground. Not floating through the air. She's already weakening. It took less time than I'd expected.

I just need to egg her on a *little* more.

"You know, maybe your power is so rare because it's kind of pointless."

Her eyes flare in rage. "What did you just say to me?"

"You're not a fighter. Not a warrior. You just throw sharp things and hope they land. You're a glorified knife thrower. It's a party trick, really. In the Mortal kingdoms, you could make an incredible living in one of those traveling circuses."

She snaps. I feel it in the way Fae magic crackles through the air. See it in the way her hands flex.

The blades lift off the ground, four of them at once. Lifting. Pointing at me.

I scan over them. Track them. Map them.

They fly at once towards me.

My heart is in my stomach as I bend backwards.

As I twist above myself.

As my hand *catches* one of those knives and throws it right back in the direction it came from.

She gasps.

No cry or scream of pain. Just a gasp as she looks down at it in shock, as if she genuinely can't believe I got lucky enough to actually hurt her.

It hadn't been luck that had driven my blade home, though.

In fact, that particular blow had been the first thing I planned out.

The dagger now stuck out of her abdomen, right through her stomach, giving her a rather precise injury. A fatal wound, but not one that promised an immediate death. The kind of wound Mara liked to inflict on her victims.

She lurches forward with a growl, running at full speed for me, pushed forward by absolute, blinding rage.

It never once crosses her mind to consider there might be another weapon hidden out of sight. She never considers the option that I might have realized she would strip me of my daggers and leave me defenseless.

She didn't think ahead, just like I knew she wouldn't.

My fingers wrap around the sword hidden behind the rocks, and I bring it down in a clear arc, cleaving her from shoulder to hip as her blood sprays across my face.

Mara falls.

She drops heavily to the ground at my feet.

There's the smallest of tugs at the sword clutched in my hand, and I almost laugh at her feeble attempt to use her magic while she lays gurgling at my feet. As if that would save her now.

"I made a promise to someone," I say, staring down at her as coldness flows through me. I picture Jeseina as I lift my blade once more. Even now, I hear the desperate gasps of air the Mortal woman had struggled to take before asking me to help her, and I let them play on repeat in my mind. "I keep my promises."

When I finally walk away from the small clearing where our fight had culminated, her blood isn't just splattered across my face. It's heavy in my hair, covering the metal of my sword, smeared down my bare arms.

Jeseina got her revenge.

HUNTYR

Under the unforgiving sun, the blood on my skin dries quickly. I lost the ribbon that had been holding back my hair somewhere along the rocks, and now it falls in heavy, damp strands over my shoulders, wet with equal parts of sweat and blood. The sound of my own breathing seems to echo now that the crowd has quieted as I move through the treacherous landscape of the arena.

I wonder what they see when they look at me.

The Mortal girl, whose face is unfeeling. Trampling through a pit of danger, wearing black leather, covered in Fae blood, with only a sword strapped to her back.

Walking directly towards the Fae woman they have all expected to win from the day she entered this damned competition.

I suppose it's appropriate that it's only she and I left. The strongest of the Fae against the most ruthless of the Mortals.

Seraphina's back is to me as I approach her.

She's trying to find a purchase in the rocks, to climb like I did earlier, but the stone is smoother here, not as forgiving.

Some warrior she must be if she doesn't even realize I'm standing right behind her. Watching. Waiting.

Running through my plan once more.

"The Fae have a rather sensitive sense of smell, isn't that right?"

She whirls around, dark eyes locking on me. My grin spreads when her eyes widen as she takes in the sight of me, as she sees the story the blood on my body tells. A story of victory.

"I'm kind of wondering." I reach over my shoulder, pulling my sword free and twirling it at the ready. "What do *I* smell like, Seraphina?"

Time seems to stop for a moment. The crowd is silent. The air is still. There's only her and I.

Seraphina's eyes narrow as she tilts her head to the side, red hair falling over her shoulders, before her nostrils flare and she takes a slow, deep inhale.

There's confusion in her expression, then understanding, then rage.

Because she's smelling *him*. His scent on me. In me.

And even if I am to die here, at least I'll have that small victory. Seraphina will get to spend the rest of her very long life knowing her husband was in my bed the night before she won the Conclave.

I'm almost surprised when she doesn't act right away, but she takes her time shifting her weight before stilling, and she smiles a bit before her hands light up in twin flames.

"Even so, he can't save you now."

I almost expect the sound of rolling thunder at that, but there's still that eerie silence around us. "I wouldn't want him to. I don't let others fight my battles."

She takes a small step forward, her moves calculated. "Do you really think that because you bested Mara, you stand a chance against *me*?"

She laughs, the sound twisted and arrogant, curling around me like an oily film. I swallow my disgust and let her continue. I let her talk her fill.

All part of the plan.

What's Seraphina's weakness?

She's impulsive. Since the day I met her, it's been easy to taunt her into anger. Then, she acts.

Her fire is obviously deadly, but she relies on it so much that she's not as good at hand-to-hand.

I just have to goad her into fighting me with fists instead of fire, and then hope to whatever Gods exist that I can hold my own against her Fae strength.

Seraphina sighs, flames still dancing around her fingertips. Aside from some dirt on her brow, she looks as polished as ever, hardly even a bead of sweat on her pale skin. No fear. No exhaustion. Nothing but that certainty in her eyes.

"I'm going to go down in history," she tells me. "You will be a body that no one will remember, and I will be a name that lives on in every history book."

Tension builds in my gut. She's too calm. Too self-assured. This isn't going to work unless I can get her to lose her temper.

"One person will remember me, Seraphina," I remind her, twirling my sword once more. "He'll remember how he roared *my* name every time he pretends to enjoy fucking you."

Her snarl echoes around me, the flames licking her palms morphing into balls of fire that she launches at me in quick procession. Adopting the same strategy that worked earlier, I dodge, duck, and jump. I move my body however necessary to avoid those flames.

Seraphina's aim is far better than Mara's, though, and she's damn fast.

One of those balls of fire licks across my forearm and I scream—a raw, guttural sound of pain—as my flesh singes with white-hot pain. *Unbearable* pain.

Not just fire.

Fae fire.

Well, fuck me.

No one told me she could wield Fae fire.

Hotter, brighter, harder to extinguish. It burns faster and hurts far worse. I didn't think there were any Fae left who could wield it. Every piece of legend I've heard said wielders who could summon it nearly always ended up dead because of its impossibility to control.

I guess it does make sense that Seraphina would be too stubborn to be killed by her own magic.

"Hurts, doesn't it?" she teases in a lilting tone, enjoying the sight of me grasping onto my arm.

Yes. It hurts.

No amount of brutality from Kristona had prepared me for *this* pain.

Still, I breathe through it. I only have one chance of living through this.

I conjure every bit of bravado I possess. Replace all my fear with the haughty attitude that's gotten me this far in life. "I'm not surprised that's how you choose to attack. I kind of expected you to take the easy way out."

Her face turns contemplative as she prowls towards me, her steps slow and measured. Lazy even, like she has all the time in the world. Like she's a cat and I'm the mouse she's happily batting around.

"You're right, killing you will be easy."

Gods, do I have to explain everything to her?

I sigh. "I meant your magic, dumbass. It's impressive, I'll admit."

She takes a few steps closer. Every instinct in me is screaming to step back, to maintain space between me and the Fae who's staring at me like a meal, but I stay put.

"I don't need your compliments," she says, her voice more like a growl.

"I didn't know about the Fae fire." The pain is like an infection, climbing up my arm. I'm damn lucky she hit my non-dominant arm. There's no way I would be able to wield a blade through this. "Being able to wield that probably does make you one of the strongest Fae of your generation."

She gives me a gentle shake of her head, lips quirking into a small smile. "Nice of you to agree that I deserve to win, Mortal."

"See, the thing is, though—" I scratch a finger against my temple. "When that magic runs out, when you're in battle and you've exhausted it, how will you defend yourself then?"

She stops walking.

Tilts her head at me.

Once again, time seems to stop, only this time my blood runs absolutely icy.

She smiles. Not an angry, impulsive grin. Not a snarl of frustration.

A knowing, lazy, pitying kind of smile.

I recognize it as the one I gave Froggy all those weeks ago before I ended his life.

It's the kind of smile that happens when you know your target is about to realize that their time has run out. The kind of smile that promises death as an inevitability.

I've never been on the receiving end of that kind of expression.

But Seraphina knows what I'm doing. She's figured out that I'm trying to bait her into a magic-free fight. And as that realization settles over her, so does my realization that I made a dangerous miscalculation.

She's going to give me the fight I wanted, because I'm not the only one who's been hiding my skills in the training yard.

The flames on her hands flicker out, and she lurches forward, faster than I've *ever* seen her do at training. She's several feet away one moment and in front of me the next.

She's taller than me.

That's the only thought that runs through my mind.

I've never stood close enough to her to actually notice the difference, but she's got at least an inch or two on me.

Then, she pulls back her arm and smashes her fist into my jaw, pouring all that anger, hatred, and unfair Fae strength into that one single blow.

Pain shoots through me, blooming from face down to my neck and back. My head snaps backward wildly before my body does, the jerk so strong that my spine protests.

I at least have the good sense to drop the sword before the world tilts sideways, before I tip over.

Then, my vision blacks out.

———◆◇◆———

There's a drop on my cheek. Then another. Tiny drips of water falling steadily onto my face.

Another.

Then another.

For a moment, I'm not quite sure where I am, *who* I am, but then Seraphina's boot slams into my stomach, and I'm thrown back so hard that my left side slams into a boulder. I come back to awareness.

"Get up," Kaia growls in my ears. *"You must get up."*

If only it was that easy. My head is spinning, the ground unsteady beneath me, but I roll onto my good side and push, kneeling first to steady myself before rising and attempting to settle myself into my stance.

It's a fight.

Just like any other fight.

I can do this.

The rain begins tumbling down, but I hardly notice as I meet her gaze once more.

There's no mercy on her face. No mirth or taunting remains. This is Seraphina in her most brutal, unfeeling form. She has her own Huntress, I realize.

She lunges suddenly. Her right foot pivots, weight shifting forward as her left hand fires off for a quick jab, and I react instinctively, dodging left and slamming my fist into her gut.

The bitch just laughs. "I don't *need* fire to stomp out Mortal trash. It's just more fun that way."

Another brutal kick to my stomach, knocking all air from my lungs.

We go like that for a few rounds, a healthy rotation where each of us manages small hits and jabs to the other. Like a game.

Because that's all this is to her.

A game.

I give everything I have to the dance, feeling fleeting moments of satisfaction when I manage to land blows to her kidneys and jawline. It seems to last forever, an endless cycle of giving and receiving. And throughout it all she hardly tires, there's still not the slightest indication of sweat on her.

That might be what bothers me most.

I'm dripping with it, and the fire-wielder looks as perfect as ever.

When her brows lift half a centimeter and her eyes sparkle just a bit, I know she's tired of the game.

And then she really attacks.

Her right hook swings wide, catching the other side of my jaw. My head snaps sideways, pain flaring along my cheekbone, and I stumble back, struggling to keep my balance as my muscles take on the weight of exhaustion. The tangy taste of blood bursts inside my mouth, nearly choking me.

There's no time to fall, though. I barely manage to get my guard back up before Seraphina is on me again.

She'd been masterful in the training yard. It had taken me some time watching her to start to pick out the few ways she might be vulnerable during hand-to-hand, but this version of Seraphina was not the one who had shown up to the fortress courtyard.

This version is impossibly more skilled and deadly than how she'd portrayed herself before.

The Fae presses forward, and her elbow drives towards my ribs. I throw down my forearm to block it, but the force sends a sharp jolt of pain up my arm, an arm already mangled from Fae fire. The pain is all I can see, feel, *think* about.

My legs tremble, ready to give out.

Her knee slams into my stomach, and a groan explodes from my lungs.

It hurts. More than I ever expected it to.

I hold my stance, though. I lock my knees.

Seraphina's fingers lock onto my shoulder and she *pulls* me right into her uppercut. Stars burst in my vision. Nausea rolls through my stomach. My pulse pounds like a steady beat in my ears, almost drowning out the violent roar of thunder.

A sharp stomp to the back of my calf.

I don't want to go down.

I don't want to lose.

I don't want to die.

But my leg buckles.

The ground comes towards me too quickly, and I feel my cheek split open along the dirt as I hit down hard on the rocks. I'm shaking, blood is coating my tongue, and I spit it out as I desperately try to rise.

"Where's your talk of Derian now?" she taunts me, stalking to where my own sword is discarded on the ground. With a wicked grin, she lifts it, testing the weight in her hands. "Don't you want to tell me how special you are to him? So special, in fact, that he's just sitting up there watching you bleed out?"

I push onto my elbows, using every ounce of my strength to hold my shaking body upright. I will *not* let her stab me while I lie helpless on the ground.

"No? How about I tell you a story then?" Seraphina comes to me, the steps of her boots heavy beats against the ground. She lifts my sword, using the tip of it to brush my hair back over my shoulder. The rain is falling heavier now, not enough to wash away the blood staining my body, but enough to cool the fire in my blood.

"When I told Derian I was entering the Conclave, I told him I would remind every last Mortal of where they belong." She kneels in front of me, and her dark eyes are practically glowing, alight with the fire she controls so easily. "I told him I'd leave you all dead on the ground at my feet. I'm *so* glad you're the one that's going to make that promise come true."

Through some impossible final burst of speed or strength, or maybe even foresight, I lift my hands just in time to catch the steel as it careens towards my throat.

The force sends me falling backward again. The sharpened edge of the sword, the edge I'd sharpened *myself* hours ago, slices through my hands and I scream.

I scream louder than I ever have before.

She's growling above me, pushing the blade down, closer and closer to my throat, and then the blade is warming under my touch, the metal burning my skin so intensely that I think that maybe I've never known true pain until this very moment.

Lightning cracks only a few feet from us, and yet neither of us turn away.

"HUNTYR!" Kaia's voice snaps in my mind for a moment before all I can hear is her roar echoing through the arena.

I've pictured my death before. In my line of business, it's hard not to imagine it from time to time. I never quite pictured it like this, though.

I wonder what my father would think about this. I wonder how he would have felt about his little girl, who he used to read to sleep every night, having followed the threads of fate to become this person, to die like this.

No vengeance in his name.

No justice for what was done to him.

Just my death at the hands of a Fae.

Just like him.

And Tyla, too. My death will inevitably cause hers. Without that tonic she won't have long. She'll be just another victim in the broken story of my existence.

She doesn't even know I'm here. Will Derian and Roland tell the Mortal Kingdoms of my death? How will that news eventually spread to our tiny apartment? My heart breaks for Tyla, for the moment that she'll have to receive that news, the news that I'm gone and she's utterly alone.

She doesn't deserve that.

But maybe…

Maybe I do deserve this.

These wretched hands that have ended so many lives deserve to be cut apart. This throat that has laughed at the pain of my victims deserves to be slit. Perhaps, this was always meant to be my fate. I let my soul turn so black with hatred that the very source of my fury is to be the one to deliver my punishment.

I deserve this.

A small, choked sound escapes me, and my fingers tremble, unable to hold on much longer.

There's roaring in my ears, Kaia's, filled with pain and anger and defiance.

The thunder cracks over my head, louder than I've ever heard before.

Seraphina pushes harder, her eyes glazed over with bloodlust, and just as I'm about to lose my grip, acceptance crashes over me, *through* me. The kind of clarity I've seen on so many faces before I take a life.

"Just give in," she hisses. "You have nothing to live for anyway!"

But I do, I think to myself suddenly.

Just as I'm about to release my grip on the sword, Seraphina's words fall over me like a heavy weight, and I just know, deep inside, how truly wrong they are.

I might deserve death, but I *do* have things to live for.

Kaia.

Tyla.

Even Derian.

And... myself. I have to live for myself.

Because the little girl inside of me, the one who had been thrown onto the streets as a child, deserves to experience something more than just the brutality I've embraced.

I have to keep going. I have to keep fighting. I'm Huntyr fucking Lachlan. I'm the Huntress.

And I'm going down fighting until the very end, no matter the odds.

I scream as I push back against the sword and thrash my legs. The sound is raw, filled with a lifetime of traumas that have all led to this very moment.

Fire snakes sharply down my spine, a heat that's a living thing, trailing through me in an electric burst. It sparks through every part of my body until I'm barely in control of my own movements. I'm nothing but that burning energy, until, with a roar of pain and anger, my hands explode into a glorious golden light.

Seraphina flies backward, her surprised scream echoing as she's blasted back several feet by the rush of that strange light, and all I can do is stare at my hands, at the way they still glow with that beautiful sheen.

I can still feel it, like a rush responding with every inhale and exhale of my lungs.

What did I do?

What did I just do?

She's still screaming, the shrieking sound piercing the silence as she rises to her feet. She rubs at her eyes, blinking rapidly, like children do when they stare too long at the sun.

And even though I have no explanation for what just happened, I don't have the time to ponder it.

This fight isn't over.

I rip my useless, beaten body up from where it had surrendered, and despite the agonizing pain, despite the utter exhaustion of both my body and my heart, I crawl forward, scraping my bleeding hands through the dirt as I pull myself forward.

Towards my sword.

Seraphina is still blinking and dazed when I manage to wrap my hands around it.

Her hands light up into flames as I step forward, those orange flickers climbing to her shoulders, but I'm not afraid of them now. I don't feel any pain anymore.

When I throw my weight into swinging that sword, slicing it across the soft skin of her throat, I let out a battle cry filled with such agony that I hardly even recognize it as my own voice.

Her body crumples before me.

Her flames flicker out.

The arena is silent, like they're all holding their breath with me.

And then a guttural sob pours out of me as I fall to my knees.

PART TWO

THE RECKONING

35

Huntyr

They look like my hands.

They feel like my hands.

But they can't be.

Because I'm a Mortal.

And Mortals don't have magic.

But for that brief moment, *I* did. It poured out of me from some deep place in my soul that I didn't even know existed.

Now I just stare at them, as if I'm waiting for them to light up and change my life again.

I hear the pounding of Kaia's paws before she launches herself onto me, nuzzling into my neck, and I don't stop myself from wrapping my arms around her and unleashing my sobs into her fur.

I did it.

I won.

I have no idea *how* I did it, but I'm alive. I'm still alive.

"It is not over," Kaia says softly to me.

My pulse rushes again, stiffening. What does that mean? What else are they going to do to me?

"The prince speaks."

I don't even have to look for him. My eyes lock onto him the second I lift my head.

The crowd is riotous. Some are sobbing. Some are red-faced and shouting.

They're all looking at me.

With awe.

With hatred.

With something that might be fear.

"Anyone moves against her," Derian's voice rings out clearly despite the thunderous roar of the crowd. He must be using some kind of Fae magic to amplify his words. "And it will be considered a direct move against me."

There's a beat of silence, a noticeable shift moving through the audience as their prince makes a decree.

He doesn't notice.

Because he's running.

Down the stairs from his viewing box, all the way to the railing that separates the stands from the arena floor. He doesn't slow when he comes to the railing, he simply throws his legs over it, and then he's stalking towards me.

I'm distantly aware of Roland and Caldren, following behind him. Even more distantly aware that while his words might have stilled the crowd, they didn't cease their rumblings of discontent.

But neither of those facts seem to matter at all when Derian's attention is locked so fully on me.

He kneels before Kaia and I, reaching for me.

But it's not his hands I see.

I see fire, and blood, and violence.

I see another Fae hand with the capability of pain.

Kaia snarls at him when I flinch, and he pulls his hand back, meeting her golden eyes straight on, no trace of fear in sight.

"Let me help her," he says softly to the Eshari. She stares at him, reading him, before lowering her head in agreement. He turns back to me. "Let me help you, Huntress."

Kaia backs away, allowing him to move another few inches in my direction, still keeping her ears folded back and her teeth exposed.

"Please." He holds his hand out towards me. His dark eyes stare into mine.

I feel frozen, stuck.

Nothing makes sense anymore.

Maybe it never did.

"Huntyr," Kaia speaks differently, too. Softer, gentler. Carefully. *"You must trust the prince."*

"I... can't."

She stares at me.

She knows why.

"Then at least, for now, allow him to care for you. It is all he wants to do."

Moving my neck to face him again sends waves of agony shooting down my spine. He hasn't moved, hasn't breathed. He's still just sitting there with his hand outstretched, begging me with his eyes to take it. I force air into my lungs and I place my hand in his, letting him pull me to my feet.

He gives me a moment to steady myself, even when that means I end up having to lean heavily on him. And while I'm trying to figure out how to breathe, he just stares at me. His eyes trace across my face, over and over again, like he's memorizing every inch of me. Then he lifts a hand and brushes back the matted hair from my forehead, his touch cool against my fevered flesh.

And then he's kissing me.

In front of everyone, in front of the entire crowd, Derian is kissing me. He's so gentle, so careful of every cut and bruise. It's so unexpected and *soothing* that I want to start crying all over again.

And I do.

He pulls back, carefully brushing away my tears with the pads of his thumbs.

A throat clears behind us, but he doesn't bother looking away from me.

"I would suggest we clear out sooner rather than later. I'm not interested in testing out mob mentality."

Caldren. That's Caldren's voice.

"We can take her to the healers, your majesty."

I seek out that voice. Rhen. I know Rhen. Rhen is my friend.

He's standing to our left. When I meet his gaze, he smiles softly and steps towards me.

No.

Rhen is a Fae.

The Fae did this to me.

The Fae broke me like this.

I flinch backwards and only Derian's grip on my waist keeps me from tumbling.

"Hey." He pulls my attention back to him with a gentle tap under my chin. Derian stares at me with those brown eyes that block out everything else and I find myself stilling again, leaning into his touch.

"You are alive," he reminds me.

I am alive.

"You survived."

I survived.

"You are safe now."

Safe.

No, I don't feel safe.

I feel raw, ripped apart, and unevenly sewn back together. Seraphina didn't just break my body, she took me to a place that ripped my very heart open and left it bleeding in shreds on the ground.

How is anything about this kingdom or these people safe?

"Huntress." His voice is softer than I've ever heard before, edged with something I don't recognize. "I need you to say something. I need to know the lights are still on inside that head of yours."

Right. I have a voice.

My vocal cords feel raw, ripped apart by screams and sobs, but under that pain is the ability to speak.

"She might be in shock," Derian says over his shoulder.

"And you might be a Fae bastard." I choke out the words, barely recognizing the fragile sound that comes out of me.

His gaze snaps back to me, and it's definitely relief that dances across his face.

He smiles. A real, genuine smile. "I most definitely am."

"Derian, we have to go," Caldren reminds him.

"Can you walk?" Derian asks me. Kaia growls at our feet and he laughs under his breath. "Of course you can."

He keeps my hand locked in his while his other arm wraps around my shoulders, turning me to guide me out of the arena.

It takes me a long time to take those first few steps.

Because everything is different.

It's just flat dirt now. All around us, it's just fucking dirt.

No stones. No spikes or lava.

No bodies or blood splatter.

No evidence of what just happened here.

No indication of what I'd just barely managed to survive.

"I guess I still haven't learned all your secrets quite yet, Huntress," Derian says quietly when I start walking.

I think he's trying to get me to talk again. And maybe I *am* in shock because stringing together enough words to make a sentence seems more impossible than the walk back to my room.

Rhen and Taric move in front of us, and I can feel the presence of others at our back. Parker, Roland, and Caldren most likely. They're surrounding us. Protecting us.

"I don't know how I did it," I whisper, staring down at my hands again.

There's no light anymore. Now, there's just blood, still flowing from the open wounds.

I still don't feel it.

There still isn't any pain.

"We'll figure it out," Derian promises, his hand on my back moving in reassuring circles.

"How?"

"Well." He pauses, sighs, searching for the answer he doesn't have quite yet. "We can start with getting you cleaned up. Then, you can tell me who the fuck your mother was."

DERIAN

"I've never seen a power like that," Cal says in a hushed whisper from where he, Taric, Roland, and I gather in the front parlor of my room, debating what to make of this situation.

Roland's brows lift as he shakes his head as if he, too, doesn't know what to make of it all. "I'm not sure what to tell the King of Velia. Should I be reporting that a Mortal won when she's not..."

"She's not a Fae," Taric reasons. "I've trained her myself. She doesn't have the strength of a Fae."

"Nor the healing abilities," Cal notes, glancing over my shoulder at her.

I can barely focus on the conversation, not when my attention is still stuck on the woman crouched in front of the fireplace. The Eshari's head is in her lap, and she's petting the beast absentmindedly, her shoulders hunched. She's still filthy from the trial.

And she's still barely speaking.

When we walked into the room, I brought her to the hearth, lit a fire, and told her to get warm.

She just sat down without a word of protest or attitude, not even looking at me as she did.

I scrape a hand over my face. "Tell the King she won. Huntyr Lachlan, the Lady of Vastile, won."

Cal levels his eyes on me, heavy with hidden meaning. "You're going to marry *her*?"

He's my best friend.

My most trusted ally.

But damn if I don't get a sudden rush of protectiveness when he says that.

He's right, of course. What happened last night aside, Huntyr Lachlan *was* sent to kill me. I can't just pretend that isn't the case. I can't very well trust her to sleep next to me each night.

"I don't have a choice." I sigh. "The rules of the Conclave are clear."

There's a tense moment of silence that falls over our group as we all collectively look over at her—the woman who looks more like a girl than ever before.

"Maybe we should leave you two alone," Taric suggests.

"Absolutely not," Cal growls.

The former Conclave winner frowns, not understanding Cal's sudden protest, not realizing the truth behind the Mortal woman who fights with more skill than she should. "Maybe he can get some kind of explanation from her before tonight's celebration."

Cal's eyes are on me, silently begging me to disagree. To explain to the two other males *why* I shouldn't be left alone with her.

"Taric's right," I say. "Go. Check the borders. If we're leaving the fort largely undefended for the next week for these celebrations and traditions, I want to know we won't have Velkai knocking down our doors."

He hesitates, waiting even when Roland and Taric bow respectfully and take their leave. Stepping forward, Cal clasps my forearm with his own.

"I hope you know what you're doing," he tells me.

"I'll be fine."

His nostrils flare as he stares at her, and I fight the urge to step to my left just to block his view. "Do *not* let her demand the favor of you."

"Ulna already explained how it works, I don't need you to as well."

His hazel eyes flicker to mine. "Then you should know *exactly* how dangerous this is, Derian. She's an *assassin*. She was sent to kill you. What will you do if the favor she asks of you is to kill your own brother?"

My stomach drops at the possibility. I hadn't even thought far enough ahead to consider that. She wouldn't...

That look on her face when Luceron was mentioned.

The calculation in her eyes.

"I won't hurt my brother," I protest. Fuck whatever magic is in this Conclave. *Nothing* in all of the Ever Realm could ever cause me to lift a hand against Luceron.

"I hope for all our sakes that's true."

Then he's gone, letting the door click closed behind him.

In the moments of silence after they're gone, I let my head fall backwards, closing my eyes and breathing deeply, desperate to ease the tension that's locked my back and shoulders.

She won.

She actually fucking won.

Against all odds. Against all reason.

I had prepared myself. Even as the magic railed against me, forcing itself out of me, I sat there and watched Seraphina beat her within an inch of her life. I practically felt every blow myself. When the killing blow was leveled towards her, though—when I prepared myself to follow my Aunt's instructions and throw my power towards her one last time—she *exploded.*

It was beautiful.

Beautiful. And terrifying. And impossible.

Absolutely impossible.

I walk towards her slowly, careful not to spook her again as I crouch down and put my hand gently on her shoulder. The Eshari glances up without moving her head, but she neither snarls nor tries to bite me, so I'll assume she's still okay with me. At least for now.

"Let's get you cleaned up," I coax Huntyr, noticing that she's still staring at her own blood-crusted hands. "My bathroom is over there. I can help."

She doesn't look back at me. She doesn't speak. She just stands and follows my gentle guidance to the bathroom.

I send magic ahead of us, filling the tub with steaming water for her, but just as we're about to step over the threshold, she halts, heels digging into the wooden floor. Then she stumbles back, looking wildly towards the Eshari, who is right on her heels.

The two stare at each other, somehow communicating without words, and I marvel at it, until I suddenly realize what upset her.

The smell.

"It's my magic," I explain. "You smell the Fae magic, right? It's me. I warmed a bath for you. That's all, I promise."

Huntyr stares at me for a long time, glancing once more at the Eshari before she nods and continues following me in.

The tub is filled with steaming water scented with jasmine. I leave her side to pull sponges and cleansing balms from the cabinets, and by the time

I turn back to her, she's already stripped her clothes, leaving them in a pile on the floor.

Gods, the sight of her.

There must be something wrong with me if the sight of a woman covered in blood instantly hardens me.

Or there's just something about *this* woman.

She stands unabashedly naked, showing nothing but lean muscles and *scars*. I didn't notice how many scars she had last night. Tiny pale divots down her arms and legs. A larger one down the left side of her stomach.

Suddenly, I realize that there's very little I truly know about Huntyr Lachlan.

I know her humor, her smart mouth, her fighting abilities, but I know nothing of her history. I know nothing of the pain that shaped this woman into who she is.

And I want to.

I want to know about every scar. I want to know every story they tell.

I'm just about to ask when she notices my staring and moves forward, lifting her legs and settling herself into the tub of water, hissing as it connects with the various cuts across her body. She leaves her arms out of the water, likely protecting the mangled flesh, scorched by Seraphina's Fae fire.

She watches the water turn red, growing even paler as it does. Impossibly so.

The Eshari sits by the door watching, tail twitching unhappily. She looks at me, as if begging me to do something.

So I do the only thing I can think of. I send another burst of magic and clean the water while I continue gathering supplies.

Huntyr gasps behind me, and my heart skips when I finally hear her voice.

"How do you do it?" she asks, her voice barely more than a rasp after her screams. "The water."

I have to breathe through the discomfort of hearing those cries still echoing in my mind. Keeping my posture as relaxed as possible, I carry the cleansing balms and towels to her. Slowly, holding her gaze so she can track what I'm doing, I lower myself to sit on the edge of the tub and gently take hold of one of her arms. She doesn't react as I turn her hand in mine and examine where the sword dug into her flesh.

It's a nasty wound, tendons and ligaments torn through. Even slivers of bone are visible. She's undoubtedly in shock if she's not writhing in pain. A wound like this would have even battle-hardened Fae fainting and screaming.

"There are certain aspects of magic that are simpler and easier to control," I explain.

With a soft exhale, I send some of that power forward, letting it settle over her palm. She stiffens instantly, even tries to pull away from my grip, but as the wound starts to seal itself back together she stills, watching wide-eyed.

"Every Fae has a unique brand of magic that we wield, but we also have a general connection to power that we can use for certain tasks, like filling tubs or—"

"Healing?"

I pull her arm, extending it fully so that I can spread that magic into the burn on her bicep.

"I'm not the best at this," I admit, focusing intensely on the task in front of me. "But yes, I can do it when I need to."

Huntyr turns away, looking out the window on the other side of the tub, and I know without a doubt that she's about to lock up again. She's about to go silent on me once more, and I simply cannot handle it.

"I can teach you if you want," I offer gently.

Her head snaps back towards me, blue eyes watering. "I am *not* a Fae."

She says the word like a curse.

I try not to be offended as I reach forward and tuck her hair behind an ear that's very obviously not pointed.

"You're also not a Mortal." I reach for the washrag and dip it into the water, smoothing it against her skin, washing away the blood on her collarbone.

Her brow furrows, her expression turning contemplative.

"My mother?" she asks, her voice barely more than a whisper as she thinks back to my previous question.

"Is it possible that she could have been a Fae? That you could be half-Fae?"

She glances at the Eshari again, her eyes locked onto the beast for quite some time. I continue washing away the filth while they talk, trying my hardest to ignore the way my cock twitches as I gently stroke the cloth around her breasts.

"I didn't know her," Huntyr tells me. "She died in childbirth. It was just my father and I. Until he died."

Such pain in her voice. Such raw, utter pain.

More pain than a Mortal girl of only twenty summers should have experienced.

"Dunk," I instruct, setting aside the rag. "Your hair needs to be washed, too."

"I can do it."

"Dunk, Huntress."

There it is. That flash of irritation. A spark in those bright eyes.

Relief flutters in my chest.

She's under the water for only a few seconds before she rises, and I pour the shampoo into my palm before pressing my fingers into her scalp, massaging in subtle circular motions.

A gentle sigh escapes her, so soft I think she might have been trying to fight it.

"Are you going to kill me?" she whispers.

I know what she's thinking. It doesn't surprise me that she's brilliant enough to come to the same conclusion I have.

If this woman is a threat to me, to my brother, to my *kingdom*, then my duty is to remove that threat.

Regardless of whether or not I want to.

"I think," I draw out the words, their weight sitting heavily between us. "We should probably have an honest conversation with one another before there's any more killing. We can start with you telling me why you were at that ball, Huntyr."

She stares straight ahead. Unblinking.

"I want to know why you wanted me dead," I continue. "I want to know why you say the word Fae like it's disgusting."

She goes silent again and this time I don't fight to keep her talking. I let her retreat into that quiet in her mind for as long as she needs it.

I wash her hair.

I wrap her in a towel.

I give her one of my tunics, large enough that it brushes the tops of her thighs.

And when there's nothing left for me to do, I wait for her to finally open up.

But there's just silence.

It's fucking unbearable.

I am not accustomed to people ignoring my requests. When I ask questions, they are answered. When I enter a room, people go out of their way to show me their strength.

Huntyr has never behaved that way, to be fair, but she always meets me with that icy hardness. She always has a retort. She *always* finds a reason to get irritated with me.

And that heavy feeling in my stomach isn't concern for *myself*.

It isn't even concern for my brother or her plans for him.

It's utter fear for her. The longer she remains this shell of herself, the more I'm starting to worry that whatever happened in that arena truly broke my Huntress in a way she won't be able to recover from.

It's not until she's tucked under a quilt on my bed, the panther pressed to her side, with a warm glass of hot cocoa in her hand, that she starts to speak.

And Gods, I hang on to every word like it's the only story that's ever mattered.

"When I was five summers old, I woke in the middle of the night from a storm. I was terrified of storms. The thunder would leave me trembling. So I ran to my father's room, but he didn't answer when I called him.

"And then I felt dampness under my feet, and I knew something was *terribly* wrong. Even as a child, I knew. I went to him, but it was already too late. He'd been killed in his own bed, and left there in the most gruesome, abhorrent way possible.

"My stepmother pulled me out of the room, and she said that the Fae had killed him. Then I heard her say she was going to sell me to one of the Madams in the city. So, I climbed out my window, and ran out into the storm."

I clench my hands, breathing through the anger, both that the woman had done that to a child and that she'd had the audacity to blame the Fae for the death of Huntyr's father.

There's no fucking way that Fae were murdering Mortals in Velia fifteen years ago. We've been very careful to stay within the limits of our own kingdom.

"I spent the next week sleeping under bridges and stealing bread from garbage cans. Then, when I was so hungry I was nearly delirious, I tried to rob some of the merchants. I got thrown out and called a gutter rat. So, I tried picking pockets. I wasn't particularly good at that either, though. One of the men backhanded me so hard I laid on the street crying for hours. No one stopped. No one helped me.

"But I was hungry, and cold, and wet from the storms that refused to stop. So, I got up, and I tried again. The next man didn't hit me, though. He looked at me, and he stared into my soul. He said that I looked just like someone he used to know, and he asked if I knew who he was. I did. I don't remember how, but I knew who Kristona Roschoff was. I knew what he did. I knew I should be afraid of him, but when he tossed me aside and started to walk away, I chased after him.

"I pulled on his coat, and I asked him to take me with him. I asked him to teach me how to kill a Fae."

I listen to every word, entirely captivated, lost in trying to picture her as nothing more than a child, abandoned, desperate for someone to help her, and hungry. There is no feeling more unforgettable than the sensation of a hollow stomach. I know that well enough.

Part of me can't even blame her for her hatred of my kind. What other choice had she been given in life?

She avoids my eyes as she tells her story, hands clutching her mug tightly to hide her trembling.

"So, he took me home," she continues, swatting away a tear. "And I became known as the adopted daughter of the assassin king. Kristona taught me how to fight and how to kill. Those lessons were brutal, painful, and merciless. Sometimes he taught me, sometimes the other acolytes did. Every night, though, he would help me into bed and read me to sleep. Every time it stormed, he sat with me until it was over."

I pull a chair to the foot of the bed, sitting heavily. "He loved you."

She nods. "Yes. He does."

The air between us is charged, almost unbearable. "So, tell me about the ball."

She laughs softly. "The princess was not as innocent as you might think."

"Oh?"

Huntyr looks at me, her brows lifted suggestively in an expression that looks so much like *her* that I almost sag forward.

"The princess had been having a very torrid affair with a nobleman in the Court. As you can imagine, he was not a big fan of yours."

My tongue darts over my lower lip as I lean forward, resting my elbows on my knees. "Because I'm cuter?"

She rolls her eyes, continuing her story. "Kristona's birthday gift to me was the contract. He gave me the job of killing you. I didn't want to do it at first, because I didn't want to step back into that part of my past. I didn't want to be a noblewoman. I didn't want to go by the name of the woman who would have sold me."

"You just wanted to kill me more?" I tease, even as my stomach is tied in knots.

She smiles sadly. "Yes. So, I went to the ball, and I found your room. When the guard walked in, he seemed so comfortable there, and his ears were pointed. I thought he was you. So, I attacked, and he was so much stronger and faster than I ever imagined. I had never lost a fight before that, but all of a sudden he had his hands around my throat, and I knew he was going to kill me."

Her eyes suddenly glaze over as her voice goes distant. Kaia lifts her head, looking at Huntyr, before nuzzling her head against the woman's elbow.

"When the light exploded, I thought he did it. Not me."

It takes every ounce of strength in me to keep my magic in check as my stomach falls and I repeat those words in my head over and over and over.

When the light exploded...

"The arena wasn't the first time it happened?" I ask, my voice impossibly hoarse.

She turns those blue eyes on me. So fucking blue.

"I didn't know. It wasn't possible. It didn't make sense."

"When else?"

She chews on her lip. "I think, maybe, in the second trial too."

I think back. I scan through the memories of that day. The maze. She'd run through the attacking vines and found Mara killing that Mortal girl. Then she'd found Alexandria and...

"Your orb," I whisper. "It was brighter than the others."

She nods.

And suddenly the story is over.

There's nothing more to know. There's no additional answers to be found within her past to help us figure out her present.

Except...

"Your headaches," I muse, scratching at the beginning of a beard on my jawline.

She tilts her head in confusion. "What about them?"

Shit, it was right there the whole time. Right in front of my face.

"You've had them since you were a kid, right?"

I stand, pacing, hands coming to rest atop my head as I do.

"Yes?"

"I told you I got headaches as a boy."

"What exactly is your point?"

The only consolation in me putting the pieces together so slowly is that my delay in answering seems to be annoying her. And the more annoyed she gets, the more she sounds like herself.

"Fae are pack animals, Huntyr. Our magic feeds off of the magic of others. The quickest way to recover from overspending your magic is to simply surround yourself with other Fae. When you're on your own, magic takes more of a toll on you physically. I got headaches because I was banished to an abandoned patch of land to train. They stopped happening once I learned to control my powers and came back around the others. Just like your headaches stopped when—"

"When I came here," she finishes, following my line of thought.

Slowly, so slowly, she takes the mug and sets it on the wooden table by my bed, exchanging silent communication with the Eshari.

"Is it possible?" I ask her. "Is it possible your mother was Fae?"

She frowns. "Did she kill my father?"

It's like she's poured a bucket of ice water over me. I actually stumble back. I hadn't even thought...

Although, I suppose it could be possible...

I run a hand through my hair, pulling at the ends in frustration as I continue my pacing, needing the movement to steady the unease building inside of me.

Kaia rises from the bed and shakes out her coat, glaring at me so violently I almost question what I did to upset the beast.

But then she turns her glare onto Huntyr and stalks right out of the room.

"What was that about?" I question.

Huntyr follows the beast with her eyes and shrugs. "I don't know, but she can be temperamental."

I take it as a good sign. If the Eshari is willing to leave her, then she must be on the road towards mending.

Sure enough, she's sitting up straighter. That furrow forms between her brows, the one that comes whenever she's thinking... or scheming.

"Huntyr—"

"I won," she says it like it's a surprise. Like she's finally come out of the fog and shock, and is thinking clearly for the first time in hours.

I don't know what it is about this woman, but I know her thoughts as clearly as I know my own. I just *know* what she's thinking, what she's realizing.

"Yes but—"

"My favor, I want to call upon my favor."

My heart is pounding, panic rushing through me. The thunder roaring outside the windows echoes the blood pumping too loudly in my ears.

"Huntyr, do *not* say another—"

"I want you to bring my sister to the Fae kingdom and give her the strongest healing tonic you have."

Fuck.

The magic snaps over me like a vice, oppressive and overwhelming. Gods, it nearly pulls me right towards her. I stumble forward, catching my balance on the back of the chair, and she flinches on the bed, thrown off by my reaction.

I only have the briefest of moments to be thankful that she didn't ask for something worse before my thoughts completely rewire.

Sister.

She has a sister?

Where is her sister?

How do I get her sister here?

Why is her sister sick?

How sick is her sister?

"Derian?" She crawls forward on the bed, leaning down to try to look at my face. "Are you all right?"

No, I most certainly am not.

I will not be all right until this mysterious sister is here drinking this tonic.

"Your sister," the words come out as a growl. "Where is she?"

HUNTYR

I didn't expect Derian to jump into action so quickly. I had barely told him Tyla's name and explained our history before he stormed out of the room, barking at me to stay put as the door closed swiftly behind him.

That essentially ceased any further conversation about my potential Fae heritage.

Kaia still hasn't come back after grumbling over the stupidity of our conversation and leaving.

So, I'm alone, in the Fae prince's bedroom.

It's noticeably larger than the one I've been staying in. His bed is easily twice the size of mine, and it sits before a tiny seating area in front of the fireplace, complete with matching sets of darkly upholstered chairs. To my left is a balcony overlooking a small peninsula of water on the other side of the fortress, and to my right is the door to the bathroom.

A bathroom that very notably has a tub sized for two.

Not that he had tried to crawl in with me or anything.

He had been surprisingly… gentle as he'd cleaned and mended my wounds.

The bath, and the conversation with him afterwards, managed to dull some of the shock. At least enough for my rational mind to kick back in, and to remind me that, despite whatever kindness the prince has shown me, nothing has changed.

The plan is still in motion.

Win the Conclave. Heal Tyla. Kill the prince.

It doesn't matter if we slept together, or if he was gentle, or if I somehow have some distant Fae relative. The plan is still in motion.

It will *not* change.

So, I need to continue playing my part.

Obviously, I can no longer hide the fact that I'm an assassin. The bastard already figured that out, so I just need to shift the story a bit. I need to convince him that, yes, I am an assassin who was sent to kill him… but now I've had a change of heart.

I'll pretend to be interested in the marriage, interested in him.

I'll pretend that this attraction between us has grown to mean something more.

I'll get him to lower his guard around me.

He already has, to some extent. He took care of me. He left me alone here in his private space, despite the fact that his closest friend, Caldren, clearly doesn't trust me. I suspect that Caldren also already knows my background given how close the two are. The fact that Derian left me here, despite his friend's warnings, suggests he might be starting to care for me.

I just have to nurture that trust a little more.

Get Tyla the tonic.

And kill the Fae prince.

Simple. Easy.

There's a knock at the door and I jump, instinctively standing and scurrying for a weapon.

But there... isn't one.

Unlike my room, which has blades, swords, and sharpened stakes of rock or metal hidden in every corner, there doesn't even appear to be a dinner knife readily available.

How does he not have weapons scattered everywhere?

I laugh softly, shaking my head to myself.

He doesn't have any weapons because he's Derian.

He *is* the weapon.

My hands tremble softly at my sides, and I clench them tightly into fists as I barely manage to squeak out, "Who is it?"

The door looms ahead of me, seemingly growing larger with each desperate gasp for air that I struggle to breathe into my frozen lungs. Pinpricks of pain shoot into my hands as I dig my nails into the newly fresh skin of my palms.

Snap out of this! You are the Huntress. Feared assassin. Winner of the Conclave.

Right. Taking another needy, steadying breath as I nod reassuringly to myself, I trample forward and rip open the door—determined not to be afraid.

Then, I look down to the round-faced older lady with red cheeks, wrinkled eyes, and a dress folded in her arms. She has pointed ears, which obviously makes her as dangerous and untrustworthy as any other Fae, but she's grinning up at me like she couldn't hurt a fly.

"You must be the future princess," she beams.

My blood runs cold. Princess. Right. Because Derian is a *prince.*

And we are, technically, to be married.

Which would make me the Fae princess.

Gods, if Kristona knew about this, he'd laugh so hard he'd start choking.

"I'm Marla," she introduces herself, then holds the dress up between us. "Prince Silverthorn asked me to inform you that he's arranging for your sister's travel now, but he'll need you to get ready for this evening's dinner. He says it's unavoidable, unfortunately. I've brought a dress for you, and I can help you get ready if you'd like, but the prince also warned me you might be a bit skittish after your ordeal today, so that's okay if you'd just like to get ready on your own."

I stare blankly at her, as if she's speaking a foreign language. He sent her with a dress? He told her to let me know the dinner was unavoidable, because he knew I wouldn't want to go? He instructed her to leave me be if I wasn't comfortable?

Reaching out, I wrap my fingers around the pale blue fabric in her hands and lift, gasping when I see the steel glinting in the torchlight underneath it.

"He also asked me to bring you this." She grins, holding out the dagger and a sheath to clip it in. "He said that if you need more, there's some assorted choices for you in the top left drawer of his desk."

My mouth is locked tight. I try to make sense of the information coming in but I just don't, I can't.

Marla is just standing there, staring up at me with such warmth and acceptance in her eyes, I know if I turn her away she'll be okay with that.

She'll do that to make me comfortable.

He did all this to make me comfortable.

I stare down at the offerings for a long time before I step back, opening the door wider and muttering the only words that come to mind. "Thank you."

The next knock on the door is more of a warning than it is a request, and Derian pushes in shortly after, already speaking before he's fully over the threshold.

"I've sent some of my most trusted men on a ship to Velia to get your sister. The most renowned healer in our kingdom is the one who services my brother in Bridgemond. He doesn't travel, but I've written to him requesting instructions for our healers here to create a sufficient tonic for her."

I stare at him wide-eyed, my hand pressed to my stomach to ground myself. His words are rushed, erupting out of him at a pace he can barely seem to maintain. Those dark eyes, the same ones that are always so teasing and commanding, are wild, flashing across the room.

"I need—" He pauses, tongue darting over his lips. "I need you to tell me that's good enough for now."

"What?"

"There's nothing else I can do, Huntyr. Until that boat arrives with her, there is nothing else I can do, so I need you to tell me that what I've done is enough. For now?"

He's looking at me with such intensity, I hardly even recognize him. This desperate, frazzled version of him is not one I've ever seen before. Frankly, it's not a version I necessarily like.

His eyes widen impatiently when I don't answer, fingers flexing and releasing in a maddening, repetitive pace. He steps forward towards me, and I fight the overwhelmingly strong urge to take an equal step back.

"Huntyr! I *need* you to actually speak now."

"Yes!" I cry, voice sharp. "Yes, Derian. Of course, that's enough."

He sags forward, gaze dropping to the floor as he takes a single shuddering breath and curses softly. Minutes pass by as I wait for him to regain some semblance of control.

"Thank you," he finally says, dragging his head up so his gaze can trail over me. His eyes heat as they do. "You look nice."

I'm dressed in the icy blue gown he had delivered to me. It clasps high around my neck, leaving all of my back bare and exposed, and falls easily to the ground in silken sophistication. A vertical opening at the front of the bodice offers a glimpse of my torso, while the slit leaves much of my leg on display.

He grins softly as he takes in the worn, but sensible, boots I insisted on wearing, and I suspect he knows that I hid some of those weapons from his desk inside of them. Not to mention the dagger strapped to my leg.

"Seriously?" I ask with a raised brow. "You trample in here like you've lost your damn mind and instead of offering any kind of explanation, all you have to say is that I look nice?"

Derian gives me a lopsided grin as he prowls past me, shedding his leather jacket as he does, and leaving it, and the shirt underneath, discarded on the bed.

I keep my gaze averted. I've seen enough of that man's bare body to last me a lifetime. Looking now will only distract me from my plan.

Again.

"Would you prefer I insult you?" he asks over my shoulder. "It would be a lie, of course, because you do look *very* nice, Huntress."

Instinct tells me to bark at him. To insist he stop his incessant flirting and just tell me whatever it is that got him so riled up.

But...

But the plan has shifted. I have a new role to play.

The role of a woman who may actually be falling for the Fae prince.

So, in that case, I suppose there isn't anything wrong with looking.

I turn on my heels, breath escaping me when I see him fully undressed, all tan skin and carved muscles. He stands tall, sorting through the clothing in his armoire, pulling things out and throwing them onto the bed casually, all the while cords of muscle ripple across his back.

He really is beautiful. It just doesn't seem natural that a Fae with such destructive power caged inside him also looks so breathtaking without even trying.

"Thank you," I whisper, mouth dry.

He glances at me over his shoulder, eyes suspicious as I slowly walk towards him. I keep my eyes on his face, even as I feel myself flushing, my eyes heating with lust that isn't entirely fake when I step into his warmth.

Derian doesn't say anything when I trail the tips of my fingers up his forearm and bicep. And though his eyes still spark with doubt, he doesn't fight as I gently push, nudging his back against the armoire, so that I can press myself more fully against him.

Gods, he's so tall.

And firm.

And naked.

When I run my hands up his bare chest, tangle my fingers in his hair, and pull his mouth to mine, he lets me. He molds around me, arms circling my waist and squeezing. He kisses me thoroughly, tongue invading my mouth in a wicked rhythm, until my stomach is clenching and my back is arching.

Then he bites me.

A gentle nip at my lower lip before he pulls his head back and looks down at me, apprehension abundantly obvious on his face.

"What game are you playing, Huntress?"

Fae bastard is too smart for his own good.

I know he wants me, the evidence of that is clearly visible, but he somehow has learned enough about me to know that he can't trust this sudden change in demeanor.

Leave it to Derian to be the only male in all of the Ever Realm to still be able to think clearly when a woman throws herself at him.

I laugh softly, backing away and tossing my hair over my shoulder as I turn away from him. There's no small sense of female satisfaction in the fact that I can feel his eyes trailing over my spine.

"Why would I want to play a game with you, Derian?" I ask, facing him as I sit on one of the chairs by the fireplace, crossing one leg over the other.

He watches me as he begins dressing, never taking his eyes off me even as his chest rises and falls heavily. He might have pulled away from me, but he was definitely affected by my little tease. "You seem to enjoy getting yourself into dangerous situations."

"Oh, but I'm so good at getting myself out of them."

"There are much more enjoyable ways to get an adrenaline rush, Huntress."

Warmth runs through me, bringing flashes of memories along with it. The feel of his hands in my hair. The promise of all the ways he wanted to have me.

Like this.

On the bed.

In the tub.

On your knees.

Now, I'm the one struggling to maintain my breathing.

"For you, maybe," I tease him, proud of my ability to keep my voice steady.

He pulls his shirt down over the line of defined abs slowly, smirking at me knowingly the entire time. "You weren't complaining when you clenched around my cock and told me that you felt perfect afterwards."

This room is too warm. The fire in the hearth is entirely unnecessary. It's too much, in fact. There's sweat forming on the back of my neck.

For what might be the first time in my life, a retort doesn't immediately come to mind. I have to pause just to clench my legs together before my brain can start working again.

"Such a filthy mouth for a prince."

Derian comes to me, moving with such predatory grace that it's no wonder he has the reputation he does. His eyes are impossibly dark when he comes to stand before me. With a crooked smile, he rests his hands on the armrests of my chair, caging me in before he leans down. He's so close I feel his breath on my skin as he says, "I'd like to prove that to you after this dinner."

It's over.

I've lost at my own game.

Gods, I have to stop myself from whimpering and begging him to prove that to me right the fuck now.

His eyes trace over my face, lingering over the curve of my lips and jawline just as his forefinger moves to run up the sliver of skin between my breasts that's visible through the neckline of my gown.

"But alas," he says, retreating back and reaching for my hands to pull me up out of the chair. "We have somewhere else to be right now."

The bastard winks at me once I'm steady on my feet before he pulls me out of the room, and he wears that self-satisfied grin the entire walk to dinner.

DERIAN

For someone who claims to hate the Fae as much as she does, she fits right in among them.

She sat next to me throughout the entirety of the meal, listening to the toasts in her honor, with the kind of detached amusement my brother would be proud of. When she finished eating everything on her plate, which I suspect she did solely for my benefit, she allowed Aunt Ulna to pull her from her seat and drag her through the room, introducing her to as many people as possible.

Now, she moves with effortless grace, no longer pretending to be anything other than what she is. Trained. Calculating. Confident. Strong. It's a sight to behold.

And I'm painfully aware that I'm not the only one tracking her throughout the evening.

Ulna loves her.

Although, that's no surprise. She has the kind of dry wit and attitude that my Aunt appreciates. Ulna has probably already demanded Taric tell her everything he knows about my new bride-to-be.

Then there are the eyes that trail her with lust—laced with desire for her body, her power, and her strength. I try to remind myself that she's the winner of the Conclave. It's to be expected that she gets this kind of attention. It would be expected even if she *hadn't* revealed herself to be half-Fae in the middle of her final trial. That just adds more fuel to the fire.

This dinner is more for her benefit than mine, in fact. It's a celebration for the victor of the Conclave, complete with a feast the likes of which this fortress has never seen before. Visitors from across the kingdom have found their way into this dining room, drinking themselves silly and filling their plates with more food than they can bear to eat. Along the far end of the room, a table stretches across the stone wall, piled high with pastries and cakes of every flavor imaginable.

Still, as much as I remind myself that this is normal and expected, every eye on her is eating me alive. It's as if I can't bear for anyone else to even *think* about touching what is mine.

Even if she isn't mine.

Even if she's been very clear that she doesn't want to be.

Even if she's still considering trying to kill me.

"He's quite possessive of her," Ulna notes to Taric as she returns to her seat.

And fuck, her being back means that she's left Huntyr with *Rhen*.

"You get used to it," Cal mutters under his breath.

Rhen's smiling at her. Grinning with those fucking dimples.

Cal snaps his fingers in front of my face.

"What?" I snap, hardly recognizing my own voice.

What is *wrong* with me?

I feel like I've been losing my mind slowly, painfully, since I took her to bed.

"We were in the middle of a conversation," Cal reminds me, pushing my drink towards me in a silent order to cool myself off. "Your bride will still be there in five minutes."

Ulna chuckles, looking wryly at her husband.

"A letter came from your brother's company today," Cal continues as I gulp down my glass of wine. "Since you want the wedding in Springhallow, he's redirecting to go there instead, and planning to stop at some of the border villages along the way to check in with the people."

"That'll extend his trip quite a bit," Taric murmurs.

It will. It'll add another week, maybe two, but at least it stops him from coming this close to the Wastelands. I suppose my strongly worded missive instructing him to stop being an ignorant bastard had its desired effect.

"That's good," I agree, glancing back towards Huntyr.

She's *touching* him. Pulling him to dance with her.

I breathe through the magic roaring inside me.

It's just a dance. She's allowed to dance.

"So, you think her mother was Fae?" Taric asks, following my line of sight.

My fingers tense around the glass in my hand, the only visible sign of my internal struggle, as I clear my throat. "That's the only explanation I can think of. It's rare that a union between a Fae and Mortal could produce an offspring, but I suppose it's not impossible."

Cal purses his lips, considering. "We should look into it more, before you let her ask for her favor."

I laugh darkly. "You're a little too late for that. Tricky little thing pulled herself together and demanded it the second the shock wore off."

His eyes flash with concern, and he's already leaning forward, resting his hand on the pommel of the sword on his hip as if he might take off right then and there to eliminate any threat she poses.

The growl that pulls itself out of my chest is enough to pause his movement.

"What did she want?" Taric asks, continuing to eat carelessly, oblivious to the obvious tension between my best friend and me.

When Taric won the Conclave, he asked Ulna to procure a house in Kilshore for his parents to live in. They had just lost theirs in a fire and had been living in various taverns along the coast.

She left that night and bought it. Spent far more than the house was worth, but his parents had a home exactly twenty-four hours after he won.

"She has a sister," I tell them, not bothering to hide the way my eyes don't leave her for even a moment. Rhen has the good sense to keep his hand at a respectable place on her back as they dance. That dress has left her entire spine exposed, though. I want to slice that hand clean from his arm for having felt her skin. "A sister who is ill. She asked me to get her a healing tonic."

Huntyr glances over at me, as if she senses us talking about her. Her eyes scan over our little group before lingering on me, and as Rhen spins her out and pulls her back in, she smirks.

And then, just before she turns her attention back to Rhen, she winks.

She. Fucking. Winks.

The glass in my hand shatters.

For a moment, the conversation around me stills and I just stare down at the offending hand. Did I really just break a glass because of a fucking wink?

Cal clears his throat, and a servant rushes towards us to clean the broken glass from the table. No one says a word, and truthfully they don't need to. I'm angry enough at myself for acting like a reckless child. I don't need them reminding me how ridiculous it is that one woman is having this much of an effect on me.

"So that's really all she wanted?" Cal asks, not acknowledging what just happened.

I nod. "Trust me, it was a surprise to me, too."

Ulna smiles at me knowingly. "And how are you feeling?"

Like my soul is being raked across hot coals. Just sitting here is agony beyond belief. I'm at complete odds with myself. It feels impossible to leave her side, and yet, *every* part of me is screaming to just get up and start running. To run until I get my own two hands on her sister and pour the tonic down her throat.

"You could have been more descriptive in your warning," I tell her dryly, sending a glare her way out of the corner of my eye.

She simply leans forward and pats my hand. "Once the favor is over, you'll feel better."

I doubt that.

I highly doubt that.

It's not the magic of the favor that's filling me with this absolutely unbearable possessive jealousy. It's *her*.

And from the way she glances at the servant cleaning the glass, before leaning closer to Rhen and whispering something in his ear, she absolutely knows it.

Cal sighs heavily next to me, glancing between the two of us with a look of pained consideration on his face. "I can't believe I'm suggesting this, but maybe you and your bride should go to bed."

I freeze, turning towards my best friend slowly. "What?"

Go to bed?

Surely he's not suggesting at a table full of people that I should go fuck her?

Ulna is snickering like the old bat she is beside me. "I'd reckon that's exactly what they need to do."

Cal leans back in his seat, folding his hands behind his head as he stretches out his back. "She's playing with you, Derian, and it's obviously working. If you don't want to get so jealous you summon a tornado and ruin the night for everyone, maybe you two should just leave."

Taric claps a hand heavily onto my back. "If I were you, I would most definitely be leaving a party early to celebrate my new engagement in my bedroom and not in a room full of others."

"If I remember correctly, you did," Ulna chirps, folding her arm into his. "You didn't even make it through dessert before you whisked me away."

He nips playfully at her cheek. "And if I remember correctly, you were very pleased with how we ended up spending the night."

Cal and I both grimace at them. The image of my Aunt being bedded on her engagement night is not something I need in my head. Not now. Not ever.

"This night is for her to celebrate," I tell them, the words tasting like bile. "After what she went through, she might as well have some fun."

I feel their suspicious eyes on me, but don't dare meet their gazes.

"Do what you want," Taric says through bites of potato. "Just try not to break any more glassware."

As if on cue, a servant rushes over with a fresh goblet for me, an obvious reminder of my humiliating display of a lack of control. I turn to take the offering, and the split second that I look away from her is enough for everything to go to shit.

Cal stiffens. Ulna gasps.

My heart sinks.

I whirl my head back towards her, searching.

The blue of her dress is stained red with wine that some drunken fool has spilled on her.

Rhen has her tucked behind his arm as he yells at the man, as if she needs his protection. Just as Rhen instructs the man to leave, though, the idiot punches him.

It's a hard, well-placed punch making even Rhen stumble back, and then my Huntress, my beautiful, reckless Huntress, is stepping forward, shoving him back.

I'm on my feet in an instant, but Ulna's arm snaps out, stopping me as a snarl rips through me.

"Leave her be," she orders me, unaffected by the rage I'm sending towards her. "This isn't uncommon at Conclave celebrations. If that girl is to be your wife, then she is to be *their* princess. They need to believe she deserves that title."

"Being beaten within an inch of her life and still winning wasn't proof enough?"

There's sympathy in her eyes, but also hardness, the kind of hardness that doesn't invite room for debate. "No, it wasn't. This is the way of the Fae. Let her defend herself."

39

HUNTYR

The drunken Fae male stumbles backwards after I push him, his too-long blonde hair flying awkwardly around his shoulders. His frame falls heavily into the woman behind him, and then she's turning around, locking her heated eyes onto him and then onto *me*.

Then she's lifting the sleeves of her dress over her forearms, and I brace myself for the feeling of being back in that arena, relying on my smarts to outthink Fae who can easily kill me with magic they possess that I don't.

Regardless of whatever unpredictable light lives within my fingertips.

My heart skips a beat, my pulse quickens, and I breathe deeply, fighting through the suddenly overwhelming fear and panic as I back into my defensive stance.

But...

There's no smell of magic in the air.

Not from her or from the several other Fae surrounding her.

She throws a jab, shoving her weight into it, and I step to the left instinctively. She loses her balance, flying past me and falling forward awkwardly.

And then she lands on someone else, and they both fall to the ground. He pushes her off and stands, leveling his glare on Rhen. Before I know it, he's tackled Rhen, and the two are wrestling violently on the floor.

And there's *still* no magic in the air.

This isn't a Fae fight. It's not a magical battle or a trial to the death.

It's a good old-fashioned drunken brawl.

Fighting for the sake of the rush.

Stupid. Reckless. Adrenaline-seeking.

Fun.

A grin splits my face, and I pull the blade from my thigh, slamming it against the dagger aimed towards my face. I jam my fist into the Fae before me, hitting them with an unforgiving uppercut.

There are people everywhere. The room has erupted in a cacophony of chaos. Screaming and grunting. Weapons flying and food splattering across the hall. All I can see are the bodies careening towards me before they fall onto the floor.

For a moment I'm back in that tavern with Flannigan starting fights.

This is probably the first time since I stepped into the Fae kingdom that I'm having true, unabashed fun.

Well, maybe the second.

Last night with Derian could be described as many things, fun included.

Rhen is back on his feet, fighting beside me, and it's totally unclear who's on our side and who's against us. I'm not even sure there are sides. It's every man and woman for themselves. We're all just lost in the bodies, flying fists, and the rush of violence.

After a few minutes, I've lost the weapons I brought into the room with me, and I'm relying exclusively on my fists and feet, using them to pound into any flesh I come into contact with.

The skin on my knuckles splits open as my fist connects with the jawline of a Fae man with a scar running through his right eyebrow and a remarkably large nose. I hardly even notice the pain because I'm already spinning, jamming my foot into the groin of another man, who hits the ground hard on his knees.

Then I'm ducking because a chair has been thrown across the room. I watch as it smashes into the head of a Fae woman, who stands nearly six feet tall, and it splinters apart. She doesn't even flinch. She turns slowly, anger painted across her face as she looks for who threw it, before she leaps into the air, diving to attack.

A laugh tears out of me.

There's a hand on my shoulder, and I don't even think. I reach back, wrapping around that arm and bending, tossing the feminine body over me. She careens into someone else, and they both hit the floor.

Someone lands a punch against my cheek, and blood explodes as I bite through my lip, the taste tangy and familiar. I wipe it away with the back of my hand before launching my counterattack, glee sparking through me all the while.

When I do find a single second that I don't have an immediate attacker to deal with, my eyes are drawn to the table at the front of the room.

The table where Taric sits with Ulna, both of them grinning wildly. Caldren is on his feet, hand braced on his weapon as if he's ready to pull it and break up the fight at a moment's notice.

And Derian is watching me.

Hands flat against the table.

Expression unreadable.

Eyes following my every move.

I lick the blood off my lower lip and watch as his jaw clenches before I throw myself back into the fray.

DERIAN

She's incredible.

Huntyr Lachlan is a beautiful woman. It's impossible to deny that. With long dark hair that contrasts against her vividly bright eyes, and her incredible curves in all the right places, you'd have to be insane not to find the woman attractive.

Like this, though?

She's completely in her element. She's practically glowing from the thrill of the mayhem. She's not even thinking. Her body and instincts have completely taken over, and I'm no longer watching Lady Lachlan with her gentle smiles and underhanded comments. I'm not even watching the Huntress filled with rage, violence, and calculation.

I'm just watching Huntyr. As she is.

And she's stunning.

Beside me, Cal sinks back into his seat, surveying the damage. "This is going to talke forever to clean up."

It sure will.

The dining room is a picture of destruction. Chairs broken, tables fractured, and food lining the floors and walls. Huntyr herself is covered in it.

Every blow she takes is like a direct strike to me, but Ulna was right. This is the kind of chaos that our people feed off of. If Huntyr *is* going to live among us, she should learn to stand on her own.

Looking at her, though, she doesn't need any lessons.

"Definitely half-Fae," Taric agrees, watching her head butt an opponent. "Where was that spunk during our days of training?"

"She was obviously faking her lack of skills," Ulna points out.

Cal and I turn to each other, both worried about what my Aunt is about to piece together. Anyone else knowing Huntyr's true identity right now could be far too dangerous.

But Ulna simply pours herself another glass of wine and laughs.

"Strategy at its finest. She made herself the perfect underdog."

I look at Cal, and he nods, silently agreeing that, for now, we seem to be in the clear on that front.

If I don't get her out of this room soon though, the chaos will get out of control. This fight will end with either blood spilled or me bedding her right in the center of the floor amidst all the carnage. And as desperate as I am for her, I'm just as desperate to keep the pleasure of witnessing her in ecstasy all to myself.

I push my hands onto the table, lifting to my feet.

"Enough!" I yell, the room stilling as I do, just as Huntyr bashes a man over the head with discarded dish ware she's picked up from the table beside her.

Everyone is silent, slowly climbing to their feet and breathing heavily as I make my way around the table. They part easily for me, creating a clear path directly from me to her.

Every step towards her has my blood rushing even faster. The closer I get, the more desperately I need her. She stares at me, panting heavily, her chest rising and falling in perfect time. Those long fingers are still clutching the dish as I finally come to stand before her.

I look down at it, nearly losing all ability to speak as I recognize what she has in her hand.

"A cake platter?" I ask, my words soft and just for her ears.

She glances down at it quickly, as if she didn't even realize that's what she's holding. Her lips quirk up, slowly at first, but then they split wide in the first true, genuine smile she's ever given me.

And then she *laughs*.

A joyful, lighthearted laugh that I immediately commit to memory.

"I told you," she breathes, cheeks flushed from the fight. "I'm remarkably adaptive."

I can't wait any longer.

I take her hand in mine and pull her away without another word. The platter falls to the ground and shatters as we leave the dining room. She's still laughing when the doors close behind us.

⁕

The door to my bedroom is barely closed before I'm pushing her against the wall, throwing my hands on either side, and caging her in front of me.

She's still fucking grinning.

The ends of her hair are covered in cake, and her dress is stained, but she's so unbelievably happy I'm about to become undone. I'm like a starving man. I've never wanted or needed *anyone* the way I need her right now.

Her joy is the most powerful aphrodisiac I've ever encountered.

"That was quite a show you put on out there," I whisper.

She bites her lip as she looks up at me, pushing against the wall so that her hips buck against mine. "You looked like you were enjoying it."

I tangle one of my hands in her hair, pulling her closer to me. "Oh, I was."

"It's a shame it's over," she sighs, even as her eyes spark even brighter. "I was having such fun."

My playful little Huntress, always making me work for it.

"Is there anything I can do to continue your fun?"

She tilts her head back, trailing those perfect lips along my jawline, and I'm impressed by my own willpower as I stop myself from ripping the tattered remains of her dress up and sheathing myself deep inside of her, right here and now.

"Well," she purrs, pulling back to level those wide eyes on me. "I believe you were going to show me what you can do with that filthy mouth?"

The fragile hold I had on my control snaps.

I close the inch of space between us, bringing my mouth down upon hers in a kiss that is neither gentle nor loving.

It's desperate.

My hand trails down her back, feeling every silken inch of exposed skin as I pull her to me. The soft whimper that escapes her mouth sends satisfaction coursing through me and I need to hear it again. I need to hear that sound over and over. I wrap my other hand around the back of her head, angling it just right so that she opens for me.

She's just as hungry for me, her tongue stroking against mine, her hands clawing at me as she works to rip my shirt over my head. Once it's off, her hands move everywhere, exploring every inch of my body that she can.

This isn't a game anymore. She's not trying to rile me up or tease. We're both lost to our need for one another.

She's perfection. She smells of wine, sweat, and that utter essence that is just her, and I'm completely enveloped by it. I *want* to be enveloped by it. I want her scent wrapped around me as much as I want her wrapped around me.

As I pull away, she whines slightly, but stills when she sees the devilish grin I give her before I slowly lower myself, dropping to my knees before her.

It's not a position I've often found myself in.

Without breaking eye contact, I hook one of her legs over my shoulder, kissing gently along the soft skin of her inner thigh and savoring the sound of her gasp.

"If I remember correctly, you mentioned something about enjoying when a man begs for you?"

She flushes, something that seems impossible considering how heated her skin already is, and her hand spears into my hair, gently pulling at the strands.

"So, Huntress, would you like me to beg for you? Would you like me to beg you to let me trail my lips up every inch of this perfect thigh, and then the next, until I reach that beautiful spot between them? Should I beg to fuck you with my mouth until I feel you quiver on my tongue?"

She's panting now as I trace idle circles along her ankle. Lips swollen, cheeks flushed, eyes brilliantly shining. "I fought to the death for you. The least you could do is say please."

Wicked woman.

"Please, Huntyr." I press my lips against the side of her knee. Then higher. Then higher. "Please give me the supreme pleasure of unravelling you with my mouth alone."

I could spend the rest of my life listening to that breathy little gasp on repeat.

Sadly though, I need more than a gasp.

I pause my movements, glancing up at her. "I need an answer, Huntress."

She's biting down on her lip, head tossed back against the wall, dark hair falling all around her like curtains of midnight-shaded silk. All I get from her is a nod. It might be all she's capable of.

And it's all I need.

I hook my fingers through the lacy undergarment separating us and bury my face against her warmth, letting the taste of her explode against my tongue.

The effect is instant for both of us. Her hand pushes me deeper as cries of pleasure echo around us, and I'm just as invested. She tastes like summertime. Like the way the water in the rivers beside the mountains in Amberhull tasted when I was a boy.

"Derian."

My name on her tongue is a song. A beautiful melody of such pleasure and wanting that I need to hear it over and over again. I need to carry her further. I lose myself in the pursuit of her climax—kissing, sucking and nipping that little bud until her thighs begin to tense.

Only then do I lift my hand, curling two fingers inside of her in time with the work of my tongue, and I feel tremors hit in beautiful waves of perfection. She doesn't bother to hide or quiet her moans, and I've never been prouder.

The leg she's standing on gives out, but I'm already rising to wrap an arm around her waist, lifting her.

"Now," she whispers. "Please."

I have absolutely no intention of waiting.

Without warning, I take her to the floor. The walk to the bed is far too long for me to wait to be inside of her, and luckily for me, she doesn't seem to mind. Desperately, she rips her dress up just as I lower my pants enough to sheath myself inside of her in one violent thrust that has her screaming my name again.

She bucks against me, taking everything I give her and throwing it back at me. It's fast and desperate. Absolutely feral. When the storm outside crashes against the window, she simply starts peppering kisses down my neck and chest, whispering beautiful words like 'yes' and 'please' and 'more.'

Damn if I don't want to give her every fucking thing she asks for.

Her fingernails claw into my back as I bury my face in her hair, breathing in that smell of her like it's the last breath I'll ever take. When she comes apart underneath me, I follow her over the edge.

In the still moments that follow, I roll off of her. We're both panting, sweating messes, staring at the ceiling. I can't help but wonder if she's just as shaken from whatever the fuck that was as I am.

"You know," she finally says, breaking the silence. Then she turns those eyes on me, and I'm instantly hard again. "The floor wasn't on the list of places you wanted me."

That smirk of hers is going to be the death of me.

I grin and pull her mouth to mine again.

HUNTYR

We can't stop.

We spend the entire night wrapped in each other.

Over and over.

On the bed.

In the tub.

With me on my knees and then him on his *again.*

We check off every item on the list and then some, and it's still not enough.

Every time we come together just leaves me hungry for more. It's a kind of indescribable need, one I'm not sure I've ever experienced before. Even when I'm entirely spent, muscles limp and trembling, I'm still begging him for more as he carries me to bed.

"Aren't you tired yet?" he teases.

He sits me on the sheets, pulling the covers back and pointing in a silent instruction for me to sit back.

"No," I lie, even as an immediate yawn escapes, exposing me.

He chuckles softly before settling into the bed next to me. "Sleep, Huntress. You've had a long day and an arguably longer night."

Right. This day started with the overwhelming knowledge that I was going to die. I'd faced the trial, won the Conclave, called in my favor, lost myself in an all-out brawl, and then lost myself in him... repeatedly. Come to think of it, that *was* a lot to do all in a single day.

Still, I glance at him suspiciously. "You're sleeping in the bed?"

He folds a hand behind his head and looks at me with a furrowed brow. "I was inside of you ten minutes ago, but the idea of sleeping next to me bothers you?"

No.

Yes.

I don't know.

Sex is one thing. Sex is fun and easy. Sex with him could even be described as mind-blowing.

But sleep?

Trusting someone enough to fall asleep next to them is an entirely different question.

Derian just watches me as I mentally debate myself before he stands, throws on a pair of sleeping shorts, and makes his way to the door. He opens it wide, and I gasp audibly when I see Kaia sitting directly outside, greeting him with an irritated growl.

"How long have you been out there?" I ask her.

"Long enough to know that if this is how you interact with everyone you plan to kill, then you must be a terrible assassin."

I toss a pillow at her, and she snarls aggressively before jumping onto the foot of the bed and curling up at my feet.

"I am glad you are not dead," she tells me. *"But it is late, and the prince is right in insisting you need to sleep. From what I heard, you had an exhausting few hours."*

"I wouldn't have pegged you for such a listener."

She growls at me, and I laugh, settling back against the pillows happily.

"There. Does it feel better knowing she's here to stop me from trying to harm you?" Derian asks, crawling back into the bed beside me.

Kaia yawns in my head. *"Tell the prince that, unlike you, I value my rest. If he were to give me any reason to wake in the night, I will show him exactly why the Vaereth trusted the Eshari as their guards."*

I nod at him. "Kaia says not to wake her up."

"That is not what I said," she grumbles.

He looks down at the cat skeptically. "Wouldn't dream of it."

For a moment, I watch the two of them glare at each other, a smile playing at my lips. "You don't like her, do you?"

Kaia lays her head down on her front paws, still staring at Derian, who shifts awkwardly next to me.

"She doesn't like me." He blows out the candle on his bedside table and pulls the quilt up to his waist. Then he pulls it up higher over me. "But if having her here helps you sleep soundly, then so be it."

"Thank you."

In the darkness he turns towards me, and I fight the urge to trace his jawline with my fingertips. So beautiful. He's far too beautiful.

And kind.

He wouldn't want anyone to notice.

Around everyone else, he's hard and mocking. His presence in a room is suffocating. His power is absolutely terrifying. Derian's reputation as a monster is not entirely unearned.

And yet, he was gentle with me today.

He helped me find myself after Seraphina broke me.

He let me fight out my feelings because that's what I needed at the moment.

He's letting Kaia sleep next to me simply because it makes me feel calmer.

Derian is a Fae. He has the same flaws as the rest of them. More than that, he's the Fae prince. Their leader. My father's death and the suffering of all Mortals falls at his feet.

Even still, though, if I allow myself to look past that...

"I think," I pause, searching for the words, searching for the confidence to say them. "I think that I might not hate you, Derian Silverthorn."

He doesn't know how sad those words are. He doesn't know that the fact I don't hate him feels like a betrayal to my very soul. He doesn't know that even though I actually mean it, it doesn't change what I have to do.

Derian reaches over, running a knuckle across my cheek. "I don't hate you either, Huntyr Lachlan. Now sleep, please. Tomorrow will be another long day."

I want to ask him what he means, what else there is to be done, but he pulls me towards him and then I'm on his chest, listening to the beat of his heart in a steady rhythm. Kaia snores softly at our feet, and the feeling of him running his hands through my hair is so calming and *right* that I'm asleep before I can utter another word.

⸻⸺◆⸺⸻

Derian is already gone from the bed when I finally wake up. Kaia remains, though, seated by the doors to the balcony, staring out at the ocean. When she hears me wake, she flicks her tail toward a stack of clothing that has been left for me and tells me Derian left it with instructions to come to breakfast when I was ready.

I dress quietly in a white sweater and cotton leggings, and from there the day takes off at a furious pace. We eat breakfast with his aunt, Taric, Caldren, and Roland. Then we're whisked back to the Arena for a memorial for the fallen competitors.

The sight of that cursed space sends a burst of anxiety rushing through me, but Kaia stays close to my side. I allow her presence to ground me as I mumble kind words about each of the women whose blood had flowed right under my very feet.

From there, I'm instructed by Roland to begin packing my belongings. When I remind him that I had been drug from the Mortal Kingdoms without warning, and therefore had no belongings, Derian intervenes and promises I'll be able to buy whatever items I need for my wardrobe when we arrive in Springhallow.

I then ask if that kindness would extend towards a set of custom-made blades, fitted for my height and hand shape, and he quips that there are ways I could earn that gift.

So, I call him a Fae bastard and try to punch him. He just dodges, flicks my nose, and walks off.

Now our little group is gathered by the stables, preparing to make our journey to Derian's home in Springhallow. Our *wedding* is to take place there.

A wedding that will never happen if I have my way.

I stroke my hands through the dark mane of the chestnut-brown mare I'll be riding for our trip, then check the straps of the bedroll and food pouch attached to her saddle.

It's early afternoon, so the sun is at its peak, but a gentle breeze blows the salted air of the sea towards us, lifting the tendrils of hair near my face that have fallen out from where I've pulled it back. The air is cool and fresh, good weather for riding. I can only hope it stays that way, since the journey is supposed to take a day or two.

"The prince comes," Kaia tells me from my feet, her tail twitching unhappily.

Kaia and the horses have not become fast friends, but they'll have to tolerate each other until we get to Springhallow.

Derian doesn't speak as he reaches me, choosing instead to bend and check the hooves of my mare.

"I *can* pick the hooves of my own horse," I grumble, resting my hands on my hips.

I'm still wearing the sweater and leggings, the air still warm enough not to warrant anything additional. The only change to my person is the sword that's now slung across my back and the addition of a blade on my thigh.

Derian glances over the sword, as if assuring himself that it's there, before scanning over the rest of me. "Do you have a cloak packed? It can get colder at night."

Okay, now I'm starting to feel offended. I lift my brows. "Since when did you become such a worrywart?"

He pauses his inspection of me, glancing away for a moment with a frown and turning back to me with a shake of his head. "I don't know, actually. I suppose I just wanted to ensure you have everything you need since we're about to leave."

I throw my foot into the stirrup and easily hoist myself onto my horse. "I'm fine, Derian. Even if I had forgotten a cloak, which I didn't, I'm more than capable of dealing with the cold. And before you ask, I also have my bedroll, a change of clothes, and *plenty* of food. Now stop being weird and lead us out. We're wasting daylight."

Derian frowns, still glancing over me for a moment longer. It's not until Kaia takes a step towards him with a snarl that he finally nods and leaves, climbing onto his own black steed without another word.

"You're such a bully," I tease.

She huffs once he's gone. *"I did not choose a simpering girl who needs a male to come save her. His constant mollycoddling of you is as unnecessary as it is annoying."*

"Can't say I disagree."

"Why would you disagree with a point that is so obviously correct?" She looks towards me, and for all her complaints about Derian, I'm nearly positive that she glances over my saddle and weapons too. *"We shall begin this ridiculous journey now."*

The second she starts moving, my horse bucks.

It takes all my thigh and core strength to stay seated as I pet reassuringly down the horse's mane, making soft cooing noises as I do. The Fae all look towards me, Taric with his hands outstretched as if he plans to grab onto the animal and physically restrain it if it doesn't calm down.

"I'm fine," I tell him when I get her to still. Then I feel the oppressive weight of Derian's stare on me. "I'm *fine*."

He takes a sharp, shuddering breath before turning and barking orders to those around us.

"Maybe you should keep your distance," I tell Kaia.

She glares at the horse. *"Ridiculous creatures."*

With a final glance back at me with brows furrowed, Derian flicks a hand and we begin moving, horses maintaining a steady pace as we do. Derian and Caldren lead us from the front, Ulna and I ride in the middle, and Taric and Roland keep steady behind us. From beside me, Ulna chuckles.

I glance at her. "Are all Fae males so overbearing?"

She simply grins wryly at me. "Only some. It's relatively new for him."

Of course it is. Of course the Fae prince waited until I was in his kingdom before he started acting like a possessive, over-protective fool.

"Lucky me," I mutter under my breath as we cross through the stone archway that marks the edges of the fortress.

I take a deep calming breath as we do, preparing myself to travel even deeper into Fae territory.

※

The ride to Springhallow takes us first alongside a river that sparkles under the afternoon sun, then through forests filled with towering oak trees, their leaves so full and vibrant that seeing the sun is nearly impossible.

By the end of our first day of travels, we reach the edge of the woods and stop to make camp for the night. Derian and Caldren hunt rabbits for dinner, and Ulna creates a fire for us using her fire-wielding magic. After a long day of travel, everyone is too exhausted to stay awake for long. Tents are quickly pitched and goodnights are hurriedly said.

And despite the fact that my body is aching and my eyes are indeed burning with tiredness, I make my way to Derian's tent and fuse my body to his until pleasure rocks me to sleep.

Too soon, the morning sun wakes us, and we're back on the road to continue our travels.

By the time we're midway through the second day, everyone is off balance. Derian and Caldren maintain the pace in front of us, talking amongst themselves. Behind me, Taric is clearly bored, his voice a never-ending droll of chatter in the back of my mind. Ulna spent much of our first day speaking with me, but now lingers by her husband. Roland trails on the end, content to watch the scenery.

And my thoughts are spiraling.

I can't stop thinking about Tyla, worrying about how she's doing and when she'll arrive. In the brief moments I stop thinking about my sister, I start feeling ridiculously conflicted about the Fae prince who trots along far enough ahead of me to give me space but close enough to reach me if he needs to.

Never mind the fact that *I* don't need him to.

I neither want nor need his constant hovering.

Just because I let him share my bed on a few occasions doesn't change anything. It doesn't change who I am or what I can do.

What I *will* do.

It won't stop me from seeking out my vengeance the first chance I get.

The only question left is how exactly I'm going to do that.

Will I rely on the skill sets that have gotten me this far in life, or will that awful unnatural magic come erupting out of me against my will again?

I wish I could get rid of it as easily as I plan to get rid of Derian.

"Have you always been able to do the light thing?" Taric suddenly asks, pulling his horse up next to mine.

I ignore the pit that opens in my stomach and avoid his gaze. Kaia glances up at me but is quiet in my mind.

"No," I mumble.

"Hmm," he muses. He waits as if expecting me to continue.

I don't. I have nothing I want to say further on this matter.

"That's interesting, don't you think? I wonder what triggered it."

Blood pouring over me.

My eyes so swollen I could barely see.

Pain everywhere.

"Probably the possibility of imminent death." I don't bother to hide the harshness of my tone.

The memory of it is still so fresh. Too fresh for this conversation to be bearable. I can feel the Fae fire eating my arm off, the splitting pain in my ribs, the aching in my head. My pulse skitters and Derian turns around to glance at me as if he can somehow sense my unease.

I glower until he turns back around.

"Do you think you could blind someone with it?" Taric asks, scratching at the underside of his jaw.

Screaming echoes in my ears. I can see Seraphina blinking rapidly. Numbly, I glance down at my hands, almost expecting to see her blood there.

"That might be pretty handy if you can."

No. It wouldn't be *handy*. Nothing about that light is useful or natural or *desirable*.

I focus on my breathing. In and out. I force that air into my lungs and limbs, force it to keep myself calm. Force it to push down the rising panic.

"We should test that out sometime," Taric continues.

We.

We should test it out.

There. Is. No. We.

"Taric," Derian barks from the front. "Shut the fuck up."

My attention snaps to him. He's not even looking back at us, but he's *listening*. Intervening. Defending me.

As if I'm his to defend.

Derian pulls his horse to a stream on the side of our path, instructing all of us to make a quick stop to water the horses. I've barely finished handing the reins of my horse to Ulna before I'm stomping away to a wooded area under the guise of relieving myself.

We should test it out.

Breathing heavily, I lean back against one of the trees and try to calm the surging irritation inside of me as I close my eyes and focus on the feeling of the gentle breeze across my skin.

We. We. We.

The word repeats itself over and over, an unwanted mantra in my head. An incessant reminder that from the second that light burst out of my fingers, the Fae started considering me one of *them.*

That light changed every part of my identity in their minds.

I can't do this.

I can't spend another night sleeping next to these creatures, who now treat me like I'm one of their own.

I'm *not.*

It doesn't matter what magic pours out of me or what they say. The way Derian looks at me doesn't matter either.

I am *not* their friend, and I am *not* a Fae.

"He didn't mean any harm."

I blink my eyes open to find Derian standing in front of me, hands in his pockets, eyes somehow both understanding and exasperated.

The others linger back by the horses, sending curious glances our way—even though they've obviously been instructed to stay back until Derian can calm me down, like I'm some ridiculously immature girl who needs a male to soothe me when my feelings have been hurt.

No, not just a male.

Derian.

Because they think he has some kind of claim on me.

He thinks he has some kind of claim over me.

My anger boils over.

"I do not need you to defend me," I hiss, shoving him.

He stumbles back a few steps, but steadies himself and clears his throat. "That wasn't very nice, Huntress."

That name. That fucking name was born from those that feared me, and he uses it like it's some cute little connection reserved for just the two of us. "And *stop* calling me that."

"You're upset."

I smile sweetly at him. "Would you like a prize for your perceptiveness?"

Derian's eyes heat, trailing down my body. "No thanks, you already owe me a prize from our last competition."

My lips curl back. "Keep dreaming."

"Do I need to?" he asks with a teasing smile and tilt of his head even as he keeps his distance from me. "You didn't have any problem fulfilling my wishes last night. Or the night before, for that matter."

It takes every ounce of my self-control not to lash out with my fists instead of my words.

But I can't.

I push off the tree trunk, moving to walk past Derian, but his arm snakes out, fingers wrapping around my wrist to stop me.

"You can't pretend you don't know."

I stare at that hand, at the place where it connects with my skin. I stare as his thumb traces lightly against my pulse. "Know what?"

"That you're Fae, Huntyr."

The sentence is like a bucket of ice being poured over me, drenching me from head to toe and leaving me without the ability to form coherent thoughts.

Oblivious to the effect his words have had on me, Derian continues on. "I spent years at Amberhull teaching the younglings to harness and control their magic. I can teach you too, if you'd like."

I can't look away from his hand on my wrist. Those fingers traced my spine last night. I'd *let* him touch me in the most delicate of places. I'd allowed myself to be so blinded by his beauty and the fleeting moments of kindness that he'd offered me that I'd let go of some of the hatred that had burrowed into my heart.

That hatred had a purpose, though. It had been born from a reality that I could never allow myself to forget. Even if the Fae responsible for my father's death was my own mother, it was a Fae nonetheless.

They were monsters, one and all.

When I level my stare on him, his eyes flash, and I can only imagine the viciousness of rage that makes up my expression. "*If* I am part Fae, I will go to my deathbed hating that part of myself. I don't want you to teach me a damn thing about it. Why would I want to harness something that makes me anything like your disgusting kind? You're bastards, every last one of you."

Ripping my hand from his grasp, I make my way back to our group, throw myself onto my horse, and ignore the question in Kaia's gaze.

Derian doesn't say another word to me, but he's obviously in a bad mood based on his tone. He barks at the others to get moving and begins to set a furious pace.

DERIAN

"You know," Cal draws out the words as he trots along at my side. We're at least twenty paces ahead of the others and have spent most of the day rotating between companionable silence and reminiscing on old memories. "I couldn't help but notice that your lovely bride-to-be made up her own tent last night."

She sure did.

She hasn't said a word to me since her outburst. I'm doing my best to give her space, to let her come to terms with this new part of her identity in her own time, but that doesn't mean it's easy. When I saw her start setting up her own tent last night, I nearly had it out with her right there in front of the others and dragged her into bed with me.

"Trouble in paradise?" Cal asks.

He's stopped insisting I be wary of her every five minutes, but that doesn't mean either of them has warmed up to the other.

"I don't know if any experience with Huntyr can be described as paradise."

Never mind the fact that I don't *want* paradise. I don't want the easy happiness that comes with domestic life. I want the push and pull. I want the fire and unpredictability that comes with a relationship built on equal strength and determination.

It's part of what is so intoxicating about her.

She isn't acquiescing or sweet. She isn't thoughtful or diplomatic. To most people, she is probably considered unlikable at best, but she is unapologetically herself. She has no qualms about evoking and facing my temper. It's not that she is fearless, Huntyr has plenty of fears, but she doesn't let them hold her back or limit her in the slightest.

"Is it—" Cal frowns, his demeanor becoming awkward, and he spares a quick glance back at her. "Did you do something?"

I balk. "Why do you assume *I* did something?"

"Well, because you're *you*, Derian. You're not an easy person to love."

I bristle at the word he so casually slips into the conversation, as if that word is a reasonable concept to attach to the pure desire that cements the foundation of my interactions with the Huntress. I'm about to tell him as much when I hear the distinct sound of another horse trotting up to us.

And then she's there, on Cal's other side, glowering at both of us like we're no better than the mud on her boots.

"You're talking about me," she assumes, her brows raised and expectant.

"Would you like a prize for your perceptiveness?" I mock, throwing her earlier taunt back at her and watching the way her fingers tighten against the reins in her hands.

"Anything you two need to say *about* me, you can say *to* me."

Cal glances between the two of us, lips twitching with the uncomfortable feeling of being *literally* stuck in the middle. I think I might even see him physically cringe.

I'm not sure whether it's sympathy for my best friend that motivates me, or the knowledge that the action will annoy her more than continuing our little sparring match, but I turn my eyes back to the road ahead of us, completely ignoring her.

I wait for her to fall behind again, or to say something particularly vicious, but she's quiet for some time before she finally speaks again.

Only this time she's not talking to me.

"I know that you know who I am. *What* I am."

Cal's brows raise as high as I've ever seen before. "I do."

He says it like a question, regardless of the fact that it's clearly not.

"Good." She lifts her chin, and I marvel at how the sunlight brings out the faint freckles splattered across her nose. I'd never noticed them before. "So again, if you have any concerns about me, you can discuss them with me directly. I'm not his pet, and he's not my keeper. I'm perfectly capable of speaking for myself."

Cal's lips curl into a suppressed smile. "You want to have the conversation out then?"

She shifts her weight on the horse, glancing over her shoulder to ensure the Eshari is still following behind, before tossing her hair back off her shoulders. "I'm here, aren't I?"

My best friend nods. "Very well. I think you were trying to kill Derian the night of the masquerade ball."

He's testing her, trying to see if she'll prove herself to be an untrustworthy liar. My huntress is too smart for that though, and she gives him the smirk that always manages to instantly harden me.

Gods, I went one night without her and I feel as desperate as an adolescent.

"Caldren," she tuts, her voice light and teasing. "I thought we were having an open conversation? I'm very aware he's already told you that."

I'm not sure how I feel about the two of them speaking as if I'm not right next to them.

Cal grins. "Alright then, what proof do I have that you're not still a danger to Derian?"

I feel her eyes on me like a heated weight even as I keep my gaze locked on the road ahead of me.

"I am a danger to Derian." She shrugs. "I'm a danger to lots of people. The truth is, you have no proof that I'm not going to go on a killing spree whenever I feel like it. So, the question you should be asking is not whether or not I'm going to do something."

"What is the question I should be asking then, Lady Lachlan?"

He uses her title on purpose, knowing it will get under her skin, and she does indeed visibly bristle. Instincts push me to intervene, to tell him to back off, but she was right about one thing during her tantrum yesterday. She doesn't need me to defend her.

Besides, they need this conversation.

"The question you need to be asking yourself, Caldren, is whether you would be capable of stopping me."

And just like that, she's won over my best friend.

He chuckles under his breath and looks over at her with something in his gaze that looks an awful lot like respect. With their mutual understanding reached, she pulls her horse in a tight circle and resumes her position next to Ulna as my Aunt demands every detail of our conversation.

Nosy old bat.

We ride for a solid twenty minutes before Cal finally laughs out loud.

"I don't know how you managed it, Derian."

It's like I can sense his next words before he says them. I take a deep breath, preparing myself for the barb that's about to come.

"You're going to be married to someone who might be even more disagreeable and arrogant than you are."

The sun is just hitting its mid-afternoon peak on the final day of our journey when we reach the small town just south of Springhallow.

I've traveled through the town dozens of times before. I've even grown particularly fond of a bakery within its small market square. It's a simple place, where everyone knows everyone. Travelers rarely cross through, and so on the rare occasions they do, they are treated with great hospitality.

More than once I've been swindled into staying in the local inn just so I can continue the conversations I've started in the tavern with some of the locals.

And yet, hardly anyone seems to notice us as we make our way through the street lined with wooden cabins. I glance behind us, seeing the same tension mirrored on the faces of Taric and Roland.

With an incline of my head, we all dismount and tie our horses to a nearby fence, making our way deeper into the town on foot. We walk cautiously through the neighborhood streets with houses that appear empty but not deserted, based on the gray smoke that still twists into the sky from fireplaces jutting out of the barren roofs.

I suppress the urge to look back at Huntyr and confirm she has her weapons drawn and at the ready. Her sense of danger is as sharply honed as my own, I remind myself, and she's already proven time and time again that she can take care of herself. I need to let her do that if only so I can focus on what's going on here.

That's when we hear the crying, growing louder and louder with each step we take toward the part of town that veers towards the forest. Cal looks to me, unleashing his sword as I gather magic inside of me, letting it rise and fill me like a growing tide.

The houses begin to clear, revealing the townspeople gathered in a cluster next to the wooded area. Women are sobbing, gathering curious children and forcing them away, while men exchange terse words.

"Prince Derian!" Ambresia, the innkeeper, recognizes me instantly, rushing towards me and grasping hold of my hands as Huntyr takes a step closer.

Tears stream down Ambresia's tanned face as she quickly takes in our group. "Thank the Gods you're here."

"What's happened?"

"You must look! I can't begin to describe it."

I look over my shoulder, first to Huntyr, then to Ulna and Taric.

"Stay here," I instruct before inclining my head to Cal in a silent instruction to come with me.

"Joseph and Kaelthyn went hunting yesterday and never came back. It wasn't until a girl went out to collect firewood that we found Kaelthyn, but there's still no sign of Joseph," Ambresia explains as she leads us through the crowd, their eyes tracking us as we make our way towards the body that lies on the edge of the woods.

Clothes torn, skin scraped and bleeding, head at an unnatural angle. I take in the scene, noting the black hollow eyes and the mouth dangling open in slack-jawed scream.

Velkai.

I turn to Cal, watching him come to the same conclusion I have. His fingers tighten and release on the scabbard of his sword once, twice, as he stares down at what remains of the woman.

I walk towards him, turning my back on the people.

"This doesn't make any sense," he whispers softly, careful not to let the townspeople overhear. "Velkai this far past the Wastelands?"

"I think this counts as our confirmation that they're expanding their territory. If they've come this far, it's only a matter of time before they infect the land."

His hazel eyes meet mine, his jaw locked in a tense and unhappy angle. "Derian, if that's true..."

I know what it means.

The Velkai *cannot* be allowed to grow the Wastelands.

If they have somehow emerged from those barren lands, if they are somehow organizing again under a new leader after all these years, then another war isn't just a possibility. It's an inevitability.

We can't leave this town undefended. Cal knows that as well as I do. If the second man is still missing, it's because whatever Velkai lingers in these woods aren't finished with him. I begin to turn, to consult Cal on a plan when—

"Oh, fuck."

My world shifts on its axis. Those two little words from that distinctly feminine voice are all it takes for my entire focus to shift to the short, dark-haired creature who now stands at my side.

I grasp hold of her arm, practically dragging her away, even as she stares wide-eyed at the body behind us.

"Would it kill you to actually do as you're instructed, instead of whatever you damn well please?" I growl at her.

She rips her arm from my grasp, stopping halfway between the crowd and our friends, both groups of people openly staring at the two of us.

"What was that?"

"That is none of your concern, Huntress. The next time I tell you to stay put, I expect you to *stay put.*"

For Gods' sake, there could be a Velkai right at the edge of these woods waiting to attack, and as formidable as Huntyr is, she doesn't stand a chance against one. She's never even *seen* a Velkai before.

"No," she says simply, as if I had asked her if she wanted milk with her tea. "Tell me what that was. What leaves a body like that?"

Her eyes are wider than I've ever seen them before, and shimmering with intensity. Not the intensity she'd had after her final trial, this is something different. Something worse.

There is pure horror on her face.

"Velkai, Huntress. Velkai kill like that."

She pauses, her mouth hanging open, before she shakes her head in disbelief. "Velkai aren't real. It's a story you made up."

"I can assure you it's not."

"It *is*," she insists. "It's a story you made up to hide your people's atrocious actions."

I clamp down on the irritated rush of anger that swirls through me, and she doesn't even glance up as grey clouds begin to cover the sun, casting shadows across her skin. I don't have the time to debate with her about whether the Fae are the true enemies or not.

Glancing towards Taric, I issue my silent command, and he nods, stepping towards her.

"Stay *here* with Taric and Ulna," I tell her. "Cal, Roland, and I will go take care of the Velkai."

She pauses, a million emotions spreading across her too expressive face. Shock. Confusion. Understanding.

Indignation.

"I will *not* stay here."

I glare at Taric. She's staying here even if he has to tie her to a fucking fence post.

She senses his approach, pulling one of the blades on her belt, and levels it at his throat with the same blinding speed she'd used when she aimed that very blade at me during our throwing contest. I should have realized that night she wasn't totally Mortal.

"Don't you dare touch me," she warns him, her voice low and tinged with menace.

He holds his hand up in surrender before inclining his head at me with a shrug. His thoughts are as clear as if he'd spoken them aloud.

She's your woman, you control her.

Except she's not. She's not my anything, and I clearly can't control her.

"I'm coming with you," she insists.

"Huntyr, this isn't the time for you to assert your independence. We're very aware how strong you are, but you are also half-Mortal. You are a half-Mortal with no experience fighting these creatures and no ability to control your magic."

Her back stiffens when I reference her magic, but she doesn't back down. She doesn't even lower the blade from Taric's throat.

Cal's hand comes to rest on my shoulder, a reminder that we need to go if we have any hope of finding the monster.

The Eshari comes to sit at her feet, looking at me with the same anger that is painted across Huntyr's face.

"Try to stop me and I will cut through every person who stands in my way."

I raise a brow at her. "Do you really think you could manage to kill Roland, Cal, Taric, the Conclave winner, and Ulna, the Silverthorn Warrior before getting to me?"

I swear I can see Cal take a step backwards as the tension between Huntyr and me becomes palpable.

Her head tilts, stubbornness so obvious in the angles of her posture. "Maybe not, but I'd leave at least one of them bleeding, which I imagine would be an inconvenience."

My temper is barely held back by the leash I've tied around it. The air thickens with suffocating humidity, curling the ends of her hair.

Stubborn, reckless, ridiculous woman.

"Fine," I growl. "You stay behind me the whole time. Daggers in both hands. If I warn you to run, it's because I genuinely think you are going to be injured if you don't run. So, if I tell you to run, you *will* run, Huntyr. That's the only way I'm allowing this."

Her arm slowly lowers, even as her other hand reaches for a second blade. "Fine."

"Fine," I spit back at her, before turning on my heels and stalking off.

HUNTYR

I'm no stranger to the idea of moving in tactical formations, of maneuvering as a group, organizing players based on their strengths or what you're trying to protect. The members of the League of Assassins work alone or in pairs more often than not, but when a group of us worked together, we were often required to move in this kind of strategic way.

I was not, however, used to being the valuable thing locked in the center of the tactical formation.

Derian prowls in front of me while Roland is to my back left and Caldren is to my back right. All three of the Fae warriors brandish their swords as we walk. They'd taken up the triangle around me without any orders being given, as if they'd all naturally come to the conclusion that I was the weakest link and therefore needed protection.

I think the uncomfortable feeling swarming in my chest might be that of being offended.

Still, I don't dare say anything against the formation as we walk. I'm very aware that another word out of me will have Derian turning back into a feral Fae bastard. He'd probably drag me kicking and screaming out of these woods.

I can't let that happen.

I need to lay my own eyes on whatever killed that man, on whatever monster had left his corpse the *exact* way my father's had been left.

Derian insisted it wasn't a Fae who was responsible, but I would be the judge of that myself.

His magic is stifling in the air around us, humidity bearing down on me and making the leather on my skin feel too tight. The tree cover leaves his clouds out of sight, but I have no doubt they are there.

Also out of sight?

This supposed Velkai.

We've been walking for what feels like an hour, and not even an animal scurries by our feet.

"This is starting to feel like a waste of time," I grumble, moving to sheath my dagger back into the belt on my hips.

Caldren moves so quickly I don't even notice until his fingers are wrapped around my wrist, stopping me, a clear warning on his face. *Don't.*

Then I feel it.

A sudden iciness deep in my chest, unnatural and incredibly *wrong*.

It's strange enough to cause my steps to stumble. Derian hears the misstep and glances back at me, just in time to see me rubbing a hand across my chest.

"What is it?" he asks, voice low.

I haven't the slightest idea how to answer that in a way that doesn't sound completely crazy. How can I possibly begin to explain a building sensation of doom growing within me with no identifiable cause?

"What luck, sisters."

I jolt, turning in time with the men to look at the woman now appearing on light feet from behind a massive oak trunk.

She holds onto the tree with one arm, swaying slightly. Her dark dress is worn, ripped around the hem and stained in blood. The dark hair shorn at her shoulders is in sharp contrast to her impossibly pale skin, also flecked with blood.

Biting her lip, she grins at Derian.

"The prince has come into our woods."

She's not alone. Sure enough, two other women emerge, practically identical to the first in every way, right down to the unnerving smile.

"The Mother will be so pleased," the one on the left says.

Derian stiffens. It's so subtle it's almost imperceptible. I notice, though.

I watch his hands flex on the sword in his hands. The tree cover above us is going to significantly limit his power. Lightning risks setting the whole woods on fire, and a tornado could very well kill us all.

It's not that I doubt his skill with that blade. I'd just feel somewhat better if he could end all of this with three expertly aimed electric strikes.

"What a surprise it is to see you beasts all back together again," Derian says, his voice carrying that razor-sharp edge it had when he killed those warriors who had taken me from my bed.

The woman to the left steps forward with a wild grin. "Yes, we're all together again, prince. We prepare for the Mother."

"The Mother is dead," he growls.

The woman in the middle waggles her fingers. "No, no, no. She waits. She waits for an offering strong enough to wake her."

"She'll be happy to know we have brought you for her," sing-songs the one on the right.

They're all speaking so fast, their voices so high-pitched and identical that it's nearly impossible to distinguish who's speaking, let alone understand *what* they're saying.

Subtly, Roland steps closer to me as Caldren steps aside. I receive the message clearly. When the fighting breaks out, stay with Roland.

The women are stepping forward, all in time, all in the same slow, jerking motions, all staring at Derian as they do.

Until...

The one on the left pauses, inhales deeply, and looks sharply towards me.

"What have you brought us?"

I swallow the sudden fear that lurches through me as all three women suddenly level their attention exclusively on *me*.

"Who's your pet?"

"What's her name?"

"What can she do?"

"Can we play with her?"

"The Mother would like her, too."

"We shall take you both."

They're rotating sentences between them, talking so quickly each word flows effortlessly into the next, as if it all comes from a single mind instead of three.

Those three women are all I can see. The woods are dark behind them, shadows covering every inch of the ground beneath their feet.

"You're not touching her," Derian growls.

They seem oblivious to him, though; their eyes are all bearing down on me as the three simultaneously tilt their heads at an odd angle.

"Don't you want to come with us?" the woman in the center asks me.

"Yes, help us kill them," croons the one to her left.

"The Mother will be grateful to you," finishes the one to the right.

I don't know what I did to deserve the undivided attention of these three monsters, but I'm seriously regretting telling Kaia to stay with Ulna and Taric.

"I can come," she insists in my head.

"You won't get here in time."

She won't, that much is clear, as the one in the center takes her final few steps forward. Derian's blade is lifted, its point now pressed into the hollow of her throat. Without moving, her eyes flash down at it.

And she laughs.

They all laugh, the sounds blending together into an eerie screech.

She lifts her hands and darkness...

I gawk as darkness rises from her fingertips.

Inky shadows fly from her fingers and wrap around the blade of Derian's sword, tugging it aside as if it weighs nothing, as if the Fae who holds it has no strength.

I barely have time to blink before the other two have disappeared into misty darkness. There one second, then gone the next. Only to suddenly reappear. One directly in front of Roland. The other in front of Caldren. Both still focused entirely on me.

Time suddenly speeds up.

Roland snakes a hand behind his back, grasping onto my waist and planting me directly behind him as vines burst from the ground, wrap around the woman in front of Caldren, and pull her dramatically away from our group. A blast of wind does the same to the woman in front of Derian.

They're drawing them away from me.

Based on the way the women look at me as they rise, they realize that, and they're not happy about it.

The fighting breaks out in full force, Derian, Roland, and Caldren all fighting against the women who are able to easily change their bodies into nothing but mist.

They evade every slash of metal, their laughter echoing as their bodies come in and out of existence.

Eventually, those shadows around them rise, forming solid blades that they wield effortlessly.

To their credit, the men around me all seem to expect their impossible movements. They wield their magic and steel in time, clearly anticipating where they will blink into existence.

And through it all, I'm standing in the middle, staring, struggling to track what's happening.

Caldren hisses to my right as the shadow blade of his attacker slices through the leather cuff of his bicep. She dances around his side, sprinting towards me, and I lift my dagger to meet her blade, driving my second up towards her gut.

She mists into shadow before my blade can strike home, appearing at my side.

"Why do you fight us?" she asks softly, as Cal's vines wrap around her waist and rip her back towards him.

"Huntress!" I hear Derian yell. "Now's a good time to run."

The woman fighting Roland lurches past him towards me just as Derian gives his command, and she grasps onto my wrist with an iron clasp.

The pain is immediate, worse than anything I felt in that damned arena. It's like my very soul is being sucked forcefully out of my body. My knees buckle and I fall heavily, crashing onto the ground and biting down on my lip to stop from screaming and distracting the others.

I can't stop the whimper though.

"You're very strange," the woman muses, tilting her head at me again.

Roland slashes his sword across her back, pulling her attention from me as she turns wildly towards him.

"Don't let them touch you!" he cries, meeting her shadow blade with his steel.

They're evenly matched. He's stronger, but she's faster. He's calculated, but she's violent.

He pivots, drawing her in front of him and putting me behind his back once again. Still, she's only focused on me. Desperate to get to me. They *all* are.

"Huntyr, run! Now."

Derian's voice is full of desperation, and it's not that I'm purposefully avoiding his command.

I just can't move.

I'm still on my knees on the ground, my body locked up and tense—entirely frozen—even as I will myself to stand. I'm suddenly too hot, a panting, sweating mess as heat rolls over me in steady waves.

I know I need to stand. I either need to flee as Derian instructed, or I need to fight. To help these three men, who are so clearly evenly matched with *whatever* these women are. Either way, I need to stand, but I *can't*.

I'm stuck because something is slowly building inside of me, rising to a suffocating crescendo, and I'm entirely helpless against it. I can't think. I can't breathe.

"Huntyr!" Kaia's voice sounds far away.

The fight sounds far away.

My head thrashes back, to the canopy of green leaves above my head, blocking any view of the sky.

Someone's calling my name.

I don't know who.

I barely even know who I am.

I am nothing but flesh and blood...

And power.

That's what this fire inside of me is.

It's *power* rushing violently through me. Down my spine, through my arms and legs, into my head. I'm blinded by the golden magnificence of it, and time loses all meaning. Everything loses meaning.

Until that golden vision fades, leaving my eyesight so sharp that I can see millions of shades in the leaves that had once simply been green. My hearing is just as heightened. I hear the ants on the ground around me, the beating of wings in the air, the cries from the village we left behind us.

I've barely gotten enough control over my extremities for me to push off the ground and stand on unsteady legs when I *hear* the skip of a heartbeat, then the sharp intake of breath, then the soft grunt.

The woman fighting Derian has leveled a blow so intense it knocks his head back.

Just like the blow that Seraphina dealt me.

My legs are moving before I even know what I plan to do.

"Huntyr, no!" Roland's voice is the epitome of panic, and I spin to face him, only to realize that those precious few steps have taken me right next to the woman he fights.

She rushes towards me, arms outstretched, and I take a panicked, stumbling step backwards.

Just as Roland grabs her forearm and yanks her from me.

I *feel* her snarl in my bones as she turns to him, knocks his sword away with a rush of shadow, and takes his face between her palms. Her eyes turn pure black, and her jaw unlocks into an inhuman gape as she *inhales.*

Roland falls to his knees, and I watch, wordlessly, as shimmering magic seems to leak from him, drawn out of him and into her. That inky darkness spreads down her cheeks and chest.

Somehow, I know what's happening. I know what she's doing and how this will end, but it all happens so quickly. Far too quickly for me to regain control of myself fast enough to act or to stop it.

I hear the click of his jaw breaking echo sharply in my ears as I watch his eyes dry and shrivel, leaving darkened, hollow holes behind.

She smiles widely as she drops his dead body to the ground.

Roland is dead.

Just like that man in the village.

Just like my *father*.

That power sparks down my spine once more, and there's no room for any logical thought once it takes hold of me. I don't know what I'm doing as I move forward, pushing myself towards her until I press my palm against her forehead and let that magic erupt.

It bursts out of me like an explosion of shimmering, intense light that is both intensely violent and filled with unspeakable relief. Her eyes widen slightly as I push that light out of me and into her, until it erupts from her eyes and ears, golden, warm, and intense.

It feels like home. Like Tyla. Like warm nights spent together by the fireplace reading books and sharing wine. Like the quiet moments with Derian after we've brought each other to the highest forms of bliss. Like the touch of Kristona brushing my hair aside and kissing me goodnight.

Like the moment before I kill someone, when I know that I alone control death itself.

She falls.

Her body falls next to Roland's. Both hollowed out. His left dark, and hers left golden.

I lose all control of my body as I heave forward and retch.

After what feels like an eternity, my hearing and vision fade back to their normal intensity, and I don't register when the fighting stops. I don't even sense the footsteps nearing me until a gentle hand pulls back my hair.

I tense, swinging my blade, but a hand wraps around my wrist and stills me.

"It's me," I hear Caldren say behind me.

No. I don't need Caldren.

Rocking back on my heels, I bring my hand to my mouth, wiping away any remnants of what just happened as I look for him.

Derian looks more like a beast than a man as he drops his sword to the ground and comes to me, crouching before me and taking my face in his hands.

Then, he looks at *my* hands. Hands that are still streaked with that golden light. I hold them up in horror, staring at the glittering light that flows under my skin, fading away ever so slowly.

"I—" The words don't come out easily. "I don't know how I did that."

"It's okay, Huntress." He brushes away my hair. "You did good."

I want to look to my side, to the bodies next to me, but he holds my face firmly.

"Roland." I don't know how to apologize. I don't know how to explain that I didn't keep his friend safe.

Derian wets his lip, looking to his friend over my shoulder. I would have forgotten Caldren was there at all if it wasn't for the reassuring circles he was rubbing along my back.

"Cal is going to take you back to the village. I'll take care of this."

"No!" I'm protesting before I'm even thinking it through, grabbing onto his wrist sharply.

Derian leans forward, resting his forehead against mine. "I need to bury my friend, Huntyr. Go with Cal. I'll be right behind you."

Caldren rises, bringing me to my feet with him.

I don't have it in me to protest as he puts a hand on my waist and starts guiding me back to my village.

"Caldren, what were they?" I whisper once we're out of Derian's earshot.

Cal glances down at me, a strand of copper hair falling over his brow before he breathes deeply and quickens our pace.

"Those, Lachlan, were Velkai," he tells me, his voice grave. "And I just held your hair while you puked your guts up, I think you can call me Cal now."

I don't acknowledge him. I can't. I'm too busy turning over those words again and again.

Velkai.

Not Fae.

The Fae hadn't killed my father.

Which meant...

That meant that my *entire* life had been built on a lie. Every horror I'd seen living in Kristona's house. Every brutal beating I'd taken in the name of training. Every atrocity I'd committed.

It had all been for a lie.

I'd spent my life turning myself into a bigger monster than the ones who had taken my father from me. My entire life had been leading to the moment that I could get my revenge on the Fae.

And it had all been for nothing.

DERIAN

I don't waste any time in getting us back on the road towards Spring-hallow. We've already wasted most of the day dealing with the Velkai, and I don't relish the idea of extending the number of nights we need to sleep unprotected like this.

This whole situation has gone to shit.

I'm pissed off enough about it that I continue pushing us well past the time the sun has gone down. I'm perfectly content to ride through the night, though, to ride until we reach Springhallow and I can sit with a stiff drink and consider everything that has happened.

If what those creatures said is true, if the Velkai queen really is alive, then we're all fucked.

I'd been suspecting it already, but now that I've seen it with my own eyes, I can't deny the fact that they're organizing. They're coming together again in groups after all these years. Initially, I thought it was possible a new leader had come to power, but if the Mother is still alive somehow...

I cannot allow her to rise.

And if all that isn't concerning enough, there is then the matter of my Huntress to consider.

I stopped feeling true terror decades ago. I have no need to fear death, nothing to lose really. If you don't fear death itself, then you have absolutely nothing to fear in life.

I've felt terror twice recently, though.

Terror consumed me when she collapsed after Seraphina hit her in the final trial. Then terror found me again today, when those three Velkai had all looked towards her in perfect synchrony.

What the fuck *is* she and why the fuck do they want her?

At some point, I'll have to figure out how exactly she managed to kill that one without beheading it. I've only ever seen them killed through beheading. Although, in my two-hundred years, I've also never met a Fae who could wield light. I suppose it's possible it could be a rather rare gift, but if that's going to make her desirable to the Velkai, we'll need to figure out why.

"Derian," Cal clears his throat next to me. "We've ridden far enough."

"We can keep going."

There's sympathy in his eyes, and pain. Roland had been his friend too. Another friend lost too soon from an enemy who is far too unpredictable.

"The horses are tired, brother. As am I. And Huntyr—"

"I know what Huntyr can take."

She hasn't spoken to me since I came back to the village. She hasn't spoken to *anyone.* Not even Ulna, who had her wrapped in an embrace when I finally returned. Her face has been carefully detached, her eyes distant and unfocused.

Gods, I hate it when she goes silent.

"We need to rest, Derian. Please trust me on this."

I sigh, swallowing down the urge to insist we keep going. He means no harm though, and he's right. Exhausting the horses isn't going to get us there any faster.

Slowing my pace, I pull us over to a wooded area and slide off my horse. I instruct Taric and Cal to check the area. Now that we know the Velkai are traveling past the Wastelands, we really can't be too careful.

Ulna readies herself, making a fire, while I begin pitching my tent. I don't bother with Huntyr's, she'll be staying in mine tonight whether she likes it or not.

The woman in question just sinks to the ground and rests her head on the Eshari next to her.

<hr>

Taric and Cal find a small pool of water at the bottom of the hill while investigating. Close enough that we can easily get back to camp if there's danger, but private enough that people can bathe without feeling too exposed.

After a few days of traveling and a bloody fight, everyone could use a bath.

Cal goes first, then Taric, then Ulna, then Huntyr. I wait to go last, knowing I won't enjoy it. My mind is still spinning too quickly, anxiety rushing through me that would only be made worse by a private bath.

"We need to send a missive to the King," Taric says, picking at the roasted rabbit meat in front of him. "He needs to know to be on his guard while traveling."

"He's been traveling far longer than we have," I grumble. "Chances are he already knows."

"Still," Cal agrees. "We can arrange for it at the next town we pass through. There should still be one more between here and Springhallow."

The night air is cool. I've stripped away most of my leathers, still too heated from the battle and the fire in front of me, and now wear nothing more than my pants and boots.

Taric and Cal have similarly made themselves comfortable. Taric wears his leather armor pants and cotton undershirt while Cal has already fully abandoned his armor for his sleeping clothes.

Ulna went into her tent nearly half an hour ago without a single word of goodnight.

It wasn't a good night. Not for any of us. Not when we are missing a tent tonight.

I stare aimlessly at the space between my tent and Cal's, where Roland typically would have set up his. The emptiness there is oppressive, and I force myself to look away. I learned a long time ago to bury down grief.

"She really said the Mother is alive?" Taric repeats. It's the third time he's asked, as if I was somehow mistaken in hearing that the most powerful, most evil being in history was still here, waiting to rise up once more.

I shift forward, adjusting the logs in the fire, watching the sparks lift and dance into the night sky.

"There is another matter we need to discuss." Cal's voice is tentative and uneasy.

Taric looks up at him in confusion, but I don't bother. I'm well aware of what he wants to talk about, and I most definitely do *not* want to talk about that.

"It's out of the question," I tell him, voice laced with threat.

"What is?" Taric asked, glancing between the two of us even as I carefully avoid looking at my best friend.

If he continues pushing this topic, I'm liable to kill him.

"Lachlan killed one of them."

Taric pauses, as if he doesn't quite understand why Cal is so serious. "And that's bad because?"

Silently, I roll out my neck, tension building in my locked shoulders. There are no adequate words to describe what she looked like in that moment. A shudder threatens to work its way through me as I picture it. Picture her.

Glowing. Golden.

That light traveling throughout her body, shimmering down her arms and through her fingers. Those blue eyes that I'd come to seek out, to rely on, brilliantly *golden*.

Beautiful.

And utterly terrifying.

For exactly the reason Cal was about to point out.

"She killed them with her magic," he says.

Taric's brows raise slowly as his eyes bounce between us. "No kidding?"

I feel Cal's attention on me as he continues, his voice soft and cautious. "If Lachlan's magic can kill them with a simple touch, then she could be a huge asset."

"It's not happening." I don't leave any room for negotiation.

Taric sighs, inclining his head to the side. "She *is* a Conclave winner. A warrior. It wouldn't be unheard of for her to fight along the borders. It might even be expected."

I grind my teeth together, hard enough that I'm sure my jaw will ache later. "I don't give a fuck what anyone expects. She just learned she has this power. I'm not throwing her onto a battlefield."

Cal shifts his weight next to me, the secret of her background burning through him. "She's more than capable of defending herself."

"Against *Mortals,*" I remind him. "This is different."

His exhale is sharp. "Derian, think clearly."

My chest vibrates with a growl. "Mind your tone, Caldren."

"No." If he were anyone other than my best friend, I would verbally eviscerate him for this kind of insolence. "If this was you, if *your* power could kill them, would you wait around on the sidelines?"

I meet his glare, leveling him with one of my own.

He knows the answer to that question as well as I do.

"My decision is final."

Silence falls over our trio as we all stare at the orange and yellow flames flickering up around the fire. It's abundantly clear neither of them is finished with the conversation, though, judging by the way they keep looking awkwardly at each other.

"What?" I finally bark.

"Well," Taric clears his throat before resting his elbows on his knees and folding his hands together. "Have you thought about asking her what her opinion is?"

I open my mouth to respond, but the words don't come out. In fact, I'm not quite sure what to say to that question, or the insinuation beneath it. I pause just as Cal starts chuckling beside me.

"What?" I ask, turning towards him. "What are you laughing at?"

He holds his hands up in surrender. "She just doesn't seem that appreciative when you make decisions for her."

Taric nods his agreement. "She's a wild one, that girl, and you seem to be trying to tame her when she isn't interested in being domesticated."

I wasn't—

I hadn't been—

Had I been doing that?

Had I been trying to chain up a woman who clearly neither needed nor wanted me to hold on to her so tightly?

My friends watch my realization, amusement dancing in their eyes as they do. The fire cracks sharply between us, and Cal tosses a burnt piece of rabbit hide into the flames.

"So," I hate myself as the words come out of my mouth. "What would you suggest?"

Taric stifles a laugh behind the back of his hand, and I level one of my darkest glares on him. He lifts a hand apologetically and gestures for Cal to take over.

"Why not start with telling her everything she needs to know?" Cal suggests. "Give her whatever time she needs to come to terms with that and then let her tell you what she wants to do."

"I suppose that's not a terrible idea."

"Yes, well then you need to *accept* her decision," Taric reminds me.

That sounds, admittedly, more challenging since she has a tendency to completely disregard her own safety.

I stiffen as something wet and warm presses against my back, and turn to see the Eshari pushing her snout into me. The beast looks up at me with its golden eyes. No snarl. No growl. Just a flick of a tail towards that pool where Huntyr went to bathe.

Where she'd gone to bathe twenty minutes ago.

The panther in front of me doesn't seem panicked or rushed, which tells me everything I need to know.

She's not in danger, at least not from anyone but herself.

And apparently, the Eshari has decided Huntyr needs me.

I don't waste another second.

"Where are you going?" Taric questions as I turn and start marching down the hill.

I don't bother responding, but I hear Cal's answer as I go.

"To her. He's going to her."

HUNTYR

I keep staring at my hands in my lap as if I'm waiting for them to explode again. The light faded away long before we arrived at camp, but I can still feel the echo of that power in my fingertips. I'm not even sure if I can summon it back. I'm not sure if I want to.

Fae magic.

That's what it is.

Undeniably.

Fucking. Fae. Magic.

The magic of the creatures I was trained to kill. The creatures I had *begged* Kristona to teach me how to kill.

Throughout all that training, fighting, and killing, I'd been a Fae myself the whole time.

What unbelievable irony.

And somehow that wasn't even the worst of it.

No, the worst of it, the unimaginable truth, was that the Fae weren't actually responsible for the day that had changed my life irrevocably.

It wasn't the Fae who had killed my father.

It wasn't the Fae who had forced me to jump from that window and run into the night.

It wasn't the Fae who had left me alone and crying on that street.

All this time, I'd been so sure. I'd been *so* positive, that I'd let Kristona take me home and claim me as his daughter and apprentice.

I'd been *five years old*.

I'd accepted every horror and committed every single monstrosity he'd asked me to, because it all served a purpose. Every person I ran my blade through prepared me for the day I could make the Fae pay for what they did to me.

All of it had been a waste.

Had Kristona known all along? He'd taken me in, become a second father to me, and told me he loved me every single day. But he also hurt me. Physically. Emotionally. Spiritually. He nurtured that hatred in my heart and used it to serve his purposes.

What kind of love drives a man to send a child to conduct such atrocities?

He is just as responsible for the blood on my hands as I am.

Blood that now stains my soul for *nothing*.

I don't move when I hear Derian approaching. I don't even look away from my hands when he crouches down in front of me.

"Get up," he orders, not a hint of sympathy in his tone.

Kaia snarls next to him, and he turns his glare onto her.

"She doesn't need to be coddled," he says to her, entirely unafraid as she bares her teeth at him. If I wasn't spiraling so much, I'd be impressed by his courage.

He turns back to me. "Up, Huntress. You'll either do it on your own or I'll lift you. I'm learning you'd prefer to do things by yourself, but I'm not opposed to taking care of you if you refuse to do so."

His voice still lacks any kindness or understanding for the fact that everything I've ever known has just crashed down around me. With difficulty, I finally pull my gaze from my hands, glaring at him with such anger that a smirk begins to play at his lips as I push to my feet.

He looks down at Kaia. "Scram, Kitty."

"Don't go," I beg her, not even sure why.

She pushes her head against my leg. *"The prince will keep you safe."*

"I can keep myself safe."

She's quiet, looking up at me with such seriousness that my stomach flips slightly.

"I do not speak of your physical safety."

With a flick of her tail and a growl in Derian's direction, she's gone, running up the hill, back to our camp, before I can ask what she means by that. Then, I'm left alone with the Fae prince, who's scanning over me with a poorly hidden grimace.

"You stink," he tells me.

I balk. "Well, you're not exactly a fresh spring yourself."

He reaches forward, undoing the belt on my hips and starting to strip my clothing. His movements are methodical and precise, his eyes focused only on the clothes he's removing as he's doing so. There's no desire in his gaze, only the focus on his singular goal of helping me out of my clothing.

When I'm entirely nude, and shivering, he wraps an arm around my waist and pushes me towards the pool of water at our feet.

"In you go."

In the moonlight, the water is near black, ominous, and overwhelming. As I step in, my bare feet connect with rocks and small divots that almost feel like seats in the ground. I feel my way around as heat rushes over the skin of my foot, a prickling sensation that dances the line between pleasure and discomfort.

A hotspring.

The sigh that escapes me sounds positively sexual, but I can't bother to feel embarrassed by it. Not when the water feels this warm. I sink into it, letting that warmth wrap around me. It works my aching muscles, coaxing them into a melting release, and I allow myself to go under for a few moments, letting the water flow over my face and through my hair.

Under the water, there's the tiniest sense of peace—of escape.

When I finally emerge, blinking my eyes open and gasping for air, the first thing I see is a hand reaching towards me. I can't stop my gasp from the sudden rush of fear, and water splashes into the air as I jerk backwards.

"Hey," Derian's voice cracks through the anxiety, and I make out his form in front of me. His hand comes to cup my face. "It's only me. I've got you."

His pants and boots lay discarded next to mine in the grass, and I can just make out the sight of the fire on the hill above us where our friends wait for us.

Friends.

Fae.

One and the same.

"I'm sorry," I mumble. "I'm not usually so jumpy."

He gives me a slight understanding smile. "I know."

Derian runs a thumb over my brow, to where the worry line has formed between them.

"It wasn't for nothing, Huntress."

I sigh heavily, no longer surprised that he's able to read me so clearly and sense what's worrying my mind. His hands run down my shoulders and begin kneading slightly, working at the tight muscles, and I allow myself to relax under their expert work.

"I'm fine," I lie, though I'm not sure if it's for his benefit or my own.

He gives me that expression that says he knows I'm lying. "Everything you've ever known about yourself and your world has changed in a matter of days. I would be horrified if you were still fine after that."

Perhaps, but I'd always been the kind of person who could pick myself up and keep going despite what chaos life threw at me. I was the woman who hid my pain away behind sarcasm and violence without ever struggling to seem unfazed.

So why couldn't I do that so easily now?

I chew on my lower lip, letting my head fall back to stare at the brilliantly shining constellations above us. The stars trail across the sky, so beautiful a painter could never quite capture their elegance. It seems wrong that a soul as ugly as mine should get to bear witness to something this beautiful.

"I've done such terrible things," I whisper, not courageous enough to admit the words with any real volume.

My mind has been playing it over and over since we resumed our journey out of that wretched town. Every job. The fighting. The torture. The killing.

I could bathe in the blood of my victims, and there would still be enough to fill a dozen more tubs. I'd managed to justify it all for so long, but now? There is no justification. No excuse.

There is just me. And the monster I've become.

Derian's hands fall to my waist, and he pulls me to straddle him as he sits atop one of those carvings in the rock. There's nothing sexual about the position. This is just for the comfort of being close to another body, and I allow myself to relish in the feeling of his skin on mine.

"You're not the only one to do heinous things, love," he reminds me.

I stare at him, stare into those dark eyes, and I know that he's telling the truth. I know he is, because his eyes are just as haunted as I feel. Derian has had decades to create his infamous legacy of brutality.

"How do you live with it?"

He sighs, looking away for a moment before turning back to me and brushing my hair back off my shoulders. "You just do. You remind yourself that every step you've taken has been necessary to get you where you are now. I happen to like where I am now."

His words hit heavily in my chest, and the tears that have been threatening to escape since I watched Roland die finally break free. I hate it. I hate that unstoppable show of vulnerability, but he doesn't flinch. He doesn't look at me like I'm weak or silly as he brushes them away with his thumbs.

"It wasn't necessary, Derian."

His fingers hook on my chin, forcing my attention back on him when I attempt to turn away. "Yes it was, Huntress. *Everything* you have done, everything you lived through, shaped you into who you are now. You are the stubborn, strong, vivacious, insufferable woman you are because of every single day in your past. It *all* led you here. To this moment. To you and me sitting here together."

I'm shaking. Even in the warm water, I can't stop the trembles that work through me. He either doesn't notice or doesn't care enough to acknowledge it.

"You are so powerful, Huntyr Lachlan, for so many more reasons than whatever magic runs in your veins. You are going to need that power in the days that come. So, do not look back on your past with hatred. Do not look at yourself with anything other than respect for the girl who fought to become such an incredible woman."

He leans forward, pressing his lips to mine. The kiss is gentle, barely more than a touch. It's a whisper of whatever bond exists between the two of us. A promise that even if I can't see my own strength right now, *he* sees it. He respects it the way he wishes I would.

That sweetness undoes me. It knits together something inside me that broke earlier today.

No, it does more than just that. It mends pieces of me that broke apart a long time ago.

This monster beside me, with a past as dark and horrendous as my own, might be the only soul in this realm who has the power to heal me.

And that knowledge sends a spark of desire coursing through me. Desire for a physical release yes, but also a desire for *him.* His kisses are still slow and gentle, reassuring, but it's not long before I'm grasping hold of him and guiding him to my entrance.

"You don't have to," he tells me, not daring to blink as he stares at me.

I don't have to. I know that. I've never *had* to.

I've wanted to.

I've wanted him to ease the burning in me. I've wanted him to distract me from the trauma and pain. I've wanted him to ruin my mind with pleasure.

And now I want him to give me some sort of connection to the here and now, to the version of life that he paints where it all connects. Where it's all important. Where I can accept myself the way he accepts me.

I sink down onto him and we begin moving together. This time it's not fast or desperate. It's not the lust-fueled passion that we've had every other time we've come together.

This is just... connection.

And there's something infinitely beautiful about that.

He holds me as I begin to lose my grasp on reality. His fingers dig into my hips as my head falls back, and I'm staring at those stars again. Then he's following me into oblivion with my name on his lips.

In the silence that follows, I remain atop him, resting my head in the crook of his neck while his hand plays with my hair aimlessly.

"I have questions," I whisper softly.

He nods against me before pressing a kiss to my brow. "Tomorrow. I'll tell you everything you want to know tomorrow. For now, let's get you to bed."

We emerge from the water, awkwardly putting on the leather that now feels uncomfortable on our damp skin. It's only needed for the walk back to his tent, though. And then we're bare again, curled up on the bedroll together.

Without warning, he pulls me against his chest, wrapping an arm around my stomach to keep me pressed there. We've shared a bed a few times before, I've even passed out on his chest when I was too exhausted after our unions to move myself away.

After everything that's happened, though, this seems infinitely more personal.

I should protest, but I don't.

Whether I'm ready to admit it or not, the weight of his arm around me, the warmth of his body behind mine, is so unbelievably comforting. It's tender, and fuck, it feels *safe.*

The entirety of the Mortal Kingdoms fears the Fae warrior wrapped around me, but I fall asleep in his arms and I don't have a single nightmare.

⚜

Derian lets me ride beside him today. Cal is a hundred paces in front of us, Ulna and Taric an equal distance behind. All of them are far enough away that they shouldn't be able to hear our conversation.

"You promised me answers," I remind him, working to keep my voice even.

We spoke little after waking up. Everyone was in a rush to get back on the road since we're so close to our destination. Truthfully, I think he was as unsure how to act around me as I was around him.

We'd spent the entire night tangled up together. Despite the fact that I'd slept more peacefully than I had in ages, my head was now spinning just as much as it had been last night, but for entirely different reasons now.

What we'd done with our bodies last night had been dangerously closer to love making than it was to simply acting out carnal desires.

And that feels...

Well, I don't know how I feel about that.

He is the Fae prince, nightmare of the Mortal Kingdoms. I'd do well to remember that regardless of what I may or may not *feel*.

"So, I did," he answers, shifting slightly on his horse. "What do you want to know?"

I chew on my lip, ignoring the growing unease in my stomach. We've been riding for hours already, and he keeps glancing at me out of the corner of his eye as if he's been waiting for me to work up the courage for this conversation.

"Where does it come from?" I ask him, glancing down at where my fingers are grasping the reins of my horse in an iron fist. "The magic, I mean."

Derian looks at me with a furrowed brow, as if he hadn't been expecting *that* question.

Truthfully, the question just slipped out, surprising me almost as much as him. I had planned to demand every detail I could about the Velkai, and I still intend to get that information, but the second my mouth opened, that other question came out.

His lips quirk a little before he turns back to the road ahead of us, and I'm positive that's relief in his eyes. Relief that exists because asking that question exposes the fact that I'm starting to realize I can't just wish away whatever light exists in me.

"We don't know, not fully. Our histories tell us that before the Ever Realm was made solid, it was made of pure ether."

"Ether?"

He nods, pursing his lips as if trying to decide the best way to explain. I don't imagine he's had to explain the details of Fae magic to many other Mortals.

Although, I'm not Mortal.

Not technically. Not fully.

"Ether is a sort of primal magical energy. Even now, ether rises from the ground naturally. Both Fae and Mortal carry ether inside of them, but Fae bodies can materialize that ether, store it, and manipulate it, in a way that Mortal bodies can't."

"For basic magic?"

He once told me that all Fae can control basic magics, simpler kinds of tricks like healing and warming bathwater, in addition to whatever specialty they wield.

Derian nods, the sunlight catching on his dark hair as he does. It's grown out quite a bit since I first met him, hanging easily over his brows now. I like it better this way, slightly too long and curling at the ends. Always a little unkempt and windblown. It makes him look more like the warrior he is and less like the prince he was dressed up to be at that masquerade.

I physically shake my head to clear out all thoughts about Derian's shiny hair.

"The ether is why we get sick if we're not around other Fae, we emit a small amount of it too. Being around other Fae helps you maintain the balance in your system, so to speak."

"Why are there differences in what you can wield?" I question, thinking back to the various abilities that Fae have.

"*Our* ability to wield develops from our personalities." He ignores when I shiver at him including me within the category of Fae. "Earth wielders, for example, tend to be very practical and dependable. They're patient but also very no-nonsense. Cal's a nearly perfect example of that."

I nod, from the little I know of Derian's friend, that makes sense.

"Fire wielders," he continues, "can be rather impulsive and quick-tempered like you saw with Seraphina. Storm wielders—"

"Let me guess," I interrupt, a grin playing at the edges of my lips. "Intense and broody? Wicked and unpredictable tempers?"

Derian hardly glances at me, even as his lips twitch into a crooked smile. "We're also rather passionate, but I think you've gathered that much already."

If we weren't on a horse, I'd have stomped his foot.

"Well, what about me?" I ask suddenly.

He frowns. "What about you?"

"The light. What are people with that ability like?"

He works to avoid my gaze, but I don't miss the shadow that covers his features or the way his posture stiffens slightly.

"There aren't Fae like you, Huntress, at least not any that I've met before. That light wielding of yours is probably an incredibly rare ability. Possibly even more rare than storm wielding."

A heavy silence falls between us. As if it isn't bad enough that I'm one of *them*, I have to be a super special one-of-a-kind Fae? My stomach clenches unhappily at the thought.

"Velkai," I clear my throat, desperate to turn the subject. "What are they?"

Derian looks at me for a longtime before he answers. I suspect he wasn't done talking about my magic. He hasn't brought up teaching me to use it again, but I have no doubt that unpleasant conversation is going to be initiated again soon.

"They're older than either Fae or Mortals," he tells me. "We don't even think they're natural to the Ever Realm."

I frown. "What does that mean?"

He shrugs, as if what he's suggesting isn't absolutely ridiculous. "We think they're from another realm. They rival the power of the Vaereth, what you know as the Gods. Neither seem to use ether the way we do. Velkai are able to take it. Naturally their bodies draw it in, that's why any patch of land they stay in for long periods of time becomes barren. They can also rob it, sucking directly from other people."

A shudder racks down my spine, and I don't bother hiding the look of disgust on my face as I picture the way the Velkai sucked the very essence out of Roland.

For a moment, it's all I can see. I'm right back in those woods, watching him fall before me.

"And these Gods, the *Vaereth*?" I stumble over the word, tongue awkwardly twisting around the pronunciation.

Once again, Derian gives me that infuriatingly casual shrug. "They disappeared during the War. They took great losses when trying to defeat the Velkai. Most believe that once the Velkai threat was handled, they returned to whatever realm they came from."

I puzzle over that, something about it not sitting right with me.

"Just like that?" I question. "They were here for longer than either Mortals or Fae and then just decided to...leave?"

"Maybe they decided we weren't worth defending after the war."

They hardly sound any better than the Velkai then. Even if they weren't seeking to harm us, standing by and watching us die isn't much better.

Still, if it's that easy to just disappear into another realm, why couldn't we just shove the Velkai through a one-way door back to where they came from?

Quiet falls over us again. He lets me think through things on my own, puzzling through memories and bits of facts as I piece together information in a way that now makes sense. The only indication that he's on edge is the slight humidity in the air.

That humidity lingers around us throughout the next few hours, but never escalates past that. Even when we stop for a quick lunch and I refuse to speak to anyone, he gives me my space.

It's only once we're back on our horses, and Cal announces that we're approaching the manor, that the final question bursts out of me.

"Why were you surprised to see three of them yesterday?"

He stiffens. It's so slight, just the smallest straightening of the spine, but I see it, and it's enough to make my blood run cold.

"Velkai don't work well in groups. They're violent, self-centered creatures. The last time I saw them in groups was when a leader had emerged among them. A queen."

"The Mother?"

He nods. "She was known as the Velkai Mother. She was by far the most powerful and vicious among them, and somehow, she managed to unite them all. They're powerful on their own, but as an army they're nearly unstoppable. The Vaereth killed her during the war, or so at least, that's what we thought."

"But if she's not dead…"

Derian meets my eyes, the intensity in his gaze enough to leave me shuddering once more. "Then the blood that was spilled during the last war was only the beginning."

A sharp breeze blows past me, lifting my hair. I wonder if he even knows he's doing it, or if his magic leaks out as easily as mine apparently does.

"You make it sound like we're all screwed," I try to joke, but it lands flatly between us.

"If they were telling the truth, and she is alive, we just might be."

DERIAN

I wish we had more time.

The thought surprises me a little, but it's true.

I want more time with her.

I want the time to teach her to harness that beautiful light of hers. I want to spend hours showing her how to use it, telling her how spectacular it is and how divine she looks using it. I want to pour sweet words over her until she isn't afraid of that magic inside of her.

Then I want to take her to my bedroom and spend days locked inside with her. I want to take her every way I can, play out every fantasy I know she has inside that wonderfully meticulous mind of hers.

After that? I want to take her back to that training yard. I want to see what she can do when she's not holding back and hiding her skills. I want to have a *true* knife-throwing contest with her.

We don't have time, though.

My brother will be here soon. The wedding will follow shortly after. Then, I'll need to go back to the Wastelands. I'll need to find out if the Mother lives, and if she does, I need to be the one who kills her.

I'm the only one who stands a chance of rivaling her power.

I'll have to leave Huntyr here. Regardless of what Taric and Cal said, I can't let her anywhere near the Wastelands. It's not because I doubt her. I know my Huntress is more than capable of defending herself. I knew that even before I saw she had the power to kill a Velkai with one touch. And yes, I even recognize that she does deserve the ability to make the decision for herself.

The truth is, *I* won't be able to think straight if she's there. I'll be so worried that something will happen that leaves her looking like she did last night.

Small. Child-like. Broken down.

I'd give all my fortune to never have to see her like that again.

"Where's he going?" she asks, nodding ahead to where Cal breaks away from the road that leads into the manor, right in front of the gates to the estate.

I can hear Taric and Ulna breaking away behind us, already heading towards one of the guest houses on the property. She watches them go, face scrunched in thought.

"Cal is going to check with the guards that monitor the perimeter of the manor. We're safe here, and perfectly capable of fending off anyone or anything that threatens that safety, but at the end of the day, I am a prince. So, it's as much their job to protect me as it's mine to protect Luceron."

She snorts, as if the idea that I am beholden to the same kinds of restrictions as any other royal is funny to her.

"Make disparaging noises all you want. You're a few weeks away from being a princess yourself."

That earns me one of those delicious glares that makes me want to peel her clothes off of her. I can't help but to wet my lips as I give her a wink. Gods, I can't wait to get her into my bedchamber. On a proper bed after sleeping in tents on the ground.

We pass through the front gates, and I lead her towards where a stable hand is already waiting to take away and care for our horses. When I grasp her hand in mine and start leading her towards the house, she doesn't protest, she just curls her fingers around my own, a simple gesture that causes my blood to pump unevenly for a brief moment as we make our way towards the house.

I have a few properties across the kingdom, but my manor at Springhallow has always been my favorite. It was passed down through the generations on my mother's side of the family. Luceron never much cared for the climate here, and has very little reason to ever leave Bridgemond, so the property became mine when she died.

Warmth surges in me as I take in the intricate stonework, arched entryways, and large chimneys. It's been far too long since I was last here. In my absence, though, the staff has been diligent in their upkeep. Every one of the various round and rectangular windows sparkle. I pay them a small fortune to make sure this home stays exactly as it did when my mother owned it.

I lead Huntyr through the front door and step aside, watching her as she takes it all in. Her eyes scan over the entryway, tracing over the coffered wooden ceiling and deep red walls. Above the mosaic rug in the center of the space sits a wooden table, hundreds of years older than I am, a bouquet of fresh tulips atop it.

Her eyes widen slightly as she takes in the fireplace to her right, topped with a carved mantelpiece and framed by a large stone archway, but she doesn't give away any indication of what she's thinking.

"May I?" she asks, waving a hand towards the rest of the house.

I tuck my hands in my pockets and nod, content to follow her as she explores. She moves slowly, carefully taking advantage of the opportunity to build her spatial awareness of this new place. I want to know her every thought, but for now I allow her this time to take stock of her surroundings, knowing she needs to know what's contained in every room, and track where all the exits are.

She needs that if she's going to find any semblance of peace here.

Allowing her this also allows me the chance to measure her initial reactions. There aren't many people I've allowed into this house besides the staff who maintain it. Cal is probably my most frequent guest, but even Taric and Ulna have only been a handful of times.

This is a place I keep to myself. One of the very few things that exists only for the sake of *my* happiness.

Until now.

Now, I'm letting Huntyr Lachlan, noblewoman, assassin, and Conclave champion, explore the house that is to be hers in a few weeks. This house is one of the many things that comes with being my wife.

She makes her way to the staircase to the upper floors, trailing her fingers against the carved railing. The staircase has always been my favorite part of the manor. It twists around the entryway, winding across the wall in a way that makes it the true centerpiece of the home, both beautiful in its splendor and grounding in its construction.

"It's incredible," she finally says softly, turning those eyes to me. There's so much warmth in that gaze. So much that I think she may truly realize how much this house means to me.

Huntyr knows how significant it is that I'm allowing her into this space.

She turns her head back to the stairs, tilting it backwards so she can peer up to the second floor landing, but the motion causes the light from the arched window above to fall across her face and I soak in the sight of her.

I've stared at her plenty of times before. I've watched her both when she's aware and painfully unaware of my attention. And yet, I don't think I've ever had the privilege of being allowed to so closely look at her when she's so relaxed.

Her skin has tanned slightly from the journey, making her natural blush seem pinker than normal. And Gods help me, those freckles. With the sun coloring her cheeks, they're so much more noticeable than before. A splattering of them across her nose and cheeks that's giving me the sudden desire to count everyone.

I'm just about to grab her hand and show her the rest of the house, the bedrooms of the house in particular, when there's a knock at the door. Cal opens it without invitation, a smile playing on his lips as he looks not at me... but *her*.

"Your guest is here."

Four words.

It takes four words for an entirely new version of her to emerge.

Her eyes spark as a glittering smile splits her face, and then she's moving. No hesitation. No explanation. She sprints away from me and through the front door with hardly a breath.

I've never seen her so happy.

I follow her out just in time to see her throw herself at the dark-haired girl walking up the pathway to the house, the Fae group I'd sent to retrieve her nodding at me before turning to the guest houses.

Huntyr is crying.

She hugs the girl before pulling back to cradle her head and look over her. They're nearly identical, standing at the same height and sporting that same impossibly dark hair. The other girl's skin is lighter, and her eyes are dark brown, nearly black, but there's no denying the resemblance.

"Do you think her sister is Fae too?" Cal asks beside me, crossing his arms over his chest as he leans back against his house.

His words send ice pouring through me.

I hadn't even stopped to consider that.

That fucking favor.

I'd been so consumed by the magic of it, pulling me to save her sister, that I hadn't even stopped to question anything about the *existence* of a sister. I don't even know the girl's name.

I don't know if she is just as formidable of a warrior as Huntyr is.

If this girl has the kind of magic Huntyr has, though, that rare magic that can kill Velkai, that's something we need to know sooner rather than later.

HUNTYR

She's here.

She's actually *here*, standing in front of me, alive and as well as can be expected.

I hold her at arm's length, examining every part of her. Her eyes are still sunken in, circled by shadows, and the darkness in her veins extends up her forearms, but she's standing tall, walking easily enough on her own.

"I could hardly believe it when Kristona told me you'd been taken to the Fae kingdom," Tyla exclaims, tears glistening in her dark eyes. "Then these men showed up telling me you'd sent for me."

I tuck a piece of hair behind her ear. "I have so much to tell you, but let's get you inside first."

She shouldn't be on her feet. I can't imagine how difficult the journey has been for her. She'll need to lie down. Maybe Derian can arrange for a warm meal and hot tea. Oh, and a pain tonic. She'll need a pain tonic too.

Derian and Cal linger on the porch, both watching the two of us with matching brooding expressions. I turn to them, feeling Derian's attention on me like a weight.

"Is there a room where she can rest?"

He nods, inclining his head in a silent instruction to follow him.

He leads us through the entryway and towards the grand staircase, but stops when I reach out and grasp his arm, concern flooding through me. Derian looks between Tyla and me, before nodding his understanding.

"I can carry you up the stairs," he offers her. "If that would be alright with you."

She looks to me first, a question in her eyes, but after a reassuring nod she thanks Derian and he easily lifts her into his arms. Silently, he carries her to a bedroom upstairs, all while she sends curious glances over his shoulder at me.

I swallow down my laughter.

The relief of having her here is nearly indescribable, an undeniable force that has seemingly erased the stress and trauma of the past few weeks.

Derian lays her down on an oversized bed with a floral blue quilt. The room is twice as spacious as the tiny apartment we shared back in Velia, and I watch Tyla's eyes widen as she takes in the polished floors, oversized windows, and massive carved fireplace.

The second he sits her down, Derian stiffens, glancing back at me over his shoulder.

"I need to get the tonic."

I frown. I'm in as much of a rush as anyone to get Tyla healed, but he hasn't even said hello to her. Before I can point out as much, he brushes past me. I'm so busy staring after him that I don't even notice Kaia has entered the room until Tyla screams.

"She seems different from other Mortals I have met."

The panther has launched onto the bed and abandoned any sense of respect for others' personal space by pressing her nose straight into Tyla's face and breathing in deeply.

"She won't hurt you." I sit next to them and push away Kaia's head. "This is Kaia, she's my friend."

I'm not quite sure how to explain the whole bonded thing to Tyla.

"She's sick."

Kaia looks at me. *"I know several Mortal sicknesses; this is not one I have encountered before."*

"What do you mean?" I demand, a jolt of fear pounding through me.

Kaia simply curls into a ball and rests her head on Tyla's lap. *"I do not know."*

Tyla stares down at the Eshari, frozen with her hands hanging in the air, terrified of touching the beast.

"I have so many questions," she muses to herself as she stares down at Kaia. "Who was that man? Whose house is this? What's happened to you in all this time?"

The questions pour out of her, each one asked in a more desperate tone than the last.

I want to tell her. I want to tell her everything, but I simply can't stop staring at those dark veins stretching up her arms. I can't stop wondering how much time she has left if this tonic doesn't work.

It has to. It just has to.

Derian's back nearly immediately, holding a tiny vial of green liquid in his hand. Cal follows closely behind him, nodding at me in greeting as he steps into the room to join us.

"I had the healers prepare this ahead of our arrival," Derian explains, walking forward. He gives the tonic to me, not to Tyla, a small gesture but one that leaves a suspicious burst of warmth in my lower stomach. He knows I would want to examine it first. He gives me a small smile as he brushes his fingers against mine before stepping back. "It's the best healing tonic we have."

I sniff it slowly, taking in the notes of basil, jasmine, and chamomile, along with other notes I can't quite identify. Cal steps forward as I take a small swig of it myself, swirling it across my tongue.

"I have to ask," he pauses, clearing his throat and looking at my sister expectantly.

"Tyla," she tells him.

"Tyla." Cal nods. "Have you shown any signs of Fae magic?"

I stiffen just at the same time Tyla gasps, the small motion startling Kaia, who looks up at the girl before turning back to me.

"She is not Fae."

I roll my eyes. *"I'm aware of that, but you also didn't know I was Fae, so how good is your judgement, really?"*

Kaia sits her head back down, always the lazy beast. *"I knew you were more than you realized."*

"Tyla and I aren't related by blood," I clarify. "We found each other as children and have grown up as sisters ever since.

Cal quirks his head at me, brows raised. "My apologies. I just assumed based on the resemblance."

He glances at Derian, and the two share a look that tells me they're communicating silently about something they know that I don't. I make a mental note to interrogate them both about it once Tyla inevitably falls asleep.

I shrug, passing the tonic to Tyla. "We get that a lot."

She looks to me, suspicion in her furrowed brow, and I know she's piecing together the implications of Cal's question and my answer. Reaching forward, I grasp her hand in mine and give a gentle squeeze, silently promising to tell her everything the second I get the chance.

"Drink up."

"Are you sure?" Tyla holds it in her hands, looking down at it with suspicion before leaning towards me and whispering, "They're *Fae.*"

At the doorway, Cal stiffens before clearing his throat awkwardly, and Derian gives me his characteristic smirk, the smallest of smiles playing on his lips as he crosses his arms over his chest and leans back against the doorframe.

I've only been gone a few short weeks, hardly anytime at all, and yet *everything* has changed.

I've changed.

The last time Tyla saw me, I was the vicious assassin who hated the Fae as deeply as I loved her, but now? Now, I am one of them. I've started considering them my friends.

And at some point, I'd stopped calling Derian a Fae bastard.

"It's okay," I tell Tyla softly. "They won't hurt you."

I meet Derian's gaze, finding an emotion on his face that I can't quite place.

"I was wrong about them."

***

Unlike the other healing tonics Tyla has taken over the years, this one doesn't seem to have any immediate effect on her. Derian examines the veins in her arms before declaring that it might be a good sign and that maybe the tonic just needs some time to work through her system.

He gives me a lingering look before he and Cal leave, announcing that they're going to look into getting us both some food after our journeys.

The second they're gone and the door is closed behind them, I launch myself towards Tyla.

Kaia snarls as I half land atop her and Tyla both, my arms thrown haphazardly around my sister as we both erupt into a fit of giggles.

"You seem different," she notices as I settle in next to her and rest my head on her shoulder. "Lighter."

I shrug. "I'm just so happy to see you. How's Velia?"

"Much quieter without its Huntress on the prowl," she teases. "Kristona dropped by every so often with coins, and Joneson delivered tonics as needed. They miss you."

"But business has gone on as usual without me?"

"Would you expect any different?"

No, I wouldn't. Kristona might have love for me in that black heart of his, but he is a businessman to his core. A *father* would have set sail to come rescue me no matter the cost. Maybe with all these realizations about the Fae also came the realization that Kristona hadn't protected me as much as I'd thought.

Tyla glances out the window at the fields of wheat growing behind the manor. "It's beautiful here."

It truly is. After weeks in that dreary fortress fighting for my life, a house like this, complete with stunning furnishings and plush mattresses, feels too good to be true. I'd almost expected something different, something as dark and stern as Derian.

Somehow, though, this fits the other version of him. That private version that I don't think he's allowed many other people to glimpse.

"So that man," Tyla starts, giving me one of those looks that suggests she's done waiting for answers. "Care to explain why he looks at you like he wants to eat you alive?"

I snort aloud.

"Probably because he does," Kaia groans in my head, and I swipe at her playfully. *"Or because he already has."*

"You are far too invested in my sex life."

"In all the years I remained unbonded, I somehow forgot the burden of having to deal with the emotions and desires of your kind. You have taken great joy in reminding me."

"I think you secretly like it."

"I do not."

I grin, reaching over to scratch under her chin. *"Oh you totally do. My emotions are your favorite form of entertainment."*

"Huntyr."

Tyla pulls my attention back to her.

For the first time in what feels like eternity, I relax next to the one person I love unconditionally, and I feel a bit of the weight on my shoulders release.

Then I begin to tell her everything that has happened since the moment I saw Derian masked at the ball.

HUNTYR

"Wow," Tyla breathes, sitting back against the headboard of the bed with a dramatic sigh when I finally finish the elaborate tale.

I spared no detail, telling her all about that initial attraction to Derian at the ball and explaining how I'd accidentally killed the wrong Fae. I told her the details of the Conclave and its rules. I told her about the monster Seraphina had been and how I'd come to view Alexandria as somewhat of a friend. She'd fought back tears as I explained each of the trials, including the final trial where I'd felt my very soul break apart and stitch itself back together again.

"I just—" Tyla pauses, rubbing her fingers over her brow. "I can't believe you're sleeping with the Fae prince."

I blink at her.

"*That's* what you're thinking about after that entire story?"

She gives me a soft smile. "Well, of course you won the Conclave, Huntyr. You're the fiercest person I know, and I definitely want to circle back to the fact that you're part Fae eventually."

"But?"

Her eyes go a bit gushy as a blush spreads across her cheeks. "He *is* very handsome."

Kaia gives the feline version of a laugh from Tyla's other side, and Tyla finally reaches down to stroke the area behind her ears, grinning as the beast lets out a soft purr and pushes herself closer to my sister.

"Don't let him hear you say that," I tell her dryly. "The last thing he needs is anyone else stroking his ego."

She shifts next to me, pulling at the collar of her dress. Absently, I notice it's a bit too large, and dirty from her trip. I'll have to speak to Derian about getting her some clothes. Mine will be too big for her, but they'll have to do for now.

"Do you love him?"

I freeze, jostled out of my thought spiral by those four little words.

"What?" I exclaim. "Of course not!"

"Well you're intimate with him—"

"There's absolutely nothing wrong with seeking pleasure in another person, even if you don't have an emotional connection."

Derian was hardly the first person I'd had sex with. I didn't love anyone who came before him, and I certainly don't love him. Certainly not.

She gives me a small sympathetic smile. "You're also marrying him."

"*Why* would you think that?"

Kaia and Tyla share a long look, and I get the sneaking suspicion that the two of them are somehow united against me in this, both understanding something that I don't.

I'm not particularly fond of that fact.

"You won the Conclave, Huntyr." Her voice is dry, as if she's pointing out a simple, obvious fact.

Which, yes, obviously I won the Conclave.

That doesn't mean I am actually going to marry Derian, though. I was never actually going to marry him. I just haven't told her about my plan yet, my very clear, well-thought-out plan, with easy-to-follow steps.

Win the Conclave.

Get the healing tonic.

Kill the Fae Prince.

Wait...

I jolt, jumping out of the bed and running a hand over my face, ignoring the urge to lock my knees and clench my shoulders together as my mind begins spinning.

I'd come here for two reasons: to get the healing tonic for Tyla and to get revenge for my father.

I'd accomplished that first goal, but the second? Knowing what I know now, killing Derian won't actually accomplish that for me. Derian and his people *aren't* responsible for my father's death.

The Velkai are.

And if I want to fight back against them, I have to do two equally important things. I have to embrace whatever magic lives inside of me, and I have to stay here to fight the Velkai.

Three facts begin ringing clearly in my mind.

One, I am going to stay in the Fae kingdom.

Two, I'm not going to kill Derian.

And three, I won the Conclave, and the winner of the Conclave gets the hand of the prince.

Shit.

I turn back to Tyla, my braid swinging so wildly over my shoulder that it nearly smacks the other side of my face.

"I'm going to marry him."

Tyla nods, grinning as if this little spiral of mine is the funniest thing she's seen in ages, even as her eyes bounce from my face, over my shoulder, and back.

"I'm *marrying* Derian!" I cry out shrilly.

"That is the plan, Huntress."

I jump a foot into the air, so wildly off-balance by the realization that I didn't even hear him re-enter the room. He walks towards Tyla, a plate piled high with meats and potatoes extended towards her. She takes it with a grateful smile.

"You don't understand." I wave an accusatory finger at him, but I'm not even sure if I'm talking to him or myself now.

"Pretty sure I understand," he says, glaring at Kaia as he steps back. "I am the other half of the marriage, after all."

No, no he doesn't understand. Neither of them understand.

"This wasn't the plan!" I'm practically screaming, pulling at the roots of my hair as I rest my hands on the top of my head and walk myself in a circle. "I never break away from my plan."

"What was your plan?" Tyla asks around a mouthful of food. Kaia scoots closer to her, nudging her with a paw, and she offers the Eshari a potato.

I force myself to breathe, quick inhales and exhales that feel impossible.

"Win the Conclave. Get the tonic. Kill the prince. It was a beautiful, effective plan."

Derian lifts a brow. "So you *were* planning to try and assassinate me again."

"Well it doesn't matter now!" I cry, throwing my hands in the air.

He and Tyla share an amused look, which only infuriates me further.

"It matters a little to me," he says sarcastically as he grins at me.

I can't stop picturing myself in one of those ridiculously puffy white dresses. Married. Me, married!

Gods, how many people will be there? Derian is a *prince* after all, there will be dozens, if not hundreds, of people there to watch this ceremony. People that will all stare at *me* as I vow the rest of my life to him.

I have *never* pictured myself as a bride.

I am not one of those women who dreamed of that day as a girl. I have always been far too busy sharpening knives and planning murders to ever worry about life-long commitments. I'm better suited to be covered in blood than I am to be draped in lace and pearls.

And that's just the ceremony! I also have to consider the marriage that comes after the pomp and circumstance.

We're going to be tied together for the rest of our lives.

Fuck, how long will I even live for?

The Fae live centuries longer than Mortals.

Granted, I'm only half-Fae, but what exactly does that mean for my lifespan?

Am I going to be married to Derian for *centuries?*

"Have you noticed the wrinkle she gets between her eyebrows when she's thinking too hard?" Tyla dramatically whispers to Derian.

"Oh believe me, I have."

I stare at them.

They stare back at me.

The corner of Derian's lip quirks into what is undoubtedly the start of one of his teasing smirks.

That's it.

I can't be here. I can't be in this room with the three of them, who suddenly all seem united in their amusement at my inability to process the inevitability of this marriage. I unsheathe two of the daggers on my belt and stomp towards the door.

"Where are you going, Huntress?"

"To find Cal."

His eyes follow my movements. "What do you need Cal for?"

"I need to fight someone, and he dislikes me enough that he won't go easy."

DERIAN

Tyla insists on coming outside with me to watch Huntyr and Calspar, so once again I lift the tiny girl into my arms and carry her over the stairs, setting her up on a wooden rocking chair on the porch before bringing her a blanket to wrap around her shoulders.

She really is a frail little thing. Nothing but skin and bones.

Truthfully, I haven't spent much time around Mortals, so I certainly don't know much about their illnesses. But whatever is infecting the poor girl appears merciless. No wonder Huntyr is so desperate to get her help.

"So, I suppose we are to be family?" she says to me as I flop down into the chair next to her.

The Eshari sits on her other side, resting her head on the girl's lap, a position that allows it to stare right at me with unblinking eyes. I should feel offended that the beast made such fast friends with Tyla since she constantly bares her teeth at me.

"I suppose so."

The sound of clanging metal echoes through the air.

I glance towards Huntyr andCal.

Cal is definitely not going easy on her. He manages to land a few good hits, including one that makes her head snap back so sharply that lightning tears from the sky and scorches the ground next to him before I even realize my magic had spiked.

Oops.

He looks at me apologetically for half a second before Huntyr shouts at me to 'stay out of it' and resumes her attacks.

"So, I should probably warn you that if you hurt my sister I will definitely make you suffer."

I look over at Tyla, once again stunned by how much she looks like my Huntress despite their lack of any true familial relation. The hair is nearly the exact same shade. Their eyes, while a different color, are still the same shape. Their jawlines are quite similar.

"You hardly look strong enough to kill a butterfly," I remind her. "You definitely couldn't hurt me, even if you wanted to."

She stares at me, blinking softly, before bursting out in high-pitched laughter. The sound of it startles Huntyr enough that she turns back to us, a mistake that earns her a sharp kick to the gut. I clench my fist instinctively. So help me, if he just broke her ribs, I'll break two of his in punishment.

"I'm so used to everyone coddling me and pretending like I'll be just fine. It's refreshing to talk with someone who doesn't shy away from the seriousness of my illness."

She watches her sister with careful consideration, her love for Huntyr so obvious.

"She tries to pretend the truth isn't written out in front of us."

I frown. "Truth?"

Tyla turns her dark eyes tome, eyes that are far too serious for a girl so young. "I don't think I'm meant to live very long, and I think, deep down, she knows that. She knows I'm going to die."

"You *will* be fine," I tell her, unblinking. "That tonic will work."

She gives me a soft smile. "I hope so. I would like enough time in this realm to decide whether or not you are worthy of my sister."

"And if you decide I'm not?"

Tyla shrugs. "I won't have to. Huntyr's always been smarter than me. She's the stronger one. She'll decide about you far sooner than I will. Gods have mercy on you if she decides against you."

I watch her fight, her movements a mix of utter strength and poetic grace. She's grinning, the kind of easy smile that's become more common in recent days, even as sweat drips down her brow. Remarkably, she's keeping Cal on his toes, a feat not many can accomplish.

Gods have mercy on me indeed.

She doesn't realize it, but she's gotten stronger. Faster, too. Whatever Fae magic woke up inside of her, it's brought with it some of our other gifts as well.

"You should go," Tyla says next to me, nodding towards the fight.

I raise a brow at her in confusion.

She nods towards Huntyr. "Your friend needs a break, and she's nowhere near finished. She can go like this for hours before she calms down."

For some unknown reason, I hesitate.

Huntyr has been through so much recently. Her entire world is upside down, and this drive for violence is just a symptom of her need to put everything back in its place again.

I don't fit into one of her neat little plans anymore. I'm one of those aspects of her life that's now confusing.

Somehow, that's a more unsteady place for us to be than when she hated me.

I feel Kaia watching me, those golden eyes focused so keenly on me as I look back at Tyla. "I don't know if I'm what she needs right now."

Huntyr's not just angry anymore. She's lost. And I don't know if she wants my help in finding herself again.

Tyla is quiet for a longtime, watching as her sister expertly begins winning the fight, using Cal's strength against him. She rocks slowly in her chair, the wood creaking softly under the movement.

"I think you might be exactly what she needs."

⸺◆◇◆⸺

Cal pauses, lowering his sword and stepping back from the fight when he sees me rise from my chair and begin making my way down the porch steps. Huntyr, merciless beast that she is, takes advantage of that hesitation, landing a swift punch across his jaw that leaves my friend stumbling back in surprise.

"That was unsportsmanlike!" he chastises her while rubbing out the wound.

She smirks. "No, it was underhanded fighting. I don't know why you expected any less."

He looks to me, as if expecting me to defend him against her.

I extend my hand, reaching for his sword. "You're fighting an assassin and expecting her to have the honor of a warrior. The Huntress prefers things a little dirty."

Those blue eyes roll dramatically when I wink at her, and the sight of it has blood rushing to my cock. The woman could be doing the most horrendous, deplorable, disgusting things, and I would still want her.

"I don't want to fight *you*," she protests when I take the space across from her where Cal had previously been standing.

The sun catches her hair, black waves of silken perfection. It fell out of her braid while she was fighting, and now hangs in a curtain down her shoulders and back, damp by her forehead where the effort of the fight has started creating beads of sweat.

She's pissed.

Rage is easy for her. At least, it's easier than dealing with how overwhelmed she is.

And despite the anger written across her face, the hatred seemingly directed at me, she's just as beautiful as ever. Maybe more beautiful than I've ever seen her before.

I marvel at it as I put my full strength into a swift swing of my sword, aimed right for her head.

She ducks just in time, the blade whistling over her head as she stares up at it from where she crouches. Already I'm moving again, swinging my sword in an arc towards her. Our blades meet with a resounding clang, sparks bursting on impact.

"Still think I'll go easy on you, Huntress?"

Huntyr looks up at me, the position remarkably similar to one we'd been in two nights ago.

Only that encounter had ended with both of us finding our pleasure, this ends with the wicked thing kicking me right in the shin.

Pain shoots up my leg, sharp and immediate, as I stumble back.

"Fuck," I hiss, tentatively taking a few steps and shaking out the leg.

She is definitely stronger than a normal Mortal.

Her grin is unforgiving when I look at her. Her gaze flickers to my leg, and those blue eyes light up momentarily with self-satisfaction.

"I prefer things a little dirty," she teases with a shrug.

Walking slowly, we begin to circle each other, our movements fluid and measured.

"You never answered my question," I remind her.

Her eyes narrow, the only indication that she wants me to clarify.

"Chocolate or vanilla cake at the wedding?"

I see the wheels in her mind spinning, see her tracing through her memories to recognize the reference, and see her exasperation when she remembers that first night at the fortress when I'd asked her the same question.

"I truly do not care." She sighs, and then she's driving forward again.

She's relentless, each strike more forceful than the last. I parry her attacks, grunting when the vibration of the blow travels up my arm. Her movements remain quick and sharp, even though she must be tiring. I divert her attention to the right so I can level my fist into her gut, and her only reaction is a sharp hiss.

I take advantage of the moment she takes to catch her breath.

"Vanilla cake then?" There's that eye roll again. I swallow down my chuckle. "No, you don't want vanilla."

She throws back her head, shaking back her hair off her shoulders, and squares her shoulders again. "I don't want to have this conversation."

"Right." This time when she swings, I don't meet her blade with my own. I step to the left, bending out of the way, then do the same when she spins to my right side. She lets out a frustrated huff as I dance out of the way of each of her blows. "So, you don't want to fight me, you don't want vanilla cake, and you don't want to have this conversation."

"Aren't you observant," she notes through a locked jaw. Her movements are coming more rapidly now, technique slipping as I start to get under her skin.

"What *do* you want, Huntress?"

Every swing of her blade is a release of the emotions she can't put into words. She fights not like she wants to win, but like she needs the reassurance of a win. Two very different motivations.

"Enough, Derian."

"It's not enough."

I watch her movements, anticipating them, and this time when she swings, I drop my sword, grasp both of her wrists in my hands, and rip her towards me as her own blade falls to the ground.

She's breathing heavily, her chest rising and falling against mine. Sweat drips down her temple. Heat radiates off of her body.

"Let me go," she demands, but her voice lacks strength. She's speaking in nothing more than a whisper.

"What do you want, Huntress?"

Her eyes flicker towards the porch, and I don't need to follow her gaze to know that Cal has taken Tyla back inside, leaving us alone.

"I should go take care of my sister."

"You should answer my question first."

"I'm serious, Derian. Let me go!"

Still, I refuse to soften my grip on her wrists. I refuse to let her run away from this.

From me.

"*What do you want?*"

"Control!" she screams, lip trembling slightly. "I want you to teach me how to control it."

Her shoulders sag as the confession echoes around us.

And yet, it's not enough.

She tugs at her wrists once more, tears welling in her eyes, but I can't let go. I won't. Not yet. Not until she releases everything that's eating her up inside.

"Why?" I ask her, keeping my tone gentle.

She stares at me for a longtime, and I think she might protest again when she finally opens her mouth.

"I want it to mean something," she admits, averting her gaze. "All of it. My father's murder, my childhood with Kristona, the awful things he made me do, and this magic. You said it all led me here. So, I want to do something with all that pain."

She pauses, finally meeting my gaze again. I stroke a thumb across the pulse in her wrist in gentle reassurance.

"I want to kill the Mother."

My body locks in tension the second the words are out of her mouth.

I breathe in deeply, swallowing down the instinctive urge that rises out of my gut, that protective aspect of my identity as a Fae male that pushes me to deny her putting herself in that level of danger. The part of me that can barely breathe when I think about her getting harmed.

Huntyr doesn't want my protection.

She doesn't need it.

She needs to make a decision on her own for the first time in her life, and she needs someone to support her in it.

Taric was right. I need to respect her decision regardless of how hard it is for me to do so.

"Then," I pause, forcing the acceptance of this even as it goes against every instinct in my body. "That's what we'll do."

She looks up at me, not stepping away even when I release her hands to rest my fingers on her hips.

"Really?" she asks, her voice uncertain.

I nod, ignoring the pang of unease in my stomach. "We'll do it together."

With another deep breath, I step back and offer her my hand. She stares at it for a long time, brow furrowed as she considers my words, before she finally takes it.

As we make our way back inside, a natural, easy grin spreads across my cheeks.

"Vengeance and chocolate cake, two things every great marriage is built on."

Her nostrils flare as I glance back at her. "Don't push your luck."

She doesn't pull her hand from mine, though. Whether she realizes it or not, she's made her choice. She's one of us now. She's mine now.

And there's no turning back.

"I'm sleeping in Tyla's bed tonight," she tells me.

I chuckle. "That's fine."

"I don't need permission."

Releasing her hand, I pull open the door to the manor and step aside to let her brush past me, breathing in the scent of her as she does. "No, you don't. Just as I don't need reassurance that you'll be back in mine tomorrow."

When she glances back at me over her shoulder, the mocking expression lacks any real bite. "Cocky, aren't we?"

I tuck my hands in my pockets, watching as she starts to make her way up the steps. "Go be with your sister, Huntyr. We'll have plenty of time for your teasing games later."

We'll have a lifetime for it.

⊸◈⊷

I wake to screaming.

High-pitched, world-ending screaming that bursts through me, wraps its hands around my heart, and squeezes until fear pours through every inch of my body.

Huntyr is screaming.

She's screaming my name.

I can't breathe, can't think. I can't do anything but push to my feet and rush out of my room to where she is staying with her sister.

I'm wild as I take in the room, searching for her. Something in me unclenches when I see the lack of blood or bodily injury on her. She's crouched on the floor, tears streaming down her face, hands wrapped over the shoulders of her sister, who's planted on all fours on the ground.

The sister who is currently vomiting black liquid all over the carpet in front of her.

"What happened?" I demand, coming to crouch next to them.

"I don't know," she shakes her head violently, her face paler than I've ever seen it before. "She was having a nightmare, talking in her sleep. I tried to wake her up, and she just started getting sick."

One more violent heave works through Tyla before her body gives out. It's only Huntyr's quick reflexes that catch the girl before she falls into her own mess. She sits Tyla's head in her lap and gasps when she takes in the sight of her now unconscious sister.

Those dark lines on her skin have made a web up her chest, climbing up her throat. I push back her hair, noticing the dark veins that extend from her hairline by her temples.

"You promised me you would help her!" she hisses at me.

This doesn't make any sense. That was the best tonic we have. It heals the worst of Fae injuries, it should have held up against any simple Mortal sickness.

"I don't understand," I mutter aloud.

Huntyr is shaking, terror written across every line of her face. "Fix this! You *promised* me. That was my favor. That was what I won the Conclave for."

I look at her, feeling an awful tightness spark through my chest at the realization that if that tonic doesn't work, there might not actually be a way to fix this.

Huntyr is right. I told her if she won the Conclave, I would give her anything she wanted.

I was wrong to make that promise.

Tyla is going to die, and Huntyr is going to hate me forever once she does.

HUNTYR

"**Y**ou should rest," Kaia says gently.

I glance at Tyla asleep in the bed, sweat visible across her brow even as I pace several feet away. Derian had no explanation for what caused her sickness; he just helped me get her back into bed and left with a promise to try and learn more.

I think I'll have nightmares about last night for the rest of my life.

I've never seen anything like it.

I never want to see anything like it again.

"I can't."

Sitting down means giving myself the space to feel all of the pain, worry, and despair that's trying to punch into me. I can't do that. I need to stay rational, logical, strategic. I need to make a plan.

"You've been pacing for nearly an hour, Huntyr."

"What good is Fae magic if it can't heal her?"

Kaia blinks, tilting her head slightly. *"There is no magic in any realm that is strong enough to fight death."*

I whirl towards her. *"Do not say that! She is not going to die!"*

Before Kaia can respond, Tyla stirs, her head twisting back and forth slightly.

"I know," she mutters in her sleep. "I see now, Mother."

Rushing to her side, I dip my hands into the bucket of cold water beside the bed and place the rag inside gently against her brow, brushing aside her sweat-drenched hair as I do.

"Was she close with her mother?" Kaia asks, settling next to Tyla protectively.

"I don't know. Tyla was young when her parents died, but she's been talking to her mother in her dreams all night."

Kaia turns to the door sharply, ears twitching as she listens to the conversation taking place in the hallway outside our door, too quiet for me to be able to make out.

"The prince has been offered an alternative."

My stomach leaps and I jump to my feet, dropping the rag back into the bucket and pushing out of the room to where Derian, Cal, and Taric stand in a tight circle, whispering softly. Derian doesn't turn to face me right away. His hands are tucked in his pockets, his brow furrowed, his lips pursed and considering.

His friends look just as grim, both with arms crossed over their chests and eyes locked on the wooden floor at their feet.

"What is it?" I demand, unflinching, as the three warriors all look at me in surprise.

"Lachlan," Cal says softly. "You should be with Tyla. We'll get you if we think of anything."

I look at each of them, taking in the soft blush on Cal's face, the worried lines on Derian's forehead, the tension in Taric's shoulders. Cal steps forward as if to cajole me back inside the room, and I step aside, moving out of his way and completely ignoring the hand Derian extends towards me.

"You've already thought of something." I level my gaze on Taric, the warrior who won't meet my gaze.

Out of our group, he's likely the most dangerous of all of us. He has the rarest wielding power of all the Fae. It's what helped him win a Conclave in mere minutes. If he wanted to, he could stop my blood from flowing and kill me in an instant. But I stare at him without any fear.

My sister's life is on the line, and if he has information that can save her, I *will* get it out of him.

His eyes flash to me and then flick away. "Back in Oxhurn, there's someone I know—"

"Taric," Cal warns, his tone laced with a threat.

I glare at him over my shoulder, fingers twitching towards the knife on my belt. Whatever he saw on my face was enough to motivate him to sigh and wave a hand for Taric to continue.

"He's a healer," Taric explains, running a hand through his already messy hair. "But he's a bit non-traditional. He doesn't exactly follow typical Fae healing methods, and he's gotten into some trouble for it. I've seen him get results where others haven't, though."

"Then we go to him," I announce. I don't care if it's against every Fae law in the book. They can lock me away when we're done, as long as Tyla is healed and okay.

"It's not that simple," Cal protests. "People like this also have unpredictable results. He could cause as much damage as he brings healing."

How much worse could it get?

"She's already dying," I remind him.

"It's a bad idea, Lachlan."

"And it's not your call to make!"

Cal and I stare each other down before we both turn to Derian in unison. He is the prince. He is the leader. He makes the decision, and so help me if he doesn't make the right one...

Derian's attention on me is a tangible weight. He stares at me, unblinking, his face entirely unreadable as he leans back on the wall behind him.

"Luceron is supposed to be arriving soon," he finally says softly.

I force down the bile that rises in my throat. So it was to be his brother over my sister then?

"Luceron is taking the long way," Taric reminds him. "We have time."

Time to go all the way back to the fort in Oxhurn and return here? Perhaps, but it would be a close call. It would depend on how long his brother stopped at the towns and villages along the way. It was very possible we *wouldn't* make it back in time.

I know how important it is for Derian to see his brother. I know how uneasy he feels about Luceron traveling so far from the protected walls of his capital city. Derian won't be able to fully relax until he is with Luceron and able to protect him himself.

Tyla is already in trouble though, and I have to protect her as fiercely as he would protect Luceron.

"I'll go alone," I tell him, not an offering, but a warning.

We stare at each other, Taric and Cal nothing more than figures in the background.

Derian sighs heavily, the motion causing his shoulders to sink at least an inch.

"I know you will, Huntress, and you know I won't let you."

It's decided then.

"We leave at first light," I decree, and I don't give them a moment to say anything else before I stride past the three of them and return to Tyla's side.

⸻◆⸻

The journey back to Oxhurn is painful. With Tyla now being pulled along in a cart, we stick to established roads and sleep in various inns along the way. It nearly doubles the duration of the journey, and every moment is like agony.

I watch her like a hawk, analyzing her every breath. She doesn't get sick again. In fact, by the time we're halfway through the journey, she's even sitting up and teasing Taric. Kaia has taken a particular affinity for her, even staying by her side in the evenings while I steal away to practice magic with Derian for a few hours.

He's a surprisingly gracious instructor. His mentorship is clear and well thought-out, and he's patient when I get frustrated at my own inability to control the blinding light the way I want to. After a few sessions, I manage to summon sparks to the tips of my fingers at will. It's hardly going to do anything more than provide a dim light in a shadowed alley, but it's better than nothing.

When I first managed that tiny glow at my fingertips, we were standing in the courtyard behind an inn we stayed at along the way. I'd been so ridiculously happy that I'd squealed, and Derian had looked at me with such unabashed pride that my stomach had flipped and my blood had heated. He'd been sharing a room with Cal and I'd been sharing a room with Tyla, so I'd pulled him into a nearby alley and demanded to be rewarded for my progress.

He was extremely generous with his praise.

He's begun teaching me basic magics, too, just enough that I'm able to heal the muscles in my legs that grow sore after too many days on horseback. As much as I'm still warming up to the idea of Fae magic, that is one particular skill I'm grateful to have.

Finally though, after what feels like an eternity, I spot the stone archway that leads through to the fortress of Oxhurn.

My blood runs cold, despite the sudden feeling of sweat on the back of my neck, and I slow my horse, hardly noticing as our party continues on without me.

I can't seem to look away from that archway.

I didn't expect to be so affected by this place.

But there it is. The sudden rush of disgust, a strange mixture of rage, pain, and anxiety. Nothing good lies beyond that archway. There's only the arena where Seraphina beat me, the training yard where Mara attacked me, the wing of the barracks that is now empty because the women who slept there are now dead.

There's a gentle touch on my lower back as Derian brings his horse flush with mine.

"We don't have to stay long if you don't want to," he tells me, reading over the expression on my face. "We can get a tonic and be on our way back to Springhallow before the day's end."

I work my jaw, watching as Taric's horse pulls my sister's cart through that archway and towards the fortress that lays beyond.

Kaia is with her. I remind myself. *Kaia will keep her safe while we're here.*

"The horses need time to rest." I exhale a heavy, uncomfortable sigh. "We all do. Cal will want to check on the fort while we're here, and Ulna hasn't been sleeping well in the inns."

I feel his attention on me and work to steady my breathing. I work to look as unaffected as I wish I was.

"You're right," he admits. "But my statement stands. Say the word and we leave."

It's just a stone archway. It's just patches of dirt and worn ground. It's just a place. *I* am the one who lived through it. I will survive this place and the memories that hide within it.

"I can't just avoid Oxhurn, Derian. I'm the Conclave winner. The Fae will expect me to be strong."

"The Fae will respect their princess regardless and keep their mouths shut about it if they know what's good for them."

A ghost of a smile plays on my lips. Such an overprotective worrywart he's become. With one more deep breath in and out, I press my heel into the side of my horse and begin trotting forward as Derian keeps pace beside me.

"If we're going to fight the Mother, this is the most strategic place to do so. Nowhere else in the Fae kingdom is this close to the Wastelands."

Derian is quiet for a moment, his fingers tightening on his reins as we walk under that archway. "I have to admit, Huntress, I'm not particularly thrilled with this plan of yours."

We'd discussed it during one of the nights of the trip. I'd gotten him properly drunk on wine and my body before I'd laid it out for him.

Once we get Tyla the tonic and we're sure she is well again, we'll travel back to Springhallow. Then we'll meet Derian's brother, go through with whatever ridiculous wedding celebration has to take place, then tell every-one we're taking a very private celebratory trip just the two of us.

Which won't necessarily be a lie.

We will be taking a trip, just the two of us, into the Wastelands.

"If your brother loves you as fiercely as I love Tyla, he's not going to let you go after the Mother."

"My brother is the King, yes, but I have a habit of disregarding his instructions."

I snort. The Conclave was a perfect example of that.

"Still. I don't want Tyla worrying about me, and I know you don't want Cal or Taric volunteering to come with us. You're the most powerful Fae alive, Derian, and I, apparently, am the only one capable of killing Velkai with magic. There's no reason for us to drag anyone else into this with us."

He might have said something else to me, but my attention is already locked in somewhere else.

In the center of the training yard, my sister is standing, flanked on each side by Taric and Cal, Kaia seated directly in front of her, as a group of the fortress warriors come to examine her.

I can't even be concerned by the warriors though.

All I can think about is the fact that she's *standing*.

"She's steady," I muse aloud to Derian.

He's watching her with the same intensity. He nods at me silently before dismounting his horse. I follow.

"Tyla," I call to her, walking quickly to join her. "Are you okay?"

When I reach her side, Taric and Cal leave to greet their friends and inspect the fortress. Derian follows, but I know him well enough to know his attention still lingers on my sister and I.

I place a hand on her elbow, marveling at the way she's standing tall, shoulders back, her head held high. Well-balanced, too. It's been ages since I've seen her so steady on her feet.

"I am." She gives me a soft smile. "I'm glad to be done riding for a while."

"She seems better," Kaia notes. *"Over the last day or so, she's gotten progressively stronger."*

Sure enough, it looks like the dark veins on her neck are subsiding ever so slightly. A kernel of hope blooms inside me.

"Is it possible the tonic's effects were just delayed?"

Kaia sniffs Tyla's feet before flicking her tail. *"Perhaps another night of rest to decide."*

Right. That was reasonable enough. It's early afternoon already. We could all use a bath and some food. I, for one, would appreciate some actual sparring after feeling trapped on a horse for so long.

We'll spend the night here and decide in the morning if the tonic has worked after all.

"It's possible though, don't you think?"

Kaia looks at me, ears flicking. *"It would seem so."*

I even catch the faintest amount of hope in her voice, too.

"Come on," I throw my arm around Tyla's shoulder, sending her a happy grin. "Let's get you inside."

Tyla walks with me, a gentle smile on her own face. The cloak I've given her drags on the ground at our feet. She's only a hair shorter than me, but she's so thin that it falls an inch too long. I make a mental note to have it laundered while she bathes.

My arm rips back suddenly as Tyla stops short, digging her heels into the dirt beneath our feet and swinging wildly to the left, eyes wide and unblinking.

"Did you hear that?"

Tyla is standing stiff as a board, eyes locked on something in the distance, brow furrowed in what appears to be confusion. I blink, first at her, then at Kaia, who looks just as confused as I am.

"Hear what?"

She tilts her head, and for a moment it's as if even though she's standing right next to me, she's suddenly somewhere else entirely. But then she shakes her head, and her distant gaze focuses back on me. "You didn't hear a voice?"

Derian stands at the pathway towards the barracks, waiting with his arms crossed over his chest. He only shrugs when I look to him for help.

"I didn't hear anything, Tyla. You're probably just tired from the journey. Come, let's get inside."

She's still for a moment, considering, before she finally nods and starts walking again. Her steps are slower now, and she keeps glancing suspiciously over her shoulder.

"What's over there, Huntyr?" she asks.

Derian stiffens as we reach him, and he falls into step behind us.

"The Wastelands," he mutters.

DERIAN

Huntyr is different around her sister. Softer. Her smiles come easier.

It helps that Tyla somehow seems to be doing better. Huntyr's relief eases any frustration that we might have made the journey back to Oxhurn for nothing.

The two of them walk easily next to me now as I lead them towards the halls where the more permanent bedrooms are. Huntyr frowned when I initially led her away from where she'd stayed earlier, but I simply quipped that I couldn't have my betrothed staying in such a dilapidated room.

Which technically is true.

But the fact that I also want her sleeping across the hall from me is just as true too.

After leading them to the room just next to mine, I open the door and stand aside to let them in. The room isn't entirely different from the one I'd had Tyla stay in at the Springhallow manor. There's a bed big enough for the two of them, a small table that they can eat their breakfast at in the morning, and windows that let in the afternoon light.

Kaia trails in behind them, examining the space for a minute before jumping onto the bed and resting her head.

I frown at the Eshari. "Do you ever do anything other than sleep?"

Her snarl tears through the room, and Huntyr tries, and fails, to hide her laughter. I lift my brows at her, silently demanding to know what the beast had to say, but she only shakes her head.

"You don't want to know," she assures me.

Based on the way the cat still glares at me, I don't doubt that. I can't believe I'm going to have to spend the rest of my life sharing my wife with that beast.

Shaking away the thought, I turn back to Tyla and Huntyr. "You two will stay here until we're ready to head back to Springhallow."

Tyla snickers. "No."

"No?" Huntyr questions, turning her gaze to her sister and crossing her arms over her chest. The action presses her breasts together, and I have to avert my gaze to keep from dragging her from this room.

It's been too long since I've been inside her. I can hardly think of anything else.

Tyla looks at me like she can read every thought in my mind as if it's written in large print right in front of her.

"Huntyr has slept with me every night since I arrived, and you two have been forced to sneak away to dark corners and alleyways because of it."

My Huntress blushes a sinful shade of pink.

"For a highly trained assassin, you're not as subtle as you think," Tyla deadpans, resting her hands on her hips. "So, I will stay here, and you will stay with him."

Say yes.

"No."

I swallow my disappointment with a heavy breath.

Tyla's brows lift in an expression of utter stubbornness that puts her sister to shame. "I'm perfectly capable of spending a single night alone."

I should leave. I should give them the courtesy of figuring this out alone without me hovering, but, Gods, I can't seem to make my feet move. Not when there's still a tiny shred of hope that I might have her in my bed tonight.

Huntyr inclines her head. "And what if you get sick again?"

Well, that kills any of my remaining hope. I recognize that tone of voice. Tyla is fighting a losing battle. That tone means Huntyr's mind is not going to change. I start to move towards the door.

"Kaia can stay with me," Tyla reasons. "I think she'd prefer it."

I pause. That is a fairly convincing argument.

Glancing over my shoulder, I meet Huntyr's gaze and find... conflict. For some reason, that causes something deep within me to clench.

"It's up to you," I tell her under my breath.

Tyla rolls her eyes and huffs. "No, it's not. It's up to me, and I've decided."

Huntyr stares at her sister for a long while before shifting her gaze to the Eshari, the two of them communicating in that silent manner. Then, finally, she looks to me.

"Okay," she agrees.

It takes all of my pride and control to stop my grin at just a smirk.

Tyla might be my new favorite person in the world.

From the sparkle in her eyes, she likely knows it.

"Alright then," I say. "I have to check in on a few things. I'll send Marta with some bathwater for you both."

I close the door behind me, but my Fae ears can't avoid overhearing bits of their conversation as I retreat.

"I can't believe you." Huntyr sighs, but her voice lacks any real bite.

"You'll be nicer after you've been laid."

"Tyla!"

"See? That's proof enough. It's not my name that you should be screaming."

"I might actually kill you."

"Derian!" Tyla teases, her voice turning high-pitched and breathy. "Oh, Derian!"

I smile all the way to the War Room.

⸺◆⸺

Cal has already begun checking in with the fortress leaders. Parker, Imani, Wyatt, and Geoff all stand spread around the map. Cal stares down at it, one hand resting on the pommel of his sword, and the other scratching at his jaw. His thick brows are drawn together so tightly that my stomach instantly plummets.

"One of these days, I'd like you to bring me some good news, Parker."

The warrior flicks his brows in agreement. "That would be nice, wouldn't it?"

I pull a wooden chair backwards towards the table, sitting and folding my arms over the top of the backrest. The torchlight flickers over the worn parchment as I take a moment to examine the new red markers that have popped up in our absence.

Fuck.

We were barely gone more than a fortnight.

Not long enough to warrant this many new sightings.

"You're not going to like what we're about to tell you," Wyatt sighs.

It gets worse?

Cal shifts beside me and sighs, looking down at me with an expression that tells me everything I need to know.

Our experience during the journey wasn't an isolated incident.

"Let me guess," I drawl. "They're traveling in groups?"

Imani and Geoff exchange a look. "How did you know?"

"We were attacked on our way to Springhallow," Cal explains, while I run my tongue over my teeth and consider our next steps. "Three of them together. They killed Roland."

Imani gasps, a hand flying sharply to her chest. She isn't one to show emotion often, but she and Roland have been... close. Close enough that I momentarily debate giving her leave, but I watch her roll out her shoulders and harden.

No, she won't want to leave.

She needs to be here, planning a counterattack. She needs Velkai blood on her hands to numb out the pain.

It's how I would respond if Huntyr—

I stop that thought before it can finish.

Parker sinks heavily into a seat across from me and points to a spot in the Wastelands a few miles to the west of the fortress. "Four here." He moves his finger closer. Too close to the fortress. "Nine here, two days ago."

"*Nine?*" Cal hisses.

"Any injuries?" I demand.

A shadow falls over Parker's face, and he leans back in his seat, letting his arms drag back against the table as he does. "Two casualties, one injury. We expect he'll make a full recovery, though."

My chest tightens. I hold onto that feeling for a moment before I release it. That's going to be the first of many casualties if we don't stop the Mother.

"Did they say anything?" Cal asks, exchanging a quick glance with me.

He's careful not to mention her to the others, a decision I agree with. No need to put that concern in their minds until we know more about whether or not the bitch is still alive.

"That's what's odd," Wyatt says, scratching the top of his head. There's a new scar stretching down his bicep. I fight the guilt that's creeping up my spine. I might have been able to stop those casualties if I'd been here.

"They weren't even trying to attack us at first," Imani continues. "If anything, they treated us like we were a nuisance in their way."

Cal frowns. "Come again?"

Wyatt nods. "They were trying to get around us. They only started fighting back after we attacked first."

That is... unusual.

"Any idea why?" I question.

"One of them, a leader, was shouting at them to keep on and not slow. He said something about her drawing closer."

I sense Cal's tension as his weight shifts next to me. "Her?"

Parker shrugs. "They just kept saying it over and over. How they sense her drawing closer."

I stare at the floor, feeling a wave of nervous magic begin swirling inside me. Cal sighs, looking to me for permission. I nod and only half listen as he tells them the full story of our attack and what the Velkai said about the Mother.

He doesn't, however, tell them about Huntyr's power. For my benefit, I suppose. He's giving me time to come to terms with the fact that as much as I care for her, Huntyr needs to be on the frontline.

Everyone's in agreement on that except for me.

Huntyr wants to go alone.

Cal wants her to fight with the militia.

The second everyone else learns what she can do, they'll all be ready to send her into the Wastelands with nothing but her newfound magic to keep her safe.

Logically, I should want that, too. The leader in me knows it's what's best. There's no room for favoritism in war. You use your assets to the best of their ability, even if that means you lose them in the process.

Huntyr is a weapon. It's ignorant not to admit that.

She's a formidable opponent. Highly trained and improving every day as her Fae strength and speed develop. Her magic, untested as it is, is unparalleled in a fight against a Velkai.

It's my job to defend my kingdom.

I'm the second-born son, farther removed from the crown with every child my brother sires. My only job is to protect this kingdom.

If the Mother rises, it becomes my job to protect the entirety of the realm.

I'll need every weapon at my disposal.

Even if that weapon is *her*.

I don't say another word for the entirety of the meeting. I can't. I can't think straight enough to speak coherently when I feel like I'm falling through the air and about to crash down heavily to the ground without anything to save me.

Plans are made to reinforce posts, and exploratory expeditions are arranged. We determine what updates will be given to the other fortress warriors and who will give them. We make a plan for expanding the infirmary. Eventually, after all strategies have been exhausted, the others rise to their feet and exit, leaving Cal and me alone staring at that map in front of us.

Wordlessly, he moves to close the door, giving us privacy.

"Thank you," I rasp. "For not telling them about her."

The only response is the sound of his boots on the floor as he walks back towards me. He rests his hands heavily on the table and sinks into the seat Parker had occupied a few moments ago, his watchful hazel eyes examining me slowly.

"I should have," he finally says, his voice notably harsher than usual. "*You* should have."

I work my jaw for a long moment before I nod.

He glances out the window to where the setting sun is sending hues of orange and coral over the training yard outside. "I'll admit Lachlan has grown on me too, but she wouldn't be the first friend we've sent into danger."

I know that. Gods, I know that. I feel the weight of every one of my lost friends on a daily basis. Roland is only the most recent addition to an unfortunately very long list.

"You didn't even know her a few months ago," he reminds me softly, as if the length of time that Huntyr has been in my life changes this situation at all.

"I know her now."

"And that changes things?" Cal demands, smacking a finger down on the table. "We've been preparing for this for decades, Derian. One girl shows up and changes all of our strategies?"

I can't bear to look at him. "She changes *everything*."

His heavy breathing takes up space in the room, the sound of it echoing in my head, a slow contrast to the heavy beating of my own pulse.

"Why?" he finally asks, pushing a hand through his hair as he leans back heavily in his seat. "At least help me understand why."

I'm not even sure how to explain it. I open my mouth, but no sound comes out.

"Why?" Cal pushes.

I finally gather the strength to rip my gaze off the floorboards and meet the eyes of my oldest friend. The confession tears out of me, surprising both of us.

"Because I'm in love with her."

HUNTYR

I can barely contain my smile as Kaia releases a long humming purr and twists further onto her back, holding her paws high so I can continue scratching down her belly. I rest my head on a hand as I lounge across the bed, watching her in amusement.

"You're really just a sweet little kitty cat, aren't you?" I tease.

"I am an immortal warrior. I could kill you before you even realize my intent."

I don't bother hiding my widening grin. *"Such a pretty little kitty cat."*

She swipes at me, but her claws are nowhere to be seen.

"So," I muse aloud to Tyla. "Did I ever tell you about that time I got tied up in a butcher shop?"

I continue scratching down Kaia's stomach until her feline eyes flicker over my shoulder. Following her gaze, I scan over my sister.

Tyla leans against the wall, arms crossed over her chest, staring out the window with a glazed look in her eyes. Her chest barely rises and falls, as if she's holding her breath.

I stare at her for a long time, but she never turns to me.

"She seems distracted here," Kaia notes, rolling back onto her stomach.

"Tyla," I call to her, repeating her name a second time when she still doesn't acknowledge me.

"What?" she finally says, pulling her attention away from the window slowly, almost painfully. "Were you saying something?"

I feel Kaia shifting next to me, her unease mirroring my own. "Yeah, I was actually about to tell you a riveting story, until I realized you weren't paying attention to me at all."

"Sorry," she murmurs, gaze already traveling back to the window that overlooks nothing but the western lands beyond the fortress. "You were saying something about a baker?"

"A butcher, actually."

Still, she doesn't acknowledge me. Her shoulders are tight, her head inclined slightly, and her gaze distant. Slowly her brow furrows, as if she's listening to something.

"Do you think it's the tonic?" I ask Kaia.

"It's possible." She jumps off the bed, shaking out her coat once she does. *"It's also possible your sister is simply adjusting to the changes in her life differently than you. She has been taken from her country, learned that the Fae can be trusted, learned that you are a Fae, and has now spent the past week traveling through foreign lands with her new brother-to-be."*

I consider her words, even as my gut twitches with doubt.

"Half-Fae," I mutter in response.

A knock on the door sounds, and I wait for Tyla to jump, or turn, or do *anything* to indicate that she even heard the noise, but she remains a statue by the window. It isn't until the knock sounds a second time that I rise to my feet and brush off my pants.

"Don't worry," I say sarcastically. "I'll get it."

Suddenly all worries about Tyla disappear as I pull open the door to see a flash of long hair, tanned skin, and bulging biceps.

"Rhen!" I cry, launching towards him to pull him into a hug. He holds me gently before pulling back and mussing the hair atop my head.

"I heard the princess was back and thought I'd come say hello."

Rolling my eyes, I hold the door open wider and allow him in. He leans down to grab two buckets of water and carries them in. Marta, the woman who brought me a dress the night after the Conclave ended, follows behind him, new piles of fabric in her arms.

"I am not a princess," I remind him sternly.

"Not yet," he quips with a crooked grin and a raised brow, before turning to Tyla. "Who's this?"

Still, she's absent, hardly seeming to notice the new additions to the room until I grab her by the hand and rip her away from the window.

"This is my sister Tyla," I introduce her. "Tyla, this is Rhen. He trained me for the Conclave."

He lifts his brow and moves to rest his hands on his hips. "I *thought* I trained you for the Conclave. From what I saw that day, and at the party afterwards, you really didn't need any guidance."

I run my tongue over my teeth and shrug apologetically. "Yes, well, you were very kind in attempting to teach me things I already knew."

"You have to show me that spin move you did when Mara was throwing the blades at you. That was incredible."

I feel a blush creeping up the back of my neck as I squeeze Tyla's hand gently. "Actually, I learned that one while I got into a sticky situation with a butcher a few years back."

She at least has the decency to hang her head apologetically.

"Well, it's nice to meet you, Rhen," she says, extending her hand towards him.

He kisses her knuckles politely before excusing himself to the attached bathing chamber to fill the tub. All the while, Marta begins laying out the various dresses on the bed.

"Prince Derian let me know you girls will be needing some fresh garments after your travels," she explains. "We had these available in the fortress already, but I can send one of the servants into town to pick up any other items you may need."

I pick at a loose thread at the hem of my tunic, turning over a sudden thought blossoming in the corner of my mind.

"Your mind is a disgusting place to be trapped in." Kaia sighs heavily in my head as my lips split into a grin.

Under her breath, Tyla chuckles next to me, already guessing where my thoughts are.

"I do have a special request, actually," I tell Marta.

⸺◆⸺

I allow Tyla the luxury of the first bath, choosing to take the time to catch up with Rhen.

"So, anything exciting happen in my absence?"

He shifts, chewing on his lip. "You could say that."

I tilt my head in a silent invitation to continue.

"I had to go into town to pick up some supplies, and there was a traveling troupe of performers. I stayed for the show and..."

I can't stop my grin as his voice trails off. "Did you meet someone?"

He blushes a delicious shade of crimson and rubs a hand awkwardly against the back of his neck. "I mated, actually."

The words are a slap, a level of brutal honesty I never would have expected from him.

I laugh uncomfortably. "Well, that's a bit more information than I needed, but good for you."

Rhen stares at me, at first with confusion—then surprise. He laughs suddenly, the sound a sharp cut through the quiet room. His laughter continues until he's clutching his side and I'm staring at him with equal parts of confusion and irritation.

"Sometimes I forget you're only half-Fae," he finally wheezes. "I'm not talking about sex, Huntyr."

Frowning, I lean back in my seat, not understanding.

"Mating is something that can happen between two Fae. It's a connection stronger than any other in the realm. Unbreakable. We think it's a byproduct of the Ether in our bodies latching onto that of another person. Mated pairs of Fae are perfect for each other in every way. When I saw Joeseph last week, the bond between us just snapped into place. It was like I'd known him my whole life. We were married two days ago."

Oh. Oh wow.

Rhen holds his left hand towards me, showing the silver band that now rests on his fourth finger with an expression of utter pride and joy.

"I don't understand," I admit. "You just looked at each other, and boom, you were ready to get married?"

Rhen nods. "We were lucky that way. Some mated pairs take a little longer for the bond to fully snap into place or to even notice it's there, but my parents were mated. I saw how they interacted with each other, so when I felt that pull towards Joeseph I just knew."

I shake my head incredulously. "I can't imagine that."

Rhen laughs softly, eyes narrowed at me. "You might be overthinking it, Huntyr. Trust me, a mating bond is typically fairly obvious to identify."

I suppose if I get the chance to see him and his new husband together, I'll be able to confirm that for myself.

"Do I get to meet him?" I ask with a teasing wiggle of my brows.

"Please," Rhen waves a hand at me. "He talks about you non-stop. The Mortal girl who gave everyone who doubted her the finger. I'd have to keep him away with a crowbar."

I laugh aloud at that, and I think it might be the first time that I've thought of the Conclave without feeling a rush of panic.

We chat for a bit longer. Well really, Rhen gushes. He tells me all about what an excellent acrobat Joeseph is, how his mate understands him in a way no one else ever has, how remarkable it is that he seems to sense Joeseph's presence even before he can see him sometimes.

He is clearly a man in love.

I'm still warm with happiness for him long after he leaves to report back to his post.

By the time Tyla finally emerges from the bathing room, though, I've put away all thoughts of Rhen and Fae mates to focus instead on one singular goal.

Me.

A tub.

Hot water to soak my tired muscles.

I charge into the bathroom and make my way to the copper basin tucked away in a small inlet in the room. I'm just about ready to throw off my clothes when I look down into the water and sigh unhappily.

The water is now cold and dark with the dirt that was scrubbed from my sister's skin.

I chew on my lip, debating how rude it would be for me to trample into the hall and ask for new water.

It's not like Derian would mind. If he were here, he'd simply march out and demand new water be brought for me himself.

Still.

It was needy. I'd bathed in cold water for the majority of my life. This was nothing new. I'd just grown too accustomed to the luxury of being provided for here in the Fae Kingdom.

I'd grown too accustomed to Derian ensuring that I was provided for.

But I don't need him to do that, and I don't need fresh warm water.

I strip my clothes quickly, repeating the sentiment over and over as if I can convince myself of it if I just say it enough times.

And yet, when I turn back to the water and lift my leg to climb into the tub, I freeze.

I just can't convince myself of it.

I want fresh water.

I step back, sighing heavily. There is, of course, another option. There is another, simpler, way for me to have fresh water without having to burden someone else with bringing it to me.

I could just clean it myself.

With Fae magic.

The thought still fills me with more than a fair amount of discomfort, but if I stand any chance of killing the Mother, I do need to get comfortable with this part of myself. More than simply being comfortable, I need to be proficient. Expert.

I need to be able to wield magic as easily as I wield a blade.

"Fine," I mutter to myself before rolling out my neck and shoulders.

Closing my eyes, I focus on the instructions Derian repeated to me over and over during our travels. I slow my breathing, relax my shoulders, and focus on the feeling of my body being grounded. I dig into myself, into the very center of my core, focusing on the swirling mass of energy I find there.

Ether.

That cosmic energy that flows in me, through me. It *is* me.

I pull, gently at first, then harder, ripping it from that deep place inside me even as it struggles against me. When we first started training, Derian assured me that eventually the ether would loosen and would be more willing to follow my guidance and shaping, but that has yet to happen. Getting it to listen is nearly impossible.

It fights me every step of the way, but I keep pulling, gritting my teeth as I do, until finally it explodes. The magic bursts out of me in a rush of air and light that sends me stumbling backwards and has me shielding my face instinctually. Water crashes through the air, splattering over the tiled floor and walls. By the time I open my eyes, dirty bathwater covers the room and drips down the windows. The clothes I'd discarded on the stool in the corner of the room are now soaked through.

What's left in the tub, though, is noticeably clean and steaming.

I'll take it.

"Needs practice," Kaia remarks from the other room.

"I have time to practice."

"You do not," she reminds me. *"Not if you plan to embark on this quest immediately after your wedding."*

Her words send a flicker of unease down my spine. She's right. Not that I'll admit that to her.

"You do not need to admit it aloud to take the warning to heart. I'm going to procure my dinner. Your sister remains."

I don't bother responding, not when a warm bath is just waiting for me. The moan that escapes when I sink down into it is positively sinful.

Taking my time in the tub, I allow the water to flow over me, relaxing every place it touches as I lay my head back against the copper lip. I breathe in the jasmine oils and allow myself to simply... find peace.

Peace that for the first time in years actually feels warranted.

Tyla is healthy.

The tonic is working.

She's here, with me, perfectly happy and healthy. We have warm water and our own beds. Tonight we'll dine with the people who I've come to consider my friends. Our bellies will be filled with plentiful amounts of food, and she'll be able to rest in a room that is all her own.

And I'll... well, I'll sleep beside Derian.

Again.

I'll let him move inside me and then afterwards I'll let him sleep beside me. I'll let him sleep curled around me in a way I've never let anyone else do.

It's surprisingly not a scary thought.

He is undeniably a Fae bastard, but somehow in the past few weeks, I've started to crave those moments between just the two of us. I've started to need them for more than just a physical release.

And *that,* well that is a terrifying thought.

Rather than dwell on it any longer, I emerge from the tub, now happily clean, and wrap a towel around me. It's still damp from my harrowing attempt at magic, but it's suitable enough.

With a happy bounce in my step, I pad over the tiled floors back to the bedroom, pausing for a brief moment when I hear Tyla mumbling. I smile, picturing her whispering to Kaia even though the cat can't respond to her.

I'm grateful they've taken to each other so well.

Only...

Kaia isn't in there.

She left to go hunt.

Tyla is alone.

Gently, I push open the door just a crack, listening as I do.

"Of course," Tyla whispers. "It all makes sense now. Huntyr will understand, like I do. I'm ready now."

Did Derian come back?

I push out of the bathroom, expecting to see the two of them conspiring, but Tyla stands alone.

She's still staring out that damn window.

"Tyla?"

She turns to me. She's put on one of the dresses Marta brought for us, a pale yellow gown with capped sleeves. It fits her perfectly, despite how petite she is.

"What do you think?" She waves an arm down her body. "It's lovely, isn't it?"

I nod slowly, glancing around the room as if needing to confirm I didn't miss some guest.

"Were you saying something?"

Tyla frowns. "No, why?"

"Because I heard you, Tyla. I heard you talking to someone."

She tilts her head with narrowed eyes and a teasing smile. "Clearly someone let the steam get to her head. Come, get dressed. You obviously need to eat something."

She pushes me towards the bed, to where the remaining dresses lay, waiting for me to choose. Tyla throws herself across the top of the bed, chattering about which ones she thinks will look best on me, but I only half listen to her.

She seems so much like herself again, hardly even glancing towards the window. But I know what I saw. Even as she shoves a dress at me, proclaiming it's *the one*, I can't shake off the odd feeling of suspicion that has settled within me.

I wasn't imagining that.

She'd been talking to herself.

The feeling of peace is suddenly gone, replaced now with concern that while that tonic might have healed my sister, it also might have had some other effects too.

<hr>

Rhen walks with us into the dining room, where a select few have been gathered to eat. Ulna and Taric are seated at one end of the table, Taric's arm across the back of his wife's chair. Parker and his partner are next to them, speaking animatedly. Derian and Cal are at the other end of the table, brows furrowed as they discuss something quickly between themselves, though Derian's attention flickers to me as I enter the room, looking first at my face, then down my body, then to where my hand rests in the crook of Rhen's elbow.

His eyes narrow, and the windows shake suddenly with a forceful wind.

I lift my brows at him.

Possessive Fae bastard.

He's on his feet in an instant, eyes zeroed in on me, hand extended for mine even as he's still feet away.

"He's got it bad," Rhen leans down to mutter into my ear.

I smirk up at him when thunder sounds outside.

"Why do you sound surprised?"

I feel Derian's fingers wrap around those of my free hand, and Gods help me, he actually tugs me away. Ahead of us, Tyla stifles her giggle under a cough while Kaia simply glares up at him.

"Why you are so attracted to this unbearably vexing creature is beyond my understanding," she mutters.

"Thank you for escorting the women," Derian says to Rhen tightly, before turning away without another word, effectively dismissing the guard.

I plant my feet though, refusing to let him pull me away.

"Actually, Rhen, why don't you stay and dine with us?" My voice is higher-pitched than normal, sickly sweet.

I feel Derian tense beside me and Rhen's eyes flicker towards his prince. "Thank you, Huntyr, but—"

"Lady Lachlan," Derian corrects sternly.

Tyla and I share a look of pure amusement before she joins in.

"Come now," Tyla insists, wrapping her hands around Rhen's arm and beginning to walk towards the table with him in tow, her narrow hips swishing as she does. "In the Mortal Kingdom, when a future princess asks you to dine with her, it's simply something you cannot say no to."

I watch them take their places across from the two that remain empty for Derian and me, a bemused grin dancing on my lips.

"Huntress," Derian drawls behind me.

I flick my hair over my shoulder as I turn back to him. "I'm starving, aren't you?"

With that, I let go of his hand and prowl forward, stopping only to run my hand along the line of Cal's shoulder as I take the seat between him and Derian. Derian's head falls back as I do, and I watch him take three deep breaths.

"He doesn't respond well to being played with," Cal warns me.

"I know," I grin. "That's what makes it so fun."

Cal rubs a hand against his temple. "You two are an insufferable pairing."

I wink at him as Derian takes his place next to me and waves at the servants to begin bringing in our food. As we wait, he rests an arm around the back of my chair, fingers tracing circles along the exposed skin between my shoulder blades.

It's one of the few parts of me that *is* exposed. I chose a gown more typical to what ladies of courts would wear, long-sleeved with a respectable neckline. A forest green fabric that falls easily to the ground without even the suggestion of a slit.

Throughout the meal, I'm careful to avoid Derian, not bothering to look his way and hardly acknowledging anything he says. Tyla glances between the two of us as the night progresses on, communicating silently with me in the way only a sister can.

You're being cruel.

I shake my head. *All part of the fun.*

"So Huntyr," Ulna cuts in. "You must be excited to plan the wedding."

I narrow my eyes at her. She knows me well enough by now to know that having a wedding is the last thing I want on my to-do list.

"Surely you have *some* ideas of what you want," Taric insists when he takes in my horrified face. "We'll start easy. Who do you want to invite?"

"Tyla," I answer quickly.

There's a beat of silence as everyone in the room glances between one another.

"Of course," Ulna agrees. "And who else?"

I frown, shifting uncomfortably. "Well, I suppose I have one friend in Velia. Flannigan. We could invite him?"

"Not Kristona?" Tyla asks from across from me.

I deliberate on the idea, still not entirely at peace with the new way I view my past with Kristona. Having a reckoning with him is something that needs to happen at some point, I'm just not sure if a wedding is the best opportunity for that.

"Not Kristona," I tell her, and Derian resumes tracing those circles on my back.

"Okay, so, Tyla and Flannigan," Taric counts them on his fingers. "That's only two, Huntyr. Anyone else?"

I shrug. "Kaia."

Ulna glances to the Eshari who is devouring a hunk of raw meat she dragged into the room.

"Okay, then," my future aunt sighs. "A small guest list."

"Small," Derian confirms next to me. "I only need my brother and the people in this room. Anyone else is up to Huntyr."

I feel a wave of relief knowing I won't be standing in front of hundreds of members of Fae society and nobility as I sign the rest of my life away to marriage.

Ulna nods as if she's keeping track of these plans, even though disapproval is evident on her face. "It's a bit untraditional, but I don't think anyone will be surprised that you break from standards, Derian."

Cal snorts next to me, and Derian glares at him.

"We'll need a dress made," Ulna continues, oblivious to the fact that Derian's hand has temporarily lifted from the back of my chair to smack Cal on the back of the head. "You and I can discuss that in private, dear. Best to keep it a surprise for the groom."

For the first time this evening, I glance up at Derian, who is already smirking down at me, his thoughts obvious based on the heat of his eyes. He doesn't particularly care what I'm wearing as long as he gets to peel it off of me at some point.

"Tyla can pick it," I say, feeling uncomfortable as everyone turns towards me in shock. "She's better at that sort of thing than I am."

"It's your wedding gown, Huntyr!" Tyla reminds me.

"Okay?" I let my shoulders lift and fall in a pronounced shrug. "It's a dress that I'll wear for a few hours and never look at again. If I don't necessarily care what it looks like, I don't see why anyone else should."

There's a momentary pause before everyone's attention suddenly turns to Derian, as if they're waiting for him to talk some sense into me. Clearly, they don't know either of us very well if they think that's possible.

Derian simply grins. "Let's not make this an ordeal. You're more than capable of throwing something together, Ulna. Huntyr and I trust you."

I'm not thrilled about him speaking on my behalf, but I'm also not dying to continue this conversation much longer, so I let it pass, nodding in agreement until Ulna finally throws up her hands.

"Fine, I'll plan it all. Some assistance from your sister would be lovely though."

Tyla grins happily. "Of course! I have so many ideas."

"Oh!" I suddenly cry out, hand flying to the table. "I do have *one* request."

Derian glances down at me in confusion, and I fight to keep my features neutral as I focus my attention on his aunt.

"If you only have a single request for your wedding, I will make sure it happens," Ulna swears.

"Perfect!" I lean back, resting a hand on Derian's thigh under the table as I nestle slightly into his side. "I would *love* chocolate cake."

Derian clears his throat next to me, shifting his weight as my hand slides higher up his thigh. "Of course you would."

HUNTYR

After the meal has concluded, we linger around the table, laughing and sharing stories. Throughout it all, I haven't bothered to move away from where I had leaned into Derian earlier, and he doesn't seem to mind. His fingers on my back have stilled, but he keeps that arm behind me.

And I can't bring myself to be bothered by it.

His jealousy over Rhen is still obvious based on the way he keeps glaring at the warrior every time Rhen says anything. Rhen even places his left hand on the table pointedly several times, but the prince doesn't seem to notice the ring that shines under the torchlight.

It's probably not helping the situation that I've been talking to Rhen far more frequently than I've been talking to Derian.

"You're going to get him in trouble," Cal leans over to mumble to me once Derian is distracted in a conversation with Taric.

Rhen meets my gaze across the table, eyes wide with concern. "Yes, you are. Please stop."

I only laugh, winking at Rhen as I do. "It's all part of the plan, boys."

And they do know how much I love my plans.

Tyla yawns across from me, barely stifling it behind her hand. "Neither of you stand a chance of convincing her to do something she doesn't want to."

I tilt my head in agreement. This particular plan was put into motion hours ago. No one can stop the wheels that are already moving now.

Rhen only sighs and shakes his head. "I hope your fun is worth the fact that I'll be cleaning out the stables for a week."

Cal rolls his eyes next to me and sends the warrior a sympathetic smile. "I'm not going to let that happen."

"Let what happen?" Derian asks, finally turning back to us.

Cal balks, and I quickly step in before he can spoil everything. "Allow Tyla to fall asleep at the table."

My sister huffs. "I was not!"

"Were too. That's why Cal was just about to suggest that Rhen should walk you back to your room."

The two men exchange glances before Cal awkwardly nods over at Derian. "Yes. That's exactly what I was about to suggest."

Derian humphs with narrowed eyes, but really doesn't need any convincing to send Rhen away from the table, and me, so he nods his approval and reminds Tyla that we'll only be across the hall if she needs us. She smiles her thanks, and Rhen silently mouths the words to me as he leads her away. Derian glares at his back the entire time that it takes for him to exit the room.

"You're a complete fiend," Cal mutters to me, disapproval evident in his tone.

Derian lifts a brow as I giggle. "Do I want to know?"

Step one of the plan was to get the Fae prince adequately jealous and riled up. I'd say that has been accomplished. Time to move on to the next phase of this endeavor.

My chair scrapes across the floor as I push back away from the table. "No, you don't."

He looks up at me suspiciously. "Going somewhere, Huntress?"

My gaze turns wicked, and I wrap my fingers around his and pull him out of his own seat. "*We're* going somewhere."

Our friends exchange amused glances as I back away from the table, dragging Derian behind me.

"Do you want us to come?" Taric teases.

"I most certainly do not!"

Their laughter follows us into the hall.

⬥

It's a bit colder outside than it has been the previous few nights, but I don't particularly mind. I lean back against the wooden fence in front of the throwing targets in the training yard and stare up at the sky. Stars dance across the expanse of it.

I point up at one of the intricate constellations. "That's the crown of Queen Esmerelda. She was the last monarch to rule when the Mortal Kingdoms were united."

He follows my gaze before dragging my finger to connect some of the stars to different points. "Actually, that's Geodric's Blade. He was King of the Vaereth."

I trace over the new image he outlined for me with my eyes. The Fae have their own constellations, I realize solemnly. They have their own histories,

stories, and beliefs that are completely different from those I grew up with in the Mortal Kingdoms.

And now I somehow stand between the two of them, trying to make sense of the strange place where they connect.

"How are the Fae related to the Vaereth?" I ask.

Derian rests his hands on either side of me against the wooden fence, boxing me in. "We worshipped them as our Gods. They were the opposite of the Velkai in every way. Where Velkai steal Ether, the Vaereth grant it. It's entwined in their being, their very souls. Our histories say that one day they took the Ether inside them and gave it form, thus creating the Fae. For centuries we lived alongside them, worshipping them as our creators, and they were benevolent Gods, encouraging peace between the Fae and Mortals, using the Ether within them to heal the injured and dying."

"Like you can do?"

Derian reaches for my hand, turning my palm so that we're both looking down at the scar that now runs across my skin. "I can do only a fraction of what they were capable of. If a Vaereth had healed you, there would be no scars."

Sighing, I stare down at that thin white line, the ever-present reminder of the Conclave and what I lived through. The battles that brought me here. Without these scars, without the Conclave, I never would have learned the truth of who I was. I never would have gotten Tyla that tonic.

And I wouldn't be standing here with Derian.

"I like my scars," I say, both to him and myself.

His lips twitch into a bit of a smile. "So do I."

Something deep within me sparks at that hint of a smile, and I pitch my hips forward, pressing into his unmoving frame, letting my own grin turn nearly feral.

"Huntress," he purrs, staring down at me. "Care to tell me why you brought me out here?"

I bite my lip as I bring my hands to his chest, trailing across the hard leather of his jacket before pushing it aside. I run them down the expanse of his firm abdominals, covered only by a thin cotton shirt. He leans into my touch, and I can practically *hear* his heart rate spike.

I want that shirt off. Immediately.

"I'd rather show you," I whisper, letting my hands slide lower.

Derian's eyes darken, and his calloused hand presses into my left hip, fingers digging into the flesh beneath my dress. "I might prefer that too."

He buries his head in the hollow of my throat, breathing me in before brushing his lips against the delicate skin, the touch sending shivers down my spine.

"I'm so glad to hear that." I tilt my fingers towards his belt and grasp onto the blade hooked there, pulling it out sharply and holding it victoriously between us, pushing him away with the tip of the dagger pressed at the skin above his heart. "I was thinking it might be time for a little rematch."

He freezes for a moment, staring down at the blade with equal parts of disbelief and disappointment. His eyes close for a moment, and his jaw works as he regains his composure before he finally steps back and takes the blade from my hand.

"I could have gotten it myself," he mumbles, reaching to pull a second one out of his boot.

I wink, noticing the way his eyes track my hands as I pull up my skirt to unsheathe the two blades strapped onto my thigh. "My way was more fun."

"Maybe I don't want to play right now," he says, crossing his arms across his broad chest. The evidence of what he'd *rather* be doing with me is still visible in the bulge at the front of his trousers. I have to fight against the need to lick my lips.

I pretend to think on his words for a moment, tapping a finger against my chin before moving sharply back towards the fortress with a shrug. "Okay, I'll ask Rhen to play with me."

Icy fingers wrap around my wrist, halting me in my path and pulling me back against his firm chest. "I've been trying very hard all night to remind myself that Rhen is a friend of mine. I don't think I'll manage to keep that in mind if you drag him out here in the dark with you."

He's so close I can almost feel his breath on my skin, and it sends a rush of anticipation over me. I'm playing with fire.

No, not fire.

I'm in the eye of the storm, pretending like the rain isn't going to come crashing down on me at any second.

It's positively exhilarating.

"And why's that?" I whisper, unable to break away from staring into those dark eyes.

"I think you know why."

I tilt my head. "I prefer when you use your words."

He's quiet, considering, but then he takes another single step towards me, coming ever so slightly closer. "Because you're *mine*, Huntress. Rhen seems to have trouble remembering that."

"I don't believe that."

"I know that."

I grin slyly. "I think his *mate* would disagree with you."

There's a flash of surprise on his face, but before he can fully register my words, I spin in the opposite direction, releasing both daggers in rapid procession. They fly through the air in elegant twirls before slamming into the wood directly next to each other, both perfectly within the center target.

He stares at them for a moment before turning his attention back to me, and the intensity in his gaze slowly starts to fade away as he realizes the way I've been playing upon his jealousy. Wind brushes through my hair, icy but not uncomfortable.

"We're supposed to take turns," he reminds me with lifted brows.

"Oops," I shrug, pushing myself up to perch along the wooden beam that serves as a fence. "Guess I got too excited."

Derian looks me over, his eyes still narrowed in suspicion. It must be killing him that he can't figure out what game I'm playing.

"Get down from there," he finally says, flipping the dagger in his hand so that the tip is pinched between his forefinger and thumb. "You're distracting."

The laugh that escapes me is low and drawn out. "Surely the almighty Fae prince can throw a tiny dagger even when a pretty girl sits in front of him."

He doesn't break eye contact as he pulls his arm back and releases. I hear the metal connect with the wood but don't bother turning around to check it. I know he landed center.

"I never even got my prize from the last time we played," he complains, centering his stance and examining the board. With three blades all sticking out of center, there's much less room for him to land in, making the game infinitely harder.

"I took care of that, actually."

He glances at me, brows raised in a silent question.

"Well," I hop off the post, taking slow measured steps towards him. "You told me I could buy anything I wanted to fill my wardrobe."

Derian returns his attention to the target, pretending to ignore me.

"So I sent Marta out to get me a few things."

My fingers trail to the bodice of my gown, to the place where the puffed sleeves meet my skin. Slowly, ever so slowly, I pull it down off my shoulders.

"I hope you don't mind the expense. After all, I only got a few *very* small pieces of lace."

His arm lifts to throw, but as it does, his gaze is drawn to me, to where the dress is slowly being pulled away to reveal the top of the black lace brassiere I managed to hide under my otherwise modest gown.

He releases the blade almost as a secondhand thought, his body turning towards me, and I watch it fly through the air.

"Ooh," I sigh, pulling my dress back into place as I look sadly at where it just narrowly missed the center. "Looks like you lost this time."

Derian doesn't move. He doesn't curse or glance at the evidence of his failure. He simply stares, eyes trailing up and down my body as he imagines what I've hidden underneath this chiffon.

Then he moves.

He prowls towards me, one hand grasping onto my hip and the other wrapping around the back of my head so he can pull my lips up to meet his.

"You don't play fair, Huntress," he breathes against my mouth.

"And what are you going to do about it?"

His tongue dips across my lower lip, pushing me to open for him, and Gods help me, I do. Together, we back towards that post, and fire snakes down my spine as he growls against me.

I could kiss him for the rest of my life, I realize suddenly.

It's not just fun or sexy or pleasurable.

It's all of that and more.

It's peace.

Kissing Derian is one of the only times my mind shuts off. There's no planning or scheming. There's no need to keep one eye in front of me and the other searching for danger.

There's just him. Just me. Just *this*.

He and I, coming together in a way that feels so natural. It's as if we were created simply for each other, for this one moment in time pressed against one another.

Derian Silverthorn is the embodiment of everything I've ever hated.

He's mercilessly ruthless. I've seen him kill with nothing more than a simple thought, and I know he's killed thousands more in wars that happened long before I was ever born.

He's unbelievably arrogant. Notably demanding. Frustratingly unserious in the worst of times.

And yet he's also been kind and forgiving.

He cares for his friends and family more deeply than anyone will ever realize.

He held me in the moments when my life shattered around me and was the only person who helped me come back to sanity.

He makes sure everyone is always fed because he can't bear to see anyone suffer in the way he's too familiar with.

Derian Silverthorn is a good man.

Gods help me, I like knowing him. I'm a better person for knowing him.

I've lived nearly every day of my life preparing for my revenge. My own needs, wants, and desires didn't matter. All that has ever mattered was that singular goal. Anything else—relationships, hobbies, plans—simply got in the way. I didn't care who I hurt in the pursuit of my vengeance, and I definitely didn't care if I made it out alive, so long as the Fae paid for what they'd done to my father.

And now?

Now I think I finally found something I *do* want.

I want him. As my friend. As my lover.

Even as my husband.

"HUNTYR!"

Kaia's scream echoes in my head, and I jolt sharply from it, pushing Derian away as fear lances through me with sudden precision. I've never heard her sound like that.

Panicked.

"What's wrong?" Derian's instantly on alert, scanning over me.

"Kaia, what's happening?"

"It's Tyla. Come now!"

Ice spreads through my veins, sudden and insidious. I can't breathe. I don't think.

I simply move.

I take off at a sprint, running faster than I ever have before.

DERIAN

In my unreasonably long life, there have been plenty of moments in which I've felt fear. When my powers first erupted from me and I brought a hurricane raining down on Bridgemond was probably the first time I'd felt the icy stillness of it. From there, there were countless times when I'd learned to control those powers in Amberhull, where fear had woven into my thoughts again. Even after I'd long since felt immune to it, there were moments in the battlefield during the war when it had suddenly struck through me.

I've felt fear several times since meeting Huntyr Lachlan.

None of those experiences, though, come close to the sheer and utter *terror* that flowed through me as I watched Huntyr's eyes go distant. As I watched her face pale, her breath quicken, her mouth tighten.

And then she was gone.

Running with the speed of a full-blooded Fae back towards the barracks as if her life depended on it.

My Huntress wouldn't panic like that in the name of her own life, though.

She would do it for her sister.

I chase after her, shouting out to one of the guards to summon a healer.

We crash into the fortress, feet heavy as we sprint through the twisting halls, back towards the suite I'd placed her sister in. It's a short distance, yet it feels impossibly long, each step sending another wave of panic over me so strongly that I can't tell if that feeling belongs to me or her.

Huntyr's legs are moving like the finely honed weapons they are. She runs so quickly she almost looks as if she's flying over the stone floor. And despite the fact that I'm a highly trained, full-blooded Silverthorn warrior, and she's a twenty-year-old half-Mortal girl, I hate to admit that I'm struggling to keep up with her.

She turns a corner and I push myself, ignoring the burning in my lungs.

Then she screams.

Thunder cracks outside just a moment afterwards at that sound, and dread echoes within it, punching through my gut.

I turn the corner, stopping short as I nearly barrel into her.

She's frozen, one hand pressed to her mouth, eyes wide in horror, staring down at the body sprawled across the floor.

Hollow eyes, black spiraling veins, mouth open at an unnatural angle, arm outstretched down the hall towards Tyla's room.

The wedding band on the fourth finger still gleams.

I don't know how I overlooked that ring all night.

A tiny whimper escapes from deep within Huntyr's throat as she looks down at the body of the Fae who had quite possibly been her first friend among us. It's the tiniest of sounds, one I probably wouldn't have even heard if I was Mortal, but it reverberates through me like a thunderclap.

"Tyla," I remind her gently.

Her gaze jerks up towards the hallway again, and she pulls the two blades from her hips as she bursts forward once more.

We skid to a halt in front of Tyla's door, which dangles open ever so slightly, and are greeted by Kaia's characteristic snarl.

"What is happening?" Huntyr screams, wide-eyed as she takes in the scene.

Tyla stands tall, her skin more flushed than I've ever seen it. The dark veins have somehow retreated, leaving nothing behind other than what seems like a shadow passing under her moonlit skin. Her hair hangs wild and loose down her back, tendrils of it hanging in the air as if suspended by static electricity.

She hardly glances at us as Huntyr barges into the room.

Her attention is focused entirely on the Eshari across from her, who now bares her fangs at Huntyr's sister.

"Huntyr!" Tyla breathes happily, a smile growing on her face. "I'm glad you're here. We should get going."

Huntyr stares down at Kaia, a million emotions passing over her face as she shakes her head gently. "No. You're wrong."

I push past the women, moving to examine the rest of the suite for any intruders as I listen in to their conversation.

"Tyla, what happened?"

"I'll tell you on the way."

"On the way where?"

The bedroom seems to be clear, no one lingering in closets or under the bed. I cross the space, pushing into the bathing chamber, and freeze.

"To our Mother, Huntyr. She's ready for us to come home. Hasn't she talked to you?"

Water floods the floor, splashing under my boots as I step inside. The air has an unnatural chill, like even the heat was so frightened it chose to flee.

I step in slowly, dread curling through me, and I feel my magic spark to life in my fingertips.

Marta is in the tub.

Head under the water.

Eyes black and hollow.

Huntyr.

My entire soul focuses on her and the fact that she is in the other room alone with *Tyla*.

Tyla, who is the only other person here.

Tyla, who walked to her room with Rhen.

Tyla, who Kaia now snarls at, despite how much Huntyr loves her.

Tyla, who suddenly seems healthier now that we're here in Oxhurn... so close to the Wastelands

"Huntyr!" I yell, rushing back into the bedroom. Tyla lingers by the door now, body inclining to leave even as she extends a hand to her sister, begging Huntyr to go with her.

Huntyr's blue eyes lock onto mine. They're brighter than they've ever looked before.

Kaia places herself between the sisters.

"She's a Velkai," I breathe.

My Huntress stares at me, disbelief clouding her features.

"No," she whispers, with a soft shake of her head.

But then the sound of a deep growl erupting from within Tyla splits between us, and Huntyr turns to her sister in horror. Tyla stares at me with narrowed eyes, looking like a picture of hatred and venom.

And I'm hit with the flash of a memory.

Of another dark-haired Velkai who looked at me that way. Their bitch of a queen had looked *just* like that when I led Geodric to her. She had stared at me with that same expression, the one that promised vengeance when he sacrificed himself to end her.

Only he hadn't killed the Mother.

And now she was summoning Tyla right to her.

Tyla turns on her heels and flees. I don't have a single second to try and stop Huntyr before she runs after her, screaming her name frantically. And her voice...

That voice, which is always so steady, even when she seems to be facing the most incredible of trials, is now filled with such pain that I feel my own heart breaking because *her* heart is breaking.

She knows it's the truth.

She's too smart not to know.

Tyla runs to the courtyard, where rain now falls in sheets from the sky, soaking us to the bone the second we step into the night air. Roaring wind tears against my skin.

This storm is natural, though, not at all brought to life by my magic. No, it seems that even the skies need to sob over what's happening. If I was calmer, I might have the wherewithal to clear the weather, but I can only bring myself to focus on the lives that now hang in the balance.

While Huntyr worries for her sister, it's my job to worry about every Fae living in this fortress. Fae who are now at risk by the Velkai in their midst.

Only a few souls linger outside this late in the evening, just those that are tending to their nightly chores.

"Run!" I command them, voice like a whip slicing through the air. "Get inside, all of you."

The fools don't react fast enough.

Tyla runs to the Fae male leading one of the horses back to the stable. He slows as she approaches, and before he can even process what's happening, she wraps her tiny hands around his face, opens her mouth, and breathes him in.

Huntyr's steps falter, and she makes a small choking sound.

For a moment, I even stumble as I watch Tyla kill him with my own eyes.

It all happens so fast.

I have to stomp down on the rush of power that flows through me demanding release as the scent of magic, of stolen Ether, fills the air and forces itself into my nose like a poison.

Then she's throwing herself onto the horse with a strength she didn't possess a few days ago as the hollowed-out husk of a corpse falls heavily to the ground.

"Huntyr, come!" she demands, more of an order than a request.

I step behind my Huntress, feeling her horror as potently as if it were my own, and I grasp onto her forearms.

"I'm not letting you put her in danger, Tyla," I say softly, somehow knowing she'll be able to hear me despite the booming thunder around us.

Tyla wipes a hand across her brow as she looks at me, and a sinister smile spreads across her face as her dark eyes trail up and down my frame.

"She has a message for you, prince."

I don't need to ask who she's speaking of.

"I'm sure she does."

"She looks forward to finishing what she started all those years ago."

"I'm not going to let that happen either, Tyla."

The girl just laughs as she shakes her head at me.

"You'll be dead." With her threat lingering between us, she turns to her sister. "You will be too, if you choose him."

Huntyr remains in front of me, feet rooted to the ground even as she lifts a shaking hand to her mouth in disbelief.

"Tyla," she whispers, a broken plea. "Please."

Tyla's features flash, and I'm not sure what I see in her eyes. Is it whatever fragment of love that she has for Huntyr? Or is it disgust? It's gone within an instant before she lifts her gaze away from us, trailing her eyes over the turrets of the fortress.

For the second time tonight, reality crashes into me.

Fuck.

I brought her here. I showed her everything. Led her through all of our defenscs.

And now she'll tell the Mother all of it.

"Fine," she growls.

She straightens, pulls at the reins of her horse, and kicks sharply into the steeds side, turning him around and running away from the fortress.

No, not away from us.

Towards the Wastelands.

"*TYLA!*" Huntyr screams after her sister and moves to take a single step, but her legs give out under her.

I wrap my arms around her waist before she can fall and pull her body to mine, twisting and wrapping her in my embrace as I finally manage to summon enough magic to send away the storm.

"Shh," I whisper as I run a soothing hand down her head. Her fingers dig into my shirt, forming unbreakable fists against my chest, and sobs rip out of her tiny frame. "I'm here."

That's all I can offer her.

My presence.

I can't tell her it will be okay. I can't tell her we'll save Tyla. Fuck, I can't even tell her if she'll ever see her sister again.

An hour ago we were all seated at a table laughing with one another. Huntyr was happy. She was planning our wedding, and for once, she didn't look horrified by the idea of our marriage.

And now her heart is shattering, and there is absolutely nothing I can do for her.

DERIAN

The alarm sounds quickly. Within moments the blaring horns begin, and the courtyard fills with warriors brandishing all manner of weapons. Cal, Ulna, and Taric are among them.

Ulna is the first to reach us, horror flashing across her face as she takes in Huntyr sobbing in my arms. She hasn't moved despite the commotion around us.

"What happened?" Ulna cries, wide-eyed.

My aunt reaches forward and strokes Huntyr's back. The gesture seems to pull Huntyr back to reality, and she finally steps away from me and begins wiping away her tears. I watch intently, noting the way she works to steady her breathing.

She's okay. I assure myself. *She's going to be okay.*

I look at Taric. "I want the guards doubled on all entry points into the fortress. Position scouts every mile from here to the Wastelands. All women and children get evacuated to the nearest town immediately."

"You think she'll attack us?" Huntyr asks softly behind me, her voice thin and uncharacteristically frail.

I only mean to look at her, but I feel my entire body shifting like she's the center of my universe and I'm helpless to her gravitational pull. I soften slightly as I take in her red-rimmed eyes. "She knows the fortress, Huntyr. We don't quite know what she'll do with that information."

"My sister is not going to attack us!"

Her voice slices through the courtyard, loud enough to summon the attention of everyone around us. I clench my jaw and keep my voice low and measured.

"She already has."

And there are three dead Fae to prove it. Three families I will need to contact and deliver devastating news to.

Marla has three grandchildren.

Had.

I have to be the one to tell them their Nana isn't coming home.

Rhen was newly mated. I can't begin to imagine the tragedy of finding the other half of your soul, only to have them ripped away so immediately afterwards.

"She needs our help, Derian," Huntyr hisses, stepping forward towards me, chin lifted in defiance. Gone is the sobbing girl. The Huntress of Velia now stands before me. "She doesn't need to be met with your weapons."

I grind my teeth together, suddenly at war with the overwhelming need to be the leader who has spent his life protecting his people from Velkai, and the need to guard the feelings of this woman who just watched her sister become one.

Cal steps forward, glancing between us as he clears his throat. "Maybe you two should fill us in."

Huntyr sends a vicious, wounded glare towards me. "He can explain it."

She stomps away, back towards the fortress, anger towards me replacing any bit of pain that just broke her apart. Tilting my head towards the sky, I run a tired hand over my face and stare at that constellation that had seemed so magical only a few minutes ago.

"What else do you need done?" Taric asks, jogging back towards me after relaying my prior orders.

The next command lays heavy in my gut.

"Send someone to find Huntyr and escort her to our room. She doesn't leave these grounds." My voice sounds hollow. I *feel* hollow. "If she somehow escapes this fortress, I'll hold every guard on the perimeter personally responsible."

Taric stiffens, dark brows lowering as he frowns at me. "We're keeping her prisoner?"

Ulna gasps.

Perhaps it's an overreaction.

But I know that woman. Gods, I know her to her core. And I know that nothing will stop her from trying to go after Tyla. Fuck, I would do the same if it was Luceron.

Running after that girl could get her killed, though.

I can't allow that. There's absolutely nothing I wouldn't do to keep that woman safe. Even if she hates me for it.

I feel Cal's attention on me before he beckons back towards the stone archway that leads back inside. "Derian would never hurt Huntyr. So, I think we can all trust he has a good reason for keeping her under close guard. Why don't we get inside and you can explain to us what's going on?"

I shouldn't be surprised to find Huntyr in the war room when we all pile in and begin taking seats around the table. Really, I should have expected her to be more than capable of evading any escort I sent after her.

She doesn't bother to glance up at us from where she's pilfering through the weapon chests, carefully examining the blades and crossbows before pulling her chosen ones out and arranging them on the floor behind her.

"Sit down, Huntyr," I order.

The rest fold around the table, taking seats even as their eyes remain on her. Behind me, I hear the sound of claws against the floor as Kaia slinks in to join us.

"No," Huntyr mumbles. "Plan your defenses if you want. It doesn't concern me, anyway."

"*Sit down,*" I bark, the sharpness of my tone cutting cleanly through the air. "Before I make you."

She glances over her shoulder at me from where she crouches by the chest, and everything about her expression has hardened. Even as she smiles, there's no joy in the taunting gaze she sends my way. She looks every bit the killer she is.

"There he is," she drawls. "There's that infamous Fae bastard who steps on everyone who doesn't do as he tells them. I can't believe I let myself forget for one second that *this* is who you are."

Her words sting, but I keep my expression neutral as I walk towards her. She rises, stopping only when a foot remains between us. "And there's the reckless assassin who is too eager for violence to realize when she might be making a mistake."

"I'm not making a mistake."

I match her taunting smile, running a finger down her jawline. "Isn't that what you thought at the masquerade? And yet here I am. Alive and well. While another male is *mistakenly* dead by your hand."

She jerks away from my touch. "I can still fix that particular mistake."

"No, Huntyr, you can't. Don't delude yourself into thinking you would stand any chance against me. As generous as I am as a lover, I am just as ruthless of an enemy."

Tiny sparks fly out of her fingertips, shooting harmlessly onto the wooden boards at our feet.

I hear Cal mumbling behind us, likely telling Ulna and Taric the truth of Huntyr's background, based on the way Ulna gasps and Taric curses under his breath. I'd forgotten they don't know who she really is. What she really came here to do.

"Ulna," I address my aunt without moving my gaze away from Huntyr. "It would seem that my betrothed isn't thinking rationally. Please get Lady Lachlan some tea to calm her nerves."

The second the name comes out of my mouth, I regret it.

She lunges. Her fingers somehow find a blade and jab it towards my ribcage. I move fast enough to keep it from sinking into my flesh, but not fast enough to avoid the slash against my skin. I hiss against the pain and look down briefly to see blood blooming against my shirt.

Her eyes flicker to it briefly, and I swear I see something almost like regret for the shortest of moments.

"That wasn't nice," I growl down at her, gripping her wrist and pressing down on the muscles so that the blade falls out of her hand. It clangs heavily against the floor.

"And I don't need *tea*!"

"You also don't need to go running off half-cocked into the night, chasing after a fucking Velkai who ran towards her homeland!"

She freezes, eyes misting for a quick second before she hardens again and takes a single step back from me.

"You don't understand," she whispers.

The silence stretches for so long that I feel like my organs are withering. "You don't *know* what it's like to love someone. Not the way I love her."

Oh, but I do know what that's like.

That's what makes this so hard.

I know exactly what it feels like to be willing to burn the world to the ground for another person. I know what it feels like to care about someone else so completely that you would rather they spend the rest of their life hating you so long as you're able to keep them safe and protected.

"Sit down, Huntyr," I command her again. "Or get out, but these weapons stay here, and the guard outside *will* escort you back to our room."

"I'm not a child."

"You will be treated like one until you stop acting like one."

Her gaze flicks to where the guards linger by the door, watching our argument. "I'm going after her."

"No, you're not," I sigh, running a tired hand down my face. "And every warrior in this fortress has been instructed to stop you if you try."

Surprise flickers in her eyes. Then anger. Then what I think might be hatred.

"Don't do this." Her voice is low enough for only me to hear.

I know that what comes out of my mouth next will change everything between us, but I can't stop it. I will protect her. Even if I'm forced to protect her against herself.

"You've given me no choice."

She bares her teeth at me, fingers clenching and releasing against the blade in her palm. I watch her chest rise and fall heavily until she pushes past me, shoulder slamming into mine as she does.

Kaia moves towards her, but even the Eshari seems to be on the receiving end of Huntyr's fury. The two exchange silent communication for a moment until Kaia slowly bows her head and retreats back towards the table, sitting next to Cal.

Huntyr stalks out of the room, slamming her blade into the wood frame of the door as she goes. It shakes for some time after she's gone.

HUNTYR

I 'd allowed myself to get too distracted.

It was a mistake I had never made before, and I would never make again.

It had been such a beautiful picture, so clear I could see it as if it had been painted right before my eyes. Tyla was healthy and happy. I had finally started to accept that the Fae weren't evil, that there wasn't anything *wrong* with the magic in my blood. I sat at that dinner table surrounded by all of them and considered myself among friends.

Worst of all, I'd let myself be too consumed by *him*, by his body and his words. By the way he seemed to be the only person in my life that actually made me feel... safe.

That might be the stupidest thing I've ever done.

I'd let myself feel safe with him.

I had been wrong to allow that.

I wasn't the only one who'd forgotten the truth of who the other was, though.

Derian, too, had gotten swept up in the fantasy of it all. He had grown too accustomed to seeing me relaxed and happy. He'd gotten comfortable comforting me. He'd come to view me as nothing more than a woman who was simply coming to terms with her new reality.

He had forgotten about the monster that lives under my skin, the darkness that hardens my soul.

And he is out of his mind if he thinks he can keep me locked up here.

The guard closes the bedroom door behind me as soon as I step over the threshold, but I linger there in the entry, listening to the scuff of the floorboards shifting under his weight in the moments that follow.

Two steps.

Just enough for him to turn and stand guard.

I snarl in the silence to myself.

That Fae bastard really does intend to keep me locked away in this room until he decides how to handle *my* sister.

"The prince only wishes to keep you safe. You're not thinking clearly." Kaia's voice is soft in my mind.

Coddling.

"You're bonded with me. You're supposed to be on my side."

"I am sworn to lay down my life for yours. I will not, however, throw my life away because you insist on being reckless."

Anger boils through me, lighting my very core on such fire that my fingertips explode in light again. Sparks fly out of them, crashing around the room. Glass shatters as crystal decanters and goblets crash to the ground.

"Are you alright?" Kaia demands, sensing my sudden rush of anxiety.

A dumb question. I ignore it.

If she doesn't intend to help me, then I have as much use for her as I do for Derian right now.

I don't need either of them.

"Huntyr!"

Moving to the desk, I rip out the top drawer on the left. Ironically, he'd been the one to tell me about the weapons stashed away in here. His mistake. He should have known better than to trust an assassin with the knowledge of where his blades were. I'd already stashed plenty on my person before he'd barged into the war room with the others, but I am taking these, too.

They're finely made. A bead of scarlet wells on the top of my finger when I tap against the tip of the blade. Good. Recently sharpened. The hilt is wrapped in warm leather, small enough to be uncomfortable for a male hand. Slowly, I look over the handle, pausing to glance at the inscription carved into it.

Thalas Vel'en

Old Fae language. Its meaning escapes me, but I absently wonder if it's a name. I've never been sentimental enough to name the daggers I kept in my personal collection back in Velia, but I suppose it doesn't entirely surprise me that Derian is.

"You cannot just ignore me."

Kaia's voice snaps me back to focus, and I don't bother responding to her as I strap the additional weapons onto my body.

"You are better than this. I chose you because you are better than this. You are acting like nothing more than a reckless child."

No, I'm not. I'm acting like a big sister.

This is who I've always been.

And I'll go down swinging if I must, but I'm saving my sister.

M y weapons are hidden under the dark cloak I've belted across my waist, and I pull the hood up to hang low over my face before moving to the glass doors that lead to the small balcony.

Outside, there's not a shred of light to be found other than that which emanates from the few torches and fires at the guard towers. Derian might have instructed them to stop me, but ultimately their attention will be turned towards the Wastelands, towards Tyla. None will be expecting anything odd to be happening on the prince's own terrace.

For someone who claims to know me so well, he's severely underestimated me.

He thinks a single guard posted outside the door can stop me, as if I couldn't just render him unconscious.

Easy as that would be though, there's no way to know if someone else might stumble into the hallway and see the scuffle. No way to ensure that I could sneak out without being caught. No, I need to be entirely unseen if I have any hope of breaking out of this fortress.

Which leaves option number two.

The stone of the fortress walls is old and weathered, covered in cracks and ledges that will serve as perfect handholds. Tentatively, I test two of the divots in the stone, sliding my fingers against them until I find a grip strong enough to hoist myself up and begin the climb.

I grasp onto my next purchase, and the stone crumbles under my grasp. I bite down on my lower lip to stop my hiss as the flesh on my palm tears, leaving hot, scarlet blood against the grey stone. My boots scratch for purchase on the uneven mortar as I struggle to regain my grasp, but I eventually find the right cracks. The small indentations that are just enough to balance on as I lift one hand above the other.

One more slip could leave me with a broken leg, or worse. So, I won't slip.

The ground gets more and more distant as I go, the height only a secondary thought that long lost its holdover me.

Kristona had made sure of that.

"I won't wear a harness?"

He grins down at me, the expression answer enough. "If you mess up a mission and find yourself on the wrong end of a chase, do you think your attackers will wait for you to put on a harness?"

I look between him and the wall next to us again before shrugging. "I suppose I just won't mess up in the first place."

Kristona laughs and gives me a gentle shove towards the wall. "Ever the arrogant one, aren't you? Climb. No harness. No fear."

But there was fear then. A great deal of it.

I fell dozens of times before I stopped fearing the pain of it.

I feel fearless now.

The rooftop isn't far. I fold my hand into an arrow slit in the wall and give one final push, swinging my body over the edge of the battlement. I land hard on the stone walkway, dirt and blood covering my bare hands.

I don't even feel the sting of it. There's no time to worry about it, anyway.

Without hesitation, I run down the parapet, keeping my posture hunched and my steps light. If my spatial awareness is correct, which it always is, I'm likely above the hallway leading to Derian's room, which means following this will take me parallel to the courtyard and above the war room.

Right over their heads.

They're none the wiser.

There's a break in the wall—a five-foot drop to the lower parapet—and I don't slow my speed. I leap, landing in an effortlessly controlled crouch.

Pain shoots up my knees, but I surge back to my feet, following the line of the turret that will lead to the very edge of the fortress.

I'll have to drop down. If my calculations are correct, I'll land before the two guards posted at this position. Silently, I move forward and glance over the edge of the fortress top to watch their shadows move. They're pacing slightly. One chuckles.

They're distracted.

I give myself thirty seconds and back away from the edge.

The fall looms ahead of me, only darkness visible past the stone walls, and I know that there's only a jagged hill slope below. No rope. No stairs.

Twenty seconds.

"This is going to hurt," I grumble to myself before pushing off the balls of my feet.

Fifteen seconds.

I jump.

Wind flies around me, pushing back the hood of my cloak, and I twist my body, landing into a roll on the ground. My shoulder takes the brunt of the impact and screams in protest, but I have only a moment to be grateful it's still in its socket before I'm pushing aside the folds of my cloak to grasp the daggers on my waist.

Somewhere in the back of my mind, I recognize the two guards that I stand to face. They struggle to recognize me, though. Their brows raise. Their jaws drop.

"Lachlan?" one asks with a surprised chuckle.

Ten seconds.

I lunge, slamming the pommel of my blade against his head before they register my intentions. His partner stumbles back before realizing my intentions and raising his sword against me. I duck under its swinging weight and jam my fist into his gut, spinning behind him as he doubles over and cracking the hilt of my dagger against his temple.

Numbly, I stare down at their fallen, unconscious bodies.

"This really was too easy," I muse as I move to untie the horse strapped to a nearby fence post. Really, I'm almost offended that Derian didn't even try to challenge me.

As I kick the horse into a gallop towards the Wastelands, I don't bother looking back.

I don't bother questioning whether he's right about my acting too rashly.

All those nights ago, he said it all served a purpose. *This* was why it had all happened. All of this—my training with Kristona, the Conclave, finding out I was Fae—prepared me for this moment.

I gave up my innocence, pieces of my soul, for this. I had to become the Huntress. For her.

For Tyla.

I came to the Fae kingdom to save her. My sister.

And that's exactly what I'm going to do.

DERIAN

The door to the war room flies open, snapping so hard that it bounces against its hinges. Our discussion of Tyla halts as we look up to the frazzled, wide-eyed Fae who's panting heavily.

The Fae who had walked Huntyr back to our room.

Fuck me.

I'm on my feet and moving before anyone can even process what's happened. My forearm slams across his throat and pushes him against the wall with a strength that leaves him flinching.

"*Where is she?*" I demand, an animalistic Fae growl tearing out of my chest against my control.

Kaia is next to me, mirroring the sound with her own snarls.

"She's gone!" He doesn't fight me, just lowers his eyes in a characteristic show of submission. Lightning flashes outside the window, too close to the window for comfort, and thunder echoes around us shortly afterwards. "I went to check on her, and she was gone. The terrace doors were open."

Of course they were.

I should have nailed the fucking doors shut.

Cal sighs behind me. "You don't think she—"

"Obviously she did," I tell him, forcing myself to release the guard and snarl at him to disappear. I don't trust myself not to hurt him if he stays in here, not when my instincts are raging at me.

She's gone.

She's in danger.

I have to find her.

I have to kill anyone who hurts her.

"What are we talking about?" Ulna asks, a worry line forming between her brows. "What did she do?"

I don't have it in me to answer her, to even process her question. My huntress is riding headfirst into enemy territory. An enemy she doesn't know, doesn't understand, and worse—trusts. Loves.

Huntyr would let Tyla push the dagger into her.

I won't.

I... can't.

"She scaled the damn wall," I growl through a clenched jaw, moving at a breakneck pace towards the stables and trusting them to follow behind me.

I hear the sounds of their voices, but I can't make out the words. Thunder sounds again, lightning splitting the sky open in a never-ending procession, and something in my chest tugs me forward, pulling me towards where I know I'll find her.

Cal's hand wraps around my arm, and I bare my canines at him, feeling my magic surging and transforming them into longer, deadlier weapons of their own.

It's surprising enough to make me stumble backwards and run my tongue over them.

They've never done that before.

"I'm not trying to stop you," Cal explains, lifting his hands in surrender. "We should bring others with us, though."

Air is hard to take in. It can't seem to move past the incredible pressure in my chest. I barely manage to nod and step back away from my best friend.

"Leave enough to defend the fortress. The rest will follow me."

I'm moving again. I can't stop long enough to wait for him to gather forces. We reach the stables, and I go straight to my steed, a thoroughbred Windmare. The fastest breed of war horse on the continent with a coat so dark it shines clearly under the moonlight.

"To the Wastelands?" Taric asks, mounting next to me.

I shake my head, already pushing my horse out of the wooden stable.

"To her."

Somehow, I know that pull in my chest will take me right to her.

HUNTYR

The Wastelands are a disgusting place. I've only ever heard them described, and somehow they're worse than I ever imagined.

The ground is grey and charred as if a vicious fire had ripped across it. The thick canopy of trees is nothing more than hard branches long-since killed and devoid of leaves. Even the sun itself seems to dim the moment I step over the line that seems to clearly divide the Wastelands from the rest of the world.

The horse Tyla had taken is dead on the ground at my feet.

I stare at it for a long time, my brain entirely unable to process what I'm seeing.

Until I hear footsteps.

My hands fly to my weapons, brandishing them with unforgiving speed, only for me to turn and recognize the loving face of my sister, her hands raised in surrender.

My chest locks at the sight of her.

"It's only me," she says with a soft grin.

It's not, though.

It's not *her.*

This version of Tyla seems taller, with a stronger spine than I've seen in years. Her skin is flushed and filled with color. The veins I've grown accustomed to seeing across her skin are nowhere to be seen. Even her hair seems thicker and glossier.

She practically looks like a stranger.

"Is that supposed to make me feel better?" I ask, still gripping the weapon tightly in my hand.

Tyla tilts her head to the side pensively. "Of course, I'm your sister."

"My sister wouldn't hurt a fly."

Her eyes flash for a moment, and she kicks at the ground by the horse. "That's a bit ironic, don't you think? An assassin giving me lessons in morality."

Again, that icy pressure fills my chest and gut, sliding over me with inky precision. Yes. I'm an assassin. I know every body that lies in my past. I've memorized every one of their names, starting with that very first couple and ending with Seraphina.

But now I'm not the only one of us with blood on our hands.

Images of more dead souls flash in my mind. Rhen, the guard, the horse. *She* did that. Tyla did that.

And suddenly all I can think about is my father.

She'd been this... creature all along, and I had trusted her with his story, with *my* story.

"Did you know?" I bring myself to ask, the words feeling like ash against my tongue. I'm not even sure I want to know the answer. "All this time, did you know what you were?"

Her breath catches, and for the briefest of moments her eyes soften and she looks at me with such love it makes the heartache of this feel so much worse.

"Tell me you didn't. *Please.*"

"Of course not, Huntyr. I never lied to you."

I don't expect the words to be the gut punch that they are. They don't ease the pain of this. Not in the slightest.

"How did this happen? How are you a Velkai?"

Tyla folds her hands in front of her, her fingers steady while mine threaten to tremble. She holds no weapon, and I realize with no small amount of horror that it's because she doesn't need one.

She steps towards me, and instinctively I shuffle backwards.

"Why is it so strange?" she questions, her voice inquisitive as if she truly doesn't understand why I feel like my entire world is falling apart. "You lived your whole life unaware of your powers, too."

"That's different."

A chuckle. "It's really not."

I force a shuddering breath through my lungs. I force myself to try and reconcile *this* version of Tyla with the girl I'd shared a bed with every single night of our childhood.

"I don't understand how we got here," I confess, unable to force the two visions of her into one.

"She and I are more alike," she tells me, staring at my feet. "That's why it's easier for her to talk to me, and once she explained it, everything became clear."

"*What* became clear, Tyla?" Riddles. She's talking in nothing but riddles, and I need *answers*. I need clarity. I need to know what happened to my sister so that I can fix her.

"That it had to be this way. It all led to this."

Her words strike through me. The very sentence I had chanted to myself on the ride here. The words I repeated over and over to ground myself in my mission, my purpose.

The two visions of her snap together.

No matter what has happened, no matter what she's done, she's my sister. She's the only real family I've ever known. The only person to give me true unconditional love. Sure, I protected her. I provided for her and maintained her health, but she saved *me* in more ways than she will ever know.

It was Tyla who helped wash away the blood from my fingers when I couldn't stop myself from picturing the horrors of what I'd done.

It was Tyla who stroked my hair when I woke up screaming from my nightmares.

It was Tyla who helped me hold onto the last shred of humanity that existed inside of me.

Now I have to do that for her.

Forcing myself to steady my breathing, I push my dagger back into the sheath on my hip and extend my left hand towards her, palm facing up. She won't hurt me. I know it. She couldn't hurt me anymore than I could hurt her.

"Come with me," I beg her. "We can fix this. We can find a cure."

All along I'd been searching for her cure. I would just keep looking.

The air between us feels heavy, charged. Time seems to stand still as she stares at my hand extended between us. She's held my hand more times than I can count through the years, and none have felt as important as this.

Take my hand.

Tyla peers up, eyes moving from my hand, to my arm, to my shoulder, to my face.

And slowly, she lifts her hand and places it in mine.

The relief is sudden, like a wave crashing over me, and I squeeze her fingers gently.

My thoughts race. I can't bring her back to the fortress. Derian won't allow it, and she won't be safe there. We'll have to go elsewhere. Maybe I can find the alternative healer Taric knows, maybe he'll know how to fix this. Someone has to know how to fix this.

I turn on my heels to lead her back to my horse—

Agony rips through me.

Everything I am *tugs*. Something is clawing its way out of me. My broken soul is unraveling thread by thread. My very essence is being ripped forcefully out of my body, and I can't see past the pain of it.

I can't think.

I can't *breathe*.

My knees buckle and slam heavily to the ground as my legs crash out from under me. A gasp flies out of my mouth, and I feel Tyla's hand clench around my own when I instinctively pull away from her.

There's nothing on Tyla's face when I look at her. No emotion at all.

"You have to understand, Huntyr. Mother needs you."

My sister might really be gone.

DERIAN

She's in pain.

Awful, terrible, overwhelming pain.

I don't know how I know, but it's echoing through me. It's ripping me apart.

"We have to move faster!" I yell back to the small army I've raised in pursuit of her.

Huntyr.

My Huntress.

My wife.

I'm coming.

Huntyr

Instincts are a funny thing.

When you've trained for something over and over and over, when it actually happens, your body reacts before your mind has time to think.

I don't have the wherewithal to realize it's *Tyla* draining the life from me. I simply process that I'm under attack and react on instinct.

I yank her hand and rip her forward, my other hand finding her throat. In an instant, I push down on the balls of my feet to surge upward, twisting my weight until she crashes hard to the ground.

And I'm left kneeling in front of her.

Tyla.

Recoiling, I swallow down my horror and crawl away from her, but she only laughs.

Tyla rolls smoothly to her feet. Her spine straightens. Her weight shifts to her heels. Her hands rise into a defensive stance.

I blink.

That's a fighting stance.

That's *my* fighting stance.

There's a crunch on the ground behind her. One.

Then another.

Then another.

Hordes of Velkai pour out from behind the trees. Crawling. Stalking. Some on all fours. All of them with dead, glossy eyes.

All of them looking at me with wide, hungry grins.

Tyla lifts a hand, and they stop.

They wait.

For *her* command.

"What is this?" I whisper, barely able to summon the words.

She sighs, almost sadly. "I want you to know that I don't do this lightly."

I feel sick. I feel like my stomach is caving in on itself.

"I never thought this would happen, Huntyr. I tried to convince her not to make me do this at first, but there really is no other way. She helped me understand that. I'm sorry, but this is your purpose. This is why you're here. It's what has to happen. You have to die to release Mother."

My head swims until all I can hear are her words echoing over and over in my mind as if my own body is rejecting what I just heard.

No.

That can't be. It's an arrangement of impossible words strung together.

Tyla doesn't know of the Mother.

I have nothing to do with the Mother.

Oh Gods, my stomach roils against me, and I suddenly can't breathe. None of this makes any sense.

The Velkai inch closer.

Tyla pulls a blade from her boot.

My blade.

My fucking blade.

The blade I refused to sentimentally name.

I stare at the steel, recognizing the unique curve of the handle, the fraying leather around the hilt, the patch of leather that's worn in color from where my fingers wraparound it.

She brought my blade with her from Velia and now intends to use it against me.

"I'm your sister," I remind her, unable to look away from it.

She nods slowly. "You are. More than you even know."

She jerks towards me, shoving that blade—*my* blade—towards my abdomen.

I didn't think there was any part of me left unbroken until just now. Because that simple movement shattered whatever small fragment was left whole inside of me.

My instincts take hold again, a hum of alertness rushing through me.

I know now that Tyla isn't interested in coming back with me.

She doesn't want a cure.

She wants to kill me.

And I don't want to die.

Which means there's only one other thing left to happen.

I reach for my belt, palming the dagger there.

"Don't make me do this," I beg her, praying to the Vaereth, to any God who might be listening, to bring her back to me, to save me from what she's going to force me to do.

Tyla huffs, and her expression doesn't change in the slightest as she sends the Velkai moving forward again with a simple incline of her head.

My lungs won't work.

"It's already done."

The Velkai rush me.

One moment I'm staring at my sister, realizing it's either her or me, and the next dozens of hands are reaching for me.

One touch and I'm dead.

So, I move.

Fingernails scrape down my arm as I spin out of the way, slamming my boot into the chest of one even as I pull the sword from the scabbard across my back.

With a single swing, the mist of blood floods the air and coats my skin.

I weave through them all, killing one after the other as I do. It's a dance, one I mastered a long time ago, one whose steps lead me carefully *away* from Tyla.

Not her. I can't face her yet.

A Velkai lunges suddenly, and I pivot on my back foot, ducking the hand that means to wrap around my throat. Another is already extending towards my waist and I twist, driving my elbow into its jaw.

A sharp pain flies up my left arm, and I gasp, glancing over to find a Velkai locking its jaw around my forearm.

"You're biting me?" I cry out in disbelief. "Seriously?"

I slice my dagger across its throat, pushing the body until it topples backwards.

"You can't fight forever, Huntyr," Tyla calls, watching it all with a vacant expression. "You might be Velia's Huntress, but not even you can kill us all."

She's right.

There's too many.

Even now, more are still emerging from the shadows around the trees.

Still, I keep moving. Keep killing. I don't know what else to do, because if I stop now, I'm not sure I'll be able to summon enough strength to keep going. Not when the fractured pieces of my heart are still bleeding inside me.

I shut it all off. All of that pain and *feeling*.

Like I did when I stood above the bleeding bodies of those first two kills and realized I had been the one to kill them.

Like I did when I ran my sword through the gut of my first lover.

Like I did when I sliced Seraphina's throat.

I shut it all out and spin towards the Velkai lifting a sword high in the air, and I raise my own against him.

Steel clashes. Flesh splits. I just keep going.

Dead leaves crackle under my footing as the wind picks up, blowing back tendrils of my hair as I continue a brutal procession of ducking, rolling, lunging, and stabbing.

Kill.

After kill.

After kill.

It's the only thing I can do right.

I didn't avenge my father.

I didn't save Tyla.

I'm just a killer.

That's all I'll ever be.

Raindrops begin to pepper my skin, and I ignore them all, catching Tyla from the corner of my eye. She doesn't even flinch when a blade strikes across my chest, ripping the skin apart.

The pain shutters through me, blinding me for an impossibly long minute. Lightning strikes down in the distance as a fist connects with my jaw and I go stumbling backwards.

My knees nearly buckle.

Not yet. I can't stop yet.

But then Tyla is in front of me.

Hands rip me back by my hair.

A blade presses against my throat.

Desperately, I claw for my last resort. I try to grasp onto that power in my stomach. I reach for it the way Derian has shown me dozens of times, but the tendrils of it slip away, over and over again.

Tyla reaches for me, and I know it's coming.

The pain.

The feeling of ether being pulled from my bones.

"I would have died for you," I confess. "I went through the Conclave for *you.*"

She stares at me. "Your death was inevitable, Huntyr. You were always meant to die for her."

The ache is instant. Torturous tiny pinpricks erupt against every inch of my skin. My body shakes. My vision blurs. My legs give out, but I hardly feel it when I slam onto the ground.

Thunder booms.

I gasp, but no air comes.

Rain pounds on us.

I'm dying.

Tyla is killing me.

She grips my face and pulls me towards her, drawing my gaze to the sky. There's storm clouds above us, darkening the skies. And suddenly, through the absolute terror and agony ripping me apart, I feel the briefest spark of relief. Relief tangled with a feeling so warm it's overwhelming.

Because I fell in love with the monster who controls the skies.

61

HUNTYR

I hear the hooves of horses crashing down behind me, and the sound is enough to distract Tyla.

She glances up to see who approaches and I don't hesitate. I don't stop to think about who she is or what she means to me. I simply drive my fist into her stomach before slamming my daggers into the Velkai behind me.

Then I'm moving again, rolling sideways, knocking out the feet of those behind me and driving down life-ending blows to each.

He's here.

The wind roars, a rage-filled sound, but the air around me is as warm as his embrace.

Without any conscious thought, my eyes snap to him, and I watch, completely enraptured, as he leads the charge towards me, our friends behind him.

But I can hardly see them. I can't see anything but *him*.

Every broken piece of me suddenly stitches itself back together when our eyes meet, and I don't feel a single ounce of pain anymore.

I can't feel anything but the overwhelming awareness of him.

His gaze crests over me, assessing for injuries. I watch him take in the blood across my chest, the scratches and cuts up and down my arms. His lips curl back over his teeth as that expression shifts from concern to utter rage.

Derian and the others all shudder suddenly as they cross into the Wastelands, their faces contorting uncomfortably for the briefest of moments. Despite whatever odd sensation this land must have caused for them, they lurch into action, taking up the fight with precise efficiency.

With practice.

They've done this before.

I snap back to attention, regaining my sense of self and turning back to the Velkai, who still all seem to focus on me. Even as Taric, Ulna, Derian, and so many others unleash all forms of violence and magic upon them, they all struggle back to me.

"Why are you doing this?" I scream, turning back to my sister.

There's no room left for hurt in me. No, that feeling left the second she sent an army of Velkai to kill me. Now, I'm pissed.

She stands from where she had been crouched, clutching her stomach after my blow. "I don't want to!"

"They seem to be following your orders, Tyla. If you wanted to stop it, you could."

"You don't understand!" Her voice is shrill, cracking as she screams. "You can't hear her like I can. She explained *everything*, Huntyr."

"You have no idea who you're fighting to free. You know nothing about the Mother."

Tyla's lip curls back, a snarl ripping out of her as her fingers curl like claws at her side. "No. You know nothing about *my* mother."

I expect her to attack me.

I even brace myself for it, readying my muscles and weapons.

But it's not me who she lurches towards.

Somehow, she senses the Fae coming up behind her, and she moves so impossibly fast.

It takes only a heartbeat.

Only a single gasp passes my lips.

"I will do whatever it takes to free my mother," she promises.

Then she twists around to face him. Her hand clasps around Derian's face with unnatural force. She opens her mouth, and my whole world tilts.

I watch as she begins draining everything he has.

His eyes dim.

And a panic stronger than I've ever felt before suddenly floods my senses. It crawls through me until my body hardly feels like my own. The sound of battle rages around us, but I can't hear it. There's only that link between him and I, the one that is threatening to disappear with every bit she drains from him.

"Tyla, *stop it!*"

My heart clenches, and I run towards her, faster than I've ever moved. I wrap around her wrist and tug against her unbreakable grip. All of my strength pushes into my grasp, and I don't care if her wrist shatters or my fingers break so long as I can pull her off of him.

He's not even looking at me.

The storm is quieting. It's fading the same way he is.

And I'm crying.

I don't know when it started, but there's a distinct difference between the rainwater on my face and the saltwater tears that now streak down my cheeks in angry stripes.

"Don't," Derian desperately chokes. There's pressure against my thigh. His hand, pushing against me. "Run, Huntress. Go."

No. I won't go. I can't. I can't possibly leave him here. Not when it feels like leaving half of my *soul* behind.

There's a roll of thunder, but it's quiet. The storm is clearing.

"Tyla, please," I beg, imploring her with my eyes. Imploring her to be the girl who would never dream of hurting someone. I need her to be my sister. I need her to come back right this minute. "Please don't hurt him."

She doesn't bother looking away from him, even as she momentarily halts her feeding. "You should be grateful for this mercy. Mother wants him flayed. This is a kindness for how he's cared for you."

She starts the process again, and Derian's body seizes, his features shifting into an expression of utter pain. Still, his hand pushes on my thigh.

"No!" I don't know if I'm screaming at him or at her.

I *can't.*

Running means leaving him to die.

Staying means making her stop in the only way I know how.

"Please don't make me choose between you."

She doesn't stop.

Derian's eyes are darkening, and I know what happens next.

I know what his body will look like.

Nausea rolls through me. My fingers shake. My entire body shakes.

Hours. It had been only hours since we sat at the table joking about the flavor of cake we would have at my wedding. I was supposed to marry this beautiful bastard of a Fae male at my feet, and she was supposed to stand by my side while I did it.

"Forgive me," I whisper.

My hand moves faster than my heart.

Finally, I grasp onto that magical spark in my gut and let it explode.

It floods through me, traveling down my spine in an instant, before erupting out of me in brilliantly warm, golden light. It surrounds the three of us, wrapping us all in its shimmering embrace.

The smell of magic is all around me.

Tyla gasps.

And I watch my sister fall.

62

DERIAN

The feeling isn't something that could be adequately described by any of the dialects in the Ever Realm. Being drained by a Velkai is brutal. A kind of severing of every single part of who you are.

And somehow it's not as painful as watching Huntyr's eyes as she delivers a killing blow to her sister.

As Tyla falls, Huntyr falls with her, clutching her and whispering words of apology and love.

The battle rages around us, but none of us pay it any mind.

"I'm so sorry," Huntyr sobs, the sound a broken, heart-wrenching echo. "I didn't want to. I'm so sorry."

Her words are slurred, laced with choked tears.

She pulls Tyla into her lap and strokes her sister's hair as Tyla blinks up at her.

"I told her it would be you who won," Tyla chokes, as golden light stretches up her veins the same way darkness once had. There's a small smile quirking at the edges of her lips. "You always were the stronger one."

Huntyr shakes her head. "You made me strong."

Tyla nods softly, fingers slowly being painted red as she presses tightly against the wound in her belly. "You don't need me anymore."

"I do," Huntyr insists, nodding feverishly. "I will always need you."

Her eyes slide over Huntyr's shoulder. "You have them."

The sounds of steel against steel and grunts of exhaustion are fading away. The battle is ending, and the others are beginning to circle around us.

"You have a family now."

Huntyr's body shakes. All I can do is place my hand on the small of her back and hope that the simple touch is enough to ground her through this. I know it won't be, but it's all I can offer her.

Tyla looks at me. "It's done now. Will you protect her?"

There's not a single thing I wouldn't do to protect Huntyr.

"With my life," I promise her.

And then, with a final, shaking exhale, the light from Tyla's eyes fades, and Huntyr's shattered screaming imprints itself on my soul as it goes on and on without any sign of stopping.

⊷◆⊶

Everything about the day is perfect.

The air is the right temperature. There's not a single cloud in the sky. My two nephews are chasing each other and laughing in the front lawn of my favorite manor.

And I can't seem to enjoy a single second of sitting on this porch.

I don't think I'll ever view this porch the same way again.

Even now, a few weeks after everything happened, Huntyr's shaken. She's managed to regain her appetite, even cracked a few jokes with Taric and Cal, but that darkness lingers in her eyes. Every night she wakes in a cold sweat from a nightmare. Then, she crawls on top of me and begs me to help her forget whatever terror she dreamt up.

I oblige her.

I give her everything she wants and then some. Food, jewels, time alone, time with others. I do whatever I can to make this easier for her.

But we're running out of time for her to mourn.

Since Luceron's arrival in Springhallow yesterday, he's been more than eager to meet the Conclave winner who is about to become a princess. I insisted he should rest and bathe before meeting his new sister, but there's only so many ways I can delay the inevitable.

Sighing, I stand from my seat on the porch.

"Anteroi," I bark at my elder nephew. "Go easy on your brother."

The boys pause their wrestling only for the briefest of moments before resuming the second I turn my back and make my way into the manor.

I take the spiraling wooden staircase slowly, each step feeling heavier than the last as I make my way to the office at the end of the hall. Luceron claimed it this morning, needing to respond to correspondence.

Based on the way his brows raise expectantly when I push the door open, though, he's been waiting for me for some time.

"Shut the door," he commands, sounding more like a King than a brother.

I do as I'm told, pushing the wooden door until it clicks shut and then folding myself into the leather seat on the opposite side of the desk.

You would hardly know he's been traveling for weeks. His face is still full, eyes still bright. The only indication is the way his skin is slightly tanned and the streaks in his hair that are so bright they're nearly silver.

"You've been avoiding this conversation," he accuses.

I shrug. "I'm not going to deny that."

Luceron stands in a rush, and a cold chill spreads through the room. He doesn't even flinch when frost covers the glass. He loses control over his powers like this often enough that it's nothing new to him. Growing up, everyone always told him it was okay. Our parents assured him that it was normal to have power rushes when you're a passionate person. So, he never bothered to learn the control they forced me to develop.

"I chose a wife for you! I spent *years* negotiating that alliance!"

"Huntyr is a noblewoman with a sizable estate in Velia. The alliance will be respected."

His hands slam down on the table. "And what if Seraphina had won?"

Bile rises in my throat as I picture her and remember the way she nearly took Huntyr from me. Not a single part of me misses that bitch.

"She didn't," I say simply, keeping my voice carefully neutral.

Luceron stares at me for a long moment before he turns away, rubbing a hand over his jaw as he looks out the window to watch his children. "I don't know why I expected anything different from you, Derian. You've always operated by your own rules."

I ball my hands into fists, forcing down the power that threatens to rise inside me. "It never seemed to bother you until you started looking at me as a pawn instead of as your brother."

Huntyr wouldn't have done this to Tyla, I think to myself. Tyla wouldn't have done this to Huntyr either. They love each other unconditionally, regardless of anything else.

Loved.

Luceron sighs. "What else?"

I glance up at him with a frown.

"There's been whispers since I arrived," he explains. "Cal has avoided me since I got here. I've yet to see your betrothed. What's everyone hiding from me?"

The war raging inside me is worse than any battlefield I've ever stepped on. Luceron is my brother, my *King*. My duty is to him above everyone else.

But Huntyr...

Huntyr is my everything.

And I made a vow to protect her.

"Sit," I tell my brother. I want the desk between us. I want to be directly between him and the door. He looks at me with an expression that tells me he's about to remind me of his position, and I roll my eyes before amending, "Please."

It's only after he's seated and my power is at the ready that I say, "Huntyr's not a typical Mortal woman."

Then I explain everything that's happened since I saw the Huntress parading as a noblewoman at a masquerade ball.

DERIAN

Luceron is quiet as he listens to it all, but the sound of his index finger tapping against the desk as I talk is making my skin crawl. I keep getting distracted by it, stumbling over my words every so often when his rhythm changes.

"And that's when you arrived," I finish with a heavy exhale.

Luceron stares at me, that finger still tapping. I can't take the sound of it anymore. I stare at it pointedly until he finally stops.

"I want her brought to me," he announces, rising from his seat. "Immediately. I need to know who we're dealing with."

I'm across the room in an instant, pressing a hand against the center of his chest to stop him. The coldness is instantaneous, freezing my fingers until it stings.

But I don't move.

"She's an assassin, Derian," he reminds me, staring down at that hand.

I speak before I think. "You even think about harming her and I'll kill you before you leave this room, brother."

That's enough to make him pause.

He steps back away from me, inclining his head in surprise as he considers me. "You'd commit treason for her? Kill your own *brother*?"

Without a second thought.

"There's nothing I wouldn't do for her."

Luceron stares at me, eyes narrowed, and I prepare myself for the very moment I've been dreading for weeks. The moment when he makes a move against her and I'm forced to betray my king, my brother.

I used to think there was nothing in this realm or any others that could make me stand against Luceron, but I had been so wrong. There had been something—someone—out there with the power to change everything I thought I knew about myself.

Huntyr chose me over her sister. I will make that same sacrifice if I need to.

Luceron doesn't make that move, though. He doesn't order me to bring her again or demand that I eliminate her.

He smiles.

A slow, knowing smile that lingers as he slinks back into his seat at the desk.

"I have to admit, Derian," he says, reaching into the desk drawer to pull out a decanter of whiskey and two glasses. "I didn't think this day would ever come."

"What are you talking about?"

He laughs, pouring two glasses and pushing one towards me. "You're mated."

The words he says so casually fall over me like a physical blow. One so forceful that I stumble back a few steps, needing to reach out and grab onto the dusty bookshelf for support.

"No," I protest. "I'm not."

Luceron simply rolls his eyes. "Tell me, when did the instincts kick in? You must have noticed the overwhelming possessiveness. The pull to her. The ability to find her even if you can't see her. I'm assuming you've slept with her?"

I can't answer. I can barely think fast enough to process what he's saying.

"I thought so." He nods. "And I bet you were in bed for days after that first time. I bet it felt like you couldn't breathe unless you were inside her. I'd tell you it gets easier after you claim each other, but truthfully, it takes about a hundred years before the bond settles enough that you don't feel like you'll die without her right at your side every moment."

My breaths are shallow and rushed.

That can't be possible.

And yet...

"Claim her?" I ask softly.

Luceron scoffs incredulously. "Did you not pay attention to a single thing we learned in school? Shortly after the bond starts to form, your fangs will come in. The bite will seal the bond."

I run a tongue over my teeth. They've smoothed out in the days since the battle in the Wastelands, but my canines *had* elongated and sharpened. Sharpened enough to break skin.

"It's not possible," I insist again. "She's half Mortal."

Luceron is quiet, and I find my way back to my seat, sinking into it heavily and pulling the glass of whiskey to me. I don't have it in me to savor it, even though I know it's one of the most expensive bottles I keep in the manor. I down it all in a single gulp.

"That girl is not Mortal," Luceron finally says, his green eyes unblinking, his expression suddenly serious.

I set the glass down, letting the thud of it on the desk echo around us.

"Think about it, Derian," he continues. "The power she carries, the light, the ability to kill Velkai with a touch. Fae can't do that."

"What are you saying?"

"There's only one power I know of that does that."

Silence falls between us.

Fuck.

I really hadn't paid enough attention in school. Not to the lessons on mating and apparently not to the history lessons either.

"The Gods." I feel the rightness of my words as they fall out. "You think her parents are Vaereth."

He nods slowly. "I don't know how, but if the sister was so closely tied to the Mother, maybe that's why they were so drawn to each other in the Mortal Realm."

They were two sides of the same power-filled coin, drawn to the opposition they felt in the other.

"I'm not going to hurt her," Luceron tells me, pausing for a moment to let the vow settle between us. "Quite the opposite, in fact. Huntyr Lachlan might be the only chance we have to defeat the Mother once and for all."

The thought is like a punch to the gut.

Because now that I know Huntyr Lachlan is my fucking mate, I can't stomach the thought of losing her.

HUNTYR

I finally manage to pull myself out of bed and comb through my hair after the sun has been hanging in the sky for hours. Outside I can hear the laughter of the children, siblings. I watched them for a bit earlier, marveling at the way they chased each other.

Tyla and I never really had the opportunity to play with each other like that. From the moment I met her, our lives were filled with difficulty and death. We had to work to earn our keep with Kristona. Then we moved into our own apartment, and I stepped out of our door each day not knowing if it was the day I'd end up on the wrong side of the blade.

I wonder if things might have been different had we ever been given a chance to *play*, to be children.

"I don't know where I go from here," I tell Kaia. She crawls up from the mound of blankets Derian set up for her next to my side of the bed and comes to sit beside me by the window.

"It will take time to heal."

I nod. I know that.

This isn't the first time I've lost a loved one.

"It's not just that." I wave my hand around Derian's luxurious bedroom, our bedroom now. *"It's all of this. I don't know how to live without violence and struggle. I don't know how to put that all away to be his wife."*

Kaia is quiet for a moment, and when I turn to sit on the foot of the bed, she follows me. *"I suspect the prince does not want you to put it away. You will be as you are."*

Somehow, I don't think it's that simple. I stare down at my open palms, at the calloused skin and the thin lines of various scars that travel up my wrist.

"I managed to find a couple of apple tarts in the kitchen."

I jolt slightly at Derian's voice, looking up to see him lingering in the doorway, a plate of pastries in his hand. He's dressed simply, just a dark shirt and pants, not a blade or weapon in sight. His dark eyes scan over me, softening ever so slightly as they do.

I can't help but smile up at him. It's the third plate of desserts he's brought me today. Apparently, his determination to ensure I'm well-fed does not require the food to be particularly healthy.

With a soft chuckle, I wave my arm towards the table and silently instruct him to just leave it there.

"You spoke with your brother?"

He clears his throat uncomfortably as he sets the plate down and remains standing by the window. I narrow my eyes suspiciously at the distance, and he crosses his arms over his chest.

I'm not sure I've ever seen Derian be awkward before.

"I did."

"And?" I ask with a raised brow, rising to my feet and resting my hands on my hips expectantly. "You don't have to treat me like I'm glass, Derian."

He releases a heavy sigh, running a hand over his face. "I know that, but—"

"But what?"

Kaia pads towards the open door. *"I suspect this is a conversation I do not need to be witness to."*

We watch her leave and Derian closes the door after her. He gestures for me to sit. I don't. My nerves are too on edge, my heart too battered. I don't have it in me to guess at what he's hiding from me.

"Things are complicated, Huntress."

Obviously.

Things have been complicated for some time now.

"Luceron doesn't trust me?" I guess.

Derian's snort implies that's an understatement.

It's not entirely a surprise. I did come to this kingdom with the intent of murdering Derian and his brother both, after all. I would be shocked if he welcomed me with open arms.

"Luceron is a King," Derian says with a dark laugh. "There's very few people he trusts. Some days I doubt even I'm included in that list."

He avoids my gaze as he speaks, his eyes flicking from the bed to the window to the ceiling, settling anywhere that isn't on me. For all his many strengths, subtlety doesn't appear to be one.

"Just spit it out, Derian," I snap.

Finally, *finally,* he looks at me, with an expression filled with such torment I almost go to him.

"You and I are to be married, Huntyr."

"I don't need you to restate the obvious."

His eyes close for a brief moment, and I can't tell if it's with exasperation or soft appreciation of my sarcasm. Perhaps both.

He steps towards me, closing the gap between us in three easy steps before he stares down at me. Gently, he pushes my long hair back away from my shoulders and cradles the back of my neck, holding my gaze to his.

"This marriage may be required because of the Conclave, but I intend to honor it as you would any other. I will be faithful to you, Huntyr Lachlan. I will protect you. I will provide for you."

"I have no need for your protection, and I care very little about your wealth."

His lips quirk slightly. "Believe me, I know that. Still, if we are to spend the rest of our lives together, lives that I suspect will be exceedingly long for *both* of us, I will not enter into this marriage with secrets between us."

Ice trails down my spine, both at the suggestion that whatever Fae magic runs in my blood may give me the long lifespan of the Fae and at the confession that he is in fact keeping something from me.

When I prepare myself to step away from him though, I pause.

Because there's nothing in Derian's expression to suggest that what he's about to tell me is *bad.* And if I try to think of whatever secret he could possibly be hiding from me, I can only think of one.

The very secret I have been holding onto for days now. Not because I felt like I needed to keep it from him, but because in the wake of my enormous grief, I hadn't given myself the space to come to terms with it.

"You've had so many changes in your life," Derian goes on, his words coming too rapidly. "I hate to spring another one on you, but you deserve to know. You deserve to go into a marriage knowing everything about our relationship."

A bubble of laughter escapes from the back of my throat.

It's the first time I laugh in what feels like an eternity.

Derian shuffles his weight on the balls of his feet, but when he steps back, I grasp onto his hands, refusing to let him go.

"I'm your mate," I say to him.

His brows raise, shock darting across his features. "You know?"

Since that day in the Wastelands.

Truthfully, I had started to suspect the day that Rhen explained mates to me, but I didn't know for certain until I saw him in the Wastelands and felt that impossible connection between us. And when Tyla started killing him, it felt like I was watching myself die.

There was nothing I wouldn't have done to save him.

I nod slightly, biting my bottom lip gently as I give him my first genuine smile in days. The tension in his shoulders lessens ever so slightly as I do.

"Why else would I want to be around a Fae bastard like you all the time if I didn't have some magical mating bond clouding my judgement?"

Derian folds his hands around my lower back, tugging me sharply against him as his mouth descends on me. His kiss is filled with longing, desperation, and so much more that we haven't given word to yet.

"I don't know how it took me so long to notice it," he says when he finally pulls back for air. I lean into his touch slightly when he tucks my hair behind my ears.

"Probably because you're terribly self-obsessed."

His thumb traces over the pulse at my throat, the touch sending jolts of anticipation through me. He's been so respectful since Tyla's death. He's barely touched me outside of the times I'm begging for him to distract me from my pain.

Now, I feel like I'm burning alive with need for him. Not for distraction. Not for physical release.

For him.

I pitch my hips into his, grateful to feel hardness against my lower stomach and see that the feeling is returned.

Something jerks my attention away from lust, though. The small indentation in his lower lip. As if he's biting down on it, even though he isn't.

Frowning, I place my thumb there and pull down slightly, gasping when I see his two elongated canines. Derian lets me explore, pulling back only when I tap my finger on the tip and hiss when it draws blood.

He sucks my finger into his mouth, licking the wound with a flick of his tongue, and wetness rushes through my core once more.

"When did you get those?" I ask, the sound nothing more than a breathy whisper.

"The mating bond has to be accepted by both parties. Typically, through a claiming mark."

My brows raise, and I suppress the urge to giggle again. "You want to bite me?"

"Yes." He winks. "And I want you to bite me, too."

He pushes forward, walking me back until my knees hit the edge of the bed. Derian jerks his head, instructing me to crawl back. Though I expect him to crawl on top of me and undo me with his fingers, mouth, and body, he simply takes the place next to me, propping up his head with his hand and staring down at me.

"Do you want this mating bond, Huntress?" His voice is soft, his eyes wide and focused on me, more vulnerable than I've ever seen him before. "If you don't want this, if you don't want me, that's okay. I'll release you from all of it. I'll send you back on a ship to Kristona tonight, if that's where you want to be."

I see it then. For the briefest of moments, I see what that life would look like.

No Fae. No Velkai.

I'd tell Kristona all the ways his lessons had come in handy in the Fae kingdom, and maybe I'd even find it in me to forgive him for the hell he put me through. Flannigan and I would go back to terrorizing local pubs. I'd sell off the wretched Lachlan estate and move out of the apartment I'd shared with Tyla because I wouldn't be able to spend a second inside without her.

I'd buy a beautiful new apartment and furnish it with the most lovely furniture and portraits. I'd spend my days reading and painting, and I'd spend my nights back in the shadows of Velia, hunting like I'd done every night for so many years.

Still, even surrounded by the people I considered family, living in a beautiful new home, and living adventurously, I wouldn't be happy.

Because he wouldn't be there.

And I need him more than I need my next breath.

"I do want this," I whisper, before pushing up to look at him more clearly. "But it's not just me who has to decide, Derian."

He tilts his head at me, eyes warm. "That's not even a question you need to ask, Huntress, and I think you know that. I think you've known that for a long time."

Still, it doesn't hurt to hear it.

I bite down on my lip, staring at him expectantly.

Derian laughs before shifting and wrapping my fingers in his, bringing my knuckles to his lips quickly.

"I've wanted you since the moment I saw you, and I wasn't able to look away," he confesses. "I want you now, tomorrow, forever. I want your attitude, your violence, your brilliance. I want you to call me your husband as much as I want you to call me a bastard. I want to stare at you when you're asleep and relaxed, and I want to stare at you while you're fighting and more alive than ever. All of it. All of you. I want it all."

My heart seizes, unable to let myself hang onto words I didn't know I so desperately needed to hear. This frustrating, impossible, beautiful Fae male laid out beside me, vulnerable, trusting, and *loving*. Loving me.

Someone who is so entirely undeserving of that.

I look away. "You're just saying that because of some stupid magical bond that you can't fight against."

Grasping onto my chin with his thumb and forefinger, he forces me to meet his gaze.

"I mean that with every broken, battered piece of my soul. I know you don't believe me because you think your past is too bloody for anyone to see beyond it, to love you in spite of it, but I do. I love you *because* of it. My history is just as bloody, and whatever heart has managed to survive the past two hundred years of violence and pain is completely yours. I am so fucking in love with you, Huntyr Lachlan, that I don't even know who I am anymore if I'm not yours."

My lower lip trembles, and I work to fight back the wave of emotion. When I watched my sister die in my arms, by my own hand, I didn't think I would ever be capable of feeling joy again, but there it was, buried under all the hurt, pain, and trauma. That spark of joy that was reserved for him alone.

"You love me?"

He smiles, pressing his lips to my brow for the briefest of moments. "I love you."

"You want me?"

Derian's eyes trace over my face, leaving tingles in their wake before he leans down to brush his lips against mine. "I need you."

The warmth rushing through me is a feeling I never want to let go of.

"Good, because I still think you're a Fae bastard, but I think I might love you, too."

I pull him to me, melding my lips to his and opening to him. Opening all of me. Not just my body, but the deepest part of me. The part of me that's felt unworthy since the second I heard my stepmother's plan to give me away.

Our kiss is slow, filled with unspoken words and promises, and when we finally pull away, I place my hand in his, then twist it so that my wrist is turned up.

We stare at each other for a long moment, the silence heavy but not uncomfortable. It's the kind of silence two people can sit in comfortably because they know the other so well. Finally, he moves, pulling both of us to sit up. He holds my gaze for the entirety of the time that it takes to bring his mouth to my wrist.

We don't look away from each other for a single second.

Not when his fangs pierce into my skin and he takes the first pull of my blood into him.

Not when light explodes out of me and unbelievable happiness overtakes every one of my senses.

Not when I feel a tingle of sensation in my own mouth as my canines extend.

Not when I latch onto his wrist and the darkness of a storm outside rivals the brilliance of my light inside.

Everything else fades away. There's just him and me, our magic, blood, and souls completely intertwined. It's a feeling so fulfilling and *right* that I can't imagine ever having said no to the bastard Fae prince who asked me to join the Conclave.

ONE MONTH LATER
HUNTYR

"How are you sleeping?" Cal swings his blade sharply towards me, no mercy in the force of his blow.

I twist out of the way and send a rush of magic to my hand, lighting up the small field we're training in so brightly that he has to back away and cover his eyes. I'm getting better at that, short bursts of blinding light. My next goal is to find a way to warm the light, find a way to make it hot enough to burn an enemy.

That would be cool.

I've been practicing with it constantly. Using bursts of light to illuminate the bathing chamber in the mornings when I clean my teeth rather than lighting candles. Using it as a second weapon on the sparring fields when I train during the day. Using it to create tiny sparks that fall around us when Derian and I make love at night.

I never want to feel the way I did that day in the Wastelands when I couldn't grasp onto it cleanly enough.

"I hate when you do that!" he barks at me, just as a vine twists itself out of the ground and pulls my legs out from under me.

I fall heavily, wincing as my back takes the brunt of the impact. Now it's my turn to blink at the uncomfortable brightness of the sun beating down on me. At this point in the day, it's at its hottest, and sweat has already started dripping down my back under the leather of my protective vest.

"And I hate when you do that," I groan, rubbing at the back of my head.

He doesn't bother lending a hand to help me up, a gesture I actually appreciate. Cal and I have been sparring nearly every day since Luceron left, headed back to Bridgemond. We're due to follow after him soon, but somehow, Derian convinced his brother to give us a few more weeks of *wedded bliss* before I have to be introduced to the rest of the drooling court fools.

His words. Not mine.

My sentiment, though.

Cal doesn't go easy on me, not like the rest of the guards in Springhallow do. These men didn't see me fight in the Conclave. They don't know me as the assassin from the Mortal Kingdoms or the woman who killed her own sister to defend their prince.

I'm just his wife to them.

It drives me mad.

"I'm sleeping fine," I mumble, staying on the ground as I catch my breath.

Cal has been sleeping in a room down the hall from us, which means he's undoubtedly been woken up by my screaming in the night.

Always at the same time.

Always from the same dream.

The nightmares started shortly after our wedding, a thankfully simple occasion. Derian insisted that with our mating being officially claimed, there was no need for the two of us to make an elaborate show of our relationship. The ceremony was kept small, with our immediate friends, his brother, and a Fae priestess. We'd celebrated afterwards with dancing and a ridiculously enormous cake—chocolate and vanilla swirled together.

Everything had been perfect for the first few days until I started having these unbearable nightmares.

I see Tyla standing in front of me, reaching for me, but when I take her hand, the ground fractures beneath her. She falls into a pool of darkness while the world shakes beneath my feet and those shadows begin to grow. They crawl out of that hole in the ground and slither around me like serpents closing in.

And then I hear it.

A simple whisper, so quiet I can't quite understand it at first.

But it repeats. Louder and louder and louder.

"Huntyr," it calls to me.

Until I launch out of bed screaming.

"Princess Silverthorn!"

I groan. Right on time.

My new lady's maid, Sheryn, waits by the door to the manor, wiping her hands on her apron and staring at me expectantly.

Sheryn also sees me as Derian's wife more than anything and has no qualms reminding me that wearing gowns would be more appropriate for my new station.

"I'm a Conclave winner," I mumble under my breath to Cal. "You'd think they would remember I quite literally murdered people to become his bride and stop insisting on having me act like a lady."

Cal rolls his eyes. "You? A Lady?"

I climb to my feet, smacking his arm as I do, all while carefully avoiding the expectant gaze of Sheryn.

"Prince Silverthorn has requested your presence, ma'am. He is in his office."

Gods, if Kristona could see me now.

"Ma'am," I hiss the word like it's poison. "I hate *that.*"

Cal takes my sword with a sympathetic smile, and I make my way back inside, taking the towel that Sheryn hands to me as I go and using it to wipe away the sweat from the back of my neck.

She trails me as I walk through the polished foyer and take the spiral staircase two at a time.

"I've laid out some new gowns to consider packing for your trip to Bridgemond ma'am. They're in your chambers."

My chambers.

Not the chambers I share with Derian.

Because apparently, royal Fae have separate bedrooms.

Which makes absolutely no sense because Derian is my mate, proven by the little white scars on both of our wrists, and I spend every night in his bed, anyway. Still, Sheryn refuses to acknowledge that.

"I already packed for my trip to Bridgemond," I say sweetly over my shoulder.

There's a pause, long enough to know that she's thinking carefully about how to respond. "You packed leather."

"I like leather," I remind her. "Prince Derian likes me *in* leather."

"He most certainly does," Derian's voice rings out.

I can't help the way my blood sings when I reach the top of the staircase and lay my eyes on him. He waits in the doorway of the office at the end of the hall, arms crossed over his chest as he leans against the frame.

His dark eyes scan down my body, from the top of my head where my hair has been tied back out of my face, to the sweat-streaked tan skin visible above my vest, to the expanse of my hips and thighs. Each place his eyes touch is left feeling impossibly hot.

I keep waiting for it to fade, the insatiable need for him. I thought it would after that first time I gave in to temptation during the Conclave, but it's only gotten stronger every day since.

"Wife," he greets me, holding out the door.

I duck under his arm to step into the office, and he closes the door behind us. His expression turns positively wicked once we're alone.

"You needed me?" I ask innocently, propping myself up on his desk.

Derian stands in front of me, resting his hands on either side of my hips as he leans down and breathes me in. "Terribly so."

"I thought you had work to do? Correspondences to send? Plans to make? War to prepare for?"

"Oh, I do." He dips toward my neck, trailing his tongue up the delicate skin there until I shiver.

"Won't I be a distraction?"

"Some people would argue that you're more productive when you take breaks to reward yourself."

A kiss to the space where my throat meets my jaw.

A kiss to the space right under my ear.

"And you would like me to reward you?"

I can't stop the tiny whimper that escapes when he tugs my earlobe between his teeth.

"Mhmm, I would."

A tug on the laces of my vest.

A squeeze on my hip.

"*Huntyr...*"

I jolt, jumping so sharply that Derian steps back, concern evident in his eyes.

"What's wrong?"

That voice.

That voice in my mind that's so distinctly different from Kaia's or anyone else's.

I stand slowly, taking careful steps towards the window.

Nothing looks different. The sun is still high in the sky, sending warmth and brightness down upon the full grass and shrubs covering the estate. Cal still stands on the lawn, talking to one of the guards. Horses still graze in the distance.

Everything is the same.

And yet, I know it's not.

"It's not over yet," Derian agrees, sensing my thoughts as he comes to stand by me, his hand tracing soothingly up and down my back.

"No," I sigh. "It's just beginning."

He rubs my shoulders, trying to work out the building tension there as I keep staring out the window. Staring in the direction of that dead land, infested by the monsters who ruined my life.

"What do you want me to do?" he asks.

I know he's desperate to help. I know that every nightmare is like a stab to his heart.

But there's nothing to be done. Not yet, at least. We have to travel to Bridgemond first. We have to have our marriage formally acknowledged by the King and the court.

Afterwards, though? Well then, I'll do whatever it takes to find answers about what happened to Tyla—to find out what hold the Mother had on her, and why.

And once I've done that, once I have every bit of knowledge I can find and I've mastered this magic inside of me, I'll kill the Mother once and for all.

I turn to face Derian. My husband. My mate.

"Be a distraction for me?"

If he were anyone else, he might have protested, but Derian knows who I am. He knows how I think and how I cope. He knows what I need better than I do.

"I'll be anything you need."

He smiles and brings his mouth to mine.

Thank you for reading *Shadows & Secrets*

Be sure to join my newsletter to get access to the bonus epilogue!

THANK YOU FOR READING!

Thank you so much for joining Huntyr and Derian's journey in *Shadows & Secrets*! Your time and support mean the world to me.

Leave a Review

Reviews are the **single best way** you can help this book succeed.
Even a few sentences can make a huge difference!

Share the Story

Love a line, a trope, or a moment? Share it!
Make sure to add *Shadows & Secrets* to your **Goodreads shelves**
Post quotes, aesthetics, or reactions on TikTok, Instagram, or Threads
Tag me so I can see your posts! @arcadiarayne

Stay Connected

Want behind-the-scenes updates, bonus scenes, and news about book 2 in
the Fatebreaker Trilogy?
Join my Newsletter
Follow me on social media @arcadiarayne

Authors Note

Omg, how are we feeling? Are you guys as warm and fuzzy as I am?

Shadows & Secrets is my fourth published book, and it's one that took root in the most unexpected way. One random Tuesday morning in early Fall — while I was recovering from a break-up and contemplating my entire future — this idea arrived and refused to let go. I had an in-progress series, a million other things demanding my focus, but this story demanded to be written. And in the process, it made me fall in love with writing all over again.

Even though we discover Huntyr and Derian are fated mates at the end of this book, I wanted to show that their love wasn't something fate forced upon them. It's a bond that grew slowly, intentionally, beautifully. It's a connection born out of mutual understanding, respect, and vulnerability. They embrace every part of one another, even in the darkest places, and I think there's something infinitely powerful in that. My hope is that you felt the magic of their journey as deeply as I did while writing it.

Now for a few quick thank-yous.

To my editor, **@syntaxandswoon** — thank you for turning this messy pile of words into something sharp, clean, and actually fun to read. I don't even want to imagine the repetitive chaos without you.

To my fellow authors and friends — thank you for being constant sources of inspiration, encouragement, and safe spaces to dream (and rant) through every step of this process.

To my family and friends beyond the page — there aren't enough words in the English language to capture how grateful I am. Thank you for letting me talk your ears off about assassins, fae princes, and deadly competitions at every possible opportunity.

And finally... to **you**. Thank you for being here, for taking a chance on Huntyr and Derian, and for walking this path with me. Your support means more than you'll ever know.

I'll keep it short and sweet, but just know this: this is only the beginning. I'll see you again *very* soon.

— Arcadia

THE STORY CONTINUES

Looking for your next read?

Try the House of Hyrax Series

The Rose in the Shadows
To the Edge of Athenia – A Prequel Novella
The Crown of the Dark Prince

Keep reading for a preview of The Rose in the Shadows

THE ROSE IN THE SHADOWS
CHAPTER ONE

"**S**top worrying, she'll be asleep for quite some time still. The sleeping potion they gave her was *strong*."

The sound of a womans laughter reverberated through my scalp, sending shockwaves of pain into my temple and the back of my neck. I tried to open my eyes, but the violent agony forced them closed once more with a wave so intense it threatened to knock me unconscious again.

"Did you see her out there? I've never witnessed anything like that!"

I didn't recognize the voice that hovered over my head, talking in an exaggerated whisper.

"Rayna, be quiet! Nurse Kira will kill us if we wake her up before the guard comes."

I wanted to call out to them. I needed to. I needed to tell them I was, in fact, awake and in pain, but my body protested.

Rayna scoffed. "Live a little, Theadora; it's not every day you get to see an Athenian traitor."

Where am I? I wondered, trying to trace back my memories.

"Ok, we saw her, so let's go. Please," Theadora pleaded, her voice tense.

"Fine, but only because I promised Samson I'd meet him in his suite in twenty minutes."

"You're going to his suite? You cannot."

"I have before and I will again. The things that man does with his hands are downright godly."

Rayna giggled again, and the sound of their footsteps echoed once more. Before I could find the strength to call out to them, I heard the sound of a door clicking shut and their steps faded into the distance.

Forcing in a deep breath, I took a mental stock of my body. I wiggled my toes and rolled my ankles. All seemed to be functional. I shifted my neck slightly, trying to ignore the stab of pain in my temples as I did so. With another breath, I focused my attention on my shoulders and elbows. They felt heavy, but otherwise unharmed. Finally, I wiggled my fingers, noticing the start of a nagging itch spreading up my hands and wrists.

Something was on me, scratching tender skin. As I focused on it, the itch grew to my forearms and elbows. It prickled until it became so unbearable that it actually... hurt.

No, *it burned.*

I shifted my arms once more and lost myself entirely to the scorching pain. My skin was burning. *I* was burning.

My eyes flew open and with a sudden gasp, I stared down at my body as if it were foreign. Someone had tied a thin, uncomfortable gown too loosely around my shoulders, and my waist and legs were strapped to a bed with leather bindings. My hands and arms, still screaming in pain, were bandaged with leaves and a pale yellow paste. I nearly gagged on the lurid smell of it.

The bed sat against the wall in an otherwise empty room. Pale white tiles covered the walls and floors that were otherwise devoid of decoration, sparing a small stool in the corner of the room. Two candles burned near the door, letting in a slight glow of light, but the space lacked any windows to the outside world. The door itself was glass, allowing me to look out.

Or rather, allowing others to look in on me. But no one hovered outside. I could only see a long hall dimly lit and trailing into darkness.

"Help!" I croaked, voice raw and tired. "Can anyone hear me?"

I struggled against the restraints, but they refused to budge even an inch and though my arms were free, the pain of my injuries kept me from being able to move them above my sides. I threw back my head in frustration as minutes turned to hours.

Until finally, after what felt like a lifetime of isolation, a nurse clicked open the door and walked inside. I jerked my head towards her, taking in the image of a small woman, wearing a simple white dress and apron with graying hair tucked back neatly. Her small square shoes hit the floor with a thud at each step.

"Why am I here?" I struggled to sit up against the straps holding me down.

"Quiet!"

I clamped my mouth shut, teeth snapping together loudly. She approached me without hesitation, pulling at the leaves on my arms and glancing at the inflamed skin underneath. My arms were covered in bruises and blistered flesh that nearly turned my stomach in the second that I looked at it before jerking my head away.

"Does it hurt?" She asked, nodding towards my arms.

"Yes," I whispered, flinching as she poked aggressively at the tender skin.

Without responding, she pressed each of her palms flat against my arms and I watched as she took a deep breath in and closed her eyes. Slowly, the air in the room stilled. Frozen, I stared as a golden glow erupted from her fingertips and spread across my wounded flesh. Warmth covered my arms and I flinched, instinctively, but she squeezed down, locking me into place under her vice-like grasp.

"Stop!" I cried out. "What are you doing?"

The glow from her fingers spread over my wounded skin, and the pain eased after a moment. The stomach-turning burn of my crisped flesh was erased from every place the light touched me.

"What are you?" I gasped.

She peered up at me through dark lashes with irritation. "Try not to move. The skin will still need a bit more time to heal completely."

Her shoes hit the floor once more as she retreated back into the seemingly unending hall outside of my room. It was all I could do to stop myself from crying as she faded from view and all that was left were shadows. She didn't even tell me her name.

Time passed. I wasn't sure how much.

———◆◇◆———

The sound of booming footsteps pounding through the door woke me from an otherwise dreamless sleep. Soldiers, ten in all, marched forward in dark vests and trousers. I wasn't quite sure what to be more afraid of, the fact that they looked ready for battle or that their eyes were trained on me alone. Then, as if practiced, they formed around me, surrounding the corners of my bed and the room door. No one spoke. For a moment, we were all still.

And that's when he came in.

Even while terrified and strapped to a bed, my body couldn't help but respond to him. Under his carefully tailored black tunic and leather trousers, I could make out the signs of firm muscle. He stood tall, broad shoulders pulled back as he strode into the room confidently. His sandy hair was perfectly combed back away from his clean-shaven face and remarkably sharp jaw-line.

It wasn't hard to acknowledge that he was attractive, but attractive men weren't always trustworthy.

As he pulled the stool from the corner of my room and sat it by the foot of my bed, choosing to prop a leg upon it than to sit, his stormy grey eyes met mine and there was no kindness to be found in his gaze. I couldn't fight the catch in my breath as that gaze travelled down my body before crawling back to my face.

"Well?" He finally asked expectantly, linking his hands together and leaning forward on his knees. "Care to explain what your plans were on that bridge?"

What bridge?

"This will be much easier if you cooperate," he growled after I failed to respond.

"I don't know what you're talking about."

"I will get answers from you before this day is over." He paused expectantly, waiting for me to agree to play a game I didn't seem to know the rules of. "Let's start with your name."

"My name?" I echoed, immediately feeling stupid.

"I won't ask again!" He snapped.

His voice sounded like death and pain, and the room had somehow heated to a nearly unbearable temperature with him in it. And yet, as terrifying as he was, it wasn't his interrogation or the ten guards who stood with weapons at the ready that made my body erupt into trembles.

It was the fact that as hard as I searched for an answer, no name came to my mind.

How could I not know my own name?

His eyes narrowed at me. "How about this? For every question you refuse to answer, I'll burn another part of your body until nothing is left of you but ash."

To prove his point, he grasped onto my wrist suddenly, ripping away the leaf and exposing a patch of still-healing skin. Without breaking eye contact, he raised a brow and jammed his thumb into the blistering wound. The pain was instant and nearly blinding as I pulled my arm away and the motion tore the fragile skin. Swallowing my sharp whimper, I blinked through the tears to glare up at him.

"Theadora," I grunted through a locked jaw, grasping onto the first name that came into my mind and claiming it as my own.

"Now, we're getting somewhere," he remarked with a self-satisfied smile that sent my blood boiling. "You, of course, know who I am."

Arrogant, wasn't he?

"And I assume you know exactly the power that I have. Athenia does not take kindly to attacks during a time of peace."

"I don't know what you're talking about!"

He moved impossibly fast. In an instant he was at my side, bent over me with hands thrown on either side of my head until all I could see were his eyes and all I could smell was his cinnamon and burnt oak scent rolling over me in waves.

"You put the lives of hundreds of *my* people at risk on that bridge, Theadora, and you will tell me why!"

Heart frozen, my gaze locked on his hands. Like my nurse, his coloring began to change. But where her fingertips had exploded in a comforting light, his did something... different.

As he spoke, the veins in each hand darkened, mutating into something sinister, leaving his fingers and hands as dark as midnight. Golden scales erupted violently from the skin and the nails on each of his hands grew into *talons* that sliced effortlessly through the cotton pillow my head rested on.

I wasn't able to swallow the scream that burst from the deepest parts of me.

"Clayton Vail, you're going to give the girl a heart attack!"

I didn't dare look away from him to see the woman who had entered the room.

His eyes. They were blazing, sparkling with shimmers of light that grew in intensity until the only color that remained was a glowing bright golden. *Unnaturally* golden.

How was that possible?

We stared at each other for a moment, both breathing heavily. Then, slowly, the light in his eyes dimmed, and they settled back to their dull gray haze. He looked away first to the stranger at the door, and I quickly focused back on his hands. He was quick to fold them behind his back, but I caught sight of them as he did. There was only tanned skin, as if I had somehow imagined the whole thing.

"Iris, you don't need to be here." He sighed, turning to her.

She was a beautiful girl, albeit a bit extravagant. Her pastel pink hair hung to her shoulders in tight curls and was pulled back from her face with a flower crown. Shades of gold and sapphire decorated the lids above her dark eyes, and she wore a long gown falling towards the floor in waves of rose-hued taffeta. Her caramel skin was doused in sparkling pink and blue glitter that caught the light in the room as she walked towards me.

"Call it moral support." She smiled at him and winked. "So, who do we have here?"

She addressed me directly, stepping forward to the side of my bed with a smile. With her head tilted, she looked down at me, and one of her cheeks dimpled as she tried, and failed, to hide a grin.

"Theadora," I mumbled, repeating the stolen name that had become my own with a glance towards the man.

Clayton, I reminded myself. That's what she had called him.

"I see," she noted. "Well, Thea, everyone is dying to know how you ended up on that bridge!"

Clayton sneered at her. "Nice choice of words."

She only grinned back fondly at him over her shoulder. As she turned her attention back to me, her wide eyes sparkled with amusement.

"What bridge do you keep talking about?" I questioned.

"What bridge?" Clayton repeated, brows raised and voice thick with incredulity. "The bridge you shook so violently it will take weeks to repair! The bridge you stood on when you attacked my people and killed someone. Am I ringing any bells?"

I froze, breath caught in my throat. No. That couldn't be true.

And yet, if it were true, then maybe all of this chaos since I woke actually... made sense.

Of course that's why I was strapped to this ridiculous bed in this painfully empty room. I had hurt someone. They had somehow subdued me and locked me up here so I couldn't hurt anyone else.

But why couldn't I remember any of this?

"I don't think I wanted to hurt anyone," I mused, unsure if I was speaking more to myself or him.

"You certainly did," he replied.

"You don't understand!" I cried, struggling against the restraints. The guards around me responded at once, each stepping forward and brandishing their weapons. I froze, raising my now fully healed hands up in surrender. The loose gown fell gently over my shoulder, but I didn't dare to try to move it back into place.

"I don't know anything about a bridge, who you are, or even where I am. I remember waking up, and that is *all* I remember!"

Clayton wrapped his hands against the railing at the foot of my bed again, but his skin did not mutate this time. I was grateful for that, at least.

"Exactly how naïve do you think I am?"

"How should I know the answer to that question when *I don't know you.*"

With a swift motion, he ripped the stool off the floor and threw it across the room. I flinched as it hit the wall with a crash and splintered into pieces before falling to the ground.

"I will find out the truth whether you want to tell me or not! So, I suggest you do so now while I'm being kind in my interrogation tactics."

"Clayton, stop!" Iris gasped suddenly as she looked down at me with an emotion I couldn't quite identify.

"Problem, Iris?" He scolded, huffing with frustration.

Throwing a glare at him over her shoulder, she strode towards me suddenly, heels clicking on the floor.

"I won't speak to your naïvety," Iris called to him, "But I might question how observant you are!"

Her nails grazed my skin as she pulled the thin fabric of my gown further down my shoulder. I flinched away from her forcefully and the guards stepped forward once more, weapons at the ready.

"Doesn't this seem odd to you?" She questioned, voice sharp and eyes locked on my chest.

The guards must have been well-trained because while each of their eyes seemed to widen in surprise their hands did not waver until Clayton mumbled for them to be at ease and took a few tentative steps forward. He didn't speak, but I saw his jaw working as he glanced over me.

A flush of unease peppered my cheeks as I strained my neck to see what had captured everyone's attention. I could just make out the dark tattoo, in the shape of a weapon of some sort, inked into the skin on my left breastbone. It had one long shaft stretching up and branching into two jagged spear-like ends.

I shifted again, desperate to see more of it. "Is that a-"

"It's a bident," Iris told me, her voice quiet and tense. "The symbol of House Hyrax, God of the Dead. That tattoo is the Mark of Hyrax."

Wordlessly, Clayton ran his fingertips over the Mark, leaving pebbled flesh in his wake. I shivered just as he cursed under his breath.

"The Dragon will want to know," Iris said softly behind him.

He was quiet for a moment, staring intensely down at me while his lips pursed. Dampness covered the top of my brow and I wondered numbly how it had possibly grown so warm in the room.

"You truly don't remember anything before you woke up?" He asked, his voice low enough for only me to hear.

I nodded, too unsure of anything to speak aloud.

He bowed his head, and for a moment, he seemed to almost deflate. It was just a split second really, but long enough for me to see concern and tension hidden under his anger. There for a moment and gone in the next. When he finally looked up, his mask had returned and he once again looked powerful and in control, seemingly unaware I had witnessed his momentary crack in composure. With a wave of his hand, he beckoned a guard to come forward.

"Have the nurses remove her bandages and relocate her to the palace cells until we can call an emergency Council meeting," he commanded.

"Yes, your grace." The guard nodded.

Iris pursed her lips when he mentioned transferring me to the cells, but she didn't speak up. Perhaps that was a battle she knew she couldn't win.

He looked towards me once more, not at me necessarily. Rather his attention stayed on the Mark on my chest. "She can't wear that to the Council."

"I'll get her some clothes." Iris volunteered, speaking up for me as if I wasn't there.

"Good," he muttered. "Nothing elaborate, Iris. Regardless of what's on her chest, the Kingdom still views her as a threat. We don't need anyone to see her dressed like you. For now."

For now?

Iris nodded her agreement, and Clayton turned to leave, his guards following behind.

"I do hope you're telling the truth," he called to me from the door before finally exiting.

And without him and his overwhelming presence, the room suddenly seemed larger and easier to breathe in. Iris and I were silent for a moment, both seeming to need time to adjust to the space without Clayton in it.

"What is happening?" I whispered.

After flicking her colorful hair over her shoulder, she leaned down to pat my knee affectionately. "Don't you worry. We'll get this figured out."

"Iris, that's your name?"

Giggling, she hiked her skirts up to her thighs and tossed herself onto the foot of my bed, leaning carelessly over my legs. "Yes, I'm Iris, pleasure to make your acquaintance. Clayton, who just left, is my cousin. Sorry he was being a bit of a bully."

Her eyes widened slightly as the words escaped her mouth and her mouth tightened for a moment before quirking in a soft, nervous smile.

"Don't tell anyone I said it. His father would consider it treasonous for me to be calling the Crown prince names, even if it is all in good fun."

Ignoring the large majority of her words, I grasped onto her hand. "You have to help me get out of here."

"Unfortunately, my dear, I can only do so much." She sighed, glancing over her nails. "You caused quite a scene on that bridge. I *can* get you a proper dress, though, and we'll clear all this up in no time."

"At least tell me what's happening!" I called out to her as she stood and began to retreat. "Please, I don't understand any of this."

She paused at the door, just as Clayton had, and nodded. When she spoke again, her voice was as serious as it had been when she noticed the Mark stamped across my chest. "I will. I promise. I'll explain as much as possible when I return, but I have to get you a dress. We can't be late for the Council, or it's both of our necks on the line. You'll have to trust me for now."

With that, she left me alone with nothing but my anxieties for company. There was some consolation in the solitude this time, though, because for some reason I did, in fact, trust her. Maybe it was because she had talked to me like a person instead of a criminal. Perhaps it was because her colorful ensemble made her look more like a child than an adult. Whatever the reason was, though, I did trust that if she said she was coming back for me, then she would be returning.